<u>REVIEW COPY</u>

Release Date: March 31, 2003

Contact: Mochi Press
PO Box 51234
Eugene, OR 97405

mochipress@aol.com

1

John Arbogast

This book is a work of fiction. All events, characters and names come from the author's imagination. Any resemblance to actual persons, living or dead, is unintended.

First Edition

Cataloging in Publication Data

Arbogast, John

       Stepping Off the Wheel / John Arbogast.

       p.   cm.

       ISBN 0-9724510-0-5

I. Title.

Library of Congress Control Number: 2002112345

813'.54-dc21

Printed in the United States of America on recycled paper

Mochi Press
P.O. Box 51234
Eugene, OR 97405
mochipress@aol.com

John Arbogast

Stepping Off the Wheel

by

John Arbogast

John Arbogast

1

RENNY

SAN FRANCISCO	KYOTO	BANGKOK	KATMANDU	LAKE TOBA	VARANASSI	IPOH

YEAR 1	YEAR 2	YEAR 3

DUMPING THE STASH

The antiseptic liquid swirls in a turbulent blue spiral around the stainless steel bowl and into the holding tank, into the irretrievable void, taking with it the last few grams of a faded dream. With a smile and a shudder, I observe the last of the cellophane covered rectangles drop beneath the hinged lid. The slurp of the vacuum, sucking it all down, subsides and all is quiet save the low hum of the engines. Muffled voices and shuffling bodies outside the tiny compartment flare and ebb. Looking up in the mirror, I know this feels as right as anything ever has, yet the absurdity of it is not lost on me. My eyes have the tired, wide-awake look of an all night driver wanting to stop, yet wanting to get there even more. I exhale and chuckle and proceed to wash the imagined residue from my hands. Imagined, because I'd wrapped the flattened slabs of resin very well. It isn't possible that any lingering crumb, or odor for that matter, attached itself to my body or clothing, though a seed of doubt persists.

All around me seems especially sharp and clear. I notice with new appreciation the smudges on the mirror and the splattered drops of water by the basin left over from a previous occupant. I want to think this is the beginning of an epiphany, so I pause expectantly. Nothing comes and I am left to my own reflections. *Yes, Greg, we have choices in this world and while I'd like to think I'm still screaming at The Man, your way just isn't my way.* I take one last swish of my fingers through my hair and splash water on my face and feel I am ready. Doing an about face in the tiny compartment, I slap the latch on the door from "occupied" to "vacant". Before opening the door, I pause once again and smirk at the whimsy of my thoughts. *I should have at least swallowed a dollop of the hashish, if only to savor that sweet taste. The distraction for the next few hours of the flight wouldn't hurt either.* Three more hours to San Francisco.

So this is my story. It all started... no, no, no. I can't tell it that way – from the beginning – because that's not the way my mind works. It would be nice if there was some objective orderliness on the subject, but it's too late for that. Let's just see what sparks will flash here and there, free association being my preferable mode of cogitation.

If anything has led me to this moment, it's been my predisposition to follow an idea or person or place, if only because it tickled my fancy to pursue it. That is to say, something intrigued me enough that I eagerly changed directions to see where it would lead. It's too generous to call it "living spontaneously" or "having a free spirit", though I have referred to it thus myself when trying to describe my ways to family and others. I've often thought of myself as selfish, though I suppose that is a little too harsh. Wishy-washy? Nope. Suffice it to say I'm just a wanderer. My range is from the territory of the Lone Wolf of Lenny and Squiggy to Dean Moriarty to Tonto to Robinson Crusoe to...you get the picture. I don't want to give the impression that I see my life in a romantic light (though, at times, I do). It's more an amalgam of a Van Gogh painting superimposed on an Ansel Adams landscape; clear and yet eyebrow-furrowing simultaneously, but judge for yourself.

ღღღღღ ღღღღღ ღღღღღ ღღღღღ ღღღღღ

Osaka and the ways of the east lay eight hours behind. The sweat of exiting through Japanese customs and then boarding the jumbo was trivial. There was the long train ride to the airport and the pass through the control checks to endure, but getting on the plane was easy. I think I knew even then, as I arrived at Kansai International Airport, that I wouldn't go through with it. The truth just hadn't hit me yet. The secret thrill of doing something illicit and the mix of excitement and fear of the consequences seem almost silly as I look at it now. That little stirring in the pit of your stomach is oddly addictive, isn't it?

Though I admit I am only a half-assed smuggler (I did transport the goods into Japan, after all), the operational part of the affair was mostly straightforward. A thorough individual with a modicum of brains can figure out most of the particulars. Some methods are even practically foolproof, requiring only extreme bad luck to go wrong. Having the nerve and just thinking it through is half the battle. The basics of avoiding detection seemed pretty simple. I read somewhere that being able to think of even fifty percent of the things that can go wrong with any operation means your thought process borders on genius. I figured I'd gotten to about a third. My preparation was mainly concerned with avoiding odor and visual detection. I had those angles covered pretty well and counted on calm nerves and good fortune with the rest.

After boarding and getting into the air, I settled into my seat, by a window and over the port wing. Unlatching my lap belt, I stretched out and closed my eyes, trying to ignore the faint odor of jet fuel exhaust permeating the air. With the practice of umpteen months of commutes on the Osaka JR Line to my credit, I easily shut out the bustle of passengers heading to the toilet, fidgeting in their seats, and settling in to watch the first movie. My focus began to drift up towards the cabin ceiling. And so it began.

From my mind's eye I see myself, sitting with eyes closed and hands in my lap, and it startles me. That is, it jars me internally and my subconscious awakens. I stare closely at my body and think for a moment that I can see the long, flat, rectangular strips of resin taped to the sides of my thighs. I instinctively reach out and feel along my pant legs and relax, reassuring myself that the heavy cotton appears normal and that there is nothing out of the ordinary that would be noticeable to anyone. My floating gaze veers upward to my face and, after lingering there for an instant at my seemingly calm expression, the image rushes inside my brain and sets off a gurgling cascade of memories. The two years that have just passed fly by in a whirl of images. It is the resulting perspective on those years, and my journey through them, that ultimately leads me to the lavatory.

I just spent the last two weeks in Kansai, in central Japan, as the final stop of this two-year, meandering excursion. I had lived in Kyoto and worked in Osaka teaching English and generally farting around for about a year – time sandwiched between first heading out and now traveling homeward. Five months ago I left a couple of boxes with Tony in Kyoto and went tramping about Southeast Asia. The routine of working in the Japan scene had worn on me and I was eager to continue traveling where I'd left off. I returned to Japan only to gather my things and catch up on the latest gossip before heading back stateside to... to what?...grad school maybe? Mom and Dad's place will be doable for a month or so, but I've already lived on that street once and it is sure to become all the things it was before and I will need to move on. I could always move back to San Francisco where I lived for two years prior to stepping off *that* wheel. I guess hanging there again is a possibility. Then there's Cheryl. Wait, why is she on my mind?

❧❧❧❧❧ ❧❧❧❧❧ ❧❧❧❧❧ ❧❧❧❧❧ ❧❧❧❧❧

Arriving in Osaka from Bangkok with a major stash strapped to your legs is good for at least a few minutes of heart-pounding excitement. Having come in at the new KIX airport twice before, I knew what to expect. Most of the time people just sail through. Occasionally the customs agent might randomly check your bags. You hear rumors of the rare strip search, but I had never met anyone who had experienced one. Speaking a little Japanese doesn't hurt. If you're all white – I am only half – Japanese customs is even more likely to be kind to you. Non-white people mostly get a strange vibe when dealing with official Japan. It's hard to pin down the feeling – probably something like walking into a blue-collar bar in a three-piece suit and penny loafers. The odor that "you're not one of us" hangs thick in the air. Of course no foreigner in Japan is ever considered to be *in*, but if you are part of an identifiable white ethnic group, life is easier. God help you if you carry a Thai or Indonesian passport. If you're a mixed breed but carry a North American or European passport, you rank up a notch, but the disapproval is discernibly there behind the polite façade. At the immigration counter I requested a tourist visa – good for three months – and it was given without much hassle. I had cleaned up scrupulously before leaving Bangkok and gave the immigration man my best smile.

I should explain something here. When I first entered Japan, a year and a half ago and through Tokyo, I also entered the country on a three-month tourist visa, the first of many in a string of comings and goings from Japan. I never did get the official passport stamp that allows one to work legally in Japan. Instead, I adopted the modus operandi of all those who seek to work in Japan without leaving the usual trail of tax documentation. We enter on tourist visas, work under the table, and leave at the end of three months for a cheap nearby destination – Seoul being as close and cheap as they come. We hang out there for a few days, usually getting shit-faced at one of the tourist spots just to be able to say you did something, and then return innocently to Japan, securing another three month visa from another customs agent at the border.

This typically works two or three times before the immigration people become suspicious. Upon seeing several consecutive tourist entries in our passports, they hassle us and potentially deny us entry. My second entry through Osaka was a breeze and the third just a light struggle. I knew that the fourth on the same passport would be akin to a twelve year old trying to buy booze with a fake ID. So before attempting the fourth incursion, I set aside a few days in Bangkok to procure a new passport. I "accidentally" washed my passport. I actually soaked it overnight in a bucket of light bleach until the photo and type were almost – but not completely – illegible. I crumpled it up for good measure, and then, forlornly, went to the U.S. Consulate. Apologizing for my abject stupidity, I requested a new passport and was well-served by the Foreign Service staff, obtaining a virgin and visa-less passport within three days.

Arriving back in Osaka, I acted like it was my first time to Japan and was welcomed into the country without a hitch or much ado. I suppose I could have run into one of the same immigration agents who previously admitted me, but the chances of that – and of him or her distinguishing me from the thousands of other foreign faces arriving there daily – were slim. At the immigration checkpoints there were six different windows to choose from and I was careful to assure myself of anonymity by selecting one where the agent barely looked up from his stamp. Between the clean passport and the dope taped to my thighs, I felt pretty good. In my mind, I just pulled off a double play.

As usual, I only had one small carry-on bag, so I proceeded directly to the customs area, bypassing the tedious and anti-climatic carousel of checked baggage. I felt some apprehension about dogs and surly customs agents, but a deep breath and a smile erased those fears. Or masked them, anyway. They waived me through after collecting my nothing-to-declare form and I strutted through the airport to the train platform feeling like one bad dude. My first truly illicit venture had passed the critical risk point and I was feeling a virtual contact high through my thighs.

I caught the next express train to Osaka, switched to the Loop Line, then to the Keihan Line and scored a seat all the way to Kyoto. I could have taken a super express train straight through, but funds were short and I had time. I knew Tony worked until nine and that he would be at The Boar shortly thereafter, this being Wednesday, darts night. I did a concentrated ten minutes of yoga breathing to calm the adrenaline jitters and spaced out on the flickering lights of love hotels and train stations for the next forty-five minutes.

❧❧❧❧❧   ❧❧❧❧❧   ❧❧❧❧❧   ❧❧❧❧❧   ❧❧❧❧❧

I stepped into the cool, May Kyoto evening air and stopped to breathe it deep. I just missed the cherry blossoms by two weeks and was only half-glad to have avoided it and the standard "aren't the blossoms beautiful?" sort of small talk that goes with it. I was also half-disappointed, because they truly are beautiful and I had missed perhaps my last chance to see them. I wandered around towards the famous Sanjo Bridge. The usual array of young couples and drunks were milling around on the concreted banks of the Kamo River. I caught a pungent whiff from a favorite and aptly nicknamed "Stinky Ramen Shop". The elegant, deep-throated refrain of a sweet potato vendor – *"yaaakii- moh, yaki-imo, yak-iiiimo"* – hung in the night air. I wandered towards the bar, humming the tune.

A couple of lonely, red-faced, gray-suited salarymen were shuffling towards the station on their way home to wives who wanted their paychecks, but not their pathetic husbands and their utterly prosaic lives. *Ain't it the same the world over?* I thought, and then chided myself for being such a cynic. I cannot abide being a cynic. As guilty as I am of too-easily succumbing to its impulses, I resent my descent into the fatalistic. I can accept that we are all pretty much fucked up, but what is the point of dwelling on it? Creeping ennui is all around and I'll be damned if I'll allow myself to give in without a fight. I sometimes think it would be cool to sit around all day in a café, keeping up a buzz on coffee and cigarettes and hanging out with people of like mind. We would all be dressed in black, kicking at every new and old idea, but never proposing anything new, just whining. But how long could I last? It makes you want to blow your brains out like Hemingway because it isn't worth doing if you can't grab it by the balls. I shook it off, exhaled and went up the stairs.

The Boar Stool is an English styled pub on the third story of a non-descript concrete building in downtown Kyoto. It was generally referred to as The Boar or the BS by the English-speaking locals, among others. It was bustling as usual with the mid-week expat crowd as I entered the bar. I use this word, expat, but I dislike it. I am not sure what defines an expatriate, I just know that it gives most gaijin (the true local's word for those not from Japan) here a feeling like they belong to some kind of exclusive club, and that feeling has a slight smell of bullshit to it.

13

Long timers can impress and welcome the newbies by throwing it around in casual conversation. But to me it signifies a pompous and condescending air of inclusion and exclusion, where in the end we fool only ourselves into thinking we have arrived at some special status because we've "escaped". Stepping out of one rut and then into another just isn't anything to crow about. Many of the guys who describe themselves this way, as expats, are assholes who use the mystery to score psuedo-rebellious Japanese babes and think themselves studs.

"Well for fuck's sake, who will they let in next?" Tony said with a big grin, setting down his mug and crossing the floor to give me a big bear hug. He cultivated a disheveled British scholar look, but he was powerfully built. He wore an odor of cigars that always lingered about him on Wednesday nights at The Boar and tonight there was a tinge of red in his eyes to keep it company. It was damn good to see him. He was standing in the darts corner with fellow Brits Mark and Mike: M and M as we referred to them. I knew them only from Darts Night at The Boar, and we shook hands.

"So, the prodigal returns," said Mark. I nodded.

"A man's gotta have somewhere to go."

"'at's the truth," replied Mike.

I put down my pack and leaned against the wall to watch my buddies finish their match. M and M were what we called "lifers" in Japan. No one was sure how long they had lived in Kyoto. Some speculated twenty years or more. They were both in their forties, consumed endless quantities of cigarettes and beer, spoke badly accented Japanese and worked good jobs at Kansai universities. This meant their pockets and their cheeks were always flush, with ample time off to make the best of it. University jobs were the best gig in town and required just seven months a year of teaching – four-hour days at that – but paid twelve months a year.

At our first meeting I thought M and M were gay, but was promptly assured by Tony that they were not. Mark always seemed to have some cute Japanese *bodycon* hanging off him. These were the local babes in supertight short skirts, heavy makeup, stiletto heels, and a constant "yes" expression in their eyes. Mark was the caricatured English gent who was "in" with the working class blokes. Mike was taciturn yet congenial, self-deprecating in his humor and dart play, and intelligent to boot. Both were hard to figure out and I wasn't sure I wanted to. Their stereotyped natures fit well in my mind and I didn't see the need to erase it with a truth less satisfying.

Tony and I had met on my first day in Kyoto. I had stayed in Tokyo for a week with my sister Charlie before heading south on the *Shinkansen*. Charlie had given me a tip on a guesthouse, the Blue Danbue – and yes, the spelling is correct – on the western side of town. I was lucky (I later found out) to secure a tiny (so it seemed at the time) six *tatami* mat room. A tatami mat is about fourteen square feet, or five and a half by two and a half feet, so the entire room came to around eighty square feet, and it was right across the hall from Tony's. The tatami mats in Tokyo are supposedly larger, though I suspect this may be folk wisdom only. Foreigners and Japanese alike love to spew this sort of arcane information. I've yet to meet anyone who knows the precise truth - if there is such a thing.

He had been living in Kyoto for a year and held a world of information for the neophyte that I was. He casually invited me to join him for some ramen at a noodle shop around the corner and we became close in no time. He was from Liverpool, but had lived in various places around England and Wales as his Father was transferred here and there. He went to a university somewhere in Manchester, studying accounting and then worked for a couple of years on contract jobs in London, never feeling satisfied with it. He described himself then as a modern day David Copperfield, wandering the streets of London trying to figure out what the hell he was doing. He hadn't found himself in the throes of destitution though, financially-speaking. He eagerly hopped a 747 to Japan when he heard there were opportunities to teach here. Anything to get away from what he was doing and venture out into the world. Being on the edge of the Asian sub-world couldn't help but be alluring. Almost immediately, he began working evenings at a chain of local private schools in or near Kyoto and started studying aikido religiously.

Tony finished up his darts game, losing badly and using it as an excuse to beg off and we made for a low table in the corner. The Boar was small in floor space, but well designed with nooks and crannies to give the feeling of privacy. Wood and brass were abundant and you would swear you were in Britain somewhere, except for the Japanese beer signs.

"Alright," he said, "out with it. What trouble have you gotten yourself into since the island?" We had spent a couple of weeks on Koh Chang in Thailand two months earlier. He had been able to finagle the time off – always an iffy proposition with a Japanese company – and came along with Charlie and the rest of the gang.

"Oh...you know," I muffled, suppressing a yawn and rubbing my hands over my face in an effort to make myself more alert.

"Christ. You look a mess. Do you want to head out?"

"That bad huh?" I said smiling, knowing it was true.

"You don't know the half, mate." He started to stub out his cigar, but I stopped him.

"One for the road first."

"Now you're talking. "Need a refill me self," he said rising. "My shout."

He walked over to the bar, pausing to jostle acquaintances, throwing and receiving barbs along the way. He returned with two glistening pints of Yebisu and sat down with an audible grunt. We did not say anything for a minute and I appreciated just being able to sit, sipping beer and watching the crowd. Tony could sense I had something on my mind and had the patience to wait me out.

"Seen Eric around lately?" I asked.

"I thought he'd be here tonight," he said. "He's been having the usual traumas with Kenji," he added, rolling his eyes and half smiling. "What's Charlie up to now?" he tossed in as if it were an afterthought. I knew better.

"She was heading for The Philippines when I last saw her in Bangkok. That would have been about a month ago."

Tony nodded his head thoughtfully. "She's going back to Shinsaibashi for a couple weeks after that?"

"Unless something's changed." I shrugged my shoulders. I wished there was more to add, but Tony already knew what I told him. He knew more about Charlie's day-to-day than I did.

"I got a postcard from Kuala Lumpur a couple of weeks ago. Sounded like she enjoyed being off and running. I think she'd split off from Marie by then."

"They were meeting back up in Manila if all went well," I gave Tony a knowing purse of my lips with raised eyebrows. Traveling with Marie, as we both knew, was like riding the dice in a crap game, whooping it up one minute and cursing the next. She could change her mind in a wink and even if she didn't, you might reconsider the plan yourself.

"You remember that poor chap who tried to give her a squeeze that evening in Koh Chang?" Tony said with a shake of his head and an amused laugh. "She practically castrated the poor bugger."

"He deserved it. Half of it." I added. We burst out laughing.

"That fuckin' guy never knew what hit him," Tony said and we chuckled some more and then were quiet for a few moments.

"Lets get outta here," I said. We drained what was left of the pints, walked a slalom towards the door saying a few goodbyes, and escaped down the stairs and out into the street. Tony offered to tote my backpack, but I declined. I'd feel lost without it on my shoulders.

The night was pleasant and we decided to walk the two miles up the river to Tony's place. Tony walked his bike and I allowed my backpack to be hung on the frame. He'd moved from the Danbue shortly before I left five months ago. He found a small flat of his own on the north side of town, just a block from the river.

"I'm carrying," I blurted out as we passed under the second bridge.

It took a few moments for what I said to sink in. He looked puzzled at first, but then it slowly dawned on him what I meant and a smile of incredulity came over him.

"You crazy fuck!" he shouted, punching me in the shoulder and grinning.

We walked on for a moment before he said "How much?"

"You don't want to know."

"The hell I don't."

"You'll see soon enough."

"Timing's good. Things have been a little tight here as of late."

"I don't think I want to sell much of this – except of course to those close friends in dire need," I said with an exaggerated air. He responded with the look of a kid promised an ice cream cone. "And even in that case, it won't be as a sale."

"Don't tell me you swallowed the stuff?"

"Naw. I couldn't bring myself to try that way." He was referring to the time-honored and popular method of ingesting small, cellophane-wrapped balls of hash – five to ten grams or so – and fishing them out of your shit the next day. Timing is everything with this method, and Japanese squatter toilets have a little platform of porcelain that facilitates recovery. I shudder to think that I have most certainly inhaled the smoke from many a bong filled with crumbs that had been filtered through various intestinal tracts. An unsavory thought now, but one easily overlooked when you're jonesin' for a toke. I'm still here, ain't I? Whenever I made a buy, I never wanted to know where or how it "passed through" customs.

I could tell Tony was still curious, but he refrained from asking any further questions. We walked the rest of the way making small talk. Tony's flat was in an alley behind a bicycle shop in one of those old style Kyoto houses with a wooden frame, mud siding, and thick, translucent glass. The whole place seemed on the verge of toppling over and yet retained its old world charm. As we approached the alleyway, Tony pointed out the row of houses on the adjacent block. They looked similar to Tony's, basically run down, but cool to us.

"Have you heard much about the *burakumin*?

"Not really," I replied. "It means 'black workers', doesn't it?"

"That's right. These are my neighbors," he said with an expansive gesture. "I think most of these folks are metal workers now, but in the past they might have worked in the slaughterhouses or in some other 'dirty' profession. I'm guessing that this pad of mine is so cheap because of the neighborhood. Most Japanese look down on these folks, from what I can tell."

"I can see why that was true in the past, sort of," I replied, "but what's the point of holding onto that idea now?"

"You really have to ask that question in Japan?"

I had to think about that one for a moment and then, of course, it didn't seem so outlandish. Japan mixes the past and the present in more convoluted ways than you can shake a stick at. Working with animals was considered dirty, especially in the harder trades like butchery and tanning. That this sentiment carried over to modern Japanese laborers wasn't so surprising. These folk are similar to the Untouchables in India, socially speaking.

We walked down the alley and parked the bike in front of the townhouse, leaving just enough room for a person to squeeze by. We entered the *genkan*, or entryway and I was transported back into the Japan of my imagination. The tatami flooring in the house was older, but still retained that wonderful grassy smell. The wooden sliding doors showed gaps in the out of square frames. I immediately went to the bathroom in the back and appreciated the open sky view peeking in from the edges of the too-small corrugated fiberglass roofing. On the other side of the concrete wall to the back, I heard someone clearing their throat and expectorating into a sink. *Pretty nice digs overall for five hundred bucks a month and no key money.* The key money, or money to get the key, was a kind of deposit that discouraged many foreigners from seeking out finer pads. Scarcity of space being what it is, Kyoto landlords often charge up to five months' rent on top of the first month's rent to let a place. And it was usually nonrefundable. Written contracts were the exception, most agreements being made with a handshake and a smile. Being vague and obscure seemed a preferred way of doing business, especially with gaijin.

Tony lived in a small one-bedroom apartment, which included a three tatami mat front room, a three mat kitchen, (sans tatami and in linoleum), a four mat 'living room' coming off the genkan and a six mat bedroom behind the living room through which you accessed the open-air bathroom area to the rear.

The entire unit was in disrepair, yet held a quaintness to it distinguishable only by the ever-so-unrefined foreigner's eye. Tony had furnished it with assorted *gomi* (literally-*garbage*) furniture that was put out on the streets every so often by Japanese families who no longer had use of it. Most pieces were perfectly usable, but were outdated or slightly nicked. Learning the ways of "gomi hunting" was an art that I never tired of pursuing.

We quickly settled in, doffing our shoes and stepping up into the kitchen and retrieving two beers before sitting on the floor in the living room. Tony refreshed me on the location of the bedding. I would be sleeping in the living room and was glad to have it. Renting a room would have run me at least fifty bucks a night and probably more, including the hassle. More than that, given my illicit pursuit, I was happy to be in friendly environs. Tony's company was appreciated as well.

By now it was close to midnight, but neither of us was ready for bed yet. Tony went into the back room and returned with a crude bamboo bong with a stem fashioned from a piece of an aluminum can. He set it on the table and gave me an expectant look. I stood up and dropped my trousers. I countered Tony's feigned look of disapproval with a flutter of my eyelids. I was wearing black bicycling shorts underneath, minus the padded crotch they had come with. Down the seam on the inside of each leg, I had sewn three long rectangular pockets. Into each pocket I fitted a series of flattened rectangular bars of hashish, wrapped carefully in three layers of cellophane and again in cheesecloth. This set up allowed me to sit or squat without the bars bulging because they hinged naturally in each line of three. The cloth wrapping hid any noise and the long johns and baggy pants any unsightly bulges. I could only be found out through a frisk and strip search by a customs guard who might have mistaken the bulges for huge quadriceps muscles, or so I hoped. If it ever came to that, I knew I was done for, but one can't help fantasizing.

Each pocket held three 20-gram bars, for a total of eighteen chunks of Thailand's finest export. I had smuggled in just a little over three quarters of a pound. Tony looked like he wanted to give me a blowjob. The value of this stash was almost twice its weight in gold. I could support myself comfortably for half a year – *in Japan* – if that were my goal, which it was not.

I pulled out each of the small packets slowly, dropping them on the table, explaining the how of it to Tony as I did so. I tossed one to him. "Rent for a couple weeks?" I knew it wasn't necessary, but what are mates for? He carefully unwrapped the bar, peeling back the layers of cellophane like he was uncovering a long lost artifact. When finished, he held it reverentially in his hands like a priest with the Eucharist. He closed his eyes and, holding it up to his nose and inhaling deeply, said "Christ that's beautiful." He broke off a few crumbs to place in the bong, kneading the resin with ritualistic intensity. There is nothing quite like that sweet emanation to set you salivating with expectations of bliss and beyond. We smoked.

2

CHARLIE

SEATTLE	TOKYO	THAILAND	LONDON	THE PHILIPPINES		INDIA

YEAR 1		YEAR 2		YEAR 3

STARTING OUT

She's lying awake in bed, peeking out at the muted morning light and thinking, *Damn. The alarm hasn't even gone off yet. This sucks. It's not even 6:30 yet. I'm tired even though I slept through the night. What was I dreaming? It's all so hazy and vague. Something about being in Pike Place Market in my underwear, only nobody noticed except me. And even I didn't notice right away. Oh lord...the dreads are heavy this morning. I'm supposed to feel lucky having a good job and living in the Northwest. Why does it feel so fake? Wake up Charlie! Stop being such a whiner!*

She forces herself out of bed and into the shower. The phone rings as she steps out and she listens to the answering machine pick up while she towels off. It is Cory, reminding her about his office party that evening.

"Hi Charlie. I'll pick you up at seven tonight. It's going to be fancy so dress up a little, ok? See you then."

She can't bring herself to pick up the phone. She dresses in her favorite light gray wool suit, which helps a little. Then she runs a new pair of stockings on her big toenail.

Damn! Nothing's going right this morning. She doesn't like the look of her long black hair falling over her shoulders and decides to pin it up. The alarm goes off..."For NPR News this is…. blah, blah, blah...." She reaches over and slams the snooze button. *Christ, I'm not even PMSing.*

She decides to go into work early to beat the traffic, grabs her shoulder bag and heads out. The sky is ash gray and she scowls at it, daring the rain to come down upon her. As she winds her dingy blue Corolla through the deserted early morning streets, she searches for something decent on the radio. She settles on a station and as she pulls into an espresso stand, it starts playing "Take it Easy" by the Eagles. She cracks her first smile of the day and orders a double mocha.

The Eagles Live album was one of her first. She and her twin brother Renny used to listen to it over and over again until they knew every word and note. It was one of the few albums their Mom and Dad liked and she can still hear Dad singing to it, off key. *"Don't let the sound of your own wheels drive you craaaazy...."* He's in the kitchen and she and Renny are in the family room cowering with embarrassment. *"Daaaad!"* A clearer, recent conversation with her father brings her back to the morning's earlier thoughts.

> *"A good job is hard to come by, sweetheart. A lot of people want what you've got, so think twice before saying you hate it so much."* And Mom's take on it: *"You can buy all of those nice things you like so much dear. You couldn't do that working for minimum wage."*

They just didn't see her point. *What is the point?* Renny could relate. She pictures him on the MUNI eight hundred miles to the south, trudging to his job at a stockbroker's accounting office in San Francisco. She imagines him with a weary, resigned look. As she sips her mocha, she is comforted to think that he has had a morning equal to hers.

She pulls into the far end of the practically empty parking lot at the square, entirely-mirrored office building she works at every weekday. She sits in her car on the upper tier, looking at the reflection in the building of her in her car with gray Puget Sound glistening in the background. It is calm outside but the building appears sinister, hued in green and with a convex quality, the reflected images curling towards her ominously, as if to swallow her up.

After a few minutes of sipping her coffee and daydreaming, she steels herself, gathers her things and walks in a hurried clip to the entrance, descending the concrete stairs and crossing the asphalt with apparent determination. She stops at the door, looking through the sign that reads: Klemmer Frozen Foods, and then glances back towards her car and the Sound beyond. The morning's uneasiness still roils inside of her and she consciously squeezes her eyes shut tight to purge it. It doesn't go away, but it does recede and she quickly darts inside. Her cubicle is on the third floor in the Marketing section in a middle grouping and measures six by five feet. She automatically opens up her planner and scans through the day's to-do list. She has a lunch date with Joan, and this makes her feel better immediately. *If anyone can give me some perspective, it's Joan.* She sets to work and the morning skips by on fast forward.

At 11:00 she tells her boss that she came in early and is going out for a two-hour lunch. She leaves the building feeling lighter than when she entered and drives ten minutes down the road to a diner with a derelict sign of half-lit neon. Inside she spots Joan in a booth by the window and hurries over. She gets only halfway up as Charlie bends down to hug her.

"Look at you, all professional and all, makes me feel like the old woman I am," Joan chuckles and squeezes her hand.

"You look better than I feel," Charlie rejoins. Joan is dressed in a white polo shirt and blue pants with an elastic waist. She is as chipper as always.

"Staying out too late, breaking hearts and bottles?"

"I wish it was so exciting," Charlie laughs back.

They met a little over two years ago. Charlie was new to Seattle then and rented the studio above Joan's apartment in the Wallingford neighborhood. Joan was eighty-six years old and owned the remodeled Victorian house that now housed six rental units. Charlie's first job in Seattle was as a waitress at a fancy steak house downtown, so she had mornings and early afternoons off. She and Joan used to sit on the downstairs porch and sip herbal tea. She loved hearing Joan tell stories of her "olden days".

Joan had married in the late twenties to an engineer from Nebraska and, to hear her tell it, suffered through five years of midwestern boredom before she up and left him. She hooked up with a hellcat named Alice and they somehow made their way to Europe, where they toured Spain and France on a motorcycle. The two fell in love and eventually settled in Seattle, running a boarding house business. Charlie related to the Midwestern and boring part, as she herself escaped to Seattle after college in Colorado and two years of clerking in Cincinnati, not far from her parents. She worked as a paralegal at a corporate law firm with a plan of going to law school. After a year, she became determined to have nothing to do with "the law" and started looking around for some other way spend her time. She visited a college buddy in San Francisco and they drove up the coast to Seattle. She liked the feel of the city and after returning to the Midwest, decided to move there.

"How's that Cory doing?"

"Oh, he's still around," Charlie says with a roll of her eyes, trying to maintain her composure, but starts giggling. They both have a good laugh. They give their order to an amused waitress and as she leaves Joan offers advice.

"Well you know, there's plenty of fish out there. You can always throw back the one you've caught and try for another." Joan always seemed indifferent to Cory, so the comment doesn't surprise Charlie.

"Oh it's not just Cory. Everything these days just leaves me feeling so...bleech." Joan looks at her intently but says nothing.

"You know how it is. Everyone is telling me how lucky I am. Good job. Cool place to live. Boyfriend, money, security, health....? If it's all so great, then why do I feel so.... so.....goddamn bored by it?" Charlie feels a tinge of embarrassment at the outburst, but not the swearing. Joan says worse. But Charlie feels a little punch drunk and chuckles while rubbing her eyes. She's not usually so forward about how she feels, but Joan accepts her as she is.

"Oh girl. You're just seeing things as they are," Joan laughs. "Sounds like you need to shake things up a bit."

"I've been thinking about that. I just don't know what should be next."

"How about doing some traveling? You know, head out and see some different things." They're silent for a moment.

"You should visit Andrea. She could help get you started on your way."

"In Japan? Oh, I don't know... it seems so...crowded there." Andrea was Joan's Australian great grandniece, just a few years older than Charlie, who had been living in Tokyo for the past three or four years, working as a hostess and teaching English. She came to Seattle a year ago to visit her Aunt Joan and she and Charlie became fast friends. Andrea was so confident and cosmopolitan. Charlie remembered talking with her about living in Tokyo and traveling abroad, but it seemed so exotic and out of reach. Charlie herself had just started her new job and moved to a new apartment at the time, which then overshadowed any interest in exploring Andrea's lifestyle for herself. But now....

"Crowded isn't a big deal." Joan reassures her. "New and different is. But it's worth thinking about. And if that's not right for you now, then maybe you'll come up with something else."

Charlie knows Joan is right, but it is too much to think about just now. "I know. I know," she replies.

I guess when you've been around, like Joan has, it's easier to put things in perspective, she thinks. At least Joan makes her smile about it. She looks closely at Joan, her brown hair heavily streaked with gray, her smile ever-present. And Joan is so patient – the mirror opposite of Charlie' internal self. The moment passes. Lunch comes and they eat and talk for another half an hour, ordering coffee and laughing over things trivial, the mini-drama submerged and forgotten for now.

Charlie offers to drive Joan home, since she had taken the bus, but Joan declines, saying she enjoys the ride. Charlie waits with her until the bus comes and they hug tightly and say their goodbyes. Charlie watches the bus pull away and walks slowly back to her car. She drives back to work with a vision of Joan and Alice (now a decade in the grave), clad in black leather and riding tandem on a black motorcycle through the French countryside, startling the locals. The thought brings her an odd comfort and her mood lightens considerably.

She returns to the afternoon of work as if in a trance. A co-worker catches her daydreaming at the copy machine and when asked where she is, Charlie can only answer "Oh, nothing," with a shoulder shrug and conspiratorial sort of chuckle. She finds herself with a break between duties during the mid-afternoon and on a whim begins surfing the web for tickets to Asia. All of a sudden it hits her.

What are you doing?! Are you really considering taking off? Yes you are. Holy shit! She looks around, feeling self-conscious and secretive.

Well, why not? What IS holding you here? Cory?! Face it girl, he is a sweet guy, but you know he's not the one. Why prolong the inevitable? And this job, and Seattle? ...You could leave it all in a minute. So what's stopping you? You've got four thousand dollars in the bank and no debts. So.....? She is interrupted by a phone call and a brief flurry of activity. When the distracting task is completed a few minutes later, she thinks again about the choice before her.

I think I'm going to do it. Do what? Go to Japan! I'm going to go to Japan! Why the hell not! She feels elated. The work and people around her suddenly seem dull to an extreme. Her suit suddenly is like a prisoner's uniform and her co-workers are fellow inmates. It is so clear to her now that she wonders how she hadn't seen it before?

Out of habit, she starts a list of pros –

- travel
- experience the world
- meet new and interesting people

27

- learn a new language
- different food

– and cons. The con column is conspicuously blank. She chides herself and makes herself put something in it. Taking cues from the pro column, she writes:

- security
- money
- safety/danger
- Mom and Dad feeling uncomfortable

She thinks more deeply about each one in turn. *Money and security are...well...overrated, and Mom and Dad will just have to deal.* As for the rest, she really is craving the unknown, and the desire for security and safety are directly opposed to that. As for money, four grand is surely enough to get started. Her skills and work ethic would keep her from ever being poor, so the possibility of roughing it abroad does not make her feel uneasy. That is good enough for now.

The rest of the day is a blur of catching up on work and trying not to be distracted and before she knows it she is in the car, driving home. She thinks about Cory. *I've got to do this now. I do not want to go to this stupid party tonight where I won't know anybody and I'll have to act perky and fake. Do it tonight.* At her apartment she changes into jeans and a sweater and starts on a microbrew. By the time Cory arrives, she is on her fourth. They peck at the door and Cory seems surprised by her attire and by her breath. She feels a brief moment of weakness shake her resolve, but she quickly steels herself. "We have to talk."

They sit on the couch, not touching. He is stiff and motionless, as if he'd known all along that this would come as she blurts out her feelings and the day's new ideas. She feels like an idiot. None of it sounds anything near to eloquent and she keeps repeating herself. Cory tries to argue with her, to erode her confidence by questioning her, but his doubts are overwhelmed by her determination. He asks her to think it over and she says she already has and will always have a warm place in her heart for him and that is that. They hug, she with sincere affection and he with zombie-like formality. He leaves fifteen minutes after walking in; she sits and cries for fifteen more.

It still feels right, and that is good. She dials Joan and tells her of the decision. Joan is excited for her and says she will call Andrea and get back to her tomorrow or the next day. Charlie then, ceremoniously, taps out a resignation letter on her laptop, rewriting it three times before settling on a simple couple of lines that say her last day will be in two weeks. She prints it, signs it, places it in an envelope and sighs deeply.

Taking stock of the day, she is drained, elated and alone. She calls her buddy Cheryl, with whom she worked at the restaurant, and finds her at home. She tells her the news. Cheryl is genuinely surprised but also confused and excited. They agree to meet at a pub a few blocks from Charlie's place in twenty minutes.

They get drunk. Cheryl pushes Charlie to pour herself out to her, revealing long silent dreams and frustrations about working, about men, and all manner of things. By midnight they make their way back to Charlie's apartment. Cheryl had driven but, being too intoxicated, leaves her car near the pub and walks home with Charlie. She passes out on the couch, but Charlie is too hyped up to sleep. She calls Renny.

She doesn't wake him up. "What's up Sir Renford?"

Renny's bright laugh. "Sounds like *you*, Miss Charles." They adopted these pet names for each other as teens. His real name was Rene and hers Charlene, which they both hated growing up, hence the nicknames. "You are sounding well lubricated. I wish my evening had gone so well"

"What's up bro?"

"Just dealing with bimbos is all. I mean, *you* know who Ralph Nader is right? Christ! I think I insulted my date outright by implying she should have and now I'm sitting here watching Charo on Letterman alone when I should be getting laid!"

Charlie laughs.

"So what's up sister? Did you just sense I needed to whine or what?"

"Oh nothing," she continues laughing. "Just wanted to tell you that I quit my job and I'm going to Japan!" She says it with a rising crescendo and is waving her arms like she is flying. Cheryl stirs on the couch.

"No way!"

"Yeah way, baby! Thought of it just today."

"What do you mean? Like, you've already told Mr. Whateveryourbossesnameis and bought a plane ticket?"

"Got my resignation right here in my hand and...and...I'm gonna buy a ticket soon. Hai!" She salutes the phone.

"More details. I need more details Diaz-san!" Renny is excited.

"Stop being so practical already." She feels a little more sober. She isn't sure of the details.

"Come on. How can you spring this on me and expect me not to want to know more?"

"Alright. Alright." She tells him of her conversation with Joan and how it all came together with how she was feeling and how she just decided.

"So, where does this leave me, twin sister?"

"In the dust, twin brother." She is airborne again, making engine sounds.

"Have you told the folks yet?"

She laughs nervously. "No. But they'll deal. I hope. And if they don't, well..." Her voice trails off and she shrugs and he feels it.

"Yeah. They'll deal. What about Cory?"

"History. Get with it man!" Her voice sounds stronger than she feels.

They talk for longer about nothing in particular. He is still bored with his job and she rubs it in a little.

"You'll just have to follow the superior intellect and intuition of our pair, as usual," she says with a snicker.

"Yeah right, does that mean I should've sold frozen peas too?"

"Hey, you do, in a way," she replies, referring to his job, "so don't act so high and mighty now." He laughs and they banter some more and when they hang up after "I love you's", she suddenly is exhausted.

She turns in her resignation letter the next day. It takes a bit of explaining and her boss acts upset, but in the end he accepts it all. She feels a burden released from her, like peeing after having to hold it in forever, as she walks out of his office. The rest of the day is a blur of informing her coworkers and explaining herself. She tries not to sound too smug, but she can hardly avoid it. She feels smug, after all. She is about to launch into the wonderful unknown and everyone in the office seems stuck there. *What is it*, she wonders, *that makes people wary and suspicious about doing something different?* Most people take her news in stride and go on about their business, wishing her the best and likely soon to forget it and her. There are a few of them, however, that give her a bad vibe: Is it disdain, or even jealousy? Maybe they think that she is violating the rule that says, "Conform or be ostracized!" She shakes off these vibes easily, but also stores them for later contemplation. Before she knows it, she is home for the weekend and already laying out plans.

Joan calls her next day, saying she spoke to Andrea and the ball is rolling. She left that on the answering machine and Charlie listens to it three times. Joan was so calm. It is unnerving and heartening at the same time. She left Andrea's phone number and a good time to call, noting the time zone and international dateline differences. Charlie calls Joan and leaves a message, thanking her.

Charlie spends the rest of the weekend visiting bookstores and making lists of things to do, such as buying luggage and checking visa and passport status and making phone calls. She finally calls Andrea on Sunday night and learns it is Monday morning there.

"Mushy–mushy!" Charlie isn't prepared for that. She will later learn the Japanese phone greeting, "moshi moshi."

"Hi Andrea? This is Charlie Diaz calling from Seattle. I got your number from Aunt Joan."

"Hi Charlie! How are you? Aunt Joan phoned a couple days ago and said you might be calling. So you're thinking about jumping ship, eh?"

"If the waters seem friendly."

"Oh, they're probably too friendly. You shouldn't have any problem. When are you thinking about coming?"

"I'm planning on leaving Seattle in a month or so and …. I'd like to travel for a month or two before coming to Tokyo." She hasn't actually worked this out yet and it just then occurs to her to travel first. She is proud of herself for being so spontaneous. "What's the best timing for finding work?"

"For hostessing, anytime is a good time. I can probably set you up with something at the place where I work. If you want to teach English, each school has its own time frame for stopping and starting up again. If you teach privates, which is what I do, they go anytime and pay better and you don't have to deal with offices and the like."

"Sounds like the way to go."

"Well, most of us took what came our way at first and worked up from there."

"Oh sure. What are accommodations like?" Charlie had heard horror stories: tiny rooms with no furniture, jumping spiders, paper-thin walls, and outrageous prices. "Do you think you could help me find a guest house or something?"

"Oh right on you. It can be a challenge, but not as bad as everyone lets on. I think you could doss at our place for a few nights until you get set up. I have to pass that by my roomie, but I don't think it'll be a problem."

"Oh thank you so much!" Charlie is ecstatic. "This is so great! I'm so excited and it's all kind of coming together." They discuss visas and money and Andrea reassures Charlie that a couple of thousand is enough to get set up. They hang up with Charlie promising to call back in a week or two with an update.

This is going even better than I had hoped. Andrea was so helpful and full of information. Charlie calls her parents. They take it pretty well, all things considered. Dad even offers to help with money, but she declines. This has to be her show, she tells him. It is a rite of passage. In the end, they are both supportive and even seem to have an appreciation for Charlie's decision.

"I always wanted to do some wandering around myself, but I had too many responsibilities and family. I can see where you're coming from." Dad tries to relate. "It won't stop me from worrying though." Mom throws in her not-unexpected dose of caution.

"You be careful with those Asian men now. I hear they think all western women are loose and they try to take advantage. Watch yourself around them." Mom is so Midwest. Charlie is relieved to have that over with and secretly appreciates their concern almost as much as their support.

As her preparations continue later that week, she finds a dizzying array of travel possibilities available. She chooses her first destination almost by accident. In her search for cheap airfares, she happens across a 'round-the-world ticket with stops in London, New Delhi, Bangkok and Tokyo. It is a unique booking at a cut rate and after thinking about it for half a day, she – impulsively she feels – purchases it. She could have obtained more flexibility with destinations and timing for a higher price, but this one feels right and she is beginning to pay more attention to her gut. Going with the flow seems more and more natural.

She has to book the dates right then and chooses one week in London, and three weeks each in India and Thailand. She would like to stay for longer in each place, but her concern over money and for getting settled in Tokyo override that idea. She books the return leg from Tokyo to Seattle on the last possible day, which is a year from the day she will leave for London.

The next couple of weeks fly by in a frenzy of activity, both at work and around town in planning for the trip. Charlie makes a point of having lunch with those few co-workers with whom she feels a true affinity. They are supportive of her adventure and she is very grateful to them for that. They convince her that she isn't crazy, just crazed – and that is not a bad thing. On her last day, her section holds a goodbye party for her with a cake that says "Good Luck" and a Swiss Army knife as a going-away present. When it is done, she feels slightly let down. It is all so anticlimactic. She wants to feel triumphant, but instead is nostalgic and even a little apprehensive. That melancholy passes quickly though, when later that day at her desk she calls Andrea and gives her the up-to-date plan. Andrea, in turn, gives Charlie directions to her pad in Shinsaibashi and a two-months-hence welcome. She feels a twinge of guilt at milking the company for the call, but it is just that.

On her way out the door, her last paycheck with accrued vacation in hand, Charlie is awash in the feeling of freedom. She'd been awaiting that tingling and she is intoxicated with it. Driving home she decides to rid herself of her planner and all it means. The planner represents, now to her, the company's need for overarching organization and control. Charlie found herself sucked into its power just a few short weeks after beginning work there. It was a gift on her first day from her new boss. From then on, it never left her side and she was lost without it. At meetings, she often looked around and compared the style and heft of hers with those being lovingly stroked and petted by their owners. As the newer electronic versions took hold, she found herself desiring one at first, then, as she thought about it, she decided she didn't want to go that route. She realized it would have been just one more step in the chain of bigger and better, and taking it would have left her farther from the road she has now finally found. All of her managers define their lives through their planners, so it seems. Getting rid of it will be fun.

Her apartment is a maze of boxes and piles of crap. She has decided to give away most of her things in a potlatch party just before departure, which is ten days away. Joan has offered to store a few boxes in her basement (but just a few!) and also to send a duffel bag of "work clothes" that Charlie will need in Tokyo once she arrives. Charlie looks around her apartment and gives in to the impulse to organize it on paper. She reaches for her planner then stops herself. *How easy it is to forget. And who gives a flying fuck how all this crap is organized?* She chuckles to herself.

She sits down at the kitchen table and slowly flips through the lambskin binder, once so elegant and now an outmoded piece of junk. She pulls out those few pages with information she needs, like addresses and scraps of paper with phone numbers. The remaining binder and pages inside lay as a gutted carcass on her kitchen table. She looks at it, sipping a beer. Then an insight comes to her and she rises from her seat and methodically gathers the following: an old metal trashcan from the basement, into which she throws a few odd two by four ends lying nearby; a stack of newspapers; a rusty half-full can of lighter fluid long since abandoned; and some matches. She brings the trashcan with its contents to her apartment and gleefully crumples up some of the newspaper and places it underneath the wood.

On top of the heap she ceremoniously places her brown leather planner. If someone could see her, she would appear like someone meditating over garbage, hands clasped to her lips and eyes closed. She loses herself in the moment for a minute or two and breaks out of it with a wide smile, shaking her head as if to shrug off cobwebs. She then walks carefully around her apartment, searching for things to add to the pile. She adds a binder from a training she gave on marketing frozen veggies – "Intermediate Procedures for Distribution and Sales of Frozen Corn in the Western Region" – and some old stacks of paid bills. She hefts the bin and its contents to the roof by way of the outside fire escape, which takes a little doing. She returns down the stairs to her apartment and comes back up with a cleaning bucket full of water.

The night is cool and cloudy and the rain has subsided. She squirts the entire contents of the lighter fluid into the garbage can and then drops a match into it. The flame erupts ten feet high with a *whoosh*, emitting an acrid black smoke, which scares the shit out of Charlie. She jumps back and hoots. She almost pours the water into the can right away, but as it settles down to a slow, steady burn, she also settles in with it. She is concerned about someone reporting the fire via 911, but then it is already too late for that, so lets the thought go up with the wispy smoke. The embers are mesmerizing. Peering into the can she sees her planner shriveling into a wrinkled black blob.

How appropriate, ashes to the old and a new start. I hope I took out everything that I needed. Oh, who cares! Charlie shouts silently to the Seattle rooftops as her inner strength finds its voice. *It's all just words on paper. Remember how proud you felt when Mr. Boyd gave that planner to you? Like you were part of the team, part of something bigger, something meaningful. What happened to that feeling? Shit – I hope no one sees all this black smoke and does call the fire department!*

She relapses into self-doubt for a moment. Then, ...*Sorry officer, I was just trying to burn this sucker down!* She breaks out in a fit of giggles that turns into a full laughing convulsion. Her eyes are watering and her sides ache. As it subsides she looks around her. *Anybody watching this would think I was a mad woman! I am a mad woman!? Or I need to be.* It starts to drizzle. She pours the bucket of water onto the flames and they hiss and pop. The sides of the can buckle but hold, and as the water seeps out the bottom, so too do her own worries and fears, for the moment. She goes downstairs, grabs her purse and keys and skips off to the pub.

༄༄༄༄༄ ༄༄༄༄༄ ༄༄༄༄༄ ༄༄༄༄༄ ༄༄༄༄༄

The following ten days wind their way through Charlie's life as a series of final phone calls, endless driving errands and the limitless details of closing up shop. She meets with friends and pays bills and delivers boxes, reads through "Southeast Asia on a Shoestring" and buys maps of everywhere on her route. On the Saturday before she departs, she hosts the potlatch party at her apartment. Cheryl helps her put it together and it threatens to turn into a full-blown rager. Starting promptly at noon, friends and friends-of-friends start coming by to select items and pull a draft from the keg. They end up staying for hours, of course, and by early evening her apartment is packed with people she doesn't know. Luckily, the keg runs dry around eight o'clock and the party dwindles to a dozen by nine. Most of those left are friends from her days at the restaurant. Jack, the Armenian chef, with whom she had a brief fling; Tara, Julie and Alicia, waitresses who all worked at other restaurants now and miraculously got a Saturday night off; Eddy and Trent, bartenders from two taverns on her old restaurant block.

She realizes how much she would miss these people and wondered why the "professional" crowd from the office lacked their sincerity. *No, that's not entirely fair*, she thinks. *We all get caught up in it, me included.* A couple of folks from the office showed up, but none remain. They are busy people with families, and she is an outsider now – a crazy, unattached, undirected fool. She doesn't feel slighted by it, but the feeling that she had earlier, of having put something over on them, has mellowed. Charlie knows she is doing the right thing for herself, but whether or not it is right for everyone is certainly in question. Cheryl comes up beside her.

"For somebody going on a long vacation you sure seem quiet."

"Oh, hey, I was just thinking about everyone here and how I'm going to miss you all."

"I think that means you need another drink." Someone had procured a few six packs and Cheryl retrieves two bottles.

"I guess it does!" She smiles. "Hey Cheryl, thanks for doing all this, and for letting me crash at your place until Wednesday, and...for...you know..." She lifts her bottle and Cheryl follows and sighs.

"I don't know who I'm going to whine to now that you're up and leaving." She looks away. Charlie puts her arm around her shoulder and they stare out into the room.

The potlatch aspect of the party is a rousing success. Most of her stuff has been carted away, save for a mattress and a couple of boxes of kitchen knick-knacks. The mattress is due to be picked up on Monday by Eddy, who is also purchasing her car. The leftover boxes are easy Goodwill giveaways. Late that night Charlie sits in her almost-empty apartment and surveys the scene. A few stuffed trash bags are all that remain in the living room. Her backpack and shoulder bag are in the closet and she pulls out the sleeping bag and lays it on the mattress. This is her last night here. She will spend the next three with Cheryl and then fly to London, stopping in Cincinnati for two days. The restaurant crowd gave her a poster collage of photographs with signed farewells. She falls asleep looking at it, reminiscing on what had been and fantasizing of what is to come.

The day before she leaves Seattle, Charlie meets Joan for lunch one more time at their favorite diner. Joan is preoccupied with a newly conceived trip to Southern California, but not so much as to detract from Charlie's big adventure. "I had to do something now that you're off. I can't let myself be shown up by you young whippersnappers."

"You said you're buying a condo in Laguna?"

"Maybe. I'll give it a good look. MK is from there and we thought to head down together." MK is a champion lawn bowler in the senior ladies division. She and Joan have been dating recently.

"I didn't know you two were so serious."

"Neither did I. Maybe we're not." She shrugs her shoulders and smiles.

"Don't go getting yourself in trouble now." Charlie relishes the role reversal.

"Hah! You're one to talk Ms. Diaz."

Charlie feigns astonishment. She is glad for the lighthearted tone. She had been worried about getting emotional and blubbery. They continue the meal, chatting about the challenges of life on the road for a single woman, and board the bus together afterwards. As they near Charlie's stop, Joan says, "I don't know how you are for writing, but I'll be expecting something now and then."

"You can be sure of it. Check your email too." Charlie had helped Joan get set up with a computer and email and they corresponded this way already.

"I will. Take care of yourself now." They hug and hold it for a few seconds longer than usual and Charlie pulls the bus cord. She steps down, waving as the bus and her friend move on.

Cheryl drives her to the airport the next day. It ends up being a rush because Cheryl gets called in to work and has to drop her off in front, avoiding the half-expected wait together. *Better this way*, Charlie thinks. They speak in the car on the way in about Cheryl joining her somewhere along the road and Charlie has a vague premonition that something exotic waits ahead for the two of them, but she doesn't mention it. Their goodbye is swift and Charlie enters the airport feeling like her new journey has begun in earnest.

☯☯☯☯☯   ☯☯☯☯☯   ☯☯☯☯☯   ☯☯☯☯☯   ☯☯☯☯☯

Cincinnati and the folks are pleasant enough. Dad is a little choked up to see her and Mom is her usual. That evening they call Renny, with Mom and Dad on the upstairs phone and Charlie downstairs on the extension.

"Do you have any ideas like your sister, Rene?" Mom enquired.

"I'm thinking about it Mom. Why not? You know."

"Here's your father."

"Love you Mom."

"Hey Ren, what do you think about your sister taking off on us?"

"Dad, I'm not..." Charlie tries to break in.

"She'll be ok Dad," Renny interjects. "If she gets into trouble, I'll help her out."

"Right! More like the reverse I think!" Charlie shoots back.

"Well just don't make me have to come get both of you," Dad says with a laugh that is half-filled with concern.

They laugh together and then there is an awkward silence. Mom comes back in with news about aunts and uncles and they small-talk the rest. Hanging up, Charlie has a peculiar sensation that she assigns to feeling like an adult with her family for the first time she can remember. It feels good.

☯☯☯☯☯ ☯☯☯☯☯ ☯☯☯☯☯ ☯☯☯☯☯ ☯☯☯☯☯

Goodbye Cincinnati, Ohio, USA. For now. She sees the airport runway recede in the distance over the wing of the plane. She fingers the wad of five hundred dollars in her pocket that Dad pressed upon her at the gate. She tried sincerely to not take it but Dad was insistent and, in truth, she was happy to have it. She changes planes in New York without a hitch and sleeps halfway to London. She is excited and numb and in the moment – ready to take things as they come.

3

RENNY

SAN FRANCISCO   KYOTO   BANGKOK   KATMANDU   LAKE TOBA   VARANASSI   IPOH

YEAR 1   YEAR 2   YEAR 3

A BICYCLE, SEX, AND A ROCK GARDEN

Returning to Japan after a five-month absence gave me a feeling of coming home. I knew I wouldn't be in-country long and wanted to savor it. After Tony went off to work, I scrounged an old bike out of a nearby park and had instant transport. Junk bicycle piles are a unique urban phenomenon in Japan and common in Kyoto parks. These bikes were either stolen or abandoned or left to rust by locals who had to make space for new ones. An average pile might consist of up to twenty bikes in various states of disrepair. Sometimes you can find a usable bike outright, but mostly you have to take various parts and assemble them into a new, personalized creation.

The official word is not to touch them, but they are an irresistible stash of salvage to the enterprising gaijin in need of wheels. With a wrench, a screwdriver and an hour, any slightly mechanically-inclined individual can put together a decent bike. You have to put up with a few disapproving stares here and there from passers-by – mostly from the old Mama-sans hanging out in the park, wondering what in the hell has happened to good, ole' systematic Japan and how did all these uncouth foreigners get in? On the flip side, putting a bike together from "garbage" also attracts the friendly curiosity of children and vagrants. It's not that there aren't Japanese who do this sort of thing, but these "unhammered nails" who have resisted being pounded down are more surreptitious about it and are of a character that does not invite scrutiny from the mainstream Mama-san.

With my newly created, truly unique machine, I pedaled down the river path. My new bicycle was a classic blue ten-speed frame with upright BMX style handlebars and a yellow seat. I stopped at a bicycle shop to purchase a cheap lock and cycled onward to a small restaurant on the north side of the Imperial Park. I was early for lunch with Eric, so I sat with a well-thumbed Daily Yomiuri English newspaper from the day before and sipped some coffee until he came. The Osaka sumo tournament was closing up and the Hawaiians were fading. I sat in the back corner and watched for Eric.

He was instantly easy to spot, not only because he was a white gaijin, but because he had an impeccable manner of dress that would set him apart in any country. He saw me and came gliding down the aisle in a long black leather trench coat. Black was in among the local fashion conscious, but that was grunge black with big boots. Eric in lambskin and Italian leather shoes was a swan among pigeons. He flashed a dazzling, practiced smile and I got up to give him a hug.

"Dapper as always," I said.

"The opposite, as always, for you my friend," he smiled.

"I don't want to challenge the stereotype now."

"Yeah. Likewise." Eric came out just before our introduction over a year ago. He was proud about being gay and could be in-your-face-about-it and graceful all at once.

"You seem to be doing well. Not working too hard, I hope."

"I'm glad the term is almost up. Hawaii for a few weeks is just the thing I need. I'm burnt out this year. But other than that, things are good."

"Kenji is still in the picture?"

He looked partially resigned. "Same as always." Kenji was Eric's Japanese counterpart and erstwhile mate. He was a quiet and graceful fellow who was openly gay in all manners, quite a rarity for an adult Japanese male, except that he was celibate. I never quite understood why this was so and it never ceased to be a topic of interesting conversation for Eric and me. "At least I've got him to watch me now." Eric, if he was to be believed (which I usually did), had the libido of a chimpanzee during mating season. I'd often argued with him that his claims were physically unlikely, if not impossible. They would go something like this:

> Me: "A guy can't come twice a day or more, every day, forever. You've got to have time to replenish. You could do it for a few days maybe, but you'd be severely depleted and wiped out at the end."
>
> Eric: "Look, I know the statistics." (I didn't doubt it.) "I think that I just have an abnormally active production capacity. I mean, I have to come twice a day or I get cranky, start sweating, and can't concentrate on anything else."

Normally I would have taken this as a boast, males being what we are and prone to exaggeration. However, Eric was so sincere and even distressed with this 'predicament' that I believed him. It was an odd, sad, karmic joke that he hooked up and fell in love with one so monastically inclined.

We went up to the counter to order the daily special and he informed me that he'd run into Louise and asked her to join us. I was delighted. Louise was teaching at a school nearby and would come as soon as her class was over. We sat down with our numbers.

"So, what's happening with the plan?" I asked.

"One more year, I think. I've got letters off to three major airlines and I'm going to a recruiting session next month." As I knew from the occasional substitute teaching stint at a larger school, major airlines held these huge tryouts for future flight attendants once or twice a year. You could tell when one was coming up when classes started to fill up with perky young women wanting to hone up on their conversation skills.

"Can you take another year without losing it?"

"As long as I get out of here every chance I get."

I nodded. Eric was a variation of the M and M class of gaijin. He worked a similar job to Mike and Mark's and generally enjoyed his life, but fled the confines of Japanese culture and the frigid winter temperatures whenever the opportunity arose. But I figured it had more to do with running towards paradise than with escaping from Japan. We were not so different in that regard. M and M pursued expat fame and found it – and a willing audience in young Japanese psuedo-rebels. Eric, with only a slight twist on the theme, sought a life where he could embrace his sexuality and express himself freely. This he could not do in his hometown of Oklahoma City. His plan was to join an airline as a flight attendant and work his way into a permanent position in first class. Me....well, I don't really know what the hell I want, but I know it's just around the corner and I pursue it with gusto.

Louise came in and we rose to greet her. She presented an imposing figure at over six feet three and a placid, unreadable, but graceful face. She walked with perfect posture and reserved demeanor, if there is such a thing, and always appeared introspective, though I knew better. She greeted me with a sincere smile and hug.

"Nice to see you Chieftess," I said.

"You as well. My you're looking tan and healthy."

"Isn't he though?! God, I have to get to the sun. Look at me. I'm a bleached bone next to you."

"You are bleached, Eric. God you really look awful. Are you ok?" She looked truly concerned.

He almost bought it, but then broke into a wide smile. "Never a break," he said, shaking his head, but still grinning at her too-good, too-dry humor.

They called our numbers and we picked up our food as Louise ordered hers.

"The practice is going well?" I asked her.

"Yes. I've picked up a few new clients and I've started a new course on introductory shiatsu. Six students signed up and I gave the first lesson yesterday. So tell me about you now. What's been happening?"

"Oh you know, same ole' same ole'" I sighed casually.

"Now that's not going to cut it Mr. Diaz." She gave me a stern look and I withered. "What's it been, five months since you left us? Last I heard you were in Indonesia at the orangutan place."

"You know orangutans practice same sex couplings," Eric chimed. "I think he's beginning to see the light." He nodded at me. She gave him the same look, but his grin remained steady.

"I went to Thailand after that for two months and now I'm here."

"So…. what, – beaches, trekking, Buddhas?" asked Louise.

"The Buddhas in Thailand are spectacular. They look like what you really think the Buddha must've looked like. And they're everywhere."

"What do you mean what he must've looked like? It's all just a crock of organized religious crap to oppress the poor folks." Eric was serious now.

I laughed and Louise said, "Come on, you don't think there's any spirituality there? They've been thinking about it for centuries. How to find peace and be at one with the things around you. And you, you're one to talk, Eric. You love Zen rock gardens don't you?"

"Yeah, because there's nothing there, that's the whole point!"

"But…" they called her number and we were, for the moment, spared the repartee.

When she returned I jumped back in.

"Anyway, the Buddhas are extremely cool. After a seeing a few, I got to see them from more of an historical point of view. You know, how the styles changed over time and from place to place. And they are usually set in peaceful places to hang out and, hey, what else have you got to do when you're visiting a place."

"How about hang out at the beaches, man?! Come on. That's where I'd be the whole time."

"With one thing on your mind too." Louise shook her head, but also smiled.

"I did some of that beach stuff too, as you can see. You can't do it all the time though. Too much of a party scene. I didn't want to stay inebriated my whole trip." I avoided Eric's inevitable comment by quickly changing the subject. "How's Alex doing?"

"Oh he's fine. He's just now finishing up his research and he's getting ready to write the dissertation this summer I think." She seemed a touch melancholic, but I didn't pursue it.

"He's writing about, something like semiotics or semantics, right?" Eric was sincere.

"Semiotics, yeah. I'm not really sure about it myself, and I live with the guy!"

"I can never seem to pin him down on what he's studying either," I said. "Not that that means anything!"

"Too much wasted brain power, man." Eric respected Alex's work but knew there was a better place to focus one's energy.

"Like you're a guy to be talking about wasted energy." I was sucked into the macho exchange.

"What are you guys talking about? We need to inject some female energy into this discussion." A pained and incredulous look appeared on her face.

"That's why I like it when you're around," I said.

"What does that mean? Female energy...hmmmpf. You're a more masculine female and I'm a more feminine male than anyone else I know" Eric spat out, righteously.

"That's why I like it when you're around too," I added.

Louise was taken aback and I liked it because it happened so rarely. With her usual grace, though spiced with a touch of aplomb, she said, "Weren't we talking about Buddhas and Thailand?"

"Some of the Buddhas I've seen have breasts.... speaking in terms of the male-female thing, that is." Eric was still goading Louise.

"Androgyny is part of the aura, I think." I had to get something in.

"So you were focusing on androgyny and spirituality in your Buddha quest in Thailand?" She was so smooth.

My turn to pause and ponder. "I hadn't thought of it that way, but I'm open to the possibility. Yin-Yang and all that. Is that true about orangs?"

"I.... wish I could say I had a reliable source." Eric backed down a bit. "I heard some Japanese salaryman using that line in a bar. My Japanese is pretty good but he was trying to pick me up and he'd been drinking and so had I. It sounded something like that. "o-ran-gu-tan" – I guess he could have been talking about oranges, but what the hell."

Louise chuckled "Oh my God," finishing it with a sigh and a shake of her head.

"So I guess you're hanging out in Kyoto for a while longer?" I asked her.

"Yeah, I think so. I'm still learning a lot and business is good. I'm not ready to live in Sydney again just yet."

This was one of the idiosyncratic realities of living the expat lifestyle in Japan, where a foreigner could never become a native. Most everyone, while leaving wherever they were from, for whatever reason – which very likely included boredom and wanderlust – framed the future in terms of when they would return "home". I was not immune to this myself, but having observed the situation for what it was, always tried to come up with something different. I'd yet to settle upon a phrase or style of discussing the future, but I figured if I kept at it, someday it would come to me.

"And what about you now? You're heading back to the states in a month or so?"

"Yeah. I think it's time to move on. I thought I'd give drag racing a try."

Dead silence.

Eric started to say something but Louise cut him off, holding her hand up. "Don't even go there." Eric looked wronged.

"I don't know what's next. Maybe grad school." This was the pat answer that always left your listeners with thoughtful expressions. They looked thoughtful.

"What would you want to study?"

"Oh ... I don't know. I did my undergrad in English Lit. Maybe I'd take that a step further. Speaking of getting *lit*, I've got something for you." I said, nodding to Eric. He gave me a severe look that said, "Shut up and be more discreet will you!" I got the point and so did Louise, though she tactfully didn't say a word.

After a short, painful silence, we lapsed into small talk about sumo and the weather. Before parting they invited me along for a group gathering – a couple of days in the Okayama countryside at a small inn. Louise and Tony and some others had planned this weeks ago, and Tony had mentioned it to me the night before. I was happy to be included.

Louise departed in a hurry to her next appointment and we walked her out. Eric and I decided to leave our bikes by the restaurant and take a walk through the Imperial Palace grounds, which we took great pride in calling The Gōshō, only slightly butchering the Japanese pronunciation.

The Gōshō is unusual, not only because it is a two square mile postage stamp of unconcreted, open land in the middle of a modern Japanese city, but also because its green grass, trees and ponds are bordered by marching-band-sized gravel parade lanes. These lanes are a hundred yards across in places and, as no motorized traffic is allowed through The Gōshō, they are always eerily empty compared to the bustling avenues outside the park. The original purpose of the grounds was as a residence for the imperial family, so the wide lanes had been designed for security and ceremonies. I loved bicycling through the park just to escape the city for a few blocks. I would go out of my way to do so whenever the chance presented itself.

We walked towards the softball fields near the northwest corner of the park and sat on a cold stone bench. We both took great pains to glance around us without making the scan obvious, though in truth, this wasn't really necessary. There was an older, hunched over couple trailing a Pekinese on the far trail, but too far out off to worry about. Out of my backpack I pulled a large, thin cardboard envelope and handed it ceremoniously it to Eric with both hands on the package, making a slight bow. "*Omedeto gozaimasu,*" I said solemnly, acting out a Japanese ritual of saying congratulations.

He opened the envelope gingerly, glancing around once again. "Smart ass. Any difficulties?"

"No, it was really kinda fun. Everything went smoothly, just like you said, only it cost an additional thousand baht, so you owe me."

He separated the cardboard, slid out the parchment carefully, and beheld his new credentials. On the virgin sheet of antique-looking vellum was a professionally embossed, very credible replica of a diploma from the University of Calgary. It stated that Eric earned a Master of Arts, received in Nineteen Hundred and Eighty Nine. He beamed as if he had truly just shook the dean's hand. Eric had been working in Japan for five years, lucky enough to get into the university teaching system when credentials were enumerated with the wink of an eye and rarely verified. But in the last year or so, much to the disappointment and occasional chagrin of bogus MA holders, university administrators were demanding legitimate diplomas, which included copies of the original. This document would help Eric out enormously.

He had asked me to check this out for him when I was in Bangkok, which is undeniably one of the counterfeit capitals of the world. Following the instructions Eric received discretely from a colleague at his school, I had no trouble locating the small sewing shop near the Khao San Road neighborhood. The tailor and I bantered around the unspoken until I brazenly requested the goods outright. He played dumb until money was mentioned. It all worked very smoothly and I was happy to do it, both for my friend Eric and for the sheer intrigue of it.

We walked back towards the restaurant to pick up our bikes. He started to give me some yen, but I stopped him. "Lets settle up in Okayama." "I think I'll end up owing you some back." We parted.

Three days later I was on an express JR train headed westward to the province of Okayama. I was riding with Tony and we were heading for a small, traditional Japanese inn, called a *ryokan*, up in the mountains. This particular ryokan was part of a provincial tourist program to lure foreign visitors out of the cities and into the gorgeous Japanese countryside. It was reserved exclusively for *tourists*, small enough to rent out in its entirety, and it was very inexpensive, by Japanese standards. We reserved the place for three nights and I was looking forward to the retreat. There isn't much opportunity in Japan to get away from the hustle and bustle of the city, outside of the little escape hatches like The Gōshō or the occasional rock garden. Being in the countryside, near rice paddies and bamboo forests, is an irresistible lure.

Four hours, two train changes, and a forty-five minute local bus ride later, we arrived. The bus wound its way up the tiny valley and stopped for us at the bottom of a short gravel drive. The driver pointed up the hill, wished us a good time and we were off. The ryokan was all on its own, on a small rise in the middle of a quilt of rice paddies. Louise and Alex were already there. Not far behind it was a densely forested hillside. They were sitting on the front decking and came down the driveway to greet us and help carry the groceries we brought for the weekend. Eric and Kenji were on their way, and late that evening we expected Miyako, Barry and Marina.

The ryokan building itself was an old converted farmhouse with thatched roofing and joined carpentry. The inside was mostly open and centered around a sunken fire pit, or hibachi. A huge beam ran along the length of the ceiling and the center of the roof was blackened from years of smoke from the fires. A modern kitchen was installed in one corner and four small rooms bordered the other two sides, all opening to the center with sliding *shoji* doors. The kitchen floor was vinyl, but the rest of the rooms had tatami mats. The three couples had dibs on three of the private rooms, and it was left to Marina, Tony and I to work out who would get the fourth room. Though the ryokan was well stocked with futons and blankets, we each brought sleeping bags and camping pads for flexibility and comfort. Some of the Japanese futons were unbelievably thin and while this is supposed to be better for your back; sometimes it just doesn't cut it.

Louise had already cooked up some rice in the rice maker and Tony and I both took bowls gratefully. Plain, white rice with a light sprinkling of toasted sesame seeds. We sat down at the table where Louise and Alex were having tea in silence. It seemed as if our arrival interrupted a serious discussion they were having out front.

I hadn't seen Alex for some time, but he seemed as furtive and squirrelly as ever. He was enormously intelligent and scholarly in demeanor. He had been in Japan for three years, gathering data for his PhD dissertation in Sociology and Linguistics. Adding to his quirkiness was his peculiar and high-pitched nervous laugh, which asserted itself at the oddest of moments. I chalked it up to Alex feeling insecure most of the time, but he and his laugh were disconcerting all the same. He spoke with a Michigander's accent and never dropped the scholars pose. Tony and I ate our rice quickly and then excused ourselves to take a short walk around the grounds.

The remaining five of our party showed up together in a taxi around seven o'clock. They ran into each other by accident at the second train station and traveled the rest of the way together. Since the bus stopped running at six o'clock, they shared a cab and arrived in good spirits. Barry brought his kendo swords with him and approached the ryokan with the bearing of a samurai. He reminded me of Richard Chamberlain in <u>Shogun</u>, and with Miyako as his lover, the comparison was complete. He spoke excellent Japanese and was fearsomely confident. I knew him only a little from evenings at The Boar, but was at ease with him and took great pleasure in kidding around, mostly because no one else would. Miyako was polite and smiling and unbelievably beautiful. I found myself wondering how Barry snagged her?

51

Marina was an Indian Brit who I knew even less well than Barry. I thought she was painfully shy the first time we met, but then she was surprisingly extroverted the second. This time she was pleasant and cordial, greeting Tony and me with warm hugs. I was curious to see who she would become as this weekend progressed.

Kenji avoided the hugs by darting into the house. He was already busy setting up and surveying. Despite being good friends with Eric for a year, I had never spoken with Kenji one on one, eye to eye, and I suspected I never would.

Copious amounts of Japanese beer had been ferried in for the weekend festivities, and it made its way out and into our hands within ten minutes. Everyone helped themselves to rice and condiments and we decided to pass on a larger dinner. As night settled in, we started a roaring fire in the hibachi with the wood provided and sat around it on the tatami floor. Tony crafted a couple of smoking pipes – one out of an empty soda can and another out of a cored apple, and then he, Barry, Eric, Marina and I smoked. I could tell it made Miyako nervous – she got up, went into the kitchen, and looked out of the window. She stayed there to talk to Kenji, who was making something sweet for dessert. Alex did not smoke, though I encouraged him to try it in the hopes it would perk up his disposition. Instead, he sniffed disapprovingly. But so what?

Louise also passed on the pipe, and in an official tone announced that she would like to give everyone a short massage during the next couple of days. She was a master of shiatsu and everyone knew that her offer was indeed a gift. We all murmured with approval and Marina jumped up to be first. They went into one of the bedrooms and closed the sliding door.

With all of the women out of the room, the testosterone began to build. Tony was looking appreciatively at Barry's *katana*, sitting in their sheaths next to the fire.

"You're an aikido man, if I recall," Barry said.

"Yes. I've been working at it for a couple of years."

"Ever tried working with one of these?" He picked up one of the wooden swords, stood up and made a few practiced downward slicing motions.

"Not seriously, but I'm fascinated by it." Tony picked up the second sword carefully.

Barry continued a series of slow twisting and cutting motions with the katana. He was showing off, but I didn't care. Alex, however, looked on with disdain and that I could not ignore.

"You don't like the martial arts I take it?" I said to him.

"They're too violent for me. I don't see the point."

"The point is self discipline," said Barry, overhearing.

"You can practice self discipline a lot of ways. You don't have to act like you want to harm someone." The nervous laugh followed.

"I thought you liked tai chi?" I said.

"Tai chi is not martial. It's about centering and balance."

"But its basis is martial, it's just slower and more controlled," Tony piped in.

"That may be true, but it's not aggressive."

"Neither is aikido. That's all about redirecting energy. It's very similar to tai chi in that way."

"Tai chi is just dancing." Barry said it mockingly and I couldn't tell if he meant it or not.

"Yeah. And kendo is just baton twirling," I threw back.

He smiled. "What do you know about it Diaz? As far as I can tell you don't practice anything."

"I am a serious practitioner of smokingdō," I retorted, reaching for the soda-can pipe and reloading it with a fresh hit. "And what's wrong with dancing?"

"Dancing is not manly." Eric chimed in with a mocking tone.

Barry leveled the sword point near Eric's neck. Eric got up on his knees and bent over so the sword was pointing at his butt. "But as you can see, kendo is manly."

Barry poked him lightly with a laugh and withdrew, saying, "Dancing is too free-form. The serious martial arts are more structured, more real. More here and now. Now aikido I can

53

respect." He nodded to Tony. "Tai chi, though, is a little too....wishy washy."

Alex missed the light hearted tone of the comment and with a flustered sigh replied, "Well I don't care if you respect tai chi or not. I'm not out to hurt anybody and I'm here now."

"So you are." Barry looked thoughtful and returned to his practice.

The door slid quietly open behind us. Louise was done working on Marina, and called out, "What's this about wishy washy and respect? Sounds like you're afraid of the softer side Mr. Crane."

Alex was visibly relieved at the help and Barry was caught off guard. He paused to collect his thoughts.

"I don't think of it as hard or soft," he recovered nicely.

Louise walked up to him and stroked his katana, smiling at him. "What *do* you think of it as?"

He raised the sword slowly upright as if the stroking was having an effect, but mostly in a mock defensive gesture. "I think it....is......time to see what Miyako is doing in the kitchen." He beat a hasty retreat, bowing to our chuckles. Louise stood with her hands on her hips and a wry, knowing smile. Alex looked righteous.

Marina walked out and sat beside me. Her long black hair hung down over her shoulders and she seemed relaxed and flushed. She reached for the can and took a deep drag.

"I like dancing," she said. I nodded and felt stupid because I couldn't think of a pithy reply. Fortunately she handed me the can so I had something else to do with my lips.

Kenji had made chocolate chip cookies and we devoured them before they had a chance to cool. He seemed pleased at the feeding frenzy and we all encouraged him to make some more. He didn't give a clear answer.

Finishing up the cookies, we sat in that mesmerized state that comes on when you sit, stuffed and sauced, around a late night flame.

"Let's go back to the self-discipline discussion," I said.

"What about it?" replied Tony.

"I've been thinking....why is it so important? I mean, I think it's a good idea in an overall sense, but then I think....why not fulfill and indulge yourself as much as you're able?"

"Because it would lead to...to...anarchy and ultimately, boredom," said Tony.

"Look at us now. Are we bored?"

"That's not what he means," said Barry. Tony looked at him curiously. "At least, that's not what I think he means. From my point of view, self-discipline is a means to be excellent at something. NOT to be disciplined is...... boring."

He looked expectantly at Tony who nodded, replying, "That's close enough."

Louise shifted her legs and said, "I don't think self-discipline leads necessarily to excellence, but maybe to balance. You can't fully experience one extreme without the opposite in perspective."

"Why can't you be fully hedonistic or ascetic and be happy in it?" said Eric.

"I think you can be if you accept that a hedonist is who you are," Marina chimed in.

"I agree with that, but only to a point. You can change yourself and you can get better at something if you want to. When I study kendo, it helps me focus and become more aware, so I don't have to accept how I am now."

"Are you saying that because you choose to focus on something it makes you more....more....mo betta than me, because I choose not to discipline myself?" I said.

"I think it's more the point that you do something because you *need* to and that's that." Tony nodded to Barry.

Alex had been itching to get in on this. He blurted out, "But you have to have a standard. Otherwise it would be anarchy. And there would be no way to judge anything."

"That's true, but who's to say one standard is superior to another? Potayto-potahto you know," Marina was brushing her hair; that and her musical Indian-British accent, among other things, drew my attention more and more. She noticed it and smiled and we started playing footsie. As there was no table, it was hard for everyone else not to notice

"That's just a matter of confidence," said Eric. "I know my shirt here is of far better quality than that rag Diaz has on. I don't care if anyone else is too uncultured to see it."

"So you are egoless my friend? I always knew we should be prostrating ourselves before you." I made an elaborate kowtow to him.

"It's about time you figured that out."

"My ego says to go to bed," yawned Louise. Alex joined her. Following them, the other couples drifted off in a slow Act II exit.

Tony went to the loo and before I knew it my fingers were running through Marina's hair. She wasn't startled by it, seeming almost to expect it. She soon maneuvered around to face me and we kissed. We both pulled back for a moment, sighing and smiling, and then plunged in to one of those tingling deep-down-in the-toes kisses. And then another.

"There's more to you than meets the eye," she teased on our next pause.

"I plead the fifth." She gave me a confused look. "It's an American thing."

"Well that explains it."

"It means...."

"Oh shut up already," she interrupted with a smile as she pulled herself up to me and we started again. We slurped to a stop when we heard Tony return and say, "I guess I've got the fucking living room then." We both smiled at him, she not making eye contact and me giving him an eyebrows up, "sorry pal" sort of look. We went to the bedroom and I threw his bag out the door, sliding the shoji closed with a thwack.

The moon provided enough illumination in the room, so we kept the light off. My rational self wanted to slow down. I didn't want to be the guy in a rush to get it done with. But our kisses gained intensity and depth as we wiggled down to the mat and the rational part of my brain shut down as our hands started roaming over each other. The steam had built in both of us. Marina started to sigh and I groaned in reply. She pulled back and looked in my eyes with a fire about to explode. She very deliberately let me undo my own shirt, as she ripped her top off over her head in one smooth motion, then in a split second was throwing her jeans across the room. She left her tiger-striped thong on. I paused in my undressing to watch her show, but was quick to catch up. In seconds we were entwined once again and rolling across the floor.

I paused to pull out the futons and some blankets out of the closet and as we settled under them, I realized I hadn't packed a condom.

"Fuck me. Fuck me. Fuck Me." I said, looking at her forlornly. "No condom." She lay back down, exhaling long and slow.

"Me neither," she replied. Then a mischievous smile came over her and she sidled up to me and she said, "I'll bet we can improvise." Her hand slid down to my crotch and we kissed some more. I put my hand over hers, but didn't remove it and pulled my mouth back from hers.

"You know I'm leaving the country in a few days?" She smiled back, sadly it seemed, and nodded her head.

"I don't want you to think I'm a loose floozy," she laughed nervously, and then said with more confidence, "but I'm okay with just being with you now." She looked sincerely right through me and I melted into her. She started stroking me and I closed my mouth over her erect brown nipples and soon exploded into her hand. I felt momentarily embarrassed at the mess, but relaxed as she smiled and handed me some tissues.

"Your turn now," I said when I was done cleaning. I cradled her in front of me and started caressing her all over.

"I'm not terribly good at this, with my hands I mean." She giggled playfully.

"I'll bet you can figure it out."

"You could show me how." She paused and half turned to look at me, and then exhaled deeply, settling back into my sitting spoon position.

"Okay." That was all she said. She guided my hands, first putting hers over mine and then switching them, with me following her motion. We swayed, grinded, and rolled our hips and thighs into each other with an ever-increasing energy. She soon arced her back in pleasure and I tried thrusting my fingers up into her deeper, but she stopped me by squeezing her legs tight around my hand so that I could feel her spasming. As we settled into a regular breathing pattern, I pulled some covers up over us.

"I think I could do that better next time."

She patted my hand and I could see her smiling. She said nothing.

About a half hour later I did do better, and with very little help. I know it's a male ego thing, but I'm proud of it just the same.

The next morning, I took the long, windy bus ride into town and bought enough condoms for everyone in the ryokan. That night, and the one after that, Marina and I continued our affair. I learned a bit about working with my hands, but I never learned much about Marina. We never ended up in deep discussion. I tried once to go into her background, but we were interrupted and she seemed glad for it, so I didn't bring it up again. She never pressed me for more either. That was fine by me. I was enchanted by her, and it seemed she with me, but we both knew reality would burst that bubble. Why destroy a fantasy in the midst of it? The irony of that first night is that by the third, Marina and I trusted each other completely. Well, enough to go directly oral. It's the first night I remember the most, though, because of its spontaneity I guess. At the end of those three nights I was wondering if maybe Eric was right?

Those three days were spent in a pleasant haze of verbal jousting, overeating and revelry among friends. The last morning, I was weary with inactivity, and so declared my intent to climb the mountain behind the inn. Eric, Marina, Barry, and Tony joined me. They trusted my instincts in following the path on the way up, but on our way down I decided to strike a new trail, and they willingly followed. We soon found ourselves on a very steep downward slope in thick, impassable brush. I knew the house was just below, but we needed to keep backtracking to find a way to get there. I enjoyed it immensely. Eric cursed and tore at the vines with a hearty vengeance, throwing a few choice words my way as well. Barry was stoic and serious and oddly businesslike. Tony and Marina were lacerated and exhausted, but seemed to enjoy it. When we finally came to a clearing, we whooped for joy and at the sight of the creek just above the ryokan. We shimmied out of our clothes to immerse ourselves in the cold spring water and soothe our scrapes. The others from the house had come up the path looking for us just then and joined us when they heard the hollering. Tony felt he needed to explain that he really wasn't that poorly endowed and that the water was really very cold. It was. We still didn't cut him any slack.

Marina and I parted after sharing the train from Okayama, and it was pretty much understood that what happened would remain where we left it. We never talked about it specifically and I wonder if that would have made a difference? We kissed goodbye before she got out at her station and that was it. Since then I keep hearing Janis in my head. *Take another little piece of my heart now baby...* I don't know what I was thinking would happen, or what I might have expected, or even what might have been possible if Marina had shown a little interest beyond the sex. It was one of those fork-in-the-road moments where my life could've taken a turn down an entirely different path. I was intrigued enough that I would have at least looked down it, perhaps even have taken a few steps, but not enough to start down it without any prodding. Marina has a piece of me now, whether she wanted it or not.

☯☯☯☯☯   ☯☯☯☯☯   ☯☯☯☯☯   ☯☯☯☯☯   ☯☯☯☯☯

Eric and I spent one of my remaining days in Kyoto visiting the Ryoanji Zen rock garden in the northwestern part of the city. The garden itself is, at first and to the uninitiated, often a disappointment. Ryoanji usually has dozens of busloads of tourists passing through it each day, the garden being among the most famous of its kind in the country. This particularly stormy day was no different. We entered the grounds and walked up the path to the main building. We removed our shoes and shuffled across the smooth wooden floors to the open air garden and sat on a wooden bench underneath the viewing veranda. All of its fifteen rocks are not visible from any one position, yet the dozens of Japanese visitors around us, true to form, counted out loud each of the garden's rocks as they walked past. Rather than being annoyed, as Tony was, I chose to hear their counting as a sort of mantra, as part of the experience. Many a tourist has sat on the viewing steps for a minute or two, looking at the dark gray stones and light gray gravel, raked and swept each day. A minute can be a long time if you're just looking at rocks. The surrounding walls and dense foliage completely closed out the city for a true feeling of escape. Of course, it has always been a magical and spiritual place and this time was once-in-a-lifetime.

Just as we settled our butts on a step overlooking the stones, a terrific downpour burst from the sky. Sheets of rain poured off the tile overhang and dimpled the immaculately raked designs in the stone. It made all the normally noisy tourists pause for a moment, keeping silent, hushed by the rain and the rocks. During the downpour, the reverberation off of the tile roof was deafening, like we were standing under a waterfall. The streams of people slowed to a halt. Like a still life portrait, the scene in the viewing area mirrored the garden – people standing and sitting like the stones, staring back and forth with passive introspection. When the shower passed, as abruptly as it started, the sun broke through, lighting a new set of shadows on the gravel and the faces of the visitors. I felt washed clean, rising with a lightness that seemed to be shared by everyone in the crowd. Some visitors were thoroughly drenched, but their chatter was surprisingly gay and smiles abounded. Tony and I rode our bikes through the streets with rooster tails streaming behind us all the way home. It was a unique and joyous afternoon.

On the day I left, Tony rode the train halfway to the airport with me. Somehow we knew the end of something was at hand, but we refused to acknowledge it by discussing it. We rode into Osaka like it was any other workday. We stopped for lunch at an obscure revolving sushi bar inside the train station in Osaka. I indulged myself by trying everything that passed in front of me that looked new. By the end of the meal, we both had a stack of empty plates a foot and a half high. Tony mumbled something about how he was the one holding things together while I was off gallivanting about, wreaking havoc. I replied that he was just griping about having to go to work and, well, that someone out here has to do the wandering about. We walked over to the connecting line, saying very little. Before going in, I gave him a big manly hug, which he returned as well as he could in the middle of a busy Japanese train station.

"Don't go off and get arrested or anything," he said.

"I'm trying to avoid it as best I can," I smiled. "Don't you go digging yourself a hole here that you can never get out of."

"I could think of worse things. But point taken." He paused. "Say hi to Charlie for me will ya?"

"You'll probably talk to her before I will. But I will." I smiled and he nodded.

"Let's get back to Thailand soon, eh?" he said with a conspiratorial grin.

"That's for sure. You get yourself stateside soon as well. I could use a partner in all this havoc I'm wreaking."

He nodded again and I walked slowly up the stairs under the weight of my backpack and the heavier weight of reminiscences of a time just now passing. I turned around at the top of the stairs in time to see him wave one more time and walk off.

4
CHARLIE

SEATTLE TOKYO THAILAND LONDON THE INDIA
                                   PHILIPPINES

YEAR 1   YEAR 2   YEAR 3

ON THE ROAD

Charlie takes the bus in from the airport to Trafalgar Square. The trip into Heathrow is easy and the transition to England from the US without incident. She finds herself slightly intimidated by the severe faces of the customs and immigration officials, but enjoys the challenge of interacting with them all the same. Despite her jet lag, or perhaps because of it, she flirts a little with the agents.

"First time to England?" Charlie nods and tries to catch his eye.

"Bringing any alcohol, drugs or firearms?" He asks mechanically.

"Oh, god, no." She shakes her head, surprised at the question.

"Welcome to England, then." He breaks out in a genuine grin. Seeing her smiles returned, she feels recharged.

The backpacker's guidebook recommended a place, The Dosser's Claim, as a safe and solid hostel, so she calls ahead from the airport. She is relieved to hear that they have space and is eager to accept sharing a room to cut down on cost. The clerk gives her directions on how to take the bus and she finds the place easily, it being just three blocks from Trafalgar Square. There are three other beds in her dormitory and Belgian girls, near her age, named Anya and Therese, occupy two of them. They immediately invite her out to dinner and she gladly accepts. It has the feel, to her, of going away to college for the first time.

They cross the Square, marveling at the odd mix of punkers who idle around and business people who never stop moving. It seems to Charlie like a surreal version of a San Francisco street corner. It still retains an edge to it, though, and feels older and more alien. The women choose the first Indian restaurant they come to because it is cheap, not so crowded, and feels right.

Anya and Therese recently graduated from a university in Antwerp and are traveling for two months around Europe before returning to look for jobs. They have been in London for a week and point Charlie in some interesting directions for sight-seeing. They act worldly in sophomoric fashion, speaking like it's all old hat already.

They talk the typical "backpacker bullshit" – exchange rates, cheap places to eat and sleep, the best beer in Europe, cautions about the digestive impact of certain foods, and so on. When they get around to discussing American culture, Charlie finds herself bristling a bit and defending US culture against the girls' innocent comments. She doesn't know why. She hasn't ever given it much thought and is surprised to be grasping for the right words.

"So, tell us about where you are from," inquires Anya. She is the more talkative of the two and laughs constantly. Charlie is disconcerted with the laughing at first, but then chalks it up to Anya's nervousness.

"America is so big, it's hard to describe in a few words."

Anya and Therese nod. They seem intrigued to actually be discussing this with an American, perhaps because they know the media images so well but not the place itself. They speak excellent English.

"I have been to New York five years ago," Anya says. "It was so exciting, but I was a little scared by the violence. I heard police cars almost the whole night."

"I haven't spent much time in New York, but I think I know what you mean. New York seems kind of scary to me, too, but exciting. I grew up in the Midwest, in Ohio, and it's very different there from New York. In the Midwest, people are more conservative." They seem impressed by this information. She continues. "I moved to Seattle two years ago and I like the west coast much more than Ohio – its friendlier, more relaxed, and there's so much to do!"

"Ah – Seattle has the music," nods Therese knowingly.

"Yeah, that's right." Charlie feels a tinge of guilt because, while she knows this is true of Seattle's reputation for the grunge scene, she has had very little experience with it personally. She owns some Nirvana and Pearl Jam CDs, but had never sought them, or others out in concert. *But what the hell*, she laughs to herself, *these girls may have never eaten a Belgian waffle!*

"I would like to go to Seattle when I have some money." Anya muses. "I have seen Pearl Jam in Brussels and it was so...fantastique!"

"I know that the states can be pretty spendy, but I hope London doesn't break me," Charlie says.

The Belgians look perplexed and after a lively discussion in Flemish, Charlie realizes they didn't understand what she meant. She explains what she meant by "spendy" and "break" and they nod appreciatively. The three of them begin to talk more intensely, like reunited schoolmates, and take the mood with them to a pub next door once they finish their delicious Indian food. At the pub they quickly get marginally drunk on pints of ale and the drug of new-found friendship. Fending off approaches from several equally drunk male patrons, they make it back to their room by eleven o'clock and sleep soundly. Charlie dreams vividly of a clear blue sky and deep, baritone laughter, interrupted by that disturbing feeling of something having gone terribly wrong – only she can't pinpoint the problem. She only half-remembers this dream as one she experienced many times before. She sleeps in until ten and feels great when she finally gets up. She decides to take it easy this first day in England, letting jet lag ease away with several short naps, a walk around the hostel neighborhood and light meals taken at the hostel.

Planning her week in London, Charlie realizes that such a short amount of time and her limited funds are indeed too little to allow her to do even half of the things she had hoped. She feels sure, however, that her money would indeed last longer here than it would in Japan. She intends to arrive in Tokyo with at least two thousand dollars. Her ticket cost just under a thousand, which leaves her with just one thousand dollars to last five weeks on the road. She had read that India and Thailand could reasonably be done on fifteen to twenty dollars a day, if not less, so she does the math and decides to stay under $400 for the week in London. God, that sounds like a lot, but she knows it will go fast. She could probably skimp in London on the beer and sightseeing and leave with more funds, *but why?* She has budgeted for it, so why not have a good time and make it a memorable adventure?

Her "London experience" becomes more like a packed-schedule tour. Knowing she has only a few days and wanting to do it all, she lays out an ambitious itinerary. It isn't until later in the week that she starts gaining some perspective on what a sustainable travel routine might look like.

The next day, she gets up early, grabs a coffee and croissant, and walks around Piccadilly Circus until the British Museum opens. She devotes most of the day to the overwhelming collections housed there, being especially curious about the Indian colonial displays.

That afternoon, she sits in a quiet café near the museum, resting her feet and going over some of the literature she picked up at the museum gift shop. She is amused with herself for liking John Lennon's hand-written notes for his songs. "She loves you yeah, yeah, yeah..." keeps echoing inside Charlie's head like a looping cassette tape. She begins to hum "On the road again..." to keep from driving herself crazy.

Just then a group of eight American tourists come in and sit near her table. She knows them to be her countryfolk immediately. They are obviously tourists, and even more conspicuous as Americans for their body size, group size, and their unselfconscious exhilaration. They plop their shopping bags on the floor, scrape their chairs across the floor, and hail the waitress with a "Hey, Miss, can we get a menu please?" Their voices carry easily across the small room and their physical presence quickly dispatches the tranquility of moments before.

They seem exhausted from all the walking, but excited by the Britishness of their surroundings and let everyone within earshot know of it. *My god they are loud...and...gross.* These folks must be the "ugly" tourists she has dreaded meeting. It is to her chagrin that they are Americans in this case. She will later learn that America has no monopoly in this area. At this moment, though, it is providential that they are her countrymen, for it sends her deeper into her own subconscious, ruminating about ingrained characteristics and expectations.

Charlie hunkers down over her tea and pretends not to notice, but in actuality observes them closely.

"Did you see those Greek statues? My Lawd they were big."

"I think the gothic paintings were flat out ugly."

"When does our bus come back to pick us up?"

"Our train leaves for France at seven."

Charlie finds disgust, nostalgia, confusion, empathy and other emotions all dueling inside of her.

Her internal assessment goes like this: *Where are they from? The Midwest or the South for sure. Those accents, my God, do I sound that bad? Do they think they're "seeing" Europe – seven countries in ten days? How is that possible?*

And then, more analysis: *Why do they embarrass me? They seem pretty innocent, and even harmless. Look, the other people here don't seem to notice them. Do they think I am like them? No. I'm being too self-conscious about this. I mean, they're just having a good time, right? They're just the hometown crowd. That's obvious. Why should I expend any energy feeling weird about this? They're...uninhibited. So why do I want to puke? Maybe I AM like them but I don't want to admit it! Oh God! Please don't let that be true! I'm not an elitist, but just look at them! I can't be like that!*

But she can't stop being judgmental: *They're so pompous! They just flash in and out of places, sucking off whatever they happen to notice. Imposing their "culture" instead of absorbing a new one. No real connection or openness for it.*

And finally, a modicum of acceptance: *Wait girl ...like you know what's the truth here. Look at you. You've been blasting around London like a maniac all day – planning on doing the same thing all week. How can you say you're any different? And these people, they're just like Mom's family. They are just regular people who want a taste of Europe, that's all. So why do you care? You don't know these people from Adam. No one else here knows you're American. Nobody else even seems to notice them. Does it matter that they are from the same country as you? Get a grip, you're losing it.*

Charlie's mind begins to pitch and twitch trying to figure this out. Not being able to take it any longer, she gets up, pays and leaves. The conflict still rages in her, but with the proximity of the tourists removed it morphs into a vague and less defined feeling of inadequacy and, simply, unresolved turmoil. Charlie decides to walk it off through Hyde Park and rounds her way back towards the guesthouse. Slowly the roiling sea of conflict subsides and she is able to look around her afresh. She walks a good mile before she realizes she hasn't been paying attention to where she's going. Finally stopping to observe the multicolored faces ambling past her and the stately trees framing the Victorian architecture, her mood lightens considerably. She hasn't figured it out at all, but gives up trying for now. She knows her few days in London are too precious to waste them with negativity. She strolls with a grin back to her hotel.

A couple of days later Charlie is full to the brim of London museums, theater, food, and drink as she catches a shuttle to Heathrow. As she waits to board the plane to New Delhi, London has already become a blur. The excitement of India looms, tempered with more than a dash of apprehension. She isn't sure of her itinerary yet and is concerned now with the details of just how she is going to get into the city from the airport and where she will stay. Sitting in the waiting area, thumbing through her Lonely Planet guidebook, Charlie's peripheral vision picks up a young woman approaching her. She's smiling, holding up the same book.

"You're traveling to India as well?" she asks.

"Yes I am!" says Charlie, looking up and being pleasantly surprised. "What are your plans there?"

"I don't really know yet. I'm just winging it."

"Sounds like we're in the same boat. I was just trying to decide where to stay in Delhi. That's as far as I've gotten." She exaggerates a frown.

"My name's Marie." She speaks with a British accent tinged with something else.

"Nice to meet you. I'm Charlie." They shake hands and Marie sits down beside her.

"How long are you planning to be in India?"

"Just a couple of weeks. Then I'm off to Thailand and then to Japan, to Tokyo, to look for some work."

"Oh really!" Marie gives her a conspiratorial look.

"Yes…..?"

"I live in Japan now, in Miyazaki – it's in the south on the island of Kyushu. I'm on holidays for six weeks and was visiting Mum in Essex."

Charlie perks up. What luck to find someone like this so early in her trip! She doesn't know what to say for a moment and blurts out, "Really!?"

Marie laughs gaily. "Yes. I was in your shoes three years ago, only I was coming from New Zealand. I imagine you're coming from somewhere in America?"

"Seattle. By way of Ohio." She whispers the last part, not knowing why, and snickers to herself for doing so.

"Would you like to sit together?" Marie pulls out her boarding pass and they compare their seat numbers as Charlie gladly agrees. They go up to the ticket counter and are able to change their seat assignments.

"So you've no plans for India?"

"Well I guess that's not entirely true," Charlie replies. "I'd like to see the Taj Mahal, and Varanassi sounds fascinating."

"That's where I'm heading. Varanassi, that is. I went to the Taj during a visit two years ago. It's well worth it, if you can stand the crowds of peddle cabbies and vendors in Agra." Charlie looks innocent. She *is* innocent – and now a little more scared.

"You'll understand what I mean later." Marie waves her hand and smiles. "Listen, would you like to share a cab into Delhi together? I don't know where you were planning on staying, but I know of a nice little hotel just outside the Nepalganj area."

Charlie nods gratefully and cannot believe her luck.

They board the plane and settle in for the long ride. Charlie notices how Marie seems so sure of herself. She is a few years older, maybe in her early thirties, has shoulder-length blond hair and a kind of contagious confidence. It turns out that Marie teaches English for a private school in Miyazaki. She started out in a large school in Tokyo, but the city life "zapped too much spirit," so she transferred to the south when the first opportunity arose. She has also dabbled with hostessing in Tokyo and doesn't think too highly of it, though she admits the money is good. There is an edge to her that scares Charlie a little, but fascinates her more. She reminds her of Joan a little; Charlie feels drawn to her.

Six hours on a plane is plenty of time to get to know someone. Marie is going to be in India for ten days before flying back to Japan. Her parents are separated, with one living in England and the other in New Zealand. She grew up on the south island, just outside of Christchurch. From what Charlie can gather, Marie considers herself both Kiwi and Brit. She describes herself as "schizo" because her mother is solidly Old World, believing in all things properly British and disdaining most else, whereas her father, on the other hand, is a tried and true New Zealander who distrusts the "motherland" and prizes independence. Marie speaks of this off-handedly, mocking both her parents without apparent humor.

Comparing Marie's background to her own, Charlie sees some similarities, but hers lack the drama. Helena Frampton met Eric Diaz during a Catholic Church retreat in Dallas, Texas in the mid-sixties. Neither had much exposure to the world outside of family. They were both in college at the time. And though she was more idealistic and he more practical, they fell in love. He, being a first generation American of Mexican decent, caused some consternation among Helena's longtime Chicago family, but he soon won them over with his intelligence and simple grace. His family in return accepted Helena eagerly, even overdoing their graciousness, happy with their first son marrying an Anglo. Helena and Eric married and started on that long and well-traveled path to Middle American prosperity. They reversed roles over time, he becoming more whimsical about life and she more conservative. Eric came to wax philosophically about the world and working and Helena became a worrier about her children's welfare and status. Charlie and Renny were their only children. Charlie's parents still loved each other and the twins loved them.

Marie nods thoughtfully at the information, without comment. The arrival of Charlie and Marie in New Delhi goes off without a hitch, but it would have been a mess if Charlie had been alone. The teeming chaos of the airport assaults every sense. Multitudes of dark heads maneuver about the pair of women, offering rides or a hotel or good deals on silver jewelry. Marie takes the lead in hailing, negotiating, and reluctantly accepting the cab driver, and they are soon heading into town. Even once out of the airport, the city traffic numbs Charlie's sensibilities and she is more than relieved to have experienced company to rely upon. The excitement and tension of dealing with so many new things is absolutely exhausting. *How would I have possibly dealt with this on my own? I probably never would have gotten out the Delhi airport!*

She and Marie have known each other for less than a day in real time, but they have become fast friends – closer, by Charlie's reckoning, than many of her long term relationships. On the flip side, they still know each other only from what their words can reveal, which leaves a lot yet to be discovered. Charlie is freed to observe her new environment without the pressure of having to perform. She feels very fortunate and slightly guilty about this. The aggressive push of the crowd and cabbies are intimidating at first, but she quickly adopts Marie's composed and somewhat cold demeanor and is less chilled by the journey. The cab makes its way through the bustling downtown, past makeshift housing and into the Nepalganj district. The stark contrast of wealth and poverty, old and new, power and helplessness is everywhere.

Marie leads her down a narrow alley to the hotel and they inquire at the front desk about a room. They had not made reservations beforehand, as the hotel does not take any. With no single rooms available, they decide to share a room, after making an agreement with the desk clerk that when another room opens up, one of them can move to it. Their room is on the second floor and well used, though clean and cheery. There are two single cot-like beds, with thin mattresses and a small window overlooking the alley. After choosing beds, they return downstairs to the attached café for a chai.

They soon fall into conversation with a few of the other guests at the hotel. Mostly they are Europeans, with a few North Americans, Australians and a pair of New Zealanders. It is with the Kiwis that they sit and join in conversation. These two, Matt and Terry, are from the North Island – Auckland to be specific – and have been traveling around India for four months. They are on their way north to Nepal after working out some visa extension issue in Delhi. This is an apparently arduous process about which Charlie knows nothing. She listens eagerly and feels novice, thinking to herself, *I hope I don't appear as green as I feel.* Looking around her, she assesses the guests to all be seasoned veterans of the travel circuit. She wants to know their stories, their fears, and their plans. *Some of them look rather run through the mill,* she observes. Even more than hearing theirs, Charlie longs to have a story of her own to contribute. This being her first real day in Asia, though, she surrenders to her exhaustion and begs off to turn in early. That night, her sleep is deep but the wild dreams surge on, with no coherent images for her tired mind to grasp, only fleeting moments of intense emotion with no apparent cause. Once again, fear and joy dance the tango in her head.

The next day over breakfast, she and Marie have a long discussion about independence, tolerance, and finances, and in the end they decide they are well-suited to travel together directly to Varanassi. From there, Charlie will take ten days to slowly wind her way back towards Delhi through Agra, while Marie makes a bee line back to catch her flight to Japan in a week. They decide to spend just one day in Delhi and leave tomorrow. They learn that Matt and Terry are going the same way, through Varanassi, on their way to Nepal. The four decide to take the bus together and make the arrangements at a nearby travel agent. Charlie and Marie spend the rest of that day roaming the area around their hotel. The density of people living in close quarters and the extreme contrasts that come with that serve up a sensory overload for Charlie, which leaves her exhilarated and exhausted at the same time. As she thinks about it later that evening, she can't put her finger on any particular vision or experience, but knows all the same that she has stepped away – in a major way – from her life of just two-months ago.

Charlie knows very little about the City of the Dead, or Benares, as her bus ticket reads. She knows it only as Varanassi, with the Ganges flowing through it, and that it is a sacred spot for Hindu people. *If your ashes are placed in the Ganges, your spirit will soar to heaven*, or something like that, she thinks

On the bus Charlie overhears that Benares is also famous among certain tourists for allowing the open consumption of bhang, or marijuana. She has never been a smoker, but has been comfortable around it since her brother became a regular consumer in high school. Marie admits that she is an inveterate practitioner; Terry likewise, and Matt is just a dabbler.

They arrive in Benares at one o'clock, after a six a.m. exit from Delhi. Charlie sleeps for at least half the ride through fields of wheat and small, nondescript towns. She awakes on the edge of town to a blaring horn. Like Delhi, the city itself is dense with people and odors and the heat is intense, but there is also a mystery to it, omnipresent, and it draws everyone to the river. The Ganges, in spite of the surface scum and apparent pollution, retains a majesty. It *is* the point where the lifeless returned to the flow. White and gray buildings, some dingy, others fresh, and none over five stories, line the northern shore while the southern side stretches away into marshy wetland and a gray-white haze.

Matt and Terry have been to this city before and know of a place to stay. By 4 pm that afternoon, the four are lounging with beverages on the hotel rooftop when the two Kiwi women light up. Charlie and Matt are drinking refreshing banana lassis laced with whisky, while Marie and Terry quaff the bhang variety, hold the banana. As the evening and the moment wane, the four travelers – Charlie likes to think of them all as travelers, not tourists, though she would be hard pressed at this moment to say why – adopt a delirious air, induced partly by the drugs but mostly by the lugubrious tension of the city, where so many of the living strain to stay that way.

Feeling the melancholy, Marie and Terry supplement their drinks with several bong hits, which Marie savors in the caricature of a true hippie. She recently quit smoking cigarettes and desperately misses the feel of the smoke in her lungs. Tuneless sitar music wafting up from tinny speakers enhances the moment. Charlie knows at that moment that *now* she is truly on the road.

Just before midnight, Matt declares his intention to walk down to the ghats, or funeral pyres, along the river. He invites everyone to join him, but Marie and Terry decline and he looks expectantly to Charlie.

"What the hell," she sighs. They leave the other two sitting contented and silent, gazing out at the river. Matt and Charlie wind their way to the river through a maze of alleyways. They are both surprised, and somewhat relieved, to find dozens of people still milling about at this hour. It seems safer with company on the streets, even though many of the open doorways and clumped gatherings are shrouded by a sinister aura. Charlie thinks she can actually see meaning in the shadows, but can't say if these are real or just her over-active and over-tired imagination.

"I don't think I could walk out this late by myself. Or would," she confides in Matt.

"I suppose not. You'd attract some attention. I think this part of the city is pretty safe though. It would be a desecration to commit a crime here."

"How much time have you spent here?"

"Oh, I've come through three times before, I think. Twice with Terry and the first time on my own. Probably a month and a half in all. I like walking about the ghats at night because I don't feel I'm interfering then."

The night is poorly lit, so Charlie can only make out Matt's outline. His silhouetted profile is stretched long and thin, with a hawked nose and tousled hair. He seems a bit broody, but is friendly all the same. Onlookers give them only cursory glances and she guesses they probably assume the two of them are a couple.

"Do *you* get hassled if you come out here by yourself at night?"

"No, not really. Once I thought I'd happened into a bad situation of two blokes arguing, but they let me be. I don't suppose you've walked much on your own at night?"

"Not really. Maybe down to the store or something, but not exploring. It sucks for women sometimes." She looks up at his face, dimly lit by a yellow door lantern, and returns his smile, letting him know it's not an issue he needs to tiptoe around.

He shrugs his shoulders. "You can't help men being what they are."

"You know what they say, can't live with or without 'em."

"I think it was a man who came up with that – about *women,*" he retorts.

"He was probably a closet queen." He looks perplexed at this and she doesn't even know where that comment came from, but they like it all the same and laugh. "Don't mind me. I'm just babbling." She looks away.

They descend a set of crumbling concrete steps and walk down a low retaining wall along the river. The water is shallow and dotted with small islands and sandbars that reflect the moonlight. They stop in synchronized silence next to one of the islets and watch in horrified fascination as a dog chews on the torso of a skeleton on the lower embankment.

The body is legless with no discernable flesh to be seen. The animal seems not to notice them, gnawing away heartily around the lower ribcage, but the skull is turned to the side, towards Charlie and Matt. Its empty sockets peer meaningfully at them. The mouth is clearly smiling. They stand for a few timeless moments, moving along only when they hear footsteps ahead, coming towards them. This has suddenly become a place not to be dawdling. They shuffle forward in what is now self-conscious silence. They pass a robed pair, not making eye contact, and walk another hundred meters to emerge onto the top steps of an empty ghat. They sit.

"I've never seen anything like that before. And I've done this walk quite a few times." Matt is clearly impressed.

"I'm...that was amazing. I don't think I've ever seen a real dead body before. Especially like that," Charlie replies. The brightening half moon shines on the horizon, just coming out for the night, and its light bounces off the water. In the distance upriver, one of the ghats is still billowing an acrid smoke. Colorless, gleaming crows circle the pyre, spiraling black-against-black in the hazy moonlit sky.

"Do you want to be cremated when you die?" he asks.

"I haven't thought about it. Do you?"

"I suppose I really don't care. I've considered having my body thrown to the sharks, or maybe left out in the desert for the buzzards."

She is incredulous at this and can't tell if he is serious or not. After a few minutes, they arise and slowly make their way back to the hotel. They feel at least a little changed by what they have seen. Terry and Marie, on the other hand, look as though they haven't moved. Only now they have been joined by Raj, the hotel owner. They are all in a hazy state but perk up when they hear about the skeleton. Raj nods solemnly upon hearing about it.

"It is a good sign. An omen, I think, but I can't tell you what of. This is the city of life and death and has been for a long, long time." He is sitting beside Marie and Charlie notices their legs touching. She is glad they were able to get separate rooms tonight. Charlie excuses herself and wishes everyone sweet dreams.

Back in her room, Charlie stares out at the city and the dirty alley beneath her window. The city is still emitting a low, buzzing hum, but is overall much quieter than during the day. She can't see the moon, but can see its light reflected off of the rooftops that stretch forever into the distance. She detects a lingering odor that she now associates with death. Lying down in bed, she assumes she will fall right off to sleep, but instead she feels curiously excited. Is it the dog at the ghat? Walking with Matt? The idea of Maria and Raj getting it on next door? It isn't because she misses Cory, alas. Feelings of self-consciousness slowly give way as she reaches down and begins to see if self-pleasuring feels much different in Asia compared to The States. She slowly and expertly satisfies herself, and afterwards is convinced that sex is definitely better on the road. She can hear the muffled groaning from Marie's room beside her and thinks she can even hear Terry and Matt across the hall, but maybe she's just imagining it. She sleeps soundly that night and can't remember her dreams the next morning.

Terry and Matt leave the next day for Nepal. They all walk together to the bus station and exchange addresses. Though she feels a friendship possibility with Matt, she suspects they will never see each other again. She has yet to learn in full the nature of friendships on the road. Intensity in lieu of longevity. The ephemeral nature of being on the road itself is its only lasting quality.

They stay almost a week in Benares. Charlie visits the ghats every day, often on her own. The numerous ghats along the river host an unending flow of mourners, heads shaven in grief and renewal, carrying the body of a relative or friend to the fire. The wailing over the burning pyres holds a morbid fascination for her.

Steps leading down to the river are interspersed between and around the ghats and she often finds a quiet place among the pilgrims to just watch, her mind often blank and her energy absorbing the vibes of the city, the river, the streams of people. It occurs to her that she also is a pilgrim, for not all come to the river to mourn the dead, but also to bathe in the purifying water. She can't bring herself to immerse her body in it or even sip the holy water, as she so often observes others doing. But she does take to dipping her fingers in it as she arrives and leaves each day, patting her forehead with a moistened hand. The first time she tries this she is self conscious, and ironically makes a sign of the cross without thinking. She realizes it immediately afterwards and laughs out loud, attracting the attention of a nearby bather. Smiling sincerely at the woman, she receives one in return and walks up the steps. *Was that blasphemy or acknowledgement?* She can't decide and it doesn't seem to matter.

Her friendship with Marie, on the other hand, is developing a closeness, similar to what Charlie knows with Joan. They spend long afternoons and evenings walking together and talking about traveling and adventures and family and whatnot. Marie is typically the teacher and prophet to Charlie's kindergarten ears. But piercing Marie's wall of certainty proves to be both challenging and rewarding.

One afternoon, the two women are checking out the silk distributors near the bus station. Charlie does not want to buy anything, but is happy to explore. Marie wants some raw silk to have a skirt and jacket tailored for her. "Clothes are so expensive in Japan!" she laments. They wander in and out of shops in the textile district, smiling at and avoiding hawkers; commenting on how every shop seems to include an extended family.

At the third household they actually enter – for they are homes more than retail shops – Marie is ready to buy and starts bargaining with the proprietor. He is a short and proper looking gent in a white Nehru jacket with matching pants. He speaks with an air of formality. He presents his wares with solemnity, as if he were a haberdasher on Saville Row and his customers rich bankers. His wife brings chai and they sit on the floor, all four of them, on an intricate and ancient looking rug in the main room. Charlie and the patron's wife are back and to the side of the two combatants, like retainers in a ritualized duel, as the negotiating begins.

Unfurled bolts of fabric lay strewn about them. As the haggling gets underway, both Marie and the elderly gentleman are cordial, but it soon turns tense. The shopkeeper holds steadfast to the fact that his silks are "only the best quality". He keeps a submissive but stern tone to his voice. Marie insists that the opposite is true and demands a better price. Her voice keeps rising, subtly, yet unmistakably. Charlie had assumed that Marie has done this before, but now she isn't so sure. Neither duelist will budge more than an inch and after five minutes of this, abruptly, Marie stands up, calls the guy an asshole, and walks out. Charlie stands up, shocked and embarrassed, and smiles to the shopkeeper and his wife as she shrugs her shoulders and follows Marie out. She is more afraid of losing Marie in the maze of the city than apologizing to the man. She catches up with Marie about half a block away, walking briskly back towards the river.

They walk in silence to a small park overlooking a plaza near the river and the ever-burning ghats. Leaning over a retaining wall, they watch a steady line of pilgrims below getting their heads shaved by a barber priest.

"Fucking men. Makes me want to smoke."

Charlie says nothing.

"Was that guy being an asshole or what!? I mean, he didn't want to give in an inch because he thought I was some rich western bitch or something. Did you see that?"

"I honestly don't know." Charlie answers carefully. She wants to appease but not give in. "I don't really know what that silk was worth. He did seem a bit rigid."

"Fucking right he was rigid. And his smarmy little wife acting all servantile behind him. Puke!"

Charlie opens her mouth to challenge her, but then thinks the better of it and says nothing. Abruptly, Marie points to the barber. "I'm going down there."

Charlie follows her down and then watches in fascination as Marie walks up to the priest and asks him in gestured English to shave her head. This causes a stir in the plaza and soon there are twenty or more pilgrims watching the scene. The barber is hesitant at first, but then seems pleased at the attention and makes a show by theatrically caressing Marie's hair. For a moment Charlie thinks Marie is going to lay into him, but breathes easy as Marie instead closes her eyes and exhales deeply. Marie makes the barber use a new straight blade and then sits, rigid and defiant, while he proceeds to shear off her shiny blond locks. He does an excellent job – no nicks or cuts at all – and Marie pays him what he asks. Basking in the moment, he points to Charlie to have a seat, but she frantically waves him off. Marie, smiling, walks over and puts an arm around her.

"Let them chew over that one." Consciously refusing to invoke a pun about the dog at the ghat a few nights back, Charlie gleefully rubs her hands over Marie's shiny smooth scalp. She is glad that the calm and collected Marie is back. With defiance written clearly on her face and extending along her smooth scalp, she is a picture of modern beauty. They look over and see the barber and some others carefully picking up the blond strands from the ground.

"I should make those fuckers pay for those." Marie starts towards them, but Charlie pulls her back and Marie relents. They walk to a café, arm in arm, and drink some lassis, *sans* bhang.

Back at the hotel, Raj is in good humor over Marie's new look, but it is short lived as she snubs him and goes off to her room. The two of them have spent most of the last week's late nights together in the throes of passion, and he seems genuinely hurt to be spurned. He looks for an answer from Charlie but she can only shrug her shoulders and sigh. They sit in the lounge and he asks the desk clerk to bring some chai.

"Is she upset with me?"

"Not with you, specifically. Don't take it personally."

"I don't understand these things."

He looks upset. Charlie observes him closely. He appears to be in his early forties and is boyishly handsome with long, thick dark hair that has a natural curl to it. She has only ever seen him dressed in a long white shirt, Nehru-style, over white pants or a wrap. He wears his clothes elegantly and against his dark skin he is a beautiful photographic negative. He smiles with a warm charm that puts one at ease quickly – good traits in his business. Charlie guesses that these types of romantic liaisons with travelers are not uncommon for him, and she therefore has less sympathy for his despair than she might have had otherwise.

"I don't know if there is anything to understand. I think she just gets angry at everything sometimes."

"Have you known her long?"

"Just a week."

"It is enough," he says, with an arched eyebrow and a knowing nod.

Charlie sips her tea.

☯☯☯☯☯ ☯☯☯☯☯ ☯☯☯☯☯ ☯☯☯☯☯ ☯☯☯☯☯

Two days later, saturated with death and ritual transition, Charlie and Marie board a westbound bus along with twice as many people as the bus should hold. As tickets for the deluxe bus were sold out, they choose to brave the next level down and Charlie experiences for the first time how sardines are packaged. She enjoys it, however, including Marie's curses. Marie is heading back to Delhi and to Japan two days hence. Charlie will be getting off at Khajuraho to visit the temples there, after which she will head to Agra and the Taj Mahal. They aren't lucky enough to get seats and spend the first thirty minutes squeezed in the aisle, sharing their armpit odors with the rest of the riders. At the first major stop, a third of the crowd dissipates and Charlie and Marie dive for an open bench.

"I've enjoyed this last week." Marie looks past her out the window. She is wearing a faded blue bandana over her head. Peach fuzz is already evident.

"I have too. It's been a great start to my trip."

"I'll look you up in Tokyo if you send me a card with your address and number once you get settled. I get up there at least twice a year for conferences and training. Here's mine." She hands Charlie a slip of paper.

"You know I will." She watches as Marie looks out the window expectantly at the scenery, anticipating Charlie's departure at the next stop.

"I've always wanted to see this place, but the timing hasn't been right."

"I'll let you know if it's worth it."

The bus stops with a jerk and Charlie muscles her way to the front door. Glancing back at Marie and smiling, she wonders if she will ever see her friend again in Japan.

Once outside, Charlie waits for the bus to sputter off down the road before refocusing her attention on her new, solo, situation. She is slightly apprehensive and mostly excited at traveling alone in India. Following Marie's footsteps, she adopts a psuedo-tough demeanor and waits for her connection.

☙☙☙☙☙ ☙☙☙☙☙ ☙☙☙☙☙ ☙☙☙☙☙ ☙☙☙☙☙

The temples at Khajuraho are famous for the many erotic bas-reliefs imprinted on the walls. All of the positions in the Kama Sutra come to life here, and then some. Walking around the grounds, Charlie is curiously detached from the images. She expected to be titillated, but now views the images with scientific curiosity. There are a few other western couples wandering about, giggling and pointing. Several indifferent Indian gents wander unusually close to her, sometimes gesturing or whispering an invitation, but she ignores them. She does allow a German fellow to walk with her for an hour and he clearly would like to do more, but no man is good company for her today, so she parts from him gracefully and leaves the temple grounds.

81

Hiking back to the little hotel she had found near the bus stop, she reflects on how the exotic sexual images were deftly carved, but left her emotionally unmoved. Some of the positions are clearly only for the truly athletic, and others physically impossible. She feels put off, rather than intrigued, by the possibilities of sex as depicted by these timeless figures. *They make sex seem more like an olympic event*, she thinks. Charlie hasn't a great deal of experience with sex and, though curious to explore more, is in no hurry. Now she's just curious about how to get to Agra. Near the hotel she purchases a bus ticket onwards for the next morning.

Marie was right about the crush in Agra. Resolutely, Charlie withstands the initial blow of tourist-seeking rickshaw drivers who assault all newcomers with cries offering assistance. She keeps her eyes forward and her pace steady, as Marie had shown her, and finds a taxi outside the station. She had befriended a Canadian couple on the bus, and after the introductory small talk, she learned they were from Vancouver and knew Seattle well. They made no plans together, but on the sidewalk outside the bus station, amid the fury, they make eye contact and decide to share the taxi. Charlie is heading to a hotel recommended by Marie, and since Paul and Sandra had not yet decided on one, they accompany her there. The Taj View is a decent place with plenty of vacancies, and Charlie is happy to have a room on her own, as she desires some solitude after the group scene in Varanassi. Later that evening, the three of them meet at the rooftop café and drink lassis together. The bleached white dome of the Taj Mahal glows like its own moon in the distance. The hotel rooftop, like many in India, offers a respite from the press of the masses. Tonight, the Taj View Café clientele is a pleasant mix of western and Indian tourists. A distinguished elderly Indian gentleman is playing the sitar by himself on a carpet in one corner. Some of the westerners are openly smoking hashish and no one seems to notice.

This first evening in Agra, for the first time since arriving in India, Charlie feels a calm, centered, *Ah...so this is India* contentment that lingers with her well into the next morning. The conversation with the Canadians is pleasant, but comfortingly superficial. The music lulls her into a dreamy state, enhanced by the moonlit dome of the Taj. Charlie realizes that she hasn't really been on her own yet in India, with Marie guiding the way for her through Delhi and Varanassi. And now more westerners could keep her from it, she worries – keep her from really experiencing the place as herself, virgin to it as she is. *If I can just manage to hold onto this "Ah, India" feeling. Can I keep centered and balanced all by myself?*

The next morning she wakes at dawn with the excitement of anticipation of seeing the Taj Mahal. She eats a quick breakfast and avoids sharing her plans with anyone before making her way to the monument. She confidently brushes off the throng of "guides" wanting to "help her" and walks through the already wide-awake and bustling streets. She finds her way to the monument indirectly, but easily.

The Taj is magnificent, simple and elegant, yet so imposing on the senses. It commands your attention. The love story behind it holds little significance for Charlie, though; an ancient prince making a mausoleum for his beloved deceased wife. More striking is the structure and setting itself. She wanders the grounds by herself all morning, sitting on the grass or along the river and letting her mind wander.

When she leaves the grounds, she notices a tall, dark Indian man staring at her and smiling from across the street. She thinks maybe she saw him that morning at the hotel, but isn't sure. She smiles back at him and then looks away and walks into a café. The man follows her in. He seems nice enough, dressed in an off white long-shirt, dark slacks and sandals, but she doesn't want company and says to him as she sits down, "I'm sorry, I'd prefer to be alone now." She is pleased that there is no fear, only a confident grace, in her tone. The man just smiles at her and sits at the table next to hers, turning the chair to face her slightly. She turns her back to him and orders a chai from the waiter. Glancing over her shoulder, she can see the man still sitting there, elbows on his knees, staring at her with a smile. He doesn't appear threatening – to the contrary, he seems almost worshipful, but she is beginning to get annoyed just the same. When the waiter brings her chai a few minutes later, he notices the man and says something in rapid and brusque Hindi to him. The smiling man then gets up and, still grinning and staring at her all the while, walks out of the restaurant. He plants himself across the street on the curb, still staring and smiling at Charlie with his elbows in his knees.

Charlie forgets about the man, browsing through her guidebook and relaxing over the spicy tea. She can still see the top of the white dome over the rooftops and the parade of people on the street makes for good watching. As she leaves the café, she notices the man again. He rises to his feet across the street and is still focused entirely on her. She quickly turns and walks up the street towards a set of shops, not looking back. She tries to put him out of her mind and is marginally successful, slowing to window shop along the way. After a few minutes she looks back and sees he is still there. Taking some deep breaths, she thinks to herself, *What the hell is going on here? What can I do about this? I don't really feel scared. I mean, I could probably kick his ass if I needed to. Look at him, he's about my size. And that stupid smile! Just what is his problem? Does he think I'm going to sleep with him if he keeps this up?! Forget about him, girl. Ignore him and he'll eventually go away.*

But he doesn't. The smiling man follows Charlie for another two hours as she meanders through the city. He keeps his distance, about ten yards behind her, and stops cold in his tracks when she occasionally stops and turns on him. But he never loses the smile. Her annoyance grows and begins to sprout into fear and helplessness. Over the course of the afternoon she becomes more and more angry, until she is consumed with thinking about the man and losing all perspective. She decides to confront him. She turns and walks toward him. He stands still in his tracks, showing a brief flash of surprise by raising his eyebrows, then settling back into the smile. Charlie stops her advance a yard in front of him.

"Please stop following me. You're making me uncomfortable. Do you understand?" She gestures firmly with her finger, pointing at his chest. The man continues to stare at her.

"Just stop it!" She tries in her best, firm voice, but there is no mistaking her anger. The flow of traffic continues around them on the sidewalk but the confrontation draws only a few stares. Charlie gives him a mean look and then turns around and walks. As she reaches the requisite ten yards, he starts again. She walks on and he persists. Panic almost overcomes her when she spots a restaurant and heads for it. Upon entering she hurries over to the well-dressed gentleman who looks to be in charge and says, "Please don't let that man come in here, he's been following me all morning." She is breathing rapidly and pointing towards the door.

The proprietor looks around in surprise and, catching on, says, "Okay, okay. I see Miss." He goes out the door, walks over to the smiling man just outside the doorway, and speaks firmly with him in Hindi. The smiling man retreats a few steps and, after a few more words from the restaurateur, crosses the street and disappears.

"Don't worry about him Miss," the proprietor says, coming back inside and looking pleased with himself. "He will do you no harm. Agra is full of these young men with nothing better to do. They are a nuisance yes, but most are harmless. Please sit down and eat something and rest."

Charlie is so relieved she wants to throw her arms around him, but knows enough by now to hold back. Instead, she accepts his offer gratefully. His kind words, in that soothing exotic accent, do as much to lift her spirits as his killer green curry does to restore her calm. She decides to be stronger in future situations. She decides not to let herself be taken advantage of.

Her resolve is immediately tested as she leaves the restaurant. The smiling man is halfway down the block, waiting for her and, once she chooses a direction, continues his routine. The distance between them is now doubled to twenty yards. He follows her to the hotel, but stops half a block away from the building. Charlie gives him a swift and searing glance as she enters.

That evening on the roof, she relays the day's events to Paul and Sandra. Both of them are genuinely horrified. Paul offers to "punch him out" and Charlie feigns appreciation, but says that won't be necessary. The white dome in the distance shines like a milky white breast ringed with diamond stars against the velvet night. Later that night Charlie dreams of it.

The dome is the breast of a beautiful Indian woman lying prone on the ground. Charlie is the same size as the woman and finds herself caressing the breast in wonder. As she does so, the ground begins to rumble violently and the woman melts into the ground. Her white left breast, gleaming, is all that is left sticking out of the ground as the trembling subsides. The city around it, which Charlie hadn't noticed before, is in ruins. A group of nondescript Indian and Western men stand on the perimeter, staring at the scene, unsmiling.

Charlie awakes from the dream with a start. It is still dark and quiet, the only sound from her breathing. She settles back down and sleeps soundly.

The next day, Charlie visits the Red Fort, home of the prince who built the Taj for his love. It is spectacular in its architecture and grace, but not as awe inspiring to Charlie as the Taj itself. The smiling man follows her throughout the day, waiting for her at the entrance to the fort for three and a half hours. He keeps his distance and never attempts to approach her. Charlie is mostly successful in ignoring him, though a seed of doubt about his purpose is always present in the back of her mind. The seed sprouts roots, however, and by the late afternoon she is once again irritated with him and with herself for allowing the situation to unnerve her. She lets the man get inside her head, but knows he is deserving of her anger for having the nerve to stalk her in the first place. She tries to view it dispassionately: *He's not really doing anything. He hasn't threatened me and I'm not scared that he'll rape me or anything like that. He's just some unemployed bozo who is fascinated by a western woman. He probably does this all the time.* And so on. This works to a degree, but not completely. When she arrives at the hotel, she decides to leave Agra the next day and spend a couple of extra days in Delhi. She books a mini-bus ticket for the next morning at the hotel desk and makes her way back up to the roof to relax on her last evening there, in full view of the Taj Mahal. As she goes to bed, a gentle thrum of light rain lulls her to sleep.

The next morning, the mini-bus stops in front of the hotel at seven a.m. and as Charlie steps out of the hotel, she spots the smiling man squatting on his heels halfway down the block. She loads her backpack on the roof rack and learns it will be another twenty minutes before the bus leaves. She goes back into the hotel for some chai and comes out fifteen minutes later.

The bus is idling and the driver standing out in front, smoking a cigarette. The smiling man is now standing on her side of the street and staring at her, only he isn't smiling now. He knows she is leaving. The previous night's rain has past; the sky is only partly cloudy now, the white and blue reflecting off of the accumulated puddles in the street.

Charlie marches resolutely and directly towards the man, cinching her daypack straps tightly around her shoulders and clenching her fists. As she approaches him, a smile breaks out on his face. Three yards away from him she picks up her pace, readies her hands in front of her, and rushes him full force, thrusting the heels of her hands into his chest and pushing as hard as she can. The man is caught by surprise and goes tumbling backwards, off the curb and into a puddle. Charlie watches him for only a moment before turning and walking quickly back to the bus. The bus driver is laughing as she boards.

She can see the astonished, formerly smiling man, staring at the bus as it drives away. He is still standing in the puddle, arms extended out in a limp cross, his stained white shirt dripping oily water and polyester pants clinging to his legs. She stares at him through the tinted window, not feeling as satisfied as she thought she would, but breathing easier just the same. *It wasn't a planned action. It just came to me, on the stairs, as I was ready to leave this place.* She senses now that the passengers on the bus are giving her a wide berth, and that is just as well.

Her time in Delhi passes slowly and without incident. She toys with the idea of rushing off somewhere else for a couple of days but decides against it, opting to chill out as much as she can on the rooftop of her Delhi hotel. Excuse or not, going anywhere in India requires a full day, and the stress of just going outside is often enough tension for a week. She admits only to herself that she is a little gun shy about walking around alone after the Agra experience. Looking for familiarities, she goes back to the same hotel she'd stayed at with Marie, spending much of her time in cafés that cater to foreigners, reading a Salman Rushdie novel, and planning her Thailand time. By the third day, she has pretty much left India, mentally, escaping into her plans to spend at least two weeks on an island in the south of Thailand. She needs an escape from herself of sorts, or so she thinks. India has been too much and too soon for her in the end, and now she fully knows it.

5

RENNY

SAN FRANCISCO   KYOTO   THAILAND   KATMANDU   LAKE TOBA   VARANASSI   IPOH

YEAR 1   YEAR 2   YEAR 3

THE AFFABLE DR. WA

"Call me Dr. Wa," he said as he introduced himself. "Because you have lived in Japan, you will understand the significance of this," he laughed heartily and took a large gulp from his glass of beer. *Wa* is the Japanese word for harmony. I still haven't decided if the word is appropriate or wasted on the good doctor. I wonder if that means that it is both?

We met in his office at Samkorn University in the Isan region of northeast Thailand, in the town of Nakhon Ratchasima. Through a roundabout series of events, I had been referred to the harmonious doctor to discuss the possibility of graduate study on Thai-Lao-Khmer cultural history. I had written to Dr. Wa when I was in Japan, about eight months earlier, on the recommendation of Larry McCall, an American professor I worked with at the University of Kyoto. I was substitute teaching an English class and had intimated to Larry that I might be interested in furthering my education when I returned to The States. Larry knew I was planning a trip through Thailand and gave me Dr. Wa's name and address.

"You should look up Dr. Wa," he said. "He has good contacts in the region and might help you find a way to pursue your studies." How right he was. Dr. Wa wrote back, inviting me to look him up when I was in the area.

I had been in Thailand for a few weeks already and had been distracted by the good time I was having – to the point of almost blowing off the meeting. Did I really want to go to graduate school to study these cultures? I had no idea. I had passed myself

89

off to Larry as more focused on school than I truly was, and now I had to pay the piper. So I called the university from Koh Chang, was connected to the doctor, and we arranged to meet in a week. Too easy.

It was late afternoon on a Friday when I arrived at the university and found his building on the far side of campus. There was no receptionist in the front office, so I took it as an invitation to peek around. I located his office with no trouble. He was sitting on the corner of a couch and apparently well lubricated, his pink eyes and ruddy cheek tone giving that away as much as the half empty glass of amber liquid sitting on the coffee table. He rose to meet me with a surprised look, guessing who I was almost immediately.

He shook my hand vigorously and then yelled something out the door. An office assistant scurried in a few minutes later with a tray of ice, glasses and beer; set it on the table, and bowed to me shyly before exiting. I joined the doctor on the couch and he fixed me a glass of beer over ice. His skin was mottled and his hair was mostly gray and he wore a similarly colored tunic and pants. As the afternoon wore on, he kept opening his tunic further down his chest, revealing a sweaty white v-neck t-shirt stretched tightly over a nicely rounded Buddha belly. The office was air conditioned, but he had opened the window overlooking the distant hills.

He spoke excellent English, with an air of nonchalant authority. I learned he had studied at the University of Washington, or "U Dub", as he affectionately called it. He was pleased that I knew the abbreviation. *Thanks Charlie!* He seemed overly jolly to me. It was almost as if he was acting a part, or trying to impress me. Lord knows why. My initial air of formality, learned over time from many Japanese business encounters, relaxed after the first five minutes, and we were soon talking casually.

"How is Dr. McCall?"

"When I last saw him four or five months ago, he was fine. He sends his...er...best wishes and said to tell you he will be visiting you sometime this year, he hopes." I lied to feign a closer friendship with Larry than I had.

"Oh, that will be just fine." He was beaming and looking off at the hills. He and Larry McCall read together in the anthropology graduate program at U Dub. Larry was on sabbatical for a year from the University of Oregon, spending it at Kyoto University. I was astonished at how much beer Dr. Wa was downing. Feeling somewhat wary of going over the top with this character and embarrassing myself beyond words, I carefully sipped my beer, not wanting to make an idiot of myself. We talked superficially about graduate study – thank god, because I didn't want to tip my hand. I really knew very little about the local region; I had chosen it because it sounded cool and, during my previous trip to the country I found the Northeast region to be the least known among the traveling crowd. I mostly nodded to his rambling monologue about Seattle and his doctoral study there. Before long, he noticed that I wasn't keeping pace with his drinking.

"You don't like to drink so much, eh?"

I fumbled for words. "I… uh… sometimes… uh…maybe… uh…." I took a large gulp, hoping that would deflect him. He gulped with me. Setting down his glass, he leaned closer, gave me a knowing look and, raising his eyebrows, said, "I bet you like to smoke the marijuana, eh?" I was speechless and tried to keep a straight face.

"I…uh…well…sometimes…uh…"

He slapped his leg and let out a rousing laugh.

"I can get you some. Excellent quality and very cheap-cheap."

I said nothing, dumbfounded.

"Yes yes, I speak truly. These hillsides are full of it." He gestured expansively to the window and became animated at the thought. He then paused and looked thoughtful before saying, "I can probably get you some for…maybe…seventy five baht a kilo, maybe a little more than that, but not much." He was serious.

It is difficult to describe how I felt at that moment. He could see from the look on my face that I was confused. He tried to wave it off as a joke.

"Seventy five baht a kilo?!" I stammered. That was about three dollars.

He nodded, pursing his lips. "Yes, truly. About that. Would you like to get some?"

Taking a deep breath – for I still couldn't believe the situation – I furrowed my brow, counted to three, shrugged my shoulders and said, "Sure."

I know this whole thing sounds ridiculous, but it honestly happened this way. It happened so quickly that I still have to shake my head and wonder about it.

"I'll call my friend. We can meet at my house. Tomorrow maybe. What hotel do you stay at?" I told him. "I will call there and leave a message when to meet."

He drew me a map to his house and instructed me on how to get there by bus. As if an afterthought, he added, "How much do you want? And how you want it? Like hashish style...?" He curled his hands around like a ball. "...or like in...?" He cupped his hands the rolled his thumb against his fingers, "Like tobacco?"

I smiled. "Like hashish style would be good. One kilo would be fine."

"I think hashish style is more expensive. Maybe twice as much."

"That's not a problem." I mimicked his serious look, though inside I was laughing. I felt like I'd fallen through a looking glass and all the rules were different now.

He rose like our meeting was over, and it was. We shook hands and he patted me on the back. Before I was out the door he had moved on to other business at his desk, seeming to have sobered up. I caught the bus back to my hotel in a walking trance.

❦❦❦❦❦   ❦❦❦❦❦   ❦❦❦❦❦   ❦❦❦❦❦   ❦❦❦❦❦

Before that moment, I had never before seriously considered smuggling. Granted, my history with herb dated back to my senior year in high school. I always enjoyed the pot high and became a regular toker by my freshman year in college. The habit tapered off by the time I moved to San Francisco after graduating. By then I only toked occasionally. I adopted a "never refuse" policy with my friends and I rarely purchased my own. But in Japan and especially Thailand, the ubiquitous presence of the herb pushed my habit back into gear. Yes, that's right, in Japan too, contrary to conventional wisdom, where everybody knows that the Japanese don't smoke much grass. In Kyoto, I wasn't an everyday toker, but I never said no and never went long without. All that said, I was scrupulously against dealing – as an occupation for myself that is. I did not begrudge those others who did deal; I even admired them. Those who take the risks deserve the rewards. I never minded paying for it, even at the ridiculous Japanese markup rates, for that reason.

Walking up the stairs to my hotel room, I kept going over the figures in my head. Three bucks for over two pounds! The street value of this was easily ten thousand dollars plus – maybe twice that in Japan. As soon as I unlocked the door and closed it behind me, the mental dialogue began.

"If you get caught, you're done for twenty years or more. You could end up in a ratty Thai jail or Japanese prison or, if you're lucky, extradited to America. Yeah! That would be better!"

"But I'd never have to buy for years if I kept it to myself. Think of all the hassle that would save. And it's easy money. Even at the wholesale price it would be easy money."

"But have you ever dealt with this level before? Dangerous money."

"I'd be the life of the party! I could just give chunks of it away for fun!"

"Japanese jail. The death penalty."

"Three bucks a kilo!"

"Are you fucking crazy? The risk is enormous!"

93

"Yeah. But the challenge is sexy. How hard can it be? People with a lot less intelligence get away with it all the time."

"And even smart ones get caught. Do you want to spend the better part of your life with them?"

"What about mailing it? Maybe putting it in a doll or something and sending it to Mom and Dad?"

"No. That's stupid. How would you explain...?"

The debate in my head continued well into the night, steering me down a long line of options for how to get it – and me – out of the country.

The next morning, Dr. Wa called while I was out at breakfast. The receptionist at the hotel gave me the note when I walked back in. We were to meet at three that afternoon and I would stay for dinner. I focused solely and unproductively on that event for the rest of the day.

Dr. Wa lived on the outskirts of town, not far from the university. As I walked the good half a mile from the bus stop to his house, I received some curious stares from villagers I passed on the street. His neighborhood was the border between jungle and village rice fields. Not many tourists get out this way. Dr. Wa's map was easy enough to follow and I soon found myself knocking tentatively on his door. The houses had no numbers on them, but I was sure this was it. It wasn't, but the elderly woman who answered didn't miss a beat when she opened her door to an unexpected Western stranger, and cheerfully pointed me down the lane. Dr. Wa must get the occasional foreign visitor after all. I found his house on the next try. It was a modest but well built brick and concrete two-story affair, typical of middle class families in northeast Thailand. Dense vegetation surrounded the place, which opened out over the paddies in certain spots for some tantalizing views.

His wife answered the door, expecting me, and showed me into the living room where the doctor and another man were, not surprisingly, drinking beer. I thought it seemed just like any number of households back in the Midwest, except back home a television would have been blasting out a football or basketball game. There was no television in the living room here, though I did glance a small one, tuned to a talk show, in the kitchen where an aproned Mrs. Wa was busily cooking a meal for us. Dr. Wa's friend turned out to be his brother. I didn't catch his name during the quick introduction (and I was too embarrassed to ask for it again). Brother Wa looked older and more down to earth than the educator. His palms felt rougher when we shook hands and his face was more deeply tanned and weathered. He was dressed in well-pressed brown polyester slacks and a button down white shirt. Dr. Wa was similarly dressed, though his slacks were light blue and wrinkled. It turned out that Brother Wa spoke basically no English but smiled profusely.

After several requisite beers and small talk about his house, Brother Wa, on instruction from the doctor, opened up a brown paper bag that was sitting on the floor by the coffee table. In it was a brown baseball-sized ball of resin wrapped loosely in wax paper. Brother Wa ceremoniously offered it to me. I gingerly accepted it with the same formality, with both hands. I then unwrapped a few of the waxed papers. I could see and smell immediately that this was the real thing. Dr. Wa brought out a small glass pipe and indicated that I should try some. I said "after you" and he declined, so I did too. I was already nervous enough. I envisioned myself wandering the outskirts of the city, half-baked, with a kilo of hash in my day pack. Despite Dr. Wa's encouragement, I declined a second time, saying I could see it was of good quality.

Dr. Wa then, with an uncomfortable sucking in of his breath, informed me that the price was higher than he thought. He explained that the process for turning bud into hash (he didn't say "bud", but I got the picture) required some arduous labor, hence the higher price.

"How much?" I asked. I was thinking, *Oh shit, so this is how it works.*

Grimacing, he replied, "I think about five hundred baht for that size." Brother Wa was grinning widely and innocently, it seemed to me, next to his brother who had a sincerely pained expression on his face. Immediately converting the figure and realizing that we were talking about twenty dollars, I nevertheless paused and looked thoughtful. Slowly, I nodded.

"I think that will be ok."

Maybe I should have bargained a bit, just for the hell of it, but I decided it was all so very absurd – possibly a dream from which I would awaken and be hashless – so I didn't push it. The doctor let out a long sigh that seemed to be more out of disappointment than relief. He was probably thinking he should have asked for more. I handed over a US twenty, which seemed to please them immensely, and they stuffed the ball back into the paper bag. I put it respectfully into my daypack.

I stayed another two hours, eating a wonderful meal and fending off beer. Dr. Wa and I didn't discuss any further the possibility of graduate study. I figured it was most likely out of the question after this little transaction. Walking back to the bus stop, I wondered what I would say to Larry back in Kyoto. I would have to gloss it over. It occurred to me that Dr. Wa might have thought he was doing an indirect favor for Larry by arranging this purchase. I had no idea if Larry was a toker, but I guessed probably not.

Back in my hotel room I locked the door, sat on the bed, opened my daypack, and stared at the ball. I needed to figure out what to do with the resin. I wasn't planning to leave Thailand for another couple of weeks. That gave me time to work out the details, as long as I didn't become paranoid about toting a kilo of hash around the country. I would be meeting up with Charlie in Bangkok in two or three days before she headed off for Malaysia and The Philippines. How would I explain this to her? Maybe I should say nothing, though I knew I would have to tell her somehow. She would know it from my vibe.

I stayed in Nakhon for another day, just hanging out and collecting myself, and then took an early bus to Bangkok. I experienced a few moments of undiluted terror, about an hour out of Nakhon; when the bus was stopped by a group of gentlemen in green army fatigues and sunglasses. I could have sworn I saw a

German Shepard in the bunch outside as well. I saw my future in a Thai jail and my heart was beating so I could feel it in my throat. Two of them boarded the bus, one with a machine gun discreetly held down along his thigh. They walked very slowly down the aisle to the back of the bus, scanning faces, then turned and left. There was a brief discussion between them and the driver outside, who then boarded and drove us onward. The consensus of the foreign passengers on board was that this was a check for undocumented Cambodians or possibly even Khmer Rouge. I had the ball of resin stuffed in my backpack and stowed in the storage compartment beneath the bus. I entertained a momentary vision of the dog sniffing through the luggage and discovering my stash. It all came to naught. I chalked it up to a lesson in remaining cool.

In Bangkok I checked into a guesthouse near Khao San Road, the Bangkok mecca for tourists seeking shopping, hair weaves, internet cafés and grilled cheese sandwiches. I asked the desk clerk about Charlie and Marie and learned that they were also checked in, but not around at the moment. I decided to go on a little shopping spree to acquire the items I would need for my international smuggling operation: bicycle shorts, saran wrap, cheesecloth, and a sewing kit. I purchased these things at a nearby department store and returned to find Charlie and Marie in the lounge. As we'd only been apart a week, there wasn't much to discuss, as far as they knew. They were about to be surprised.

I invited them up to my room. Marie, being one of the every-day-all-day-if-and-when-you-can tokers, sat down and started rolling a joint of her own miniscule score of hash. She rolled her joints European style, sprinkling crushed hashish over tobacco. I couldn't stand smoking this way. She knew it and offered me her ceramic pipe. The guesthouse was fairly accepting of all this, Marie assured me, but discretion was appreciated.

We talked some more and then Marie begged off to take a nap. After she left, I showed Charlie my newly acquired softball and told to her the story of Dr. and Brother Wa. Charlie never liked to toke, though she was tolerant of my habit. She was amused until I mentioned the bicycle shorts. Then she was horrified.

"*WHAT* are you gonna do with that?" she asked incredulously.

I showed her all of my recent purchases and explained my plan as best I could. I hadn't worked out all the details yet, but it was mostly there.

"Are you fucking crazy Ren?! What do you need to do that for?"

"Come on. I think I got it worked out." I acted like it was no big deal.

"Don't 'come on' me!" she yelled. I waved my arms for her to pipe down. "I can't believe this. What.... why? I don't get it."

"I don't know. It seems like an interesting thing to try. That's all."

"That's all?!" She gave me a withering stare, which I withstood with a smile.

"Really Char, I know I've never done anything like this before, but it gives me a...a....feeling of doing something really different. Maybe I'll make some cash on it too." I hadn't decided this yet, still thinking I might keep some for myself and give the rest away to friends, but the strike-it-rich angle was some needed ammo for this fight.

"That's weak, Ren. There are other ways to make money. And what feels so *different* about it? It looks like you're picking up where Greg left off," she said sarcastically.

"We've known some other folks who've done this sort of thing, that's true. It was scary but kind of exciting, too, right? And, of course, I've done my share of "different" things, but I've never really pushed up against anything, really. I've never felt this kind of challenge, so I figured, 'why not?"

I shrugged my shoulders. This was the first time I'd tried to articulate my feelings on the matter. I didn't feel I was doing such a good job of it. Maybe it was Greg coming out in me? I knew I felt something that was truly profound, for me, but I couldn't put the thing into words yet. When I tried it sounded trite. I wasn't saying that smuggling dope was a profound thing. But what it represented to me – the idea of going against the grain of my life, the standard, the straight and narrow – now *that* felt profound. This would probably sound idiotic to experienced rebels, but it was a very big deal to me.

Charlie looked long and hard at me, then scooted over on the bed and put her arms around me, taking a deep breath. She could feel the tension in my back and shoulders and squeezed tighter.

"Shit, Ren. I just do not want to be visiting you in some Japanese jail."

"What about a Thai jail?" I quipped to try to relieve the tension. She responded by punching me in the shoulder.

"I'll try to be sure that doesn't happen," I added, seriously. We were both getting close to teary eyed. I laugh-sighed and said, "If it does turn out that way, at least I'd finally have to cop to your being right. That'd be a first." I punched her arm in return, lightly.

She pushed me away, wiping her eyes and smiling. "I'd let you rot in there knowing it's always been that way." She became serious again. "Don't...well.... you know how I feel." She blew out a long breath, lifting horizontal a long twist of hair that had come loose from the pinned up strands on her head. We were silent then, listening to the fan whirring overhead and staring out the window at the corrugated roofing and hanging laundry across the alley. It started to rain.

We didn't talk about it anymore over the next couple of days. Charlie acted as if she didn't know about any of it. I methodically sewed the pockets on the inside of each leg of the bicycle shorts. Then I reshaped the resin ball into flat slabs about three by six inches that would fit snugly into the new pockets. It amazed me that I could only fit about half of the ball into the pockets I'd sewn. I wasn't too bothered by it, though – in fact, I was able to make a morbid rationalization about it: if I *was* caught, with this being less than a kilo, now, the penalty would be lighter than if I was carrying the whole load. Stupid. I figured I could give the rest away during the next couple weeks, spreading joy among the travelers I would meet.

And I would do just that. I fancied myself an altruist of sorts – leaving marble-sized balls of resin on restaurant tables where unsuspecting tourists would eventually come upon them. It was a weird and wonderful social experiment to watch people sit down at these "seeded" tables and observe their faces and reactions as they realized what they had. Some would look around, warily, and then surreptitiously pocket the marble. Others would be horrified and place the marble in the ashtray. Once a couple didn't even notice it on their table. Still others – and I was most surprised at these people – would handle the marble, sniff it, and still seem to have no clue as to what it was. One time, a woman tossed the marble into the street, grimacing, probably thinking it was a piece of dung. I always retrieved it – from the ashtray or the street – and reset the experiment for the next guinea pig. I fancied myself an anthropologist of sorts during those few days, but in the end it was just an amusement.

Three days after I met them in Bangkok, I escorted Charlie and Marie to the train station for their trip south into Malaysia. Charlie was in good spirits, heading off to a new adventure. I was planning to hang around Bangkok for a few more days, then go north to Chang Mai for a couple of weeks before coming back to Bangkok and onward to Japan. Marie, as far as I could tell, knew nothing about my amateur smuggler status. I planned to give her some of my bounty, but knowing she was going into Malaysia, thought the better of it. They hang drug traffickers in Malaysia, after they beat them silly. Walking with these two lovely women through the train station, I noticed how they attracted attention, a sassy and confident blonde and the exotic brunette, also confident in a new way. I'd never before thought of my sister as beautiful, but I had to admit she is. We'd discussed before how challenging it could be for women traveling in these parts, alone or together. Having heard of her experience in India, I didn't doubt it.

We stood around on the platform waiting for the train. When Marie took off for a last pee in a stationary toilet, Charlie took my hand and we stood there for a few moments, not making eye contact. I don't recall her ever having done this in our adult lives, yet it seemed very natural. Anyone watching would have thought we were a couple feeling the melancholy of an impending departure. It wasn't obvious we were brother and sister, let alone twins. We were both dark haired and tan of skin, but I was shaggier and much less refined of posture and demeanor. Charlie's features were more striking, she having inherited Mom's angular nose and cheekbones while I sported Dad's, more fleshy and bulbous. Marie returned a few minutes later and Charlie slipped her hand out of mine. As they started boarding, I gave Marie a quick hug and she hopped on, saying she would find their seats. That Marie always had a certain grace in spite of her aggressive posturing. Charlie and I hugged. "I'll see you next stateside, I suppose," she said.

"Yeah I guess so."

"I am *not* going to worry about you." She frowned and smiled.

I smiled back. "Likewise." We hugged again for good measure and she boarded.

"I'll say hi to Tony for you back in Kyoto." I gave her a raised eyebrow and she looked thoughtful, nodding her head. She gave me another of the frowning smile looks that only she can do and only I can read with any level of certainty. I would convey the sentiment to Tony. She boarded the train without a look back and I walked very slowly through the station. I decided to skip the bus ride and walked the hour and a half back to the hotel, letting the buzz and heat of the city lull me.

The following day I caught an overnight bus north to Chang Mai. I had been to the north before and was eager for the cooler air and tribal vibe. I decided to adopt the pose of the loner these next couple of weeks. I needed to be focused and certain of myself. It was difficult in the evenings to remain alone at a dinner table when new acquaintances were near.

On my second day in Chiang Mai (I slept most of the first owing to a lousy overnight bus ride), I got up early and made for

Wat Umong, a meditation temple to the north of the city. The temple grounds were vast and quite accommodating to my desire to be alone. I wandered about the temples and gardens all morning. Around lunchtime I found a small hut off in the trees by itself. It beckoned me inside. It was a simple, single room, bamboo structure on stilts, with no adornment whatsoever. I boldly walked up the porch stairs and, looking inside, saw that the walls were covered with sketches of the hills, of Buddhas, of bamboo and other trees, and one in particular of what appeared to be the hut itself. It was a very simple drawing, done in charcoal, yet it captured the solitude and intimacy of the place completely. After a good forty-five minutes in the small hut, where I ate my simple lunch of fruit, bread and cheese, I stepped outside to try to find the spot from which the artist did the drawing. I couldn't find it, oddly enough. You'd think something like that would be simple, and yet it remained elusive. I went back inside to study the drawing again and then back outside for another search. No luck. After a few minutes longer I left, leaving ten baht in an empty bowl by the door.

My one foray out in a group setting provided a little comic relief and a story that gets better with time. I met a British couple, Peter and Anne, having a beer one evening in the lounge of our hotel. I had been in town a week by then, taking daylong excursions and returning exhausted to my room. I made a point of eating at different restaurants every night and midday, to ensure and underscore the loner vibe. I had seen Peter and Anne in passing the previous few days and we had nodded to each other – that was as far as we'd gotten.

That evening, though, I came down to the lounge after a long cold bath and was sucking on a big bottle of Singha. The "lounge", a sparse gathering of couches and chairs around a low table just to the left of the reception area, had been empty. Peter and Anne returned from a dinner out and stopped for a beer. They sat down across from me. We struck up a conversation easily. Peter and Anne were an entertaining pair. He had a rock star look with shoulder length, naturally curly blonde hair worn loosely around his shoulders. He also sported a well-groomed goatee and liked to imitate – badly and he knew it – a Texas drawl. He would mangle lines like, "Wull Aah'll be" or " Ain't that a pickle" so inexpertly that all I could do was wince. Anne would reply with a similarly mangled "Yessirree, Bob" or "Ain't that the truth". She would always giggle, her own curly locks quivering around her temples, giving her a girlish coyness that was not wasted on me. These lines would pop out at the oddest moments, with no context, which made them even more painful. But as a couple they were young and in love and gave off a healthy and envious glow. After our second beer, we learned that we were both planning a trip to the caves near Doi Inthanon, the largest mountain in the northern part of the country. We agreed to go together the next day.

Early the next morning we caught a minibus to the eastern outskirts of the city. At the stop to the caves, we left the minibus, fended off a dozen pleas from local teenage entrepreneurs to guide us up the mile-long road, and made our way along. The jungle consisted of bamboo and other exotic vegetation that was lush and thick all around us. The morning was cool, with a breeze coming down off the mountain to the north. But we knew the day would soon heat up ferociously. Looming to the north and west were mysteriously rounded pinnacles of black basalt shrouded in layers of green. Wisps of white cloud circled the upper reaches of these in an otherwise clear blue sky.

Before long we arrived at the cave entrance, lined with stalls selling sugar cane juice, hand-drawn maps of the area, little carved Buddhas and other necessary tourist accoutrement. And again, the inevitable crush of affable and mercenary children and women surrounded us, offering to guide us through the caves. We had read a little about the site in our guidebooks, it being famed for housing Buddhist hermits in centuries past, with a network of caves winding for miles deep into the hillsides. One book mentioned an inaccessible underground stream that came out on the other side of Chang Mai, some twenty miles or more away. After a short discussion between the three of us, and some animated haggling with the cleverest looking adult in the bunch, we bought a map and hired a guide to show us the way. We requested a roughly two-hour journey into the mountain and back.

The first two hundred meters of the cave were well lit and our crude map was unnecessary. We each felt that touch of chagrin, wondering whether or not we had been duped or worse, fallen into the trap of "being tourists". We were soon reassured that our decision to hire a guide was prudent, as we were led through a maze of unlit side tunnels that led to larger caverns. We soon found ourselves alone in a huge and deep cavern, with only the guide's gas lantern for navigation, feeling an equally deep sense of wonder. Our guide, Patana, looked to be around thirty-five. She was a gritty tribal woman in jeans and a dirty white blouse and with vividly stained red teeth – the mark of years of chewing betel nut. She would stop every two hundred meters or so to point out an interesting feature or human marking, such as a primitive altar. We would stop and gawk and rest. Peter's Texas drawl gave way to serious British appreciation for the artifacts and awe of the history and culture here. Patana spoke very clipped English and didn't smile much, but seemed to know what she was doing. After about an hour, we stopped for a break and some of the snacks we brought. Then Patana indicated it was time to return.

"Go back price seventy-five baht. You pay now." We paid her seventy-five baht originally for the full trip.

"I don't think so. We've paid in full." Peter assumed the full height of British indignation at Patana's feeble attempt to swindle us.

"First price one way one way" She said with a stern, unflinching look.

"You can't be serious?" Anne said in a wonderfully incredulous, innocent-but-classy tone in that accent that makes American knees go weak. I would have done anything she asked for at that moment, but Patana said nothing. Peter and Anne looked to me. All I could do was smile and wonder, saying, if only to keep the situation light, "Come on Patana, we agreed already." Patana abruptly turned around and walked about ten meters away, saying, "You go back by self." She stopped, concealing her lantern from us with her body. She was good.

We looked at each other in the oozing darkness and agreed to ante up. We knew our tiny mag lites were woefully inadequate for these huge caves, as was our knowledge of the route. I knew we wouldn't die in there, but we could spend several uncomfortable hours for the price of a bit of dignity and a dollar each. Yes, we were being had in that way that many are for a pittance in this part of the world. I'd learned in India that a little *baksheesh* smoothed the way on many a road, and that indignation was at times a worthless luxury.

After receiving her extorted fee, Patana moved quickly and kept up a steady, brisk pace, keeping well ahead of us. The three of us kept mostly silent, except for huffing and puffing to stay within the sphere of Patana's lantern. Towards the end of the route out, the mood lightened fully and we started joking about it.

"Well ain't we in a pickle, by gum," said Peter in front.

"Yessirree Bob," replied Anne, next in line.

"It is downright preposterous," I finished in my best imitation of an Englishwoman, done in a high-pitched and grating Monty Python style. It didn't sound right and the other two were silent and I felt pretty stupid, but it was pleasing to give them a taste of their own medicine. As we reached the last two hundred meters and could see the light of the entrance, we paused to allow our eyes to adjust. Patana scampered off and disappeared. We stopped outside the entrance for a rest and refreshment and were able to warn a group entering about our experience. At one of the makeshift stalls I bought a small figurine of a laughing Buddha, hands raised in the air and bare belly exposed to the world. It was an appropriate souvenir of the day. The world is an unpredictable and absurd place and all you can really do is throw your hands in the air and laugh at it all. We walked back to the main road in good spirits and made our way back to the hotel in the same minibus that brought us out.

After a shower, the three of us went to a nearby restaurant, walking slowly to window shop along the way. Anne had earlier bought a deep red top with a colorful rainbow, stitched in a hill tribe pattern on the front and back. Happy to support the local economy again, she wore it to dinner. At the dinner table, Peter asked to see my Laughing Buddha, which I still carried in my daypack, and I obliged. He was a stout six inches tall, including his heaven-stretched arms, and was made of some kind of coated plaster. After looking him over, saying nothing, Peter handed him to Anne, who also made no comment other than, "cute." After she passed him back to me, I set him down on the table to watch over our meal. But when the food was finished, the waitress knocked the Buddha onto the ground as she was clearing the dishes. The fall broke off his arms and put a divot in his head. The girl, completely mortified but clueless as to what to do about it, scurried off to the kitchen, never to return. I retrieved the now four inch tall Buddha and set him on the table. He stood there, armless like a plundered Greek statue, but still smiling irrepressively. We toasted him silently and I left him on the table when we departed.

Back at the hotel, I began mentally preparing for my return trip to the US, via Japan. I'd worked out most of the smuggling details by this time. I was set to leave Chang Mai in two days, spend two more days in Bangkok and then be off. I had a bit more shopping to do, but that was more of a chore for me than a pleasure. There was the pickup of the bogus diploma for Eric, and the mass purchase of bootleg CDs at a buck apiece to enhance my collection and give away as gifts. I'd already done the passport exchange, so that was one less illegal thing that needed doing. I sat on my bed that evening trying to slog through some posthumously published Hemingway, unsuccessfully. Not that it was a bad read, mind you; the difficulty was the preoccupation in my unsettled state of mind. And even that was compounded by the gent two doors down and across the hall.

He had arrived two days earlier and though I had seen little of him, I knew his voice. He was an older chap, maybe in his early sixties and of indeterminate, though probably European, descent. He was completely bald, but with bushy white eyebrows. The few times I had seen him he was walking around the hotel bare-chested and in a tattered green and white checked sarong, preferring to hold the cloth around his waist with a fist rather than tie it up properly. His eyes were glazed over, as much as I could tell, since he wouldn't make eye contact. His body was deeply tanned beneath a mass of wispy white hair on his arms and chest. All through the day and night he would stumble around and mumble in a soft tone, "Jesus Christ...Jesus Christ...Jesus Christ." It seemed to be a litany, his mantra, with the syllables softening and trailing off toward the end. He would say this at least a few times an hour, never ceasing, and all of the hotel guests were obliged to listen, since the walls were thin and the windows always open. Did he sleep? I think not. Every once in a while the refrain would become more fervent, as if he was fending off some inner demon. In my somewhat altered state, his ranting conjured up the image of that monastic hut – the one I spent such a sweet, silent hour in at Wat Umong three days earlier. What was the connection?

But maybe it was another hut I was thinking of. I'd seen it just a few weeks earlier, on Koh Chang. A young boy, Pipop, was about eight years old and must have been the son of the owner or a worker at the bungalows we were staying at. He was a happy child, always engaged with the tourists and always drawing in the afternoon. He would draw on anything he could find – napkins, brochures, and scraps of paper from the trash... And he would draw with any implement he could find lying around – pens, crayons, and pencils... We all took a liking to him and encouraged him to sketch and show us his work. He could draw people, still life, and landscapes – anything. Before leaving the island, I bought him a set of colored pencils and gave him some paper from my notebook. In return, he gave me a drawing on a napkin of my hut at the primitive bungalow complex where we were staying. I kept the drawing with my plane tickets to protect it. Now that loony man's chanting was making me ache for the peace of the monastery and the revitalizing sun of the southern beaches. I took out Pipop's drawing out and mentally transported back to the island.

"Jesus Christ…. Jesus Christ…Jesus Christ!"

6

CHARLIE

| SEATTLE | TOKYO | THAILAND | LONDON | THE PHILIPPINES | INDIA |

| YEAR 1 | YEAR 2 | YEAR 3 |

DANCING IN THE SAND

Today I have ventured to a new part of me. Looking up she sees the rays filtering down through the water, clear on the sand and tufts of seaweed under her feet. She wriggles her toes inside her flippers and sand clouds billow around them. She's floating in a loosely assembled group of six, deep in tropical bathwater, each with a tank strapped on. Five are amateurs, learning from the sixth.

She rises to the surface and through her mask the images alternate from air and through water, retaining their clarity as the liquid covers her mask, though altered by the refracted light. She enjoys the effect, accompanied by the exaggerated breathing through the regulator, and bobs up and down on purpose to enhance it.

Thierry beckons to her.

OK, I get to go first. She launches herself the five meters over to him and they swim out another ten meters to deeper water. He looks to her, pointing down with his thumb. They sink five meters to the bottom and she settles into a solid posture, facing him. He makes a tugging motion on his mask and she gives him a thumb up. She's ready. He turns her around by the shoulders and then abruptly yanks off her mask, dropping it on the sandy bottom. The cool water feels refreshing on her face but the world is a turquoise blur. Better get moving. Taking a couple of deep breaths through the regulator, she locates the mask at her feet, reaches down and grabs it. She then wrestles her floating hair through the strap and cinches the mask over her eyes, blowing the

109

water out by forcing air through her nose. Once she is reoriented, she gives him the thumbs up sign again. They go through the same procedure with her regulator, and Charlie is both relieved and proud once she's breathing again. Thierry's eyes are smiling. Test passed. The four others go through the same exercises, but two of them panic and have to do it over again. Thierry is patient and methodical, and soon it's thumbs up all around.

Twenty-five minutes later the group is back on the dive boat, peeling out of their neoprene and excitedly discussing the day. Tomorrow is the final open water dive and certification, after four days of training. Thierry comes over to Charlie and gives her a teasing pinch on the upper arm.

"Pretty good, Charlie. Like a pro." She rolls her eyes at him and gives him a nudge with her hip. He looks away slyly and goes over to the Israeli girls, Mona and Deirdre. They are young, maybe twenty, and are happy to flirt with him. Thierry sticks to business, discussing why Mona had to repeat the regulator exercise. The other pair, Klaus and Monica from Munich, is next and review the exercise with Thierry in German. When they are finished, Thierry gives Charlie a quick glance and a wink when he thinks no one is watching. Everyone on the boat knows they have had a thing going these past few days, but Thierry insists on keeping relationships professional on the boat and Charlie agrees. It was awkward enough that they had to be dive buddies once the sixth student backed out at the last minute. Cupid smiles on new love.

A few minutes later the boat revs up and points them back towards Koh Tao, about a mile away. The acrid black diesel smoke billows out behind the boat and the motor roars and sputters, so Charlie makes her way forward to the bow. Before long Thierry joins her and they just sit, legs dangling over the edge and a breeze blowing their hair back. The Gulf of Thailand is a breathtaking turquoise jewel and the afternoon sky just a shade paler. The docking pier comes into view too soon and they pull alongside. Thierry jumps out to pull the boat in and Charlie goes towards the back with the others to help unload gear.

Everything gets rinsed off at the fresh water drums at the end of the pier, everyone acting like an old hand after three days on the boat. Thierry gathers the five students together one more time to remind them about the written test that evening, and then they are dismissed. As the others drift away, Charlie and Thierry fall in side by side and walk down the pier together. They plan to meet for a late lunch at their favorite café after he finishes some chores in the boathouse. This leaves Charlie free to meander slowly, confidently, and wistfully down the lane to "their place" – a rickety bamboo shack with two weathered picnic tables out front.

Charlie sits at the empty one and orders a banana shake by pointing at the picture on the menu. She has ordered the same thing every day for a week now – and is slightly annoyed that they still don't know the routine. She dismisses the thought, and stares out over the water, reveling in this moment's paradise, until Thierry joins her and they both order some pad thai. The meal comes quickly, since the diner keeps a constant wok-full of it cooking all throughout the afternoon. They down their lunches – ravenous from the morning's dive – and consider splitting another order.

Instead, they sit for half an hour longer, holding hands but not talking much. A small flock of seagulls swoops noisily around the other picnic table as a little German girl throws scraps into the air for them. Her mother watches her closely, but lets her enjoy the excitement. The little girl screams with delight as two gulls tussle over a piece of bread, sending the surrounding flock into a flapping titter. Thierry and Charlie are playing footsie under the table.

"You are ready for the test?" He gives her a sideways glance, cocking his chin towards the bickering gulls. His Belgian accent is thick, sounding to Charlie like a mixture of French and German.

"The test'll be easy." She shrugs her shoulders. "But maybe I could use some...extra help." She tries to look bashful but her twitching eyebrows give her away. "After a shower."

They pay at the shack counter and walk down the beach to Charlie's bungalow. It is a one-room bamboo structure propped three feet above the sand by round wooden posts. The double bed takes up most of the floor space. They go inside and straight to the added-on cement bathroom in the rear, peeling off their bathing suits. They begin the ritual by sluicing the sand and sweat off each other with buckets of cold water from the cistern. Thierry beats her to the soap and she lets him lather her up first. Before long the grooming becomes sensual as they slip and slide against each other playfully. She swirls the creamy foam over his untanned white butt and feels his readiness against her stomach. She reaches over to a bathroom travel kit and pulls out the small, square packet, as he rinses the soap out of the way. She puts the condom on him clumsily, which he loves. They do it standing up on the tile floor, with her back staying cool up against the cement wall. She will deal later with the abrasions on the backs of her shoulders. Afterwards they sluice off again, this time paying more attention to actually getting clean. They shampoo each other's hair and then wrap themselves in sarongs, allowing the cool breeze to dry them.

In the front room, Thierry twists and ties up the mosquito net suspended over the bed. Charlie turns on the overhead fan, opens the screenless windows, and puts some moisturizing lotion on her drying skin before joining him, stretched out on the bed. She curls over to half spoon him, and they cuddle without a word. Before long, they are napping contentedly.

Thierry leaves an hour later to prepare the diver's final exam and Charlie goes out to the front porch to swing in the hammock and watch the waves lap the beach. The ocean breeze flutters her sarong and she feels a world away from India, or anywhere else mortal, for that matter.

Ten days in Thailand and thank god I only spent two of them in Bangkok, though it was good to get mail at the GPO. I wonder what Renny is doing now? I'll bet he's down in Southern California at Greg's funeral. He sounded okay about it, but I know it must be weighing on him. Oh well, for me, staying here on Koh Tao for the rest of my time in Thailand is the best decision I've made yet! She mentally pats herself on the back for enrolling in the diving course as well. *I needed something to focus on and scuba was just the thing. I suppose I should count meeting Thierry as an added bonus.*

He flashed her a shy smile when she first enquired at the dive shop, and that was the clincher. The next day, still two days before the class started, she ran into him on the beach and they drank banana shakes together. The next day, they met for a walk around the island, a little snorkeling, and finally a passionate kiss good night. It wasn't until after the first day of class, however, that he walked her to her bungalow and, well, one thing led to another.

Every so often Charlie still gets a flashing image of the smiling man in Agra, standing in the puddle, stupefied. With the passing of a little time, she has become mostly amused by the incident. But she still struggles to understand it.

How is it I can be so captivated by Thierry's smile and sent into a rage by the smiling man's? On the surface, they aren't all that dissimilar. Thierry may be a little younger and clearly more handsome, but both have dark skin, both smile naturally and sincerely, neither is American.... Could it be significant that one is western and the other not? When it comes right down to it, I suppose the smiling man disturbed me because he wouldn't engage. He just smiled or gave me that empty stare. I wonder if my sleeping with Thierry so quickly is related to that incident in India? I've never hopped into bed with anyone after knowing him for only a couple of days. Not that I'm regretting it...

The written diving test that evening is a breeze. They find out the results within half an hour and everyone has passed easily. Their final open water dive is scheduled for the next morning, so everyone splits up to celebrate privately after learning their grades. Thierry and Charlie spend the evening reading on the hammock, he some material on advanced diving in German and she a tattered copy of Du Mauriers' <u>Jamaica Inn</u> she found in her bungalow.

At the break of dawn, Charlie is up and off to breakfast, leaving Thierry to sleep a little longer. The dive is to begin at 11am, but the students arrive at the boat an hour early to get into their suits and help with the gear.

The dive is in the same area where they trained, only a few hundred meters further out. It is the first time they can relax and enjoy the coral and darting fish. They meander in a close group of three rows of two. As they near the end of their time, Thierry gathers the group at ten meters down and indicates they are free to roam for ten minutes before needing to return to the boat. The pairs peel off and Charlie and Thierry find a large and lonely specimen of orange fan coral. They both hover above it for the rest of their time and Charlie is contented in her newfound world. They return to the boat. Back at the dive shop, they are presented with temporary diving cards and the class comes to a close. The group agrees to meet later at Klaus and Monica's bungalow to celebrate. Charlie heads back to her bungalow to take a nap – she is exhausted! Thierry will be by to pick her up around seven to go to the party together.

As she walks back to her place, along the beach instead of the lane, she suddenly remembers a wonderful trip the Diaz family had taken to the Ozarks that summer when she and Renny were thirteen. Their family met up with another family that included two kids, Jeremy and Alicia. He was about fifteen and she was about eight.

The four of us are walking on a trail along the river, about a half-mile from the cabin. I want to call it the Missouri River, but no, the Missouri is bigger. We stop at a small embankment to skip rocks across the swiftly moving current. Jeremy is better at it than the rest of us, even Renny. And Alicia isn't really interested; she just wants to play in the flowers by the side of the trail. All of a sudden, I see a yellow cap floating in the middle of the river. The bill is bobbing up and down in the air. I yell and point it out to the others, but they just freeze and watch it go by.

"I'm gonna get it!" Jeremy says, peeling off his shoes and shirt.

"I don't think that's a good idea." Charlie warns him. The water looks deep and dangerous. And fast. Renny says nothing and Alicia, such a child, squeals in excitement.

"It's no problem. Meet me downstream!" Jeremy plunges into the water headfirst and starts angling towards the escaping hat. I am so scared and awed; my heart is a pounding mallet in my chest as I watch his strong swimmer's strokes.

"Come on!" Renny yells as he scoops op Jeremy's clothes and races up the trail with Alicia scampering behind him. I don't want to let Jeremy out of my sight – he is at least twenty yards downstream already and getting farther with every stroke. But I hurry after Renny and Alicia and just as I catch up to them, they see Jeremy intercept the hat and wave it in the air with a triumphant whoop. He quickly surveys the riverbank, pointing downstream to an opening on our side of the stream. The three of us take off for it and by the time we get there, Jeremy is waiting for us. Renny hands him his clothes and Jeremy slaps the dripping hat on his kid sister's head. She squeals again with delight and pulls it off, beaming. It is a yellow mesh baseball cap with the word "Mack" imprinted in black above the bill. I just gawk at Jeremy's dripping, lean body and the darkened cutoffs sagging around his hips, streaming water. His long dark hair is matted to his forehead and he is breathing heavily. We are all in awe, for different reasons, as we follow Jeremy back towards the cabins.

Charlie is still smiling to herself as she leaves the beach and climbs the stairs to her bungalow. *Yep, that was the first time I ever felt in love.* Nothing ever came of it, of course. That week in the Ozarks came to an end and Charlie never saw him again, but the memory is still as clear and warm as the tropical Thai air. She unlocks the door to her home sweet bungalow and lies down to take a nap.

Later that evening, the group of diving students and their instructor are gathered in the restaurant located in the middle of Klaus and Monica's bungalow complex. They have eaten a large meal, enhanced with Thai beer and local whisky. Charlie has been quaffing Mekong Whisky shakes all night and is feeling flushed in the cheeks. Klaus is consuming bottles of beer at an incredible rate, and Thierry is not far behind him. Monica and Mona are following Charlie's lead on the whiskey shakes – though at a more sustainable pace – and Deirdre is not drinking at all. The lively conversation drifts off for a moment, giving Monica and Deirdre an opportunity to retire for the evening. The remaining four decide to play cards and continue on. They decide on Euchre and it's the women, Charlie and Mona, against Klaus and Thierry.

"Mona, tell me – what's it like to serve in the Israeli Military?" Charlie is genuinely curious. Mona and Deirdre divulged on the diving boat that both recently completed their mandatory two-year stint.

"Oh, it is really difficult for some, but for me it was easy. I served in a transportation department in Tel Aviv. It was mostly filing and office work."

"But you still had to do basic training, right?"

"Yes. That was hard, physically." Mona laughs and looks to Thierry. "Look at me. I had difficulty with the diving. But the boot camp, as I think you call it, was still fun, being with people your own age. We all have to do it in Israel, so we don't really mind."

"You never have to shoot at anyone?" Klaus comments, only half interested.

"No. Not like others who patrol near Lebanon or in Jerusalem sometimes. Those people are hard soldiers. Deirdre served a year in Jerusalem, as a driver. She saw some bad things."

"I served two years also," Klaus said. "For the Forestdienst. It's a land management program by the government. It's an alternative to the military that we have in Germany. And you two, you never do?" He looks to Charlie and Thierry.

Thierry laughs. "No. I grew up in Brussels playing *futbol*. No army for me."

"Me neither," adds Charlie. "I never even considered it. My Dad was drafted to go to Vietnam. He didn't talk about it much, but it was hard for him. Hard for him to get back into American life after what he saw." They seem impressed.

"But then America is big and your military is big too. You can tell everyone else on this planet what to do and we have to do it," says Klaus, slightly caustic. Charlie had never heard this perspective before. She doesn't know what to say and so says nothing.

"I think we all do what we want," says Thierry, coming to her defense. "Look at us. Here we are, halfway around the world from Europe and America, and it doesn't matter much to us here what goes on back home."

Klaus nods. "But still it effects us. It will be there when we go home. There are American soldiers in Germany, France, Spain, the Middle East, Japan, and the Philippines. It is The U.S., which controls things. There's no question about that."

Thierry shrugs his shoulders but says nothing, a pacifist at heart.

Mona chimes in. "I think it is just the way things are. Look at Israel; we are surrounded in our own country by people who don't want us there, so we have to fight. There is nothing else to be done."

"Yes, yes I suppose, but it is all so crazy. There is no use for it, no solution to it. You can't fight forever." Klaus gazes at Mona and then back down to the table. He takes a long swig from his glass and beckons to the bar for another.

"Maybe this is true. There are many crazy Arabs around the Middle East, and Israelis too. They will fight a long time," replies Mona.

"I've always wondered if I could shoot somebody, like another soldier in a battle? I don't think I would ever put myself in that situation," muses Charlie aloud, wanting to steer the conversation away from controversy and into the generic.

"Sure you could shoot someone. I think it just happens. The mind switches off and you do what is necessary to live." Klaus is serious and matter-of-fact

"I think like Charlie," says Mona. "I think about it for real because I might have needed to do it. I'm glad I didn't, of course. I guess I would have if it was necessary, but it wasn't, so I don't have to….to….guess about it."

"I never thought about it before." Thierry is thinking about it now. "I think I could do it, but why? It is pointless to think about something that is not likely to happen. I think about if a shark tried to bite me, maybe. Of course I would fight back, kick it in the nose or something, but to shoot somebody? You can't know such a thing before it happens."

"Right, you would kick a shark in the head!" Charlie is teasing him. Thierry raises his hands, palms up, in defense. "Yes, I think so."

"I think I would pee my wetsuit." Mona starts giggling, trying to lighten the mood.

"I saw a man get bit by a shark once." They all fall silent and look at Klaus. "Well, I didn't see it exactly, but we were in the water together. He was maybe fifty meters ahead of me. There were four of us snorkeling at a reef in the Bahamas. We saw a shark, a big one," he makes an expansive gesture with his hands, "and two of us swam like hell back onto the reef, but our friend didn't see us. His head was down in the water. We were..." He holds his hands out as if to hold a rifle and makes to pull the trigger with one finger.

"Spear fishing," Thierry helps him out.

"Yes. We had some strings around our waist and our friend who got bit had a fish on it. The shark tried to take the fish but bit him in the ass." Klaus breaks out into a laugh, and then takes a long pull from a new glass. The others laugh in amazement with him. "He took sixty stitches in his ass." He chuckles again and then grows serious.

"I remember being scared like crazy when our friend did not swim up with us. When we got to shallow water, where we could stand on the reef, we looked around for him and waited. Then we saw him, standing knee deep on top of the reef maybe a hundred meters away. He was crying in pain and holding his side." He made a grabbing motion at his behind. "…and blood was running down his leg. He had to swim to us across the water to get to the shore, and this is a dangerous thing to do in water if you are bleeding. I was terrified. I couldn't swim in the ocean for months afterward. And now you must realize how I feel to have completed a diving course. At least sharks are not a problem in Germany." He bursts out laughing again and everyone joins in.

"How big was the shark?" asks Charlie, enthralled.

"Oh, maybe two meters. But it looked really big in the water. Bigger than me."

Thierry nods knowingly. "Everything in the water is bigger and faster than we are. We are…" He makes a puffing sound and shrugs his shoulders. "…like fish out of water in the water. At their mercy."

"Oh good. And I am supposed to have confidence now to dive?" Mona says, teasing.

Thierry starts to reply, but then stops, smiling instead.

"What about this card game? Are we scared to bite the ass of these women?" Klaus demands of Thierry.

"Maybe you are terrified of this also?" Charlie challenges.

Klaus snorts. "Let us see. Monsieur Belgique? Are you ready?"

"I am terrified anytime of playing with women. Deal the cards."

"You should be." Charlie acts serious and Mona is delighted. The men win the first round and act like it doesn't matter. The women know better.

❧❧❧❧❧ ❧❧❧❧❧ ❧❧❧❧❧ ❧❧❧❧❧ ❧❧❧❧❧

Charlie stays on Koh Tao for another two days, snorkeling on her own or diving with Thierry. But since she is now a certified diver, she explores the freedom of roaming around the undersea world as she pleases. She avoids worrying about sharks or how to say good-bye to Thierry, instead planning the next leg of her trip.

She decides to island-hop southward over the next week – a few days in Koh Phangan and then a couple more on Koh Samui. From there she can catch a flight to Bangkok just in time to connect to her flight to Japan without having to go back into the city.

Thierry is pleased to be invited to join her on the first island but he has to return to Koh Tao after that – back to work. She would be on her own in Koh Samui, the Las Vegas of Thailand's islands, or so she hears. Before leaving, she exchanges addresses with her diving friends and hopes that she will at least keep in touch with Mona. Then she and Thierry board the short ferry ride to Koh Phangan.

Thierry knows the island well so she lets him guide her to an isolated beach on the northwest corner. They easily find a set of bungalows with a vacancy. They consciously decide to avoid staying on the southern part of the island, as it will be packed with throngs of young hippies and wanderers seeking the famous Full Moon Party, scheduled for two nights later. Thierry and Charlie debate attending, since she is curious, but Thierry has been several times and thinks it a waste of brain cells. They compromise on just visiting the beach for the night of the debauch, and rent a scooter to get there and back.

They spend the first couple of days in strict beach bum fashion. They wake with the sun but lounge in bed or hammock until mid-morning, when it is time for breakfast. Tropical fruit salad can motivate even the most vacationing tourist to the closest café. After breakfast they go for a swim or a long walk on the beach. They return to the bungalow and make love in the afternoon, napping afterwards until the sun begins to set. After dark, they wander the beach, stop in to socialize with other castaways at one of the many beach bars, or lie in bed reading. They sleep soundly each night. Charlie thinks to herself that this must be what a honeymoon is supposed to be like.

She and Thierry do not discuss anything beyond these days on Koh Phangan, and she doesn't want to jeopardize the perfect romance it is now, where they are both fully *in the moment* and the future is only their next meal or a spontaneous caress. Outside of each moment lurks a black hole that emits nothing and sucks you in if you venture too close. The question of "What next?" can only bring discussion, expectations, and probably a heartful of hurt for her. She chooses not to risk it, and Thierry says nothing as well.

The night of the full moon party, they ride their rented scooter to the south, slowly weaving along the winding, narrow road. Charlie drives first, but Thierry's weight on the back is too awkward for her to handle and after a close call with a gravelly curve, they switch. They wear no helmets and the night breeze is cool. They park the motorbike at a small restaurant with a party that is already in full swing. The crowd looks a bit young, so they walk down the beach to see what the other options are. It is already close to midnight and the beach is alive and crawling with people. There are dozens of cafés and bungalows on stilts, built very near the water line. With the tide on its way in, Charlie and Thierry wade around some of the pilings to get past them. Most of the nightspots are blaring rave music and pulsing with laser lights. "Gross." Charlie manages under her breath, and they walk on towards a darker and more mysterious stretch of the beach. There are still bungalows in this area, and the scene is still alive, but jazzier and mature, as opposed to the head-banger intensity they had just rejected.

Thierry sees a couple of guys he knows – divers from the other islands. They greet each other like brothers and speak in rapid French as Charlie tunes out, content to observe the many other scenes playing out on the beach. She removes her sandals, leaves them by Thierry's daypack now resting near his chair, and wanders out into the dark water. She wades in up to her knees, gaining some space for perspective, and turns to watch the beach. She can see up and down the long curve and notices dozens of small groups and several larger ones, tripping and giggling. All manner of drugs are available and in use. Thierry waves to her and she slowly walks back out of the water towards him. They all sit down at a small table in front of the next restaurant and order drinks. Thierry continues talking to his diving mates for a few minutes and then turns to her.

"Do you think you would like to try some mushrooms?"

They had discussed the possibility of experimenting with one drug or another this evening. Charlie is inexperienced, other than over-drinking many times before, and she is curious – her one experience with cocaine in college never amounted to anything. Thierry rarely does any drugs anymore – it is no good to mix drugs and diving – but he had snorted, smoked, or swallowed his share of mind altering substances at some time in his past.

"What do *you* think?" Charlie doesn't want to seem too eager.

He shrugs. "Sure, why not?"

She smiles back at him and caresses the back of his hand with her fingertips. "Okay, why not? Just promise you'll stay close by me."

He nods. "I'll be back in a minute." The divers all get up and disappear into the restaurant. Charlie is left alone at the table. Two very high, very young men come along and try to start up a conversation with her. They are both distractingly bare-chested, with long hair and far away looks in their eyes.

"Hey, sister, what's up? Aren't you looking hot tonight." says the blond surfer dude with an Australian accent.

"Yeah, we were wondering if you might be persuaded to accompany us…." his dark-haired friend adds, putting his forefinger and thumb to his lips in the universal symbol of the toke.

It is comical, not scary at all, and when she laughs it encourages them. She tries to wave them away several times but they don't leave until Thierry returns five minutes later. He comes back, making inquisitive eye contact with Charlie, but relaxes when he sees the mirth in her eyes. Once the boys scurry off, Thierry sits down and places his beer and her banana-Mekong shake on the table. Then, ceremoniously, he opens his fist and shows her four small dried mushroom caps, each about the size and texture of a small fig. She picks two of them up gingerly, leaving the other two for him.

"Chew on these and swallow them. Make sure they are really moist before you swallow."

"You've done this before I guess."

"Once or twice." He smiles and pops the caps into this mouth. She does the same. They taste awful, but she does as she is told, rolling them around in her mouth to moisten them, and then chewing the caps into small bits before washing them down with her shake. Charlie then realizes that Thierry had come back from the bar alone.

"What happened to your friends?"

"They went off somewhere else. I'm sure we'll run into them again later. Besides, I'm here with you. I could see you are bored with diving talk. And maybe you couldn't understand the French?"

"A little. But thanks, I'm glad it's just the two of us." She smiles at him and he reaches over, touching his fingers to her lips. Just then she is convinced she loves this guy, even if she doesn't really know him. "You are a sweet man." She blushes and looks away. She had glimpsed into the black hole for a split second but pulled back, knowing again it isn't the time to go there.

They sit for a half hour, watching the people pass, enjoying the evening, and waiting for the 'shrooms to kick in.

"Lets take a walk," Thierry suggests. Charlie nods and they both rise from their seats and head toward the lapping waves.

Meandering slowly in and out of the surf, Charlie begins to feel a warm fuzziness seep into her awareness of the night. The sand under her feet begins to feel grittier and the sound of the surf becomes almost musical. She looks over at Thierry, who had stopped to look out to sea. He is staring at a fishing boat moored fifty yards off the beach. She sidles up against his arm.

"I think it is coming on now," he says, his gaze not shifting.

"Yup. I think so too. Lets get further away from all these people."

She guides him further along the darkened beach to where groups are fewer and farther between. They find an empty space between two stacks of washed up logs and sit down in the sand. Charlie's thoughts begin bouncing around: the beach, her life on the road thus far, her life back home, and the possibilities ahead in the universe. She suddenly sees flashing lights in the sky.

Was it a UFO? Her inner voice kicks in loudly.

No, don't be silly.

I'll ask Thierry!

No, don't be stupid. And so on. In the end, she is too embarrassed to bring it up with Thierry whom, she can see, is off in his own wonderland. They sit for who-knows-how-long before she is inspired to get her feet wet. She hops up, startling Thierry out of his revelry, pads over to the rolling surf and deliberately steps in. Around her feet, bright pinpoints of iridescence blossom, outlining her steps and seeping up towards the surface. She is startled by this at first, but soon becomes mesmerized playing in it, moving her feet to dance with the lights. She finally can't contain the fun of it anymore and calls to Thierry.

"Hey, come look at this!"

He comes running and lets out a sigh of awe as he realizes what she has found.

"It is the plankton, glowing from our heat." He is equally entranced by the effect.

She looks up in surprise and frowns. "No way, I'm not going to believe scientific explanations just now. It's something else, I think. It's something else entirely." She does a little jig in the water, holding up the bottom of her shorts, and prances around like an elf.

"What do *you* think it is then?"

"It's the ocean talking to us."

"What is it saying? Maybe it wants to know who is this crazy lady dancing in the sand?"

She laughs merrily. "The ocean doesn't know that I'm a woman or you're a man." She says it like it is obvious.

"How do you know such a thing I wonder?"

"So many questions! I can tell, that's all. Just listen to it." She points to the water.

He looks down at the glittering trails of purple light in the water as they glow brightly and fade almost instantly. Charlie's sparkling footprints fade as soon as she makes new ones. "I don't hear anything that I can put in words."

"Maybe it's asking us what's up? Why are we here?"

"You mean, why are we here at this moment? Or as in philosophie...why are we here at all?"

"Could be both. What are we doing here, Monsieur Monger?" She curtsies to him.

He formally bows back. "We are dancing in the sand. That is all."

"Is that just now, in the moment, or are you talking philosophie?" She holds out her hands, one gesturing to the night sky, and the other out to him, as if to accept his invitation to waltz.

"Both, Mademoiselle." He takes her hand and they perform a comical pas de deux, entertaining the few passersby on the beach, who they don't notice at all. The glowing sand is all about them in tiny roiling clouds. Their waltz dissolves into a slow dance, Charlie clasping her wrists behind his neck and resting her head against his chest. They stay like this for an eternity. When they emerge from this bewitched moment, the full moon still shines brightly as it sets behind the coconut palms. The beach scene is still happening, but the intensity has crested. Charlie and Thierry wade back to dry sand and sit in the spot between the driftwood.

They decide not to try to ride back to the bungalow tonight, and before long they are curled up around each other and fast asleep. Thierry has his daypack as a pillow and she has his chest.

Charlie will long remember her dream that night for how vivid and surreal it is.

She is at a formal party in an estate house. Dressed in a long black silk gown, she wanders around, watching the costumed people chitchatting, so animated. In their champagne glasses is a thick pink liquid. Charlie doesn't have one but wants one. She finds a faceless waiter with a tray of drinks and grabs one. It is foul tasting, like dirty kidney beans, but she doesn't mind. It also doesn't matter that she is among strangers – not a face does she recognize. She drifts outside to a balcony and sees the garden as a wild mass of movement and color – swaying green and yellow stalks, as tall as she, and moving mounds of blue and purple moss. She is intrigued and continues walking out into it. The garden becomes an undersea coral garden, replete with swarms of tiny darting insects – are they fish? – feeding on microscopic creatures smaller still. The carpet of astrobrite yellow and green is moving to an invisible current. Charlie glances back at the balcony, now very far away, and there is Thierry, flirting with a gorgeous golden-haired nymph. They walk off together, arm in arm. Rage, jealousy, and physical pain flare through her veins, and she starts after them. But the pain is short-lived. She stops herself. What does it matter? Instead, she glides over to a group of people gathered in a corner of the garden watching a cockfight. Only the combatants aren't cocks, but huge wormlike creatures – the size of dogs and with human teeth. They bite at the other and draw pus-colored blood. She feels a wave of nausea and turns away, only to stand face-to-beak with a pair of winged creatures hovering above her. Surprisingly, she feels calm, not sick or angry or disappointed or scared, though the creatures look fierce. They regard her with curiosity and she gives them the same eye. They are powerful and grotesque, like hungry buzzards, only larger. They flap their wings and create a wind that stings her eyes and whips her hair back. As they turn and fly away, she calls out to them. Wait! No response. WAIT!!! Please! One of them pauses and looks back. Charlie feels confused, not finding the words to ask her question. The creature hovers, waiting, and then cocks its head, smiling faintly, it seems, before turning and joining its mate. She watches them fly into the distance, and as their image recedes so does her emotional turmoil. She turns to walk back to the house but the people and party have disappeared. Instead, the garden stretches out in front of her as far as she can see, and she starts walking out into it.

She is still walking when she feels something stinging her face. She awakes with a start to the quiet calm of the morning-after beach. The morning breeze is blowing tiny grains of sand on the sleeping lovers. The sky is brightening and she blinks hard, both to adjust to the light and erase the grogginess. She looks back at Thierry and meets his smiling eyes. She pushes off of his chest and sits up to stretch and look around. Scattered along the sand, for as far as she can see, lay last night's revelers snoozing or lounging in front of their breakfasts or doing yoga under the palms. She and Thierry are just barely out of sight in the shadow of the driftwood around them.

"Wow. What time is it?" she asks.

He rubs his bare wrist. "I don't know."

"Have you been awake long?"

"Just before you." He sits up beside her and snuggles his face into her shoulder to clear the sand. She smoothes out his hair. "You hungry?" he asks.

She thinks about it for a second before realizing she is.

"Ravenous!" She nods and he gets the meaning, though he doesn't understand the word.

They rise slowly and slap the sand off their clothes as they make their way down the beach to the closest open restaurant. Charlie is still dwelling on her dream as the intensity of it begins to fade. She feels strangely contented, even as her body tells her she has just ridden six hours down a dusty, rutted road in the back of a pickup. Had she only spent a night sleeping on a sandy beach in the arms of her lover?

They find an open restaurant in three minutes and sit down in the rickety bamboo chairs. He orders for them as she locates the bathroom. Washing her face and combing her hair with her fingers, she smiles at her reflection in the mirror. *You're a strange woman Charlie Diaz*, she thinks to herself, and then: *good thing*.

They eat without much talking and then return unceremoniously to their motorbike. Someone has draped a hot pink bikini top over the handlebars and they both laugh at the sight of it. Thierry ties it to a tree and salutes it grandly. They ride north to their bungalow and sleep the afternoon away.

The next day they never get farther than the beach in front of their bungalow, but lounge there as contented as they ever are to be. Ignored is Thierry's return to Koh Tao the following morning and Charlie's move to Koh Samui the day after. With the sunset of the perfect day comes an evening of honest reflection and affection. They sit on the porch of their bungalow by candlelight and cautiously approach the black hole.

"You'll be in Japan in just a few days."

She nods but continues to gaze at the water. "Will you stay on Koh Tao for long?"

He stares at the ground. "I don't know. I'll go back to Belgium for a couple months this summer and decide then if I'll come back." She looks at him, then he at her, and they both chuckle. He starts to say something else, but stops himself. She lets the moment pass and doesn't ask what he had begun to say.

Instead she is content to hold his hand and sit watching the sunset.

The next morning they ride the motorbike down to the ferry mooring. Charlie wears Thierry's pack and he drives. They both intuitively know to avoid talking, which can lead to words that could not be unsaid. They settle for hugging tightly and kissing passionately before he boards and she watches the boat chug away. Thierry stands at the stern and watches her too. Neither of them wave, but both are smiling. She feels a lump rise and tears well, but forces them down, folding her arms over her chest tightly and taking a series of deep breaths through her mouth. When the boat becomes a speck on the horizon, she returns to the scooter and rides back to the bungalow.

She continues to breath deeply all day as she re-packs her things, writes a few postcards, finishes her book, and generally keeps busy. It is an effective way of avoiding the darkness of the black hole, and it works for her. She amuses herself over the next two days touring around Koh Samui on a rented scooter. She drives fast and forgets Thierry for the moment, letting herself get excited about the next leg of her journey. Almost before she is ready to leave the islands, she flies to Bangkok and catches her connection for Japan.

7

RENNY

SAN FRANCISCO   KYOTO   THAILAND   KATMANDU   LAKE TOBA   VARANASSI   IPOH

YEAR 1   YEAR 2   YEAR 3

ISLAND LIFE

"Western women are trouble. Plain and simple." The old soldier poked the cigar back into his mouth and slouched back into his chair. Tex, as I silently nicknamed him, was a stout ex-military man from Abilene with a pale, pockmarked complexion and arms burned a semi-permanent crispy red from too much tropical sun. I was enjoying my third beer in a bar in Laem Ngop, at the eastern point of the Thai coastline, waiting for the ferry. I was heading to Koh Chang, the island a few kilometers off the coast that was part national park and part backpacker Fantasy Island. Tex was the barkeep and owner of this establishment on the wharf, and had been entertaining me since I ordered my second bottle. Now he exhaled a thick plume of cigar smoke towards the ceiling fan.

"That's why I married me a Thai gal. Don't have to deal with all the baggage." He had lived in the country for more than two decades. Since Vietnam, I suspected. He looked to me, expecting a reply.

"I don't know how to answer that one. I'm screwed whichever way I answer," I said, looking around to see who might overhear.

"How do you reckon?" He looked perplexed.

"I can only answer because no western women are around." He harrumphed and I continued. "If I say they aren't trouble, you might think I pretend to understand women, and we both know that isn't really possible. On the other hand, if I say they *are*," I continued, nonchalantly glancing around again, lowering my

130

voice, "then I admit that there is something wrong with my country women, and that ...would be unwise. In truth, I'm not sure who has the problem – me or the women – so I would rather just keep my mouth shut." I drank my Singha.

"Well see, that just proves my point!" He leaned over the table on his elbow, tilting the surface awkwardly towards him. I grabbed my beer as it began to slide away.

"Just the fact that they make you to think there is a problem means that there *is* one. You just don't have the balls to call a spade a spade. This fuckin' PC world is crap, man. I'm tired of it. You and your hippie friends got it all turned around." He banged his open hand down on the table. Case closed. His point was not debatable and so I didn't try. I didn't find him intimidating or belligerent, just a man too sure of where he stood and without inclination to explore otherwise. I thanked him for the beer and paid up, half-relieved it was time to board the ferry. The other half of me had enjoyed the repartee, if you could call it that, and the simple presence of the caricature of Tex in Thailand.

The converted fishing boat offered hard plank seating with little comfort for the butt or room for the legs. But the ride was short and pleasant, so no one complained much. The boat was partly filled with tourists like myself, but mostly with locals doing their shopping on the mainland. Large bags of rice and onions and other assorted vegetables were stacked about the deck, interspersed with backpacks. The ferry dropped everyone off at the rickety wooden pier on the north side of the island.

"Where you go? S'cuse me, sir, where you go?" The hawkers descended upon us to take us to the "most beautiful beach" for a "cheap cheap price." I found one that would take me to the beach I wanted. He tried to talk me out of going to the Escape Bungalow, probably because the commission for him would be more if he brought me elsewhere, but I insisted. We boarded the makeshift taxi – a truck with more plank seating along both sides of the hauling bed – along with a half dozen others heading that direction as well. We were soon hustled away from the paved port road for the roller coaster ride to the other side of the island.

The southwest side of Koh Chang offers a relatively uninhabited slice of heaven. At least, that is what I'd heard. I was headed for a small, secluded bay that the backpacker's grapevine said had only two sets of bungalows on it. One of them – the one *not* specifically recommended by the guidebook, was Escape Bungalows. I picked it for the name, not because it also had no running water.

The taxi dropped me off at the roadside and I hiked the short road to the beach. I emerged from the trees to a set of a dozen or so bamboo and thatch bungalows lining a beautiful stretch of white sandy beach. I noticed no concrete enclosures attached to each bungalow and walked around a bit to learn more, confirming that there were no bathrooms attached to any of the huts. The shower area was a flat rock under a small waterfall coming out of the hillside about 100 yards down the beach. Latrines were attached to the main bungalow, situated in the center of the line.

I approached the makeshift "front desk", which was really just a small counter. I waited while a young woman cleared one of the nearby tables, indicating it would be just a moment. I noticed a couple sets of fins and a flimsy looking mask and snorkel hanging on the wall behind the counter. When the woman finished, she showed me what was available. Only ten of the twelve primitive bungalows seemed to be inhabited, so luck was with me, or so I thought. There was no electricity in the entire complex, and therefore no fans or bulb lighting. There were no mosquito nets either, to my initial worry, but I shrugged it off. "Perfect," I said out loud, and paid for two bungalows when we returned to the central hut – one for Tony and me and one for Charlie and the girls. I'd have it all to myself for a day, as they should arrive tomorrow.

Other guests were eating or drinking or reading at one of the dozen bamboo tables, or lounging in one of the colorful hammocks tied up nearby. Most looked like they had been here for some time already, given away by their tans, relaxed postures, and satisfied expressions. And why not? Who could blame them?

The water was crystal clear, the sand was sugar-white, the breeze cool and soothing, and the palms full of coconuts. These happy slugs appeared to be mostly European and completely uninterested in my arrival.

The owner of the bungalows, Uab (which sounded like 'Wab'), however, was quite interested. He came out when I was signing in and introduced himself. Extremely gregarious and helpful, he gave me a short tour of the area and explained how meals worked. He expected us to eat primarily at his restaurant and not at the other restaurant ten minutes' walk down the beach. There seemed to be a long-standing rivalry between the two places and I nodded to indicate I was on his side. We needed to order dinner by noon to give the cook enough time to buy the ingredients and have them delivered by four. Coleman lanterns and candles lighted this central hut with the restaurant after sunset, and all of the cooking was done on propane burners.

Since it would soon be noon, I ordered dinner, choosing fresh fish instead of chicken, and then decided to explore the scene. Walking around my bungalow, I noticed a couple of women showering down at the waterfall. Yes, they were naked, rather than covered with a sarong, as Thai women would have done. Both of them caught me looking but seemed uninhibited and unconcerned that I could see them. I liked this place.

I donned my swim trunks and played on the beach for the rest of the afternoon. The snorkeling was decent and Uab let me borrow the snorkeling gear for free. At dinner, I ate with a pair of Canadians whom I'd met on the beach and thrown the Frisbee with. They were a couple, Spencer and Walt, in their mid-thirties, and had been in this place for five weeks already with no plans to leave soon. They were both extremely tanned and gay in both senses of the word. I took them for European at first, the way they strutted around in yellow Speedos.

At the next table over, four very laid-back-looking Frenchmen and one woman were huddled together taking bong hits. Walt had developed an obvious dislike for them.

"Friggin' Eurotrash. They're filthy and about as friendly as snakes." Spencer smiled at this and rolled his eyes. These Canadians were, I should have known, not only vegetarians, but also health nuts. They didn't drink or smoke and ate strictly vegetarian meals. I wondered why they were in Thailand, an herb and whisky heaven. They were both in excellent physical condition, with sinewy, toned arms and legs. Spencer was on sabbatical from his job teaching at a community college in Ottawa. Walt quit his job as a concierge to join him on this trip. After Walt's hissing at the French, I decided to avoid going down that lane, so we chatted about the beaches and the snorkeling and the recent weather. I looked around often but didn't see the two women from the shower. After dinner, Spencer and Walt invited me along on their usual walk on the beach to aid digestion. I briefly considered joining the unfriendly bong-tokers instead, but thought better of it and agreed to the walk. The sunset over the water was remarkable and we continued to watch until the stars appeared in multitude.

As it turned out, Walt's assessment of the French guests wasn't without grounds. I tried breaking the ice with them a couple of times the next day, but was solidly rebuffed with half nods, some inadvertent eye contact, and an unmistakable grunt of dissatisfaction. One of the fellows and his girlfriend (I guessed from their body language) smiled with potential friendliness, but the group was always together and seemingly sealed tight, which equated to unapproachable from my standpoint. I expected Charlie and the others to show up that day, but they didn't. I made the best of it by indulging myself with privacy, solitude, and acquiring my own stash and bong from Uab's cousin "Pat", the man who maintained the grounds.

The gang showed up on my third day. Charlie, Cheryl, and Marie led the way down the path from the main road, with Tony in tow not far behind. The women had waited an extra day for him in Bangkok, and I was glad to have everyone there at once. Since there were only two bungalows available when I arrived, we all had to cram into them. Tony and I shared one and the three women bunked in the other. I had met Marie about a year earlier in Tokyo. We'd bantered like old friends then. I suppose the both of us knowing the other through Charlie gave us the lead in to that. I knew of Cheryl, Charlie's confidante, co-conspirator, and helpmate in Seattle, but this was our first in-person meeting. She was still living in Seattle and this was just a couple of weeks of vacation time for her. It was her first time out of the U.S., and she carried that keen edge of new wonder that 'old' road hounds knew and wanted to get back. Am I in that category now? Her warm smile, sharp wit, and overall spirit were captivating.

After the newcomers settled in and stopped bitching about the abundance of inconveniences, we all met for beers in the restaurant. Charlie immediately wanted to know about my adventures in Malaysia, since I had just come from Penang and she was heading that way after our two weeks here. Between where I had been and where she was going, we spent the better part of that day and the next catching up. Besides, we hadn't seen each other for some time, since I left Tokyo six months ago, in fact. The others gracefully left us to our sibling bonding, but filtered in and out of the conversation occasionally. Marie was also keen to hear the Malaysia info, but got seriously distracted trying to move into her own bungalow. She charmed and pestered Uab and he gave in to her and handed her the next one that opened up the following morning.

Unbeknownst to me, three German men had been sharing a bungalow together since they arrived a week earlier. It must not have been working out, since one of them was expecting to take the next opening. I wondered why he hadn't taken the extra one I reserved, but thought it would be best not to bring it up. As soon as the three heard that recent-arrival Marie had gotten her own bungalow, the restaurant hut became a battleground.

The German chap who expected a bungalow all to himself was clearly pissed off, gesticulating wildly and spitting as he swore at Uab in heavily accented English. He pointed often and aggressively towards Marie, who was sitting with us and doing her best to ignore the tirade. Uab withstood the blasts as the picture of serenity, unperturbed and unyielding. The German, whose name we later learned was Kris and who didn't look a day over twenty, switched between English and German to suit his sentence, perhaps not knowing enough curses in the former. Marie finally could not contain herself any longer and got up to join in.

"Look, friend." She put her hand gently on his arm. He went quiet. "I don't know you, but there has clearly been a misunderstanding here. And I don't think you're going to solve it this way."

"How to solve it then!? Will you move out?" One hand was on his hip and he waved the other one over his head.

Marie put both of her hands on her hips and shook her head. "No. That's not an option. Sorry dude." She sounded sincere but looked to Uab and shrugged. Uab smiled.

Charlie snickered quietly next to me and whispered that the German stood no chance.

Kris let out a string of obvious curses in German. Marie took a half step back, kept her hands where they were, and looked to be sizing him up. "How about I buy you a drink? On me." She completely ignored the focus of the conflict. Kris looked warily at her. "Come on," she persisted. "Let's move on." He was defeated by her quiet persuasiveness after a few more seconds of eye contact and relented completely. The French group at their bong table acted as if no battle had been fought at all. True ennui.

As it turned out, Kris ended up spending quite a few nights in that bungalow after all. Even when another one opened up a week later and Uab offered it to him, Kris declined. Marie was a girl who got what she wanted.

One day, a new set of guests checked in with a rumor fresh from the ferry. It seemed that the Khmer Rouge was reorganizing over the border about ten kilometers away, and that led to some animated discussion. Almost everyone's idea of the Khmer Rouge insurgency came from The Killing Fields. We didn't know much else and envisioned the rebels as Nazi-like killers and criminals. In truth, I also thought of the rebels as just that, though

I knew there must be more to it. Most of the tourist crowd thought these insurgents needed money and would kidnap westerners for ransom. It sounded vaguely plausible to me, but what the hell did I know? I tried to press Uab about it, but he waived it off as not being worthy of discussing. "You just stay here. Have good time on Koh Chang. No worry about Khmer. They not here." The dichotomy of perceived versus real, east versus west and right or wrong led to a lively discussion that evening.

I pride myself on being calm, neutral, and balanced in my approach to the world, though I am not always successful. That next morning, however, I blamed the lack of a hot shower and too many mosquitoes for my cynical mood. After five days on the island, escaping to this paradise seemed more like being in a prison cell. I was restless. Tony could see it in me and, like a true friend, kept poking at it. I was irritated and grateful to him: No real friend lets his pal stay in a funk too long without calling bullshit.

"Another beautiful day in paradise and poor little Diaz can think of nothing to do." Tony said from his reclined, position baking in the sun.

"Fuck you." I threw some sand in his direction. We were sunning on the beach and reading, as we had done every afternoon for the last three days. "Let's go take a walk or something." He was on his feet before I was.

"The mountain?" He asked with a gleam in his eye. We had both noticed the hill behind the bay and knew each other well enough to assume we would make an adventure out of it. Uab answered our questions about the trail system going up it but he wasn't very helpful. It was as if he never climbed it himself – impossible, I thought. He acted like we were idiots for wanting to hike up "the big mountain."

"Nothing to see, nothing to see! Stay on beach. Drink beer. Much better."

"There must be a great view of the bay from up there." Tony was convinced. Uab didn't answer; he just shook his head and continued working.

We approached the others with the idea and like Uab they looked at us like we were crazy. Charlie and Cheryl were stretched out, oiled up and not ready to do anything more strenuous than lounge. Marie was walking in the surf looking for shells and thought about our invitation for a second, but decided it was too hot. We were on our own.

We loaded the water bottles, put on shoes for the first time in three days and started out. It should take two to three hours, round trip, or so we assumed from our wealth of experience as hikers. We took the marked trail about half a mile and then decided to head up, bushwhacking through the underbrush. The vegetation was pretty sparse at first, just ferns and small trees, which were easily beaten back with our hands. But soon the greens became thick and heavy, and the way was fully clogged in all directions forward. We backtracked when given no other choice and used bamboo poles to turn the larger branches aside. We even cut and swung on vines for short distances, letting out our deepest Tarzan calls. And we sweated profusely.

Halfway up the slope we heard puffs of snorting off in the bush, which stopped us dead in our tracks. One of us uttered the obligatory, "It's more scared of us than we are of it," and we whacked on. We reached the top an hour later – at least we deduced it was the top when the terrain flattened and began to slope down again. We were sorely disappointed to have to agree that Uab was right. The canopy was dense in most places, and we couldn't see through it, let alone as far as the bay. We roamed around, looking for any little clearing, but gave up the hunt for a view and settled for feeling good from the workout. After we'd caught our breath, Tony pulled out a joint and pointed it expectantly at me.

"What the hell." We lit up, inhaled twice each and were immediately baked. With this altered perspective adding renewed energy to the pilgrimage, we headed onward and discovered that we had been on a false summit, the real one still lying about a quarter mile further up. We decided to tackle it and spent another half an hour slogging through the brush until we reached another spot that looked remarkably like the first. This was the true summit, we deduced again by the same criteria as the first. We found more hanging vines to play Tarzan with, and this time we were old pros. Pushing one of his outward swings several pounds past its limit, Tony went sailing down the hill as the vine snapped off just over his head. I laughed at first, holding my belly and hooting like a hyena. But he was slow to get up and rose cradling his arm, which stopped me in mid-cackle. His grimace and whiney, "Aw, man, c'mon – I think I broke my fuckin wrist!" were my permission to laugh again, so I howled until he joined me, though without real enthusiasm. I sobered somewhat at that.

"Nice one, Limey. They all as coordinated as you back on The Isles?"

"Shit like this always seems to happen when there's a Yank around." He winced.

"That's right. Place the blame elsewhere. Very British, if I do say so." I threw in a pretty good snooty accent at the end, and was visibly proud of it.

"Stop your bloody jackin' off and give me a hand."

I bent down and clasped his good hand. He bounced up to level ground and I inspected the damage. It was pretty bad – red, swelling and bruised, but probably not broken because he could move it without an increase in pain. We decided he needed to tie it to his body for protection, so I pulled off my sweaty shirt and helped him tie it around his shoulder and arm as a sling.

"I need another friggin' smoke."

"I think that had something to do with why we're standing here like this in the first place."

"What the fuck do you know?"

"Not much, but I ain't the hurtin' one, brother."

"All right then. But lets get back to the trail."

I nodded. We gathered our things and started the bushwhack downward. My torso now shirtless, soon became as lacerated as my arms and legs. I suppose I was lucky to have very little in the way of broken skin though – the spiky, clinging vines and snapped-back branches resulted in mostly welts, bruises and light scrapes. Descending was fun. Tony was able to forget his wrist for a few moments as we leapt and slid down like children skidding down a snowy hillside. Before we expected to, we met the path not far from where we left it and promptly celebrated with a slug of water and Tony's delayed smoke.

Back at the main hut we came upon our three women friends and the two Canadians sitting around a table drinking shakes. Charlie saw Tony's wrist, now swelled up like a small melon, and she immediately began cooing over him. Cheryl joined in and Tony ate it up. Marie just rolled her eyes. I was tweaked.

"Jesus Christ, it's just a sprain. Don't go bonkers on the boy."

"Shut your trap, Diaz." Tony wanted to milk this, and who could blame him?

Cheryl looked up at me and saw the red welts on my chest.

"Look at you! My God!" She edged over to me and gingerly dabbed her fingers on one of the scores of abrasions on my arms and ribcage. "What were you guys thinking?"

On cue, I winced and moaned. I leaned up against her, for strength.

"For Christ's sake. I'm the injured one here!" said Tony, not to be upstaged. Charlie gently held his arm at the elbow.

"The stupid one maybe. Stop your whining," I replied.

"Pathetic. That's all I have to say. The lot of you." Marie gave us her Betty Davis eyes; hash cigarette perched between her fingers and smoke curling around her ears. She took a deep drag and forcefully exhaled it upwards and away from us.

"I'll see if Uab has some ice," Spencer volunteered.

"Was it worth it?" Walt asked sincerely.

"Standing here now, I'd have to say yes," I replied with a smile to Cheryl.

"No bloody view though, just trees and vines. Weak ones at that." He held out his arm.

"George of the Jungle here was in classic form. He has a nice swing, but needs to work on the dismount."

"Oh my God!" Charlie laughed. To Tony, "Is that what you were doing?" He shrugged his shoulders so she squeezed his bicep and tousled his hair like a little boy. I could see his mind trying to think of more truant acts to be scolded for harder, later. I asked Cheryl if she would help me rinse off at the falls. Tony gave me an unmistakable roll of his eyes as we walked off. As Cheryl and I finished up, I returned the glance as he walked into the shower area with Charlie.

Later that evening, we were gathered again in the main hut. We ate a late dinner and were imbibing in the après delights of drink and dope. Kris and Marie had been off for a sunset walk on the beach and had just returned. The Khmer Rouge topic surfaced again and Kris joined right in as a defender of the principle of going against The Man.

"They are acting as they need to. Their culture has been dominated by Europeans and Americans and they are fighting to get it back."

"But one doesn't rebel effectively against an outside force by killing your own people," Spencer said.

"Who are we to know? We live in a different world." His articulate approach was unexpected from one seemingly so young.

"I agree they are right to resist the west, but for different reasons." Tony's wrist was now wrapped with an ice pack.

"And those are?" I asked, on cue.

Tony explained. "Just look around us. Their lifestyle is far superior to anything we've attained in the west. They have a wonderful climate and environment, great food and the people seem genuinely contented. Look at us. We seek it as an alternative because our lives in the west are not satisfying."

"But look at the Thais, they are in a headlong rush to become like the west. They have caught the disease we have. Only they don't mind the dis-ease that comes with it." Walt chimed in.

"And so the Khmers are seeking to avoid western culture like the plague that it is. Yes their methods are radical, like Mao's cultural revolution, but maybe it's the only way," said Kris.

"Grass is always greener." They all looked at me as I spoke it simply. "We all want what the other has. That's been true since day one. The reality is that we all get what we want, regardless of the circumstances."

"What? What does that mean?" Charlie said it and Cheryl and Spencer agreed with nods.

"Just what I said – we all get exactly what we want in the end."

So you think a Cambodian family that has been 'cleansed' is getting what they want?" Cheryl challenged in a voice several notes higher than her normally soothing pitch.

"There is some luck, or lack of luck, involved, but essentially yes. Put it this way, most people have choices. Many of those choices are subtle and people don't recognize them as that, but they make them all the same. That Cambodian family makes a choice to stay in their village and be a part of what's going on around them."

"But that's crazy!" Charlie burst in. "You can't say that we control the unpredictable forces around us – the weather, epidemics, political motives. A boatload of soldiers could come to this beach tomorrow and we'd be up shit creek. That wouldn't be my choice."

"Chance does play a part…." I admitted.

"A big part!" she retorted.

"…but it is less a factor than you think." I finished. But I was not as confident.

"There's something to what he's saying though." Spencer came to my rescue. "We all do choose to be a certain way and we have to take responsibility for that. I know it's true that bigger events overtake people at times, but look at us again. As part of western culture, we've all been generally free of that sort of intrusion."

"So what's the point of all this?" asked Marie, stubbing out her cigarette. "So we all make our own lives. I don't disagree with that. And some people are fucked from the start. That's just bad luck. You gotta play the cards you're dealt."

"That still doesn't defeat my point that everyone ultimately gets what they want. In an existential way I mean." I felt a confidence boost.

"You're still on that?" Charlie looked at me with dismay.

"Your existence is a question unto itself," snorted Tony.

"I'm talking about choices here. Let's say you're that Cambodian family. You make the choice to get married, have children, become a farmer and whatever else." A press-conference flood of interruptions arose and I quelled them with two outstretched palms.

"Just hold on and let me finish. You can say those aren't choices because you are compelled to act a certain way by culture or family or hormones or anything you want. I have to say bullshit to that. Everyone is free to choose. If your personality is such that you go the route of tradition, then that means you ultimately want the things that come with it. You just have to look deeper at motivation is all."

"But like Marie said, the cards you're dealt can vary widely from person to person. Someone born in a slum in Calcutta has a greatly different set of opportunities available to them than a high class birth in Britain, say." Charlie retorted.

"That doesn't mean the Brit is going to be any happier than the Indian though." Walt said. "I think what Tony said earlier rings true. Just because you are born into circumstances that make a lot of material things available to you, it doesn't mean your life will be any better. In fact, it is very likely to be worse."

"My life feels worse now from the headache I have listening to you all prattle on." Marie stood up and said goodnight. Kris followed her and then Walt went soon after, leaving the die-hard debaters to rest and regroup.

☯☯☯☯☯   ☯☯☯☯☯   ☯☯☯☯☯   ☯☯☯☯☯   ☯☯☯☯☯

We were silent for a time after the others left, soaking up the night air and listening to the surf lapping the sand with a gentle hiss. A light breeze shushed through the palms and the sky was clear, the stars twinkling. Without talking about it, the group decided that a change of venue to the beach and the distraction of the stars would enhance the continued discussion. Spencer peeled off before the first throat was cleared, though. The four of us that were left took our beers to a deserted spot and sat. Only after the last speck of sand resettled along with us did Charlie begin.

"You're absolutely right about this lifestyle out here being better than what we've created back home." She was talking out at the night sky.

"It's awful difficult to compare them though," said Cheryl. "I like this well enough, but I also need to be able to watch a video or surf the web or take a drive."

"It gets complicated though." Tony looked deep in thought. "The different perspectives, I mean. I guess you can't compare the two in the end. To each her own. In that regard I guess we do all make our own bed. If this beach life is really what you or I wanted, we would do it."

I asked the obvious question then.

"So why are we going back?" They looked at me like I had just said, "why is the world square", but Charlie was the only one to laugh.

"Do you want us to just say you were right?" she asked.

"Well....yeah....but I also really want to know. I mean, this situation is Edenlike and we all admit it, but none of us would stay here forever. So we must need something else in the mix to satisfy us."

"Maybe we don't know what we want. I sometimes think that I do, but I don't want to look at it too hard because I don't want to know that I don't know. Shooting star!" Cheryl pointed to the sky and we all looked up but missed it.

All four pairs of eyes stayed glued to the sky after that.

"What do you think *you* want?" Tony asked Charlie with a boldness that surprised me.

She frowned in thought and then said, "Some security, someone to be with, kids maybe, some nice things around me also, like a house and a car...you know...The American Dream. The security thing is important, but I loathe myself for it."

I could have mouthed the words for my sister, until that last phrase. It was a surprising thing for me to hear coming from Charlie. Growing up, she was always the one more inclined towards the mainstream. She actually saved part of her allowance. I'll bet she didn't even go into debt to fund this trip.

"Why's that?" asked Tony, unable to conceal his sincere interest.

"Because it doesn't feel right to have security be a primary thing. I know we all need to – or *want* to – know where our next meal is coming from, but security blocks spontaneity. What if I said that twenty years from now you'll find yourself married, with two kids in high school, a mortgage that eats a third of your take-home, and an eight-to-six job that is marginally satisfying? Does that sound appealing? There's something satisfying about it, I guess, but it's an end in itself – one that you can't change once you've got yourself there. That's where I see a desire for security leading."

"That was a mouthful," I chided.

Tony replied, "I suppose that on the surface it sounds monotonous and even frightening, but you've gotta admit it also doesn't sound too bad in another way. We live for a very short time, so we try to enjoy it and that's all we can do. I could think of worse things than taking care of the garden and watching football on the weekends. Taking your four week holidays once a year and so on." Another shooting star punctuated the point, and we all just happed to be looking there at the same moment.

Charlie buried her hands in her face and shook it theatrically. "My God! I don't want to know what my life is going to be like in twenty years. I mean, yeah I want to win the lottery and not have to worry about having to work a tedious job and all that, but I want to know that *that* is not the only option!"

"So what would another option be?" I asked. "Jet-setting around to Paris and London, buying nice shit, having a lover in every port?" She interrupted me with a swift jab of her heel to my leg.

"You know that's not it. I don't know what I want but that's sort of the point. I don't want to know. I want my future to be spontaneous. Challenging. FUN! I want all those things, but you can't plan spontaneity," she chuckled at the joke, "and needing security leads to a limited life."

"It's a paradox," Tony said and started rubbing her shoulders and she smiled at the familiarity of it. "You know that Dire Straits song, 'Money for nothing and your chicks for free'?" He sang it in a passable Mark Knopfler voice and sounded not half bad. "Everyone wants the good life, but none of us are really sure what IT really is. Or even why we want it. If you're rich, so you watch TV on a bigger screen sitting in a bigger chair. What's the big deal?"

"What do you mean?" I shot at him. "Because it's *easy*, that's why. We all want to get laid and have 'the good life', and the easier the better."

"That's true, I guess," Cheryl said, "but easy is not always good. It's usually empty. Think about the most satisfying times you've experienced. I'll bet they came from doing something hard. Overcoming the *challenge* was the thing." She smiled and paused, scanning the group. "I still wouldn't mind winning the lottery though. So there's your paradox again."

"Yeah, we can all cop to that spiel about how "the journey is more important than the destination" and all that, but I'm not so sure. Sure, you want to have a good time along the way, but getting there – arriving at happiness or luxury or whatever is the real goal, the real important thing. The overnight bus from Bangkok to here was an interesting ride – even fun at times, but I would have skipped the journey if I could have gotten here by snapping my fingers." I snapped, genie-like. Nothing happened.

"Touché on the literal example, trite as it may have been. Buddha said there is no path to happiness. Happiness is the path."

Tony was giving me one of those "what the hell do you know?" looks.

"Maybe," I responded, "but think about it. Actually being here – *having* a thing – is better than not having it or wanting it and trying to figure out how to get it."

"Maybe the point is to *not have* it and not *want* to have it." Charlie said this slowly, as if the significance of it increased the gravity around her. Even Tony paused with the massage he'd started on Charlie, contemplating the comment. She took this as a signal and stood to switch places with him.

"I like the sound of that," said Cheryl. "I'm just not sure if it's possible to not want anything. Then you'd be Jesus or the Buddha or something."

"Or just enjoy what you have and not desire what you don't," said Tony.

"C'mon, you guys have been reading too much new age gobbeldygook." I said, refusing to let this get too philosophical – I was more interested in hearing about life in the real world. "Those are all nice sentiments, but this is the real world. Tell me which one of you doesn't crave something."

"Geez, Ren. What a wet blanket," Charlie chided me.

"Tell us what you crave," asked Cheryl.

I instinctively opened my mouth to spew forth wisdom but found that the well was dry. The straight question shut me right up. I craved a lot of things, of course, but didn't know how to put it all into words. I stammered a few syllables and then covered for myself with an exaggerated shoulder shrug and drag on my beer.

"Nice to know you're not so sure of yourself after all," Tony said, ignoring my middle-fingered response.

Charlie pretended to defend him. "Be nice."

"I guess I have really no fucking idea what I want. I mean other than a nice meal and some good company. I guess this is it then. I'm in nirvana now!" I opened my arms to the heavens and Tony toasted me with a bottle. Charlie was shaking her head in smirking dismay, trying to keep it light but I could tell she had more thoughts on the subject. Cheryl was smiling right at me, which I took as an invitation. I touched my knee to hers and let it linger.

The conversation petered out after that, but we sat there for a few minutes longer, glimpsing two more shooting stars and marveling at the clarity of the night sky. Charlie curled up in Tony's arms and Cheryl and I were snuggling like tentative high schoolers. A dog barked up the beach. As if on cue, we all got up, dusted off the sand and walked back towards the bungalows. For a moment, I thought there was some chance that perhaps the night's sleeping arrangements were due for a change, but Charlie's peck on Tony's cheek punctuated the end of romance for the evening. Cheryl and I just squeezed hands before parting and nodding good night. I could see Tony was whipped. We decided to walk back over to the main hut for another drink.

"You don't mind, uh...?" He asked cryptically, looking towards the bungalows.

I glanced in the direction of his and paused. "It's not my business and no, I don't mind. She could do better, obviously, but hey, there's no accounting for taste." I shrugged my shoulders. "How's the wrist?"

"Throbbing a bit, but not bad, all considered. Swelling's gone down some."

Uab and two other Thai men were sitting at a table drinking with Marie. They made room for us. They all seemed in jolly good spirits and Uab got two more bottles from behind the bar.

"I thought you were in for the night?" I asked Marie.

"Nope. Too wired. Had to get out and then saw these guys and here I am." She smiled and yawned.

"Where's Kris?"

"Wore the poor little bastard out." She said this as a matter of fact and without pride.

We laughed and Uab and his friends laughed too. They laughed because we did, I suspected, and not because they understood the joke, except for Uab, maybe. The two friends didn't speak English too well, but the party didn't seem to be hindered by it. They had obviously been drinking for some time, judging from their candy-apple cheeks and eyes to match. Uab explained that these were fisherman from the next bay down and had taken a late night paddle over to see him. He pointed to their boat pulled up along the pier. I nodded my understanding and thought that if they were half this drunk rowing over, it must've been an interesting ride. We sat silently, except for occasional throat-clearing and the clink of bottles against the table, stretching out like nocturnal sloths.

Simple conversation eventually returned, drifting between the English and Thai speakers, with Uab occasionally translating for either side. Marie's chair was next to one of the fisherman – Naaj, I think his name was. She had stretched her long legs out onto another chair in front of her, with one knee bent up. Her sarong slipped back to reveal the panties of her bathing suit. She was unselfconscious about this and, had it been any other time, I wouldn't even have noticed. Naaj sure noticed. I saw him notice. I knew what was coming, but I was too late to stop it. Unseen, or so he thought, Naaj reached out and slid his hand gently up under Marie's thigh. Uab, his other friend, and Tony missed the movement, blocked by the table between them. Marie grabbed Naaj's arm and flung it hard back at his face. The conversations abruptly stopped.

"What the fuck do you think you're doing?!" she yelled at Naaj, who recoiled but smiled widely, in apology and nervousness, I thought. Even I knew that Thais often smile when confronted with anger or an embarrassing situation. That smile was clearly different, to me, from a genuine smile of happiness or pleasure. That subtlety was lost on Marie. She shot upright and, seeing the smile, became enraged.

"You goddamn fucking pig!" she screamed and unleashed a volley of slaps at Naaj. One connected solidly on his cheek, getting through his arms raised in defense, and sent him off his chair to the ground. Marie pursued him and kicked viciously at his back and legs. Naaj was clearly unsure of what to do in response to the onslaught of this unpredictable foreign woman. I thought he must have been trying to figure out how to save face.

The rest of us froze in shock. Somehow we were all standing and gawking at this unbelievable scene. Since Marie showed no signs of stopping her attack, I lurched into the breach between them – not without trepidation, mind you – and received a few of Marie's powerful blows for my effort. Once I was able to grab one of her wrists, she regained her senses and backed off, shaking badly as she stepped back. Uab helped Naaj get up and then he bowed to Marie, eyes lowered and hands together in Buddhist supplication, and said he was sorry. Marie pursed her lips and looked away in disgust. Naaj regained his smile, sort of, as the second fisherman bowed to us and pushed him away towards the boat. I hoped to God that Marie hadn't seen the smile. She didn't, making only a half-hearted effort to break through my block and get back at him. She finally waved it off, cursing his retreating form. Uab persisted in his apology and I put my hands together in reply. This seemed to make him feel better. Tony and I flanked Marie and herded her out towards the beach. She stayed a few paces ahead of us and when we'd gone a hundred yards, she turned around and sneered, "You don't have to fuckin' baby-sit me!"

Tony held his arms out and joked. "This isn't babysitting, sister. I'm just tagging along to see you take on the next bloke." Marie stood staring at us, chest heaving up and down, arms and fists at her sides defiantly.

"I'm with him," I said, pointing his way.

"Fuck you both."

"That's what poor Naaj wanted. If I'd have known it was this easy, I'd have told him." Tony put on a huge smile. Marie took a few steps towards us and I put up my hands, palms out, in a classic self defense posture. She saw this and stopped.

"Don't worry, pretty boy. I'm not going to kick your ass tonight."

Tony laughed.

She looked at him. "Don't push it." We both looked down, concealing our smiles. The three of us headed down the beach.

"Do you have any idea what a pain in the ass your gender is?" she started in.

"I apologize for all men. Everywhere on the planet," I said. Marie gave me a murderous glance.

"At least we're straightforward," said Tony, taking some of her heat off. "You lead us around by our dicks and the rest is easy."

That got a loud "Hah!" from Marie. "That's why you all suck. You can't think any other way than through your fucking penises."

"Now women, there's a straightforward topic for you. They always say what's on their mind. They're very predictable. Maybe I should just get a sex change, you know, cop to the superiority of women. If ya can't beat 'em," Tony winked the pun over to me, "join 'em!"

"You couldn't handle it as a woman, you jerk."

"I think I'd do quite well really." He started strutting like he was striding down a fashion show runway.

"See what I mean?" Marie said to me.

"I think he looks fetching."

"Then you can have him. I think he'd have problems with being lesbian in any case."

We walked on silently until Marie blurted out, "I could've killed that pervert!"

"You practically did," replied Tony. "Not that he didn't deserve it."

We turned around after a bit and headed back. Maybe we said all there was to say, or maybe she had forgotten about the brawl already, but we said nothing more about it. Back at the bungalows, we walked Marie to her door.

"You guys really didn't need to escort me."

"I know," in unison.

"Nothing better to do," Tony added. She smiled and rose on tiptoe to kiss each of us on the cheek.

❀❀❀❀❀ ❀❀❀❀❀ ❀❀❀❀❀ ❀❀❀❀❀ ❀❀❀❀❀

I spent another week on Koh Chang. Cheryl left two days before anyone else. She and I flirted for a week – to the point of madness for me. On her last night, we spent a good hour kissing and groping on the beach, but she was reluctant to do more and I, a gentleman despite my reputation to the contrary, respectfully and somewhat painfully abided by her wishes. I've never been good at forcing the issue. I know that no is no, but "I don't know" is sometimes yes. I liked Cheryl and, especially with her so close with Charlie, I didn't want to screw it up. Not having a private shower or the privacy to relieve myself made the discomfort all the more awkward. I told myself I was training for a prizefight – "no dames to weaken the legs." I even ran a few lengths of the beach one day to relieve some of the physical tension, which raised the eyebrows of Charlie and Marie. I could overhear just enough of their wisecracks to know that they had sussed out the situation with some accuracy.

Tony, Marie and I spent our final two days on the island in a stoned out stupor. Charlie spent most of her time studying up on Malaysia unless Tony was inviting her attention. They seemed to be approaching couplehood. Tony finally spent a night in her bungalow after Cheryl left. I didn't ask any questions, but found myself lying awake that night, wondering.

Charlie and I had shared a room until we were twelve. That makes for an enduring closeness, and we're to this day each other's confidants. Occasionally I tried to make the mental connection that is supposed to have come with sharing a womb. But we have never had a telepathic connection that I'm aware of. When we were around eleven, we tried, sincerely, to read the other's mind from across the yard. We thought we had something when we both were thinking about dinner, but later realized it was coincidental. We've never been able to make it work. I do believe it exists, but that it is not an exclusively twin-specific phenomenon.

I may not be able to read her mind, but at times I know what Charlie is feeling. It *could* be just a subconscious reading of body language or voice intonation. Mom used to say we would get headaches at the same time when we were teenagers. I don't remember that. When I broke my arm in seventh grade, Charlie had sympathy pains in hers. Mom thought it was silly but I believe it was real. I could see Charlie liked Tony, but still had something else on her mind that was keeping her from going with it fully.

Marie stopped seeing Kris – or, more accurately, allowing him to share her bed – the day after the Naaj incident. Kris and his buddies left shortly thereafter. Spencer and Walt were ever-present fixtures at the restaurant and the beach and probably still there. On our last morning, the four of us caught the same ferry across to the mainland. We split on the pier. I took off north towards Nakhon, to meet up with Professor Wa. Tony rode the bus with Marie and Charlie west to Bangkok and caught his flight back to Japan the same evening. I visited Tex at his bar on the pier for a drink before catching my bus. He remembered me from two weeks earlier, but not the conversation. We small-talked some more, me not wanting to allow the topic of women to come up. He gave me some pointers about traveling in the area and we bullshitted about the people we'd met and the places we'd been. He hadn't gotten out much in the last few years, preferring his little bar to anywhere else. He hadn't been stateside in over a decade. I told him I'd just come two weeks ago from Malaysia, and India before that.

"Malaysia, eh?" he crooned. "What's that like these days?"

8

CHARLIE

SEATTLE	TOKYO	THAILAND	LONDON	THE PHILIPPINES	INDIA

YEAR 1	YEAR 2	YEAR 3

LIFE IN NIHON

Dear Renny,

It is SO true what they say about Tokyo. You would not believe how crowded it is here! My first day in the central station was overwhelming. I've never seen a more bustling place in my life. The people here are amazingly polite and friendly, though. I have to tell you about this strange thing I saw yesterday.

I had taken the subway back to Shinsaibashi (where Andrea lives) and was standing on a street corner, trying to get my bearings. (It is such a zoo here I get lost all the time.) When the light changed, people – well, actually, it was more like a mob – started crossing the street. But just then one of the cars waiting at the light edged forward a few feet and hit this woman! Her shopping bags went up in the air, her legs flew out from under her, and her butt hit the pavement hard. But then an even more amazing thing happened. Nobody helped her. No one even stopped! They just parted around her like a school of fish. I just stood there with my mouth open. I didn't know what to do! Well, gradually the lady got up on her own. She smoothed out her dress, collected her bags, and seemed calm. She didn't seem hurt, either. The driver of the car looked to be a middle-aged woman, though I couldn't see her very well. All during this, she was sitting up tall, gripping the steering wheel with both hands and staring straight ahead and not moving – as if nothing had happened! As if she hadn't done anything! The woman out in the crosswalk then turned to the driver, bowed once to her, and then hobbled off. All this time the people on the sidewalk kept walking around the scene, making as if they are not even aware anything was going on! Talk about surreal! When I got home, I asked Andrea about it and she said something I never would have thought of. She said it was probably about saving face. The old woman bowed to the driver as an apology for having put her (the driver) in such an embarrassing position. Is that twisted karma or what?! I get to see this stuff everyday here. It's like a different planet – you'd like it here, bro!

I've been in town for five days now and already I have a line on a little apartment not far from Andrea's. She's also set me up with some evening work at her hostess club, so I'll start that next week. I need to get some cash lined up, but I also want to delay the work-a-day world as long as possible. I still have a lot of Tokyo to get acquainted with. Seriously – every time I go out it's a new adventure. It really fried me at first – having to steel my nerves to go to the corner store to get some milk! – but now it's truly an adventure every day.

The only scary thing is the prices. It's true what they say about that, too. Yep, Tokyo is crowded and pricey! You think San Francisco is expensive?! Count your blessings, pal. Hey, did you get my last letter from Thailand? I wrote it from Koh Tao. I'm a certified diver now! And I got some "private lessons" from a certain instructor... I loved it all! I don't know when I'll get the chance again, but it's high on my list. Gotta go – I'll finish this later......

Back again – four days later. A lot is going on Ren. I was able to get that apartment. It's a tiny little place, about eight by fifteen feet square, including the kitchenette, plus a small bathroom. OK, so I have only one small window that looks out onto an alley, and the rent is around $800 a month (if the yen rate holds steady), but I am ecstatic to have it! Lots of places don't even rent to gaijin (that's foreigners in Japanese). The floors in my place are this spongy reed mat stuff called tatami. It's so cool – like having straw under your feet. And of course you can't wear shoes on it. The best thing about the place is that I didn't have to pay a deposit, which is good because that would have cleaned me out. Andrea knows the guy who owns this place and he was easygoing about it. I guess he goes to the club where I'll be working. That makes me a bit wary of the deal they must've struck, but I'll cross that bridge when I get to it. You can't look a gift horse in the mouth. I've been able to scrounge a futon and some dishes from a new friend, but mostly the place is empty, which is how I want to keep it. That's the Japanese way, you know.

So you have a place to crash in Tokyo now. What're you waiting for?! You've got to be ready to quit by now. The last letter I got from you was at the Poste Restante when I was in Bangkok. Sorry I didn't get to write you back from there – I'll have to fill you in more about Thailand the next time we're drinking in the same bar in the same country. Calling The States from Japan is really expensive, so I don't think I'll be able to do much of it in the near future. I probably won't be getting a phone for a little while yet. Surprise, surprise – it costs a ton of money to BUY a phone line, which gives you the privilege of paying for monthly service, so I'll just have to do without for a couple of months. Hey, major bummer about Greg. How was the funeral? It sure makes you think about how quickly it all goes by.

Write me back soon, Ren. I could use the mail. Hurry up and quit will you?!

Love, Charlie

Shinsaibashi is one of the entertainment hubs of central Tokyo. During the day it appears like any other dense city area, but at night it blossoms into a sparkling disco ball of nightclubs and bars and noodle shops. Pachinko parlors jingle in the night air, competing with music blaring from electronics vendors and restaurants. Bar WhyNot is tucked into one of the side alleys off of the main drag running through Shinsaibashi. The building is a six-story edifice of cement and tinted windows looking out across the twenty-foot wide alley at another building that could be its sister. The bar, Charlie's new place of employment, is on the third floor and accessed primarily by an elevator the size of a public bathroom stall. Of course there are stairs not ten steps away, but they are seldom used for the up journey. That there exists an establishment up above is not apparent from the street level, save for the small backlit sign by the elevator.

Bar WhyNot caters to senior level Japanese salarymen. Senior salarymen are good customers – loyal, predictable and of the old school. These men spend four out of five weeknights away from home, using their abodes almost as a locker room. They look with disdain on the younger employees who now desire to return to their homes almost every night to be with family and create a life apart from work. And they are the most able to afford the price and style of beauty that WhyNot offers. An evening of having your drink poured, cigarette lit, jokes laughed at, ear whispered into, and, on a lucky night, thigh brushed up against, runs a couple hundred dollars per person, not including the tip.

The décor is plush red carpeting, with black velvet stripes on the walls and black leather chairs huddled around low glass tables. A large one-way mirror window – you can see out but no one can see in – looks out over the alley below. A sleek, well-polished ebony bar runs the length of the far wall. Jazzy music wafts through hidden speakers.

Andrea and two other western women sit at one of the low tables at the far end of the room, waiting for the first guests of the evening to arrive. When Charlie walks in, Mr. Soto gives her an approving look, which makes her feel queasy and unsure of herself. She is dressed in a black, sleeveless cotton dress that stops just above the knee and is tight in most of the right places, flattering her figure. She borrowed the dress from Andrea, since her box of work clothes has not yet arrived. Andrea chose the dress and the look for Charlie with a knowing eye. Charlie had worn a similar borrowed dress of lavender a few days earlier upon meeting Mr. Soto. He spoke with her then for maybe five minutes in clipped English, and then indicated to Andrea, who sat quietly nearby, that Charlie would be suitable. He left it to Andrea to explain the details and that was that.

"Don't worry." Andrea can see the discomfort in Charlie's face. "Remember, don't let them touch you or do anything you don't want to do. Just be pleasant and speak slowly so they can practice their English on you. Follow my lead."

Charlie lets out a long breath and wonders just what in the hell she's gotten herself into. She is happy to be starting work, sure, and also dreading it. The money will relieve some pseudo-poverty blues, true enough. It is time to start generating some funds. The bar pays about a hundred dollars a night and Andrea swears that Charlie can easily double that or more with tips. The other girls, Tanya the blond South African and Julie the Aussie with the dark curls, are friendly to Charlie and seem unconcerned about the competition. They are both dressed like Charlie, though their hemlines are a couple inches higher than hers. Tanya smokes a little brown cigarette – a *beedie*, she calls it – like the ones they smoke in India. It has a strong clove smell, and Charlie is glad for its incense smell above the tobacco. They all sip coffee.

All the girls start at seven o'clock and are expected to work until one or later if the customers demand. She doesn't have much training to call upon, but her job, as best she can make out, is to keep the clientele happy by topping off their drinks at every opportunity, laughing at their jokes and talking with them about whatever they want to discuss. Andrea warned her that tipsy patrons will occasionally "let their hands get the better of them" but the management does not tolerate this. If she complains, the boss will ask the man to leave. Any after-hours arrangements between clients and hostesses are, however, private matters. These occasions are infrequent, Andrea assured Charlie, because Bar WhyNot is mainly an after-work hang-out for overworked executives who need a place to talk turkey and unwind before going home, even though the wife and kids are usually in bed by the time he arrives home. As a true dreamer, Charlie romanticizes her role to be a gaijin geisha. She is here to use her western, womanly ways to entertain the gentry and ease their otherwise painful and weary lives.

Her first clients that evening are Mr. Shinmura and his three coworkers. Mr. S is clearly the head honcho, as evidenced by how respectful, deferent and polite the other men are to him. He is in his late forties and wears a nondescript gray suit of expensive make, which matches his hair color. When Andrea introduces him, he warmly grips Charlie's hand with both of his. She expects to be subsequently introduced to the other three, but Mr. S seems to forget them as he guides her over to one of the tables. The others follow discreetly.

He asks a lot of questions and drinks a lot of whiskey. He is interesting to talk with and his English is pretty good. Charlie begins to believe that she might like this job. Normally, hostesses don't "work" any single particular client per se, unless the customer is a regular and requests his favorite. Hostess protocol requires that each woman move about the bar, entertaining the singles, pairs and groups that need attention. On this night, Charlie ends up spending the entire evening with Mr. S's group, snacking on *edamame* (roasted soy beans) and other delicacies that the customers order. Charlie wonders if she is eating too much, but the gentlemen encourage her and are happy to explain the Japanese food and customs, so she doesn't worry about it. Before they leave, just after ten o'clock, Mr. S. slips a small envelope containing a five thousand yen note into her hand. She smiles and gives him a sincere "thank you" before she wanders off to greet a pair of new customers.

At the end of their shift – tonight it is two in the morning – Charlie and Andrea walk slowly back home through the still-bustling streets. A few drunken salarymen weave past them, but overall, the crowd has switched over to the night people, dressed in wilder fashions, though still predominantly in black. The rave scene has a strong following in Shinsaibashi. Mini skirts and leather stream in and out of clubs and the music blares with a techno beat. Despite being exhausted, they are both still wired from the night and decide to stop off for a nightcap at a place Andrea knows well. Charlie does not miss the irony of the situation: working at a bar all evening and then going out to one afterwards to forget about work.

They choose a quiet little table near the door and order beer.

"It'll take some getting used to, the hours that is. That and the temptation to eat all the time or get drunk with the customers." Andrea gives her that knowing look.

Charlie laughs. "I think I overdid it tonight already. With the food anyway."

"Mr. Soto doesn't mind, trust me. It makes the customers buy more food. Those little dishes of mushrooms, for example, cost twenty dollars apiece. Did you do well with tips tonight?"

"I made an extra five thousand yen on top of the four thousand we got from Soto-san at the end." There is a group tip jar that gets divvied up among the staff after the customers leave.

"Good. That's about right. Sometimes you can make a killing. I got fifty thousand once. The chap had just gotten a fat bonus and was happy to share."

Charlie does the math in her head: four hundred and fifty dollars at the current exchange rate. She lets out a low whistle. "Wow."

"You can get screwed too, though. We feel it when the country is in a recession. You get used to the nice tips but when times are hard it sucks because you start to see the customer as a dollar sign only and not a person. They see that real fast, and that just makes the night interminable and the tip jar dusty."

"I still feel a little…strange about this job." Charlie's contorted face hints at pain, or at least confusion.

"You mean you feel like a prostitute?" Andrea has come to grips with this long ago.

Charlie nods, and waits for the rationalization.

"Think of it this way. And I do know what you mean, by the way." Andrea squeezes her arm. "When you teach English in Japan, you make about the same per hour as we do, and both jobs are pretty much the same thing. English teachers here like to think of themselves as professionals, but shit, most of them have degrees in English – how hard must that have been for a native speaker?! – and they teach *conversation*. Not grammar or literature or Shakespeare. What *we* do is teach conversation in real time, real situations – real conversation! We have to look nicer, we pour their drinks and light their cigarettes instead of correcting their grammar and making them talk about the weather and holidays. English teachers can be quite slutty, too, let me tell you. Schools usually encourage teachers to socialize with their students to get them to take more classes. If that's not prostitution…" Her voice trails off and she pauses before concluding, "When I first arrived here, I intended to go the English teacher route. I even got a job at a small school with my own classes – kids, college students, and adults. But after a few months I saw that the owners were only interested in the money, not the progress of the students or the professionalism of the staff, so I quit. In this country, you feel like a whore one way or the other."

Charlie laughs again. "I guess that makes me feel better."

"There are some English school horror stories out there, and you'll hear them all. You just have to keep your eyes open. Don't have any illusions about it. It ain't glamorous, it ain't the theater, and it can get boring fast. You have an interview tomorrow for a school job don't you?"

"Yeah, at Kando Academy. They teach grade school kids, I think. Sounds like it would be fun. It was a funny thing. I met this guy in line at the post office a few days ago. He's Canadian, named Arthur, who works at this school. We struck up a conversation as we were waiting and the next thing I know, he asks me to drop off my resume so he can pass it along to the school director. It turns out they have an opening they want to fill right away! So I met the director when I went in, we had a short conversation, and he asked me to come back tomorrow for an interview."

"What time?"

"Ten."

"We'd better get you home then." They finish off their beers.

Andrea has become Charlie's older sister and it suits them both just fine. They walk home arm-in-arm, hardly noticing the dwindling nightlife and the lightening sky.

❧❧❧❧❧ ❧❧❧❧❧ ❧❧❧❧❧ ❧❧❧❧❧ ❧❧❧❧❧

The interview at Kando goes very well – so much so that they offer her a job right then. That takes Charlie by surprise so she says she will have to think it over. When they add that the school will sponsor her for a one-year working visa, she finishes thinking about it and says OK. *This all just seems too easy. Where are the reference checks, the other candidates, or the application form??* She agrees to a twenty hour a week contract at 250,000 yen per month (the minimum requirement for a working visa), which she calculates to be about $2400. She will work from eleven to three, Monday through Friday, teaching English to four and five year olds. She will have three classes a day, each fifty minutes long. There is a set curriculum to work from – mostly songs and memorization games – and she can shadow Pauline, an Irishwoman who has worked at the school for two years, for the first few days. Charlie's first day will be in ten days, a necessity for the school's paperwork needs and a luxury for Charlie, who really does not want to work at all.

Charlie rearranges her hostessing hours at Bar WhyNot to allow her to continue working there two or three nights a week. Mr. Soto is not happy with it, preferring to have complete control over her time, but he also knows she will be good for business and so is inclined to compromise. Charlie thinks about quitting the hostessing racket altogether, but feels she owes it to Andrea to stay with it, and besides the money is good. Looking back on her time thus far in Tokyo, she is amazed how things happened so quickly. It has been so much better than she hoped. She already has a place of her own and two jobs in hand. *Has it really only been two weeks?*

In the next week, Charlie dives headfirst into Tokyo life with a zeal that she has not felt since first moving to Seattle. She begins studying the language, which is no small task considering there are three writing systems. She spends afternoons visiting the famous sites around the city: the Imperial Palace, Asakusa, and the fish market. She borrows teaching materials from Pauline to prepare for her classes and spends evenings going over lesson plans and teaching herself the material. In ten days, she is able to teach herself hiragana and katakana, the syllabic systems for reading and writing Japanese, as well as a few kanji, the Chinese ideograms that present a monumental hurdle to those learning to read and write Japanese. Andrea waves off Charlie's anxiety about mastering the kanji, focusing her on the three dozen symbols that are essential for day-to-day life, but encouraging her to ignore the other 6000 of them for now. If she at least knows the symbols for "men" and "women", she can choose the right public restroom. This will be a great improvement over her former technique: keeping her legs crossed until someone else goes in or out of one.

Shadowing Pauline for three days proves invaluable. While confident in her ability to do many things, Charlie felt some trepidation about teaching; fears that are both allayed and confirmed in her training days with Pauline.

Pauline is easygoing and flippant, with long dirty blonde hair that hangs alongside her face in a way that makes her look like an elf. Her humor is self-deprecating and her laugh an impish cackle that can cease as abruptly as it started. She is tall and thin and has an ability to engage the children that is truly a gift. She easily modifies her class activities to include Charlie and this care and feeding soon gives Charlie the confidence and skills to take on her own classes. She is sure she will even enjoy it. The two teachers fall into the habit of going out for coffee after work at a small café near the school.

"I've tried to get me Mum to visit, but she can't get herself to leave Dublin. Just as well I suppose. This might all be too much of a shock for her."

"Have your parents ever been outside of Europe?"

"My Dad's got a girlfriend in Florida somewhere. Some old cow he visits once a year or so. I'm surprised he keeps coming back to the Irish rain. Must be the Guinness."

"He still lives with your Mom?"

"Sort of. We're a pretty mixed up bunch you see. She's a serious catholic and won't stand a divorce and he's sworn off on the church and they keep separate bedrooms." She sighs an exaggerated melancholy, but the sparkle in her eyes gives her away. "All of us wantin' the pot at the end of the rainbow and all that. I don't think the rainbow ends in Ireland, though."

"But you plan on going back someday?"

"Who knows? I like it here well enough, but I don't think I'll stay forever. The economy at home is doing well now, but there are too many Irish there for my taste, damn fine people that they are, mind you." She raises her coffee cup in toast.

Charlie laughs. "I'm like that about the Midwest. I love seeing family and going back to reminisce, but then I am reminded that you can't escape your roots. I leave vowing to try."

"To try to what?"

"To not be the conservative, good Christian, family-raising, football-watching type of people I grew up around. It feels too limiting, especially now that I've seen a bit of the world. Do you know what I mean?"

"I don't know what anybody means these days, sister. But I catch your drift. We're all wanting something greener over there, or at least *not where we've been*."

Charlie nods. "Japan's fine for now. Tokyo is fascinating for me and the work is interesting – enough to distract me for a time."

"Don't let it distract you too much, now. Our student kiddies need your full attention." She sips her black coffee and they both stare out into the street. "But here's an unavoidable distraction: tonight is *gomi* night!" Pauline answers Charlie's knitted brow with a lecturette.

"The Japanese practice "out with the old, in with the new" in a very literal sense. You know they love the newest gadgets, right? And did you know that they are not at all into second-hand goods, so recycling shops usually aren't an option. And you know their houses do not allow for the kind of pack-rat mentality that plagues our cultures back home. Well, yours anyway." She winks and continues, "There's no place to store it until little Toshi goes away to college even if he would consider watching a ten-year-old TV. So the only sane thing for them to do is chuck out their old stuff when they buy something new." Charlie nods that this makes sense. Pauline continues.

"Now, the beauty is, the Japanese don't have the means to truck their fridges, futons, TVs, and so on, to the dump – even if there were a junkyard to take it to. I think they just dump it in the bay, if you ask me. Their solution is to place it neatly on the curb – making sure it's clean and well marked as *dai gomi* (that's "big garbage" in Japanese) and wait for the trashman to come by in the morning. So, late at night, it's a treasure hunt for us – every scavenger for herself!"

By this time, Charlie's eyes are wide open, with visions of a new futon or maybe a bicycle dancing in her head. They talk a while longer about Pauline's gomi scores from the last few years, and then part, vowing to meet at ten 'o'clock that night.

At the appointed hour, Pauline joins Andrea and Charlie for a *"gomi hunting"* extravaganza. Charlie is surprised to see legions of foreigners on bikes – and some in vans! – as well as a few Japanese in cars scouring the streets for goodies. The three of them stick together, picking through the many piles of treasures in front of several houses on each block. Andrea scores a blender, two lamps, a small end table and some blankets, and then bets Charlie a sushi dinner that all of them will be in perfect working order. Charlie – feeling cheekier than she thought possible – borrowed a wheelbarrow from her building maintenance man and they pile the stash into it as they move along. They are sorely tempted by a pullout loveseat, but have to pass on it because of its size. The scene of three gaijin women hoisting a loveseat on top of a full and wobbly wheelbarrow would have caused more than a few snickers from the Japanese watching discreetly from their windows. They move on, Andrea guiding them expertly through the neighborhood to as-yet undiscovered piles with pristine pickings.

As they pass a small park, their plucky mood is sobered by the sounds coming from a couple quarreling by the swing set. The woman, about 30 years old and dressed for a night on the town, covers her face with one hand, but it is clear that she is crying. The man has a grip on her other arm and is saying something in sharp, staccato Japanese. The pair struggle against each other, almost comically, with the man tugging at the woman's arm as she tries to retreat further into the park. Charlie becomes concerned and starts walking towards the feuding pair, not knowing why or what she can do, but compelled just the same.

They both look up at the same time and see her approaching. The man looks down and the woman waves her hand frantically at Charlie, saying something that Charlie doesn't understand, but takes as a call for help. It is only once she stands in front of the woman that Charlie realizes the wave was meant to signal her to go away – a wave like one she would have used to shoo away a fly in front of her face. Andrea and Pauline haven't moved and Charlie backs up towards them slowly, confused. Once she reaches her friends, they each take one handle of the wheelbarrow and begin rolling it down the street.

"Do you think she'll be okay?" she asks.

"Probably not," answers Pauline, "but she doesn't want us involved. It would just complicate it for her."

"Pauline's right. I know it seems weird, but that woman might suffer more emotionally from our intervention than from that man hitting her a few times. It would be shameful to her to bring the attention of an outsider into her personal life."

Charlie is dumbfounded, looking back towards the park. "But what if he hurts her? Its not right!"

They can still see the couple's drama unfolding under the cherry trees, the man puffed up more now, self-righteous and in charge. The woman seems even more distressed, a pleading in her voice and her body language, but she is no longer retreating.

"Don't fight it, love." Pauline puts a hand on Charlie's shoulder.

"I've seen this type of thing before," Andrea says, taking the wheelbarrow herself now. "We foreigners just have to suck it up and hold our peace sometimes. Can't go around assuming that we know what's best for everyone else. In Japan, they've got a different way of doing things, and it seems to work for them."

They walk in silence back to Charlie's apartment, stopping to browse the gomi piles that are not entirely picked clean of treasures. Andrea claims some dishes and cooking pots along the way, and Pauline is thrilled to discover an old calligraphy set in a drawer of a dilapidated desk. Once they cart the goods into Charlie's apartment, she makes her friends some tea and they sit to examine the night's haul, admiring each other's cache.

Charlie tries to dissect the incident. "I don't know why I needed to insert myself into that situation back at the park. Back home I don't think it would have occurred to me. I might have called the police or something, but I wouldn't have approached them like I did. Especially since I didn't know them at all." Andrea nods and tries to be reassuring.

"Your mind works differently here, I think. It's the same in Sydney. A man like that – angry and acting like a jackass – might hit you for butting in if he could get away with it. But here, you don't feel so threatened by the men, even though men are really the same here as anywhere else. Here even the police wouldn't get involved so easily."

Pauline adds, "The Japanese are closed to us in that way, I think. Their culture is not all on the surface, and it's so hard for westerners to grasp the subtleties. The men here are hard to figure – they put up with a lot of shit, but we don't usually feel sorry for them because they seem to give a lot of shit, too. Yes, they drink a lot and pee on the street, and are closed books when it comes to discussing anything emotional. But they're still living with the remains of the bushido system." Pauline pauses to catch her breath.

"What's that?" Charlie asks.

"In the olden days, a man became a samurai – a retainer – for his master, usually a warlord. The samurai did whatever they were told to do, never questioned an order, and were fiercely loyal. But they had no choices. Then the system changed and the warlords were gone. Samurai without masters were called "ronin" and they wandered the country almost like beggars – lost without a master to serve. Well, today the company is the master and the salaryman is the samurai. Pretty much the same set of expectations, and it leaves them – the men – just as few choices as the samurai had, unless they want to become ronin, which none of them do."

"But that woman. Do you think she was denying him sex but he wasn't taking no for an answer? Why didn't she just walk away? We gave her the chance!"

"There's no telling what they were arguing about," says Andrea. " It could've been sex or something else entirely. But one thing's for sure, neither one of them wanted us to be there."

"Sometimes I feel like….like….an alien here!" Charlie sighs between sips of tea.

Andrea chuckles. "And you always will, even if you live here for ten years. The Japanese are fond of saying that foreigners cannot possibly understand them truly. I think they're right."

Pauline laughs and nods her head as she adds, "Well, *I* feel foreign everywhere I go. It's damned frustrating, I tell you. In Dublin, the men and women seem like aliens to me. I remember walking around with this feeling that everyone in my school was onto something and I couldn't figure out what it was. Same here and everywhere I go. It sucks but what are you going to do?"

Charlie empathizes with Pauline. It is the same for her and she, too, has begun to accept it.

And so goes Charlie's introduction to life in Japan. Within another month, she settles into the routine of her teaching job, enjoying the interaction with the children and the challenge of keeping their minds occupied. Her evenings at the bar prove to be interesting and lucrative, but a routine nonetheless. She knows she is learning more about Japanese culture than her students or clients are learning about hers. The work is not hard – more like living, speaking and being friendly in her own natural way; getting paid is a bonus that in many ways she isn't sure she earns. Sure, there is the occasional lecherous creep to deal with – she firmly guides his wandering hands away and smiles. Being firm usually works and is honestly no different than how she would deal with men back home, though the age group at the bar is older than she would have encountered at home.

She writes to Renny regularly, confirming her safety and health and teasing him about his own. Over and over again she invites him to take the leap and join her in Japan. After four months, he finally decides to make the jump.

Her daily routine now also includes writing to Renny over an afternoon coffee, prepping him about all the rich culture he's soon to be experiencing. She chooses a comfortable, quiet, spacious café located near her school. It is primarily a meeting place for housewives and students during the day. There are rarely other foreigners in the place, which adds to its charm and Charlie's comfort. She can escape into herself on these afternoons – recording her journal in letters to her brother – or trying to study the culture by clandestinely watching other customers to see how much she can understand from their body language alone. She also loves the wall of second story windows overlooking the street below, which affords a cityscape of high rises that reminds her it is a big city out there. Charlie adopts a particular table by the window and often sits there for two hours, spacing out on the scene outside. On the street level is an open-air market, packed with vegetable and fruit vendors in tiny stalls. Their welcoming calls – "Irrashai, irrashai, irrashai!" – are muted through the window but she can still make out the competing chorus of hawkers, luring customers to their stalls like chirping cicadas in mating season. She loves this spot for the activity and the color, and for the stark contrast of the neat and colorful food stalls in the shadow of massive skyscrapers.

The street is not crowded at this time of the afternoon, by normal standards, but this being Tokyo, a steady parade of shoppers passes by continuously below. On this afternoon, by chance Charlie spots a young western woman in a long dark coat down in the market. Her dark hair is tied back in a tight bun and she drags slowly on her cigarette as she peruses the fruit vendor's goods. To Charlie she seems nervous, looking around with quick, furtive glances left, then right, then left again. With a quick but smooth motion she grabs two apples in one hand and shoves them both in her jacket pocket. No one but Charlie sees the theft, and before she can process the scene, the woman crosses the street out of view.

Well, that's something you don't expect to see everyday, she thinks to herself. Less than a minute later, the woman-thief enters the café and takes a seat with her back to Charlie, two tables away. She orders a regular coffee by pointing to the photo on the menu. Charlie tries not to look at her, but can't help sneaking several glances. *The woman is shaking, so she might be feeling guilty or scared,* Charlie wonders. Her coffee comes and she hunches over it, seeming to savor the warmth. Her coat is still buttoned up to the collar; she sips noisily from the cup and sets it down. She is sniffling, Charlie can see, and then with alarm, Charlie knows that she is crying, silently, with her head down. Her shoulders shiver ever so slightly, like she has a chill, but then the bout subsides. She takes a deep breath and sips her coffee again, with less noise this time.

The urge is too strong. Charlie is curious, of course, but also feels compassion for the woman and just needs to do something. *Here we go again. You'd think I would have learned my lesson about interfering with total strangers from that gomi hunting night in the park, but what the hell. Here goes nothing.* She gets up loudly from her seat so as not to startle the woman and approaches her table.

"Excuse me. I'm sorry. I couldn't help noticing you seem....distressed. Is everything ok?" The woman gives her a look of surprise, but says nothing. "My name is Charlie. I work nearby. I stop here almost every day after work." She extends her hand, but the woman hesitates to take it.

"I'm Marta," she says abruptly. They shake hands warily.

"Would you like to join me by the window?" Charlie offers. Marta hesitates again, then nods and rises, picking up her bag and coffee.

"Where are you from?" Charlie asks nonchalantly.

"Southern California. But I was born in Poland and my parents immigrated when I was six." Charlie thinks she detects a hint of an accent. "And you?"

"My family lives in Ohio, but I'm most recently from Seattle." She says this in that peculiar American way of casually transferring one's place of origin without hesitation.

Marta glances out the window and then takes a deep, audible breath. She still hasn't removed her jacket. She looks over at Charlie with an intense gaze.

"Did you see me out there?" she asks, indicating towards the street with a movement of her head, her voice trembling slightly.

Charlie looks away down the street and then back to her. "I was just staring out the window and... I saw you, yes."

Marta looks down. Her face is crimson now and another tear wells up in her eye. She wipes it away with a defiant gesture. When she looks up again, it is with pursed lips and a cold expression on her face. "I don't have to explain myself to you." She directs her attention out the window as she says this, only barely avoiding eye contact.

Charlie looks down and sips her coffee so she has something to do with her hands. An odd memory strikes her just then – something a high school English teacher made them memorize about Americans not having any natural state of repose. She knew at that moment exactly what he meant as she fidgets self-consciously, unable to remain motionless in her discomfort. "No, of course you don't," she replies.

They are silent for a couple of minutes. Marta cradles her coffee cup and seems lost in some thought, perhaps unsure of what to make of Charlie's kindness. Charlie watches Marta's faint reflection in the window closely, intrigued with her story but put off by her strangeness. She wonders, *Has she fallen on hard times? Maybe she's just a clepto?* As if she heard Charlie's thoughts, Marta abruptly sets down her cup. "I should go." She starts to rise.

"Please don't." Charlie rises quickly with her and holds out her hand, palm down as if to touch her, which she doesn't. They freeze in place, Marta clinging to her bag protectively and Charlie with her extended hand. For an instant, they eye each other, then Marta eases back down to her seat and Charlie does the same.

"I am not what you think I am."

"I wasn't thinking one way or the other."

"And what ways are those?"

Charlie shrugs with both shoulders and gives Marta a look that says "I'm not your enemy."

Marta exhales and releases the top two buttons on her coat.

"For some reason, things haven't worked out like I thought they would." Her voice softens quite a bit and Charlie feels her own tears welling up, and then is annoyed with herself for being so emotional.

"I came to Japan two and a half months ago, thinking I would find a teaching job and maybe study some *shodo* and it's all been a...a bad dream. I think it just wasn't meant to be." She looks up and smiles. "I'm going to go back to LA. I decided that this morning."

"What went wrong, do you think?"

"I really don't know. I just don't have what they want." She blurts this out, as if she has held it in for a long time. "I'm not *genki* enough or pretty enough, or I'm too tall. I was at an interview this morning – my tenth one, at least! The man basically told me "no" as soon as I sat down. I asked him why and he politely lied that they had already decided on someone else. I've heard that one before." Her hands are balled up in tight fists now and her voice is rising. "So, I really don't know." She gulps back a sob and looks away, saying, "I'm sorry. I'm sorry." Charlie hands her a napkin. Marta dabs it at the corners of her eyes to regain her composure and forces out a smile. "So what about you. What's your story?"

Charlie feels embarrassed and momentarily at a loss for words. "I've been in Tokyo for about three months. I just started a job teaching children." Marta nods. "I also do a bit of hostessing on the side. I was thinking, maybe I could introduce you....?"

Marta smiles again and shakes her head. "I've already tried that route. Look at me. I'm not the sort that inspires Japanese men to talk." She says this with a self-deprecating humor, shadowed by the painful realization that it was, indeed, true. Charlie smiles back with a conspiratorial nod that says it may be true, but it isn't just or fair. The black hole looms before her again and she pushes it away with an inkling of comprehension that the dark side has many forms. She realizes anew that the world isn't what she'd idealized.

"Can I buy you lunch?" Charlie offers.

"You don't have to do that."

"I know. I want the company." Charlie lies – she knows Marta is hungry.

Marta slowly nods in assent. They order.

They don't speak anymore about Japan or work, choosing instead the lighter realms of movies and the news. Marta puts a mask on over her pain and Charlie speaks to the mask, knowing that she is wearing one of her own. As they finish the meal, Marta looks at her watch like she's forgotten something. She rises quickly.

"I'm sorry, but I have to run. I have an appointment in half an hour." She gathers up her things in a hurry. "Thank you so much for the meal." Charlie rises with her. They squeeze hands and pause a moment. Marta leans over and places a light kiss on Charlie's cheek. "Good luck to you," Marta says and turns to go. But Charlie holds onto her hand and Marta turns back again. They gaze at each other a moment longer and smile. Marta breaks away and hurries out the door. Charlie looks down and notices the two apples perched on the chair.

9

RENNY

SAN FRANCISCO	KYOTO	THAILAND	KATMANDU	LAKE TOBA	INDIA	IPOH

YEAR 1	YEAR 2	YEAR 3

AFTERIMAGES

His arm was raised in the air in a perpetual "Pick me! Pick me – I have the answer!" But his face was calm. His face appeared contented and focused and he had, supposedly, been waiting for the teacher to call on him for the better part of two decades. Such was the posture and fate of the Indian Sadhu. Kellen and I just descended the western half of the Annapurna circuit, taking a break from the trail in central Nepal after trekking two and a half weeks. We were in the town of Tatopani, a small enclave of restaurants and hostels with a wonderful hot spring along the river running through by the village.

We were delaying the last few days of our trek. We had met and bonded seventeen days ago on the bus ride to Besi Sahar, the first stop on the eastern side of the circuit. We'd both climbed up to the top of the bus to enjoy the air and the view as much as to avoid the bus interior crammed with people, luggage and assorted dried goods protectively clasped and defended by locals having just made the supply run from Pokhara. We got to know each other while being jostled against the other rooftop cargo as the lumbering diesel giant swayed like a chrome elephant over the pitted dirt road. Kellen was a half-Vietnamese, half-Black former bank clerk from Michigan. His parentage resulted in the same nonspecific ethnic look as mine, and this let each of us recognize the other right off. We both knew the 'I-don't-know-what-you-are-so-I'm-not-going-to-deal-with-you' response to our faces and instantly appreciated a kindred spirit. Even in Nepal, land of dark faces and mixed ethnicities, discriminating stares were common.

People everywhere try to peg what they observe and if they cannot, become wary or indifferent. The all-white, or all-black or all-Asian was the expected. Deviations like us were acceptable, but treated with an almost imperceptible air of disdain. Almost, I say, because having dough is the universal ticket.

It turned out that Kellen and I also made good trekking partners, both preferring to hike in silence and at a similar pace. The past two and a half weeks was a pleasant medley of tantalizing glimpses of distant peaks and deep gorges, endless quantities of dhal baht (the omnipresent lentil stew of the Himalayas), and beautiful smiling Nepali and Tibetan faces. Walking the circuit was comfortably challenging and exhilarating.

Now entitled to the reward of comfort and delicacies, we decided to stop in Tatopani for a few days. It was a no-brainer to choose the first hotel that advertised homemade apple pie near the hot springs, which is where we found the eagerly posed Sadhu. I had read about the life of a Sadhu and the many varied forms of meditation and devotion for which they are justly famous. But this fellow was my first encounter up close. I would have liked to hang out with this one, but the man didn't respond to our attempts at conversation. We were speaking to a stone wall – not even a hint of recognition – and that is as it should be, in retrospect. So we settled for relishing the healing embrace of hot, holy mineral water that melted tension, aches, and two weeks of mountain dirt out of our pores.

"Do you think his arm is just locked in place like that after all these years?" Kellen whispered.

"My guess is he couldn't let it down even if he wanted to."

"I wonder if he eats any of the pie from the hotel?"

"Not from the looks of him." The man was gaunt, with ribs visibly outlining his sides. But he also had a healthy looking long gray beard and clean, papery, sun-darkened skin.

"He hasn't picked a bad place to hang out."

"I wonder if he's really been doing it that long?" Kellen had gotten some information on the Sadhu from the desk clerk at our guesthouse. This man had been in Tatopani for fifteen years, sitting daily in the same corner of this hot spring pool regardless of the weather or crowds. He meditated with eyes open, though not seeming to observe. He was clad in a dirty white loincloth and a brown yak wool shawl.

"I want to ask him if it's worked," I muttered.

"If what's worked?"

"If he's had some light go on inside. If it has been worth stepping off whatever wheel he was on to stick his arm straight up in the air and keep it there? It must've hurt like hell at first."

"I don't think he wants to tell us."

"Just as well. I'm not sure if he would understand the question, or if I would understand his answer. Everyone's gotta do what they gotta do."

"I think I could go that route" Kellen said, "only I'd try it with a couch and maybe a TV and a fridge nearby."

"With what sticking up in the air?"

"Just my toes on the ottoman and after that, whatever came."

"You're a twisted human being with no reverence," I said to his mischievous smile.

He shrugged. "I reckon that is so." He submerged his head into the steaming water and blew bubbles to the surface.

We soaked in the pool for an hour more, watching the Sadhu and the other tourists who kept their distance from this odd-looking man. We were careful to respect his space and his meditation as we shared his pool, keeping quiet and spacing out contentedly. We savored the last of our trek through the wild and contemplated the reentry into the hordes.

Three days later we were back in Pokhara, a small city with the same amenities as Tatopani times a hundred. I stayed at the Butterfly Lodge, along the lakeside with a clear view of Machhapuchhre and her sister peaks. We arrived on the last day of Kellen's visa, so he took off immediately for the airport to hop the next flight to Katmandu and make his connection to New York. I stayed in Pokhara for another three days, rowing on Lake Phewa, meandering around the neighborhoods, snacking on ganja cookies and feasting on buffalo steaks. In those few days I recalibrated my funds, time, and interests and decided not to return to Katmandu, but catch the next bus for Varanassi. Charlie had primed me for The City of the Dead in her letters and I was eager to delve into the secrets of India. I was ready for something truly different and while Nepal was wonderful, there were just too many westerners around to be uncomfortable, and that is what I wanted to be – *un*comfortable. You can't really figure anything out if you are too much at ease, or such is my reasoning. All the old patterns remain in place unless they get jolted about. I am not sure what it is I wanted to purge or shake up, but India seemed a good place to find the right stimulus.

The bus ride cost $15 and took 16 hours to cover 300 miles. I snagged what I thought would be a comfy seat with a good view right behind the driver. It turns out that those two aspects of local bus riding in rural Nepal are incompatible. The more you see, the less comfortable you will be. It was a mixed blessing that the trip began at dusk and continued through the night. Along the mountainous roads leading down and around, the bus would labor and squeak and careen from one side to the other. We were in the biggest vehicle on the road, so lesser souls scattered before us like chickens.

I slept on and off. Many travelers chose to take sleeping aids, since valium was available over-the-counter in Nepal, but I don't like to be any more dopey when traveling into unknown places than I am normally. We passed through the border before dawn and all the foreigners jumped through the hoops of the professional Indian soldiers and clerks without incident. As the morning sun lightened the sky, I could see we were speeding through an expanse of flat plain, scattered with traditional orange and white mud houses among the fields of rice and wheat. The bus jerked to a stop for a short break at a small roadside stand that looked like an abandoned corrugated shed with a broken gas pump in front. I got off along with everyone else for a drink, a pee and a stretch.

To my eye, it seemed that someone had uprooted part of the Ohio River Valley and set it down halfway across the world. With only the very distant backdrop of the Himalayas and the occasional sari-clad farmer's wife to dispel the image, American wheat fronds rustled far into the distance, interspersed with unknown elms or oaks finding root here and there. Crows soared and squawked overhead and a faded painted coca cola sign hung above the front window of the dilapidated roadside stand. It was real and surreal at the same time, due as much to the exotic unknown of the moment as to my residual fogginess from intermittent sleep on the bus. I ordered a glass of spicy sweet chai. When we reboarded, a dark Indian woman and her young teen of a daughter had materialized to occupy the seats across the aisle from me. They were stunningly dressed in colorful sari, the mother in bright metallic lime green and the daughter in yellow with a fringe of purple and gold. The mother had pulled her long, thick black hair back into a tightly braided, shiny bun, had elaborate jewelry on her fingers and a bright red *tikka* in the middle of her forehead. The daughter's hair, thick and black like her mother's, was braided down her back and she wore clattering bangles and many rings distributed over her fingers, toes, ears, and nose. The girl took the aisle seat and sported the excited eyes of someone going to the big city for the first time.

I had moved to the middle of the bus and I was the only one in my row of seats – a luxury I did not question but might attribute to my foreign smell or size – and with the high chair backs I had a false, but nonetheless comforting, feeling of privacy from the rest of the bus patrons. Privacy in a public place is so rare in this crowded part of the world. I relished it. Within five miles the mother fell asleep, but the daughter remained wide-awake, curiosity driving her glances around the bus and the countryside slipping by the window. She soon caught my eye, which had been watching her for several minutes. I was sitting with my back propped against the window, legs folded up on the seat. She gave me a sweet, innocent smile and then looked down in shyness or embarrassment as I returned it. A strawberry hue

179

blushed beneath her milk chocolate skin, and I think we were both glad her mother was asleep and unaware. She was beautiful beyond anything I could describe – fresh and smooth with innocence. I was momentarily in love. She must have known enough about flirtation to give me only passing glances, flashing her deep brown eyes at me only briefly as she pretended to look out the window behind me. Her eyes were large and animated, the shape of almonds, and I couldn't resist looking into them.

The bus stopped again after an hour for a fifteen-minute break. Like the last stop, a few shabby huts offered food and drink to those with rupees or dollars to spend. Most of the passengers stayed aboard, preferring to sleep, but I took the opportunity to stretch my legs. Mother and daughter came behind me with a few others. I bought a couple of doughy meat snacks from one of the cleaner-looking stands, and proceeded to eat them at a small bench.

Or, that is, I started to eat them. A pair of very small and dirty kids, a boy and a girl, immediately sat beside me and gave me one of those wide-eyed imploring looks that belong in a National Geographic spread on starvation. Neither had had a wash in months, it seemed, and both were barefoot and in rags. They did, however, have that cute childish demeanor that all children do when they're around three or four years old. Soon enough, the little girl held her hands out, one on top of the other, asking for food. She stuck out her lower lip and somehow made her eyes look even sadder. Her brother did the same. I looked up and around and realized that I was the only foreigner who had gotten out of the bus. The mother and her beautiful daughter were sitting about ten yards away, eating their own snacks. The kids were silent but persistent – pros. I tried waving them away with an unconvincing grunt, but they only sidled closer to me.

You're just boned when something like this happens. I gave them the food with a resigned air and watched them devour the treats in seconds. The boy gave me a stuffed-cheek smile, crumbs dotting his lips and grease dribbling down his chin. That smile alone was worth submitting to the con, but I sighed like it wasn't.

180

One has to keep up appearances. I looked over at the daughter and found her looking at me with admiration. She held my gaze for a few moments before lowering her face in a smile. That made it even more worth it. The kids were my buddies for the next ten minutes, and I bought them both some candy before hopping back on the bus, keeping a piece for myself too.

Back in my seat once again, I soon became very sleepy and started to nod off. The girl was giving me more overt and playful looks now, her mother asleep again. I smiled back and kept her in my line of sight, fighting off the nods, but the drone of the tires on the pavement proved to be too much. A flurry of images passed through my consciousness and I let them come. Images from Herman Hesse's opus, Magister Ludi, one of my favorite books, caught my mind's eye. The girl across the aisle had triggered the imagery, no doubt. I lingered on the story of the dreamlife of the young prince-monk, casting the girl in the yellow and royal purple sari in the lead role and making the story my own.

We were living in a rural Indian village long, long ago. This beautiful girl-child was the prized jewel of the town and I was her proud, newly betrothed. We farmed a small plot and were on our way to prosperity. Soon a child came along and then another and before long I felt only the heavy burden of supporting a family. The business of farming went well and I worked diligently, but the family's needs and desires were endless. My wife needed new and nicer saris and the kids needed clothing, books, and toys. There were appearances to keep up, status and comfort required, and I became resentful. She and I quarreled over petty things – the quality of the dishware, my lack of ambition. My resentment grew steadily. She compared our lives with those led by others, with ours always lacking. The world slowly became a spinning ball of despair. One day, I discovered she was having an affair with a man who I had thought to be my friend. He offered her more luxury and riches than I could manage. In a rage, I went to his house and beat him to near-death, then fled the region in shame, becoming a hermit in the far mountains. I became a brooding and mean-spirited hermit, not one at peace with himself and the world. This transformation bothered my real self, and I felt this clearly even through the sub-conscious veil of the dream. I woke up, feeling vaguely disturbed.

The girl and I exchanged more glances during the rest of the trip, but the mystery was dissolved. She, or what I idealized as her character, had changed completely in my mind and I was subsequently wary of ever engaging her – in glance, conversation, or more. Her mother eventually noticed us eyeing each other and gave me a disgusted, dirty look. My silent voice responded, *Look Ma'am, I want no part of it, though your daughter is gorgeous.* Maybe she heard the voice, for she turned away and gave me no further attention.

The bus arrived in the outskirts Varanassi and the mother and daughter got off at the first stop. The daughter gave me what I prefer to think of as a long, longing look as she waited next to the bus for her bags to be tossed down from the roof. I returned the look and the longing, feeling my heart swell a bit and feeling foolish for it. We all long for the world of our dreams, but mine felt too close to a reality I could actually create, and that was too strange to contemplate. Not that I wanted to create a life with this girl, mind you, just that I had the world open before me with infinite possibilities and I needed my feet on the ground to know where to step. As I got off at the main station in Varanassi, I felt changed somehow, like I was outside myself and more aware and not aware at the same time

I remembered a tip that Kellen had given me about traveling in India, and reached into my knapsack to pull out the formerly white, now beige towel. I wrapped the towel around my head in a makeshift turban. At first I felt a bit silly, as if I was trying to be something I was not, but once I noticed its effect, I relaxed and appreciated it. My dark skin and longish hair set me apart from the expected tourist profile. I had often been mistaken for a wide range of ethnicities on the road – Indian, Filipino, Thai, Japanese – and I was quite happy to reside in that mystery category of unknown origin. Despite my 6'1" height, I had already been taken for a Bengali on a number of occasions, and intended to stay as anonymous as possible in India. If the hawkers and dealers and stealers were unsure of your nationality, they were less likely to approach you. Towel-headed and striding confidently, I ventured into India.

Starting with Varanassi, The City of the Dead, I tried to melt into the crowds. I do believe that none of the vendors I bought from, restaurant staff where I ate, or hotel clerks who gave me room keys would remember my face or my presence. I, myself have no distinct recollections of the three weeks I spent wandering the ghats in Varanassi, the narrow dirt streets of small villages, or even the manicured paths of the Taj Mahal in Agra. The stories that Charlie and Marie had told me of their trip to India a year and a half earlier became my memories as well. I stayed in the same places they did, and felt the same distracted fascination with the burning ghats, but most of all felt apart from my body, like I was floating above the world, watching me and those around me going through the motions of life. It's not that I was bored or disinterested, just detached. Perhaps it was just my natural reaction to the crush of the crowds, the foreign smells and sounds, and the completely alien way of life lived in India. I watched and observed and, in turn, blended in and became one of the cast and caste in this giant theatrical drama where I was the playwright, performer and audience.

Certainly after the tourist frenzy of Agra, I needed environs less hectic. Given the uncountable numbers of people I had seen, smelled, touched, or heard in the previous three weeks, I doubted that a quiet, rural, unpopulated town even existed in India. But the town of Pushkar held potential. True, during one week in early autumn when Pushkar is host to the annual Camel Fair, tens of thousands of visitors go there to celebrate. But rumors and guidebooks had it that the town was otherwise serene and unremarkable, and now being two months past the Camel Fair, it could be the place I was seeking.

Pushkar is a town dedicated to Brahma, the chief deity of the Hindu pantheon. The town is centered on a small lake, the primary place to worship, or perform *puja*, to Brahma. The whole area is situated on the edge of the vast Thar Desert, neatly tucked in against a hillock. Pushkar itself is a cluttering of short, white, stucco buildings nestled up to each other along dirt roads and pathways that run this way and that towards lake and hill or sometimes just peter out into the sand.

I saw only two other foreigners upon my arrival – and they were leaving town on the bus I rode in on. I took this to be a sign of good fortune and right choice on my part. I located a small hotel recommended by my guidebook as "quaint" and found it to be practically empty.

The Blue Hotel was white and spartan. The hotel – and I use the term loosely for it was just a house with a few extra rooms for let, despite the "Hotel" hand-written on the side – was cheap and quiet and located just a block from the lake on the west side. The owner was a guy of forty or so named Prip. He showed me a small private room with a straw mat on a platform (this was the bed) and a small window affording a second-story view overlooking the street below. At three dollars a day, it was a deal and I was glad to have it.

The next morning I observed first-hand the chief trade of the local hawkers: to take tourists down to the lake, sell them the necessary accoutrement to perform *puja*, and then show them how to worship Brahma properly. This consisted mostly of rubbing colored chalk over your face and bowing towards the lake, where Brahma supposedly resides, in part anyway, for he is everywhere, so I'm told. Walking down the street, fending off these well-meaning (if self-appointed) emissaries of the Hindu faith became my daily routine, pleasing to Brahma or not. I prefer to worship my own gods in my own way.

Perched on the highest hill outside of the town was a quaint little monastery, apparently uninhabited and idle at the top of a long series of stone steps. I watched this beacon of faith shine in the sun at midday and reflect the moonlight at midnight for several days before I made a vow to make my pilgrimage to it. The next day, my fourth in Pushkar, I awoke at five and set off. The town was still sleeping – quiet except for the snores of the soon-to-be-arising-for-work and the occasional sound of litter turning over in a street breeze. The air was cool enough for the hour's hike up the hill, and I figured to be back in time for breakfast. I pointed my feet towards the bottom of the hill, meandering through the maze of narrow streets and held my direction by keeping the monastery in sight. Soon the house yards grew bigger and the streets slightly wider, but rather than breathe deeply of the calm morning, I began to feel something was amiss.

I instinctively turned around and noticed that a couple of dogs had begun to follow me. They were roughly thirty yards away and paused when I stopped to look at them. I gave them my most menacing look and a few rapid waves of my hand, and then continued the hike. Within a few minutes, the two mutts had multiplied into four and my thoughts strayed from Brahma homage to self-defense. The lead dog, a dun-colored beast of about sixty pounds and intense black eyes, seemed in too-good-health compared to the other mutts I had seen around town. His companions also seemed well fed and sturdy. I tried to ignore them as best I could and picked up the pace. I could hear them shuffling in the gravel path behind me, and that sound was getting louder. I turned to face them again and to my surprise, their numbers had grown silently to eight, and they were getting ready to rumble. Needing a few more seconds to think, I turned to walk further on, steeling my nerve and doing my best to mask any fear they might smell. After another brisk hundred yards, I stopped in my tracks and faced them. Meaning to meet the challenge head on, I barked and snarled back at them with the meanest pit bull voice I could muster. That checked them for a moment.

I knew they wouldn't be completely discouraged so easily, but my confidence was bolstered by the success of my own intimidating growl, and I meant to complete my hike. Continuing towards the bottom of the hill, I kept one ear cocked behind and scanned the surroundings for weaponry. I found a pair of baseball-sized rocks on the side of the path and picked one up in each hand, comforted by their size and weight. I didn't want to use them, really, I thought, but on the other hand, I wondered how much aggression I had built up in myself these last few weeks.

The sky was lightening to blue-gray with the imminent sunrise, revealing a desert brush landscape dotted with small, corrugated shacks and tumbled down fences. There were no lights in any of the windows, so the thought that the neglectful owners of these hungry dogs would soon call them home for breakfast was laughable. When I felt the dogs approaching to within ten yards, I turned for the face off. The lead dog was now fully aggressive, barking in full-throated power, teeth bared and hackles raised. One cohort flanked each side, falling into full backup mode. I barked out again, feeling foolish but wanting to give non-violence one last try. The dogs were less impressed this time, the lead dog taking a few steps closer and almost daring me to attack first. Out of fear or anger or pride, I obliged. With my best Nolan Ryan wind up, I cranked my arm around and zinged the first rock at the leader. "Ball one" hit the dirt, skipped off the ground and smacked Dog Number Two hard in the jaw. The entire pack retreated en masse for ten yards or so, the struck dog yelping and hopping in a frantic circle of pain. I walked onward, giving them a chance to disperse, but not counting on it.

The animals began to approach again, and I pumped another fastball at them and they scattered like spilled crackerjacks. They never gave up tracking me completely, but I sensed that the trouble with them was over. I turned to glance behind me every so often, keeping up my stride. And that spooked them briefly each time. I picked up one more rock just in case and stuck it in my pocket, chuckling to myself at the incident, though my heart was pounding from the adrenaline and my brow was moist with the sweat of competition. If that had been the end of my man vs. nature adventures that morning, I probably would have forgotten the whole episode, or it would have been relegated to the far recesses as, "a funny thing happened to me in India one morning..." As it turned out, the morning's lesson was far from over as I started to climb the stairway to the shrine.

The sky was becoming lighter with each step and I hustled to reach the top before the sun breached the horizon. At about the halfway point, I heard skittering and chattering in the branches and bushes alongside the steps. For a split second, I wondered if dogs in India could climb trees, but in a flash of limb and tail I knew that a new morning visitor was interested in me. Monkeys! They were the golden color of the dawn desert, but with pink butts and hoary faces. There seemed to be about a dozen of them, each about the same size as the mongrels I had left at the bottom of the hill. Here the desert shrubs had given way to sparsely leafed trees and short, scrubby brush.

I also noticed a nice selection of throwing rocks along the side of the steps, should the need arise again. The stairway itself was five feet wide, crumbling concrete, with a single metal handrail along each side. I had a healthy respect for monkeys – for their strength, ferocity, and tenacity – based on many travelers' stories and more than enough TV specials.

Near the top of the stairs, I looked ahead and saw a monkey mother and her baby, sitting on the right side railing. Behind them were about a dozen more, crouched on a rock outcropping, peering from behind the bushes and hanging from the trees. The mother let out a piercing screech for every step I took towards her; they got louder and more panicked the closer I got, even though I moved over to the far side of the stairs and slowed to a crawl. The creatures in the bushes thrashed about on both sides of the steps as I approached. Compared to the close-encounter with the dogs, this felt like an out-take from the Planet of the Apes. I stopped in my tracks, but couldn't tell if that was what they wanted or if it made matters worse. The mother was soon joined by what I feared was her mate and his middleweight older brother. They perched on the railing and on the ground on either side of the mother and child and did not look friendly.

They looked like baboons, but I couldn't be sure. *Mutant chimps, made desperate by the poverty and cruelty of India* was what my fully-engaged imagination told me. What I couldn't image was how to get out of this mess. The two protectors screeched and bobbed, baring their teeth and pounding their fists on the railing and in the dirt. My heart fluttered and my inner voice told me to get-the-hell-outta-there. I considered turning around, but knew I couldn't do that without showing fear, which I assumed was a no-no in these situations. I walked slowly onward. The male on the ground hissed and made a motion toward me, but stopped when he saw I didn't react. As I passed in front of the aggressive trio, I shot them a full-face, menacing glance of my own, which sent them all flying off the rail and into the bushes in unison, mother clasping baby as she leapt. The bushes on either side came alive with an angry storm of shaking and ranting as I quickly trotted past, and I hoped it was all-bark-and-no-bite for them today. That remained to be seen.

Behind me the big male – Daddio, as I later dubbed him – was following me up the stairs, about twenty paces back. Like the dogs at the bottom of the hill, these guys were not easily put off. Several others joined in behind him silently. *Oh, Jeeze*, I thought. *There are no other people around for miles and not enough baseballs to pummel them all, even if I was Nolan Ryan.* The white stones of the shrine were just up ahead. As I reached the top, the monkeys remained on the stairs, keeping their distance, and me in their sights. So I also kept and eye on them as I inspected the shrine and sought a safe vantage point to watch the sunrise. I spied the perfect place – a rock outcropping beyond the shrine and just a bit down the opposite side of the hill. I made straight for it, arriving with just a couple of minutes to spare before the sun crested the horizon in a blaze of red over the gray, shadowy desert.

After a quarter of an hour or so, I turned to find Daddio staring at me and blocking my return path through the shrine to the stairs. As I approached, strengthened by the light of day, we made eye contact and he let out a shriek to wake the dead, followed by a growl that threatened to finish the job. From my pocket I pulled the back-up rock from my encounter with the dogs and I wound up as if to throw it. I was surprised to see that the movement alone was enough to send the monkey scurrying off into the bushes. But in that moment I heard what the monkeys must have heard as I was winding up my fake pitch. The soft padding of worn sandals on concrete forewarned the appearance of an elderly monk coming up the stairway. He was partially wrapped in a simple white sheet around his waist and one shoulder – the caretaker, I guessed, from his sense of familiarity with the place and what I sensed was the monkey's familiarity with him. I crossed the shrine grounds and we smiled as we passed, he holding his hands together at this chest in the traditional greeting. I returned it in kind. There was no sign of the monkeys as I descended the stairs, nor of the dogs as I made my way back to town. It was full light by the time I reached the city streets, with people stirring about and roosters' cockadoodling.

The morning incidents weighed heavily on my mind the rest of the day, and for a long while after. I called upon my insufficient knowledge of psychology, philosophy, and meditating to discern the meaning of it all. The aggressive posturing of the animals was some kind of warning, I was sure. About what, exactly, I was less sure. I never felt in danger from them, though I can't say how much of that certainty I really felt while I was standing on those steps. But I think they were telling me to "be careful of traipsing into unknown territory too lightly", or perhaps to "keep your guard up and your eyes open, for you know not what lies ahead of you." While I appreciate the advice, the fact remains that *I don't want to know* what lies ahead of me. What would be the point of that? Predictability seems a desirable quality, but is it really? That doesn't mean that there's no such thing as monkey wisdom, however.

That evening, as I had done every other evening, I went to the lakeside to watch the sun set across the water. When I returned to the hotel, Prip waved an invitation to join him on the makeshift couch in the shabby hotel lounge. He was smoking from his chillum and posed a question between pensive puffs.

"What do you go to see every evening?" he asked.

"I like to watch the bats skim over the water at dusk." He looked at me thoughtfully. Every evening at sunset, large brown bats came out and flew about the lake, hunting down insects I presumed. They would occasionally flick the surface of the calm water and create a buzzing sound and concurrent ripple. I found the effect peaceful and mysterious.

"They are holy things. Messengers from Brahman."

I nodded. "They do have a deep effect on me. I can't really describe it."

He repacked the chillum and offered me some. I asked him to go first so I could watch how it was properly done. He had me light the match as he cupped his hands and sucked in heartily, creating a dense cloud around his face and exhaling directly into my face. I blinked hard and tried not to react. He could see it surprised me and explained.

"This is the holy way to smoke from chillum."

I followed his example, and chuckled as I blew the smoke into his face, but since he remained solemn and even reverential, I repeated the rite with appropriate ceremony the second time. We passed the pipe back and forth, dropping into a deep, almost spiritual silence. The quiet was broken by Prip's curiosity.

"So you are a Christian?"

"I was raised Catholic, but I don't really practice anything anymore."

"Do you not believe in greater powers?" He swept his hands and eyes around the room.

I thought about this carefully and replied, "I guess I don't *dis*believe in. ...something greater – like nature – but I don't put a face to it anymore. What about you?"

"We are in the city of Brahman. Of course I believe!" He proceeded to list through the powers and personalities of Brahma and Vishnu and Shiva and how they were all interconnected. It was interesting from an academic viewpoint, but I was not awed or redeemed by it, and this was clear to him, and unsettling.

"Don't you want to know who made the sky and the rain and the land?"

"I don't care who made it," I replied. "I only know that it is here and I enjoy and respect it and I don't worry about the rest." He was flummoxed by my answer and let out a series of exhalations and snorts.

"What do you mean you don't care? How can that be so?"

"I mean, I don't think we – *I* – *can know* what it is, other than from a scientific point of view, so I don't speculate about it otherwise." He snorted again.

"This is the problem with you…you Americans! How can you not wonder about these things? You said yourself that the bats on the lake had – what did you say – an *effect* on you. How can you not see God in this?!" He said this with passion, but without offense to me.

"For me it is enough to see and feel the beauty of it. And I do have a sense of wonder about these things. I think places can be spiritual and wonderful without having to add anything about a god to it."

"So you think this about Pushkar? That there is no god here?"

"I don't think one way or the other. I respect how the people here think and what they believe, but it isn't part of *me*. I haven't done *puja*, like other tourists do. I don't think they're sincere and it would be a kind of lie if I did it."

"Ahhh." He nodded his head and a faraway look came into his eye. "You should do the *puja*, then maybe you would understand."

I laughed at this and he laughed in return. "I speak the truth," he said, standing. "We should go now. It is a good time to do your first *puja*."

My face must have given away my surprise and surrender, for Prip never paused. A walk would do me good and the chillum smoke clouded my reasoning enough to melt any resistance. Besides, wasn't I always open to a new experience? When the street baptistery tried to sell me the *puja* experience, it seemed false – like buying a confessional pardon or buying a scalped ticket through the pearly gates. But Prip's offer was personal and sincere, and I was intrigued.

There were no bats to be seen, replaced by a half moon shining over the lake. We walked the few blocks to the lake, quietly descending the white steps to the water's edge. The town around us was quiet and the streets were deserted. Prip mumbled a few prayers in Hindi, eyes and face cast upwards and hands together in prayer. I stood by quietly, watching and listening with interest. He moved to the water's edge, squatted on his heels and beckoned me to squat beside him. He leaned forward, cupped some water from the lake in his hands and poured it slowly over his forehead and then my forehead, chanting a Hindi phrase. He repeated this ritual several times, soaking my hair and his, as well as the front of my shirt, and then we stood up. I wiped the lake water from my eyes and face with my shirtsleeve and then he painted my face with some white chalk dust he drew from a bag he carried at his waist. He painted his own face the same way. We both stood there in silence. After a few moments, he turned and I followed him up the stairs.

"Don't worry about the lie. Brahma knows and he is larger than we are," Prip said without turning to me.

I trusted him on that and was happy to be off the hook. I wouldn't want the Hindu pantheon on my tail for insubordination. He didn't ask me how I felt, and I appreciated that. I had secretly hoped for an epiphany – perhaps I was to be born again into Hinduism (as a Brahmin cast member, preferably!), but nothing happened because I truly didn't expect anything to happen. We went back to the hotel and I went up to bed.

I stayed in Pushkar another two days, trying and not trying to think about the meaning of god and life, as taught by Brahma and monkeys. With no revelation in the offing, I made my way back north to New Delhi to catch a flight to Malaysia. The entire Indian part of my trip; ceremonies, adventures, and lessons never before imagined by me in my little cubicle in San Francisco, melted together and resisted analysis like a half-remembered dream.

☯☯☯☯☯   ☯☯☯☯☯   ☯☯☯☯☯   ☯☯☯☯☯   ☯☯☯☯☯

A dozen hooks pulled tight through the skin on his back, creating two rows of mini pup tents down each side of his spine. He leaned forward against the pulling of the ropes, a glazed look in his eyes. The hooks were attached to the ropes, which were in turn attached to the harness of a rolling cart, high upon which sat the carved figure of the colorful, bejeweled, and marigold-strewn wooden image of the goddess Kali who, despite the fanfare, looked angry underneath the elaborate gazebo.

The struggling man wore a turban wrapped around his head and a loincloth at his waist – both pure white – and nothing else. The crowds urged him along as he pulled the cart through the narrow dirt street towards the temple. The meter-high wooden wheels creaked and moaned with each step. Alongside him walked half a dozen other acolytes in various stages of pierced devotion. One woman had long pins forming the sign of a cross through her cheeks and lips. She held her hands together in front of her, praying as she walked. Another had silver charms and bells hanging from strings attached to hooks at various points around his torso. I winced at their sacrifice and marveled at each step they took. Beside me, Anton was clicking away furiously, changing lenses every few shots to create a different effect.

"What do you figure that cart weighs?" I asked as quietly as possible to still be heard over the din of the devoted.

He looked up with a puzzled furrow of his brow. "Maybe forty or fifty kilos. The road is also not smooth, so the friction would add to the weight." That seemed to give him another idea and he hunched down to take some close up shots of the road.

I didn't travel with a camera and this was one of those infrequent moments I wished otherwise. I reminded myself to ask Anton later for some copies, as I was certain we would be discussing the day's events at the guesthouse all night long.

The man pulling the cart stopped for a few moments to rest. He had pulled the cart about 100 yards so far. One of the other followers came up alongside and handed him what appeared to be a giant spliff. The man sucked away vigorously on it, surrounding his head in a veil of white smoke.

"I would like to know what is in that...cigarette," Anton commented. I nodded. Being in central Malaysia, on the outskirts of the town of Ipoh, we knew the laws against drugs of any kind were draconian. A joint could get you ten years in jail and probably a solid rattan caning to boot, if you believed the propaganda. Then again, the Muslim Malay minority enacted those laws, and this was a Hindu festival in an Indian neighborhood. I was curious how the ethnic groups reacted to policing each other.

Chang returned from the temple area. He was a longtime acquaintance of Anton's and represented the Chinese third of the Malaysian ethnic triad. He had put it to us simply: the Malays control the government, the Chinese manage commerce, and the Indians provide the labor. Anton was still curious about what the pierced man was smoking, so he repeated his question to Chang.

"It is tobacco and hashish, I think," he replied. He saw my puzzled look and added, "Malaysia's strict drug laws are not enforced in a situation such as this. This is an Indian affair and the authorities will not interfere."

Anton scratched some notes on his pad and replaced it in his breast pocket. He had the classic photographer look; multi-pocketed vest with two cameras hung over his shoulders. He wore an old safari hat over his balding head and his khaki pants were baggy and wrinkled. Standing next to him, Chang provided the ultimate contrast, with his full head of neatly combed black hair, snipped at a perfect horizontal line above his light blue, pressed button down shirt and creased gray slacks. His shoes – leather loafers with white socks, completed his costume as Anton's scuffed hiking boots completed his.

We followed the procession to the temple, but left shortly after the presiding clergy decoupled the pierced man from the cart and the ceremony took on a more subdued and reverent tenor. Anton and I were impatient from the long ceremony and dripping from the heat and humidity, though the temperature seemed to have no effect on Chang's physical or mental composure. He guided us two blocks north to a small Chinese restaurant tucked away in the middle of a block between a bicycle shop and what looked to be a bookstore. The block was entirely packed with three story townhouses of pink, yellow and gray stucco. All of the houses had some sort of business on the lower floor, with the proprietors living above. We sat in front and outside on a round concrete table, just in front of the accordion metal security gate that still remained half closed. Drying laundry hung from red plastic hangars on the gate.

Over curried potatoes and rice, I learned Chang's history and the source of Anton's love of the region. Chang's full name was Matthew Hong Chang. His family immigrated to Ipoh three generations ago from somewhere north of Canton and opened a corner store. Now they ran a grocery distribution business with over a dozen stores nationwide. Chang met Anton while studying photography in London in the mid 1980's. At that time, Anton had been working as a clerk in London for a German firm based in his hometown of Stuttgart. That had been twelve years ago. Anton and Chang developed a symbiotic friendship – Anton learned all about Malaysia from Chang and Chang about European culture. Chang had not been back to Europe since he left London, but Anton had visited this part of Asia every year since. He was an aspiring freelance photographer and journalist. I met Anton at the guesthouse two days earlier and when he mentioned this festival he could see that he just *had* to invite me along. So now I took the opportunity to ask Chang about the Malaysian ethnic situation. He spoke with a strong British accent.

"We are all different ethnically, but we are all Malaysians," he explained. "Each group leaves the other to its own devices. It is not like America where everything gets mixed up." He said this with a tone that implied mixing things up led to a less desirable outcome. I disagreed and thought about arguing but refrained, more out of fatigue than lack of conviction.

"The British colonization of Malaysia created both a harmony and tension that continues to this day." I nodded to show I understood well how a country could be both admired and despised. America assumed this mantle from the British and I was just beginning to appreciate the implication of that.

"In Germany we are all white, except for a few Turks. That is why we need to travel so much. We are all too the same and so we get sick of each other and it leads to craziness." Anton said this matter-of-factly as he wolfed down his curried lunch.

I had overheard this before from a German man in India. He stated, very directly and seriously, that the explosion of Germans on the international travel scene in recent decades was the direct result of Germans having been so insular in the past. Newer generations were determined to shed the ghost of Hitler and better understand and embrace the ethnicity that is the world. Anton echoed this point of view, though without political conviction. He was, as he stated, just a regular guy wanting to see the world. Chang nodded in empathy and I understood at once their connection. Chang drove us back in the family taxi to the guesthouse for the now routine afternoon shower and nap.

Later that evening, Anton and I were joined for dinner by an English couple, Ashley and Nate, from Surrey. The four of us discussed the events of the day, and Anton gave a less enthusiastic account of the hooks and needles than I would have. The two Brits were a middle-aged pair and very proper. Perhaps Anton's play-by-play was tempered out of respect for their maturity, an accommodation I would have been less likely to make. I had met these two a week previously in the Cameron

Highlands and they had recommended this guesthouse to me when I was ready to leave the coolness of the mountains. Nate and I had become acquainted while being shaved and coiffed by the same barber. He and his wife were on holidays for two months and had fashioned their trip along the route of Anthony Burgess and Somerset Maugham. We were all getting a little tipsy from the Tiger beer and gin and tonics. I was waiting in friendly ambush, eyeing Ashley's third cocktail, when the topic of the pierced man's hash smoking arose.

"It seems rather like cheating don't you think?" Ashley took a pull from her G and T and self-consciously flattened out her pink sleeveless dress.

"Yes, I'd have to agree," chimed her husband. "Neither of you are bridge players are you? Damn. A fine game. You should learn it, if only for my pleasure." He was smoking a cigarette from an ebony holder that extended the ash a good four inches. I thought a monocle and ascot would complete the picture, though his open white shirt and flip-flops were more suited to the warm evening.

"I think putting six or eight hooks in your back entitles you to a little indulgence. So I'd cut the guy some slack." I spread myself out languidly in the soft chair. Ashley gave me a curious look and Nate chuckled.

"I think it is as it is. It is not for us to judge the man," Anton said.

"Oh there you go, just like a Bavarian. Don't be afraid to speak your mind now." Nate signaled for another drink.

Anton rose up a couple of inches in his chair. "I am not afraid to speak so. I am sure the man about whom we are speaking doesn't care what we think." He said this in precise but accented English and it didn't sound as challenging as I anticipated.

"I am certain you are right there, old chap." Nate lifted his glass and Anton tipped his beer bottle towards him, grunting in assent.

"I see you've become gun shy since our visit to the barber." He was looking at me while rubbing his hand over his smooth cheeks. He was referring to the straight razor shave we'd both received in the Highlands. It had been my first ever and I had been astonished at the closeness of it. The barber took off a few layers of skin that gave the aftershave a sting like I had never felt before. Since that slightly painful experience, I neglected shaving entirely, and by now my beard was a thick, stubbly hedgerow. Laziness, rather than intent, had more influence on my grooming habits these days. I smiled at him, rubbing my chin. "It's the rough traveler look – it keeps the locals guessing I'm more dangerous than they are."

"I think it suits you," said Ashley. "You should let it grow out. It covers up that darling baby face of yours, but it also makes you look older."

"And looking older is a good thing?" I feigned displeasure.

"If you're a man. Of course not for a woman, but who ever said things were equal. Now those ladies you saw today. I can't imagine why they would do such a thing to their bodies – piercing with hooks and knitting needles."

"Devotion is a powerful motivator," said Anton. "And it's good that they pay less attention to vanity than we."

"Do you really think so?" Ashley questioned sincerely. "I would guess that vanity is present everywhere you go."

"I suppose that piercing your face is a form of vanity in itself. Maybe the exhibition of it is designed to attract?" Nate wondered aloud.

"Just look at all the young ones piercing and tattooing themselves today. Your guess might very well be right, my dear."

"Why can't we just accept it as a demonstration of devotion to their faith?" Anton said, sounding a little frustrated. "It is not like they do it for our benefit. I prefer to think of it as pure, as a form of meditation and very private. It is nicer that way."

"But why so publicly?" I asked. "You would think a pure act of devotion or faith would be done in private. You know, the pious fasting man who should comb his hair and go about his business unnoticed, as opposed to the "look at me!" kind of fasting man who wears tattered clothes and wails about his god."

"Oh dear. You're not going to thrust scripture upon us now, are you my boy?" Nate was giving me a warning look that I knew was in jest.

"I might if I knew any, but I don't. So I won't," I shrugged.

He raised his glass again and I answered the gesture.

"I do not think what we saw today is so different from a Christian ritual." Anton maintained a somber tone, which I respected. He studied religions as a serious hobby and very likely knew much more about it than any of us did.

"How so?" asked Nate.

"Christians are notorious for hurting themselves – physically and mentally. And they, or I should say, *we* like to make a show of things too," said Anton.

"Yes. You have a point, but..." started Nate.

"I can't make sense of any of it. Christian, Hindu, Muslim or any of the rest." Ashley said in a matter-of-fact tone. "It's all about power and money in the end. I don't mean to belittle those chaps you saw today, but really, I don't see why all that is necessary." She made a sour face and slugged back the rest of her drink.

We took the cue and diverted all attention to the less-controversial realm of playing cards. Nate tried to teach Anton and I rudimentary Bridge, but we failed miserably and his patience wore thin as the drink thickened our tongues. I gave up all hopes of a debate of any depth with these folks, though I think Anton would be a willing devil's advocate in other circumstances. I knew I would never see Nate and Ashley again after that evening, and I was right. I had hoped to see Anton again on the road somewhere, but two days later I left for Thailand to meet up with Charlie.

But the stunted conversation had planted a seed in my subconscious, and I went to bed thinking about Catholicism – the religion of my birth. My family belonged to a large and very traditional church – our Lady of the Immaculate Conception. Charlie and I went to parochial school up through the eighth grade and were oriented to the nuances between mortal and venial sin and the guilt of sinners. There was no question of my becoming an altar boy when I turned twelve and I signed up with great excitement. Wearing the black and white and carrying the holy water was, for me, akin to wearing the school colors as a basketball jock, at least when I was a pre-teen. My favorite part of the service was the candle lighting, which is where I think the pyromaniac in me first surfaced. But my first day was not the open-armed entry to the fold that I had anticipated

A junior priest, Father Vega – but he let us call him Father Mike – and two senior altar boys were the trainers that first Saturday. Two other boys were training with me, and we were all to serve mass together the next day. After a short lecture on the Three Ps – piety, promptness and paying attention – Father Mike went away, saying he would return in an hour or so to check in and test us. We newbies were then at the mercy of the two senior boys, seventeen year old high school juniors named Tommy Pearson and Stanley McBride. I assumed that one could not be an alter boy and a bully at the same time. My learning curve was steep when I was twelve. At first, they made us kneel on the stone steps that led to the altar platform while they explained how we should pay attention. Tommy draped himself over the priest's chair, legs swinging over the arms, and Stanley hopped up to sit on the altar. They reveled, in my mind's eye, at our gasps of surprise at their heretic ways. I told Stanley that it wasn't right to sit on the altar and he promptly hopped off, slapped me sharply on the ear, and hopped back up.

"Any other comments?" he asked. We three shook our heads in unison. They then took us through the routine of entering with the priest, placing the candles and assisting the priest with hand washing. When we got up to the point of the serving the Eucharist, Stanley went in the back to the sacristy and returned with a small box of communion wafers. He proceeded to eat them like potato chips, to my utter horror. I had never imagined such blasphemy, though I didn't know it was called that back then. Stanley read the dismay on my face like an open book, and once again walked over to me as if he would hit me again. Instead, he just continued to crunch and chew the wafers three inches in front of my face. I wasn't able to look him in the eye. I was scared and angry and ashamed.

When we heard Father Mike's footsteps, Stanley quickly hid the box and Tommy moved from the priest's chair over to the altar boy's bench. Stanley gave us a clear "keep quiet or else" glance and we understood the significance of it despite our innocence in everything else. We all looked up, little angels, as Father Mike took us through the routines once again. This time we newbies actually performed the rituals. Cory, one of the other trainees, messed up the hand-washing bit by dropping the drying hanky and this earned him a gentle rebuke from Father Mike and unreserved snickering from the two older boys. I couldn't bring myself to snitch about the wafers, and in that moment I joined the secret order of altar boys and would never look at Catholicism the same way again.

My career as an altar boy lasted three years. By the time Charlie and I were juniors in a public high school, where our parents thought we would be "broadened", other interests – mostly girls and soccer – began to rank higher on my priority list, and Mom and Dad finally surrendered to the inevitable and let me give it up. "Altar-boying", as Charlie used to call it, yielded some great experiences – like seeing my first dead body, close up, while serving a funeral, or getting twenty bucks for a wedding where all I remember doing was flirting with the bridesmaids. I couldn't shed some of the more nerve wracking memories, though – like smashing the wine cruet in the middle of a service once – it slipped out of my hand and splintered on the hard stone floor. That is still my most embarrassing day to-date. That first training day stands out, though, among all of the learning experiences I had in high school. I occasionally wonder what Stanley is up to, but assume he is in jail for petty theft or behind the front desk at a seedy motel, either way catching his karmic boomerang.

My own boomerang, arcing its way in and out of Japan and South Asia, appeared to be under a similar karmic influence. I seemed to keep finding myself in situations that challenged my idea of how the world and relationships are supposed to be. The fifteen months I spent in Japan prior to going on the road a second time certainly held its own dramas and adventures. Why is it that certain events, while comprising only a small space in time and even significance, weigh heavier than others in the makeup of our psyches? A seemingly unrelated conversation or observation can have a greater impact on the future than an intended, well-designed symbol or event. Japan and the many small, fleeting, and memorable events I lived through there gave me that feel. I was circling on a wheel of my own making and not trying to get off.

10

CHARLIE

SEATTLE   TOKYO   THAILAND   LONDON   THE PHILIPPINES   INDIA

YEAR **1**   YEAR **2**   YEAR **3**

'COME HITHER'

"Aren't you Charlie Diaz?"

The question surprises her and rouses her out of her train ride coma. It is mid-afternoon and she is half-reclined in an aisle seat, rocketing via *Shinkansen* toward Osaka at 200 miles per hour. The patchworked rice fields whizzing past the bullet train windows suddenly come into focus and Charlie looks up. The comment came with a southern accent from a pretty brunette standing next to her in the aisle. Charlie has no idea who she is.

"Uhh, yes I am," she says, hesitating and sounding official. The woman smiles and holds out her hand.

"I'm Brenda Brilson." Charlie shakes her hand, the name reaching back deep into her memory and grabbing hold of familiarity with a physical jolt. The Brilsons were family friends, back in Ohio when she and Renny were in the third or fourth grade. Their parents had been close and the families spent many weekends and a few holiday dinners together. But the Brilsons moved to California one summer, and though her mother mentions them every now and then, Charlie hasn't seen any of them in fifteen years or more.

"Brenda! My God, what...this is amazing!" She rises from her seat and they hug, unaware of the smiles and frowns of their Japanese audience.

"How did you recognize me?"

"Your Mom and mine still send Christmas cards every year with family pictures so I could pick you and Renny out of a crowd!"

"What are you doing here?" Charlie looks around the train car. The seats are all taken, mostly by salarymen, dozing or reading newspapers.

"I'm on my way to Nagoya to catch a plane back to California. I was just passing through to the bathroom. I'm in the next car back."

"Are there any empty seats back there?"

"The one next to me. You want to join me?"

"Of course. Pick me up on your way back from the bathroom."

When Brenda returns, Charlie gathers her things and they bump their way to the next car. The Nagoya stop is coming up in about a half an hour, so their catching-up speeds to double-time. Brenda has been in Tokyo for a week on a business trip for her publishing company. Charlie gives her a quick synopsis of her last few months of traveling, working, and settling into Tokyo life. They both lament not having known the other was in Japan.

A sudden flash of memory flares across Brenda's face and her smile is conspiratorial.

"What are you remembering?" Charlie asks curiously.

"Remember when we all got caught in that thunderstorm? And Bobby wanted to hitchhike?"

Charlie's eyes wander to the car ceiling for a moment and then a bigger smile spreads across her face. "Of course," she says, nodding once. "I remember Bobby jumping up and down in the middle of the road trying to find a car to take us home. Do you remember him screaming "Hitchhikers over here! Look this way! Hitchhikers here!" Charlie cups her hands to her mouth in a mock yell, and they both fall into a fit of giggles thinking about that day.

In her mind's eye, Charlie can see his skinny, ten-year-old frame, drenched to the skin and arms flailing. He looks like a drunken carney plying his trade in the hell of a deserted roadbed. No cars ever came. His three companions – Renny, Charlie and Brenda – are huddled together under a tall tree, trying to keep dry until Brenda, at twelve the eldest, realizes that the most unsafe place to be in a lightning storm is under a big tree. She insists that the group seek shelter in a ditch. In Charlie's memory the thunder peals right over top of them as they run from under the giant sycamore and across the field to a roadside ditch.

"He could be such a doofus," Brenda replies, fondly, "and we were pretty stupid to get ourselves in that situation!"

"I remember you tried to make us squat in that gross ditch filled with muddy water. We should have been scared silly. We were so young!" They both laugh at the memory, fondly recalling the distant images of youth.

"Renny, always the good soldier, heeded your warning and went into the ditchwater up to his knees before we told him to stop." Charlie narrates.

"And as a compromise," Brenda picks up the thread, "we all went to lie down in the open field instead."

Charlie smiles at the memory. Both of their families had moved into a new suburban subdivision around the same time, and the kids had become as fast friends as the parents. It had been a habit for the four to wander to the far reaches of the subdivision – where the streets were cut but not paved, and the fences petered out into grassland. They had been about a mile from their houses when the storm broke, and to avoid the tree and ditch dangers they walked out into the waist high cheatgrass and dandelions and reluctantly squatted down together to wait it out. They got soaked through and through, but the air was warm and the storm passed quickly, so the details didn't seem to matter.

"What is Bobby up to these days?" Charlie asks.

"He's working in Dallas as a computer guy. He's married now, with a kid on the way. It's due in two months or so."

"Oh, good for him!" Charlie is glad to hear it.

"I remember us lying together there in the grass," Brenda continues. "That one really close lightning strike and crash of thunder that made us go deaf for a minute. I can hear it like it happened yesterday."

The downpour had been torrential, lasting longer than they had expected, with the sky a ferocious black overhead and bright stabs of lightning on the horizon. The kids were, unlike their parents back at the house, not scared of the phenomenon in the least, at first. They even enjoyed the excitement of it, the spectacle of it, until the lightning started to creep closer to them. They waited for it, rather than risk a dash in the open. Blinding flashes lit right overhead, static electricity chilled their wet skin, and then the instant thunder cracked and boomed to deafen and overwhelm them. Charlie remembered screaming and grabbing onto Renny and Brenda. Bobby, outwardly unperturbed, kept on screaming in mockery of her until she yelled at him to stop. Brenda finally bonked him on the forehead and he piped down to fake whimpering. The rain increased in intensity before it finally let up, fading to a drizzle and then slowing to nothing. They could see the lightning moving away across the plains and their fear subsided with it, leaving them holding onto each other a moment longer.

"What about Renny? What's he doing now?"

"I just heard from him a couple days ago. He quit his job in San Francisco and is traveling. He'll be coming through Tokyo in a couple months or so."

"So, you guys turned out to be traveling types. Who would have guessed?"

"Not me," Charlie chuckles and shrugs. Memories of that stormy day continue in the background of Charlie's mind as the two women reminisce. The four of them started to walk home as the sun came out. Steam rose from the wet blades of grass where the sunlight hit them, and the ditches were full and noisy with runoff. They walked the half-mile down the gravel roadway, joking and laughing as if the sun had shone all day. When they reached a main street, they saw Mrs. Brilson's red pickup driving toward them. She hid her worry in her anger at their being soaked and foolishly caught out in the storm. They took the verbal lashing with heads down, then hopped in the back of the pickup. She made a u-turn in the road and as she rounded out of it they saw the bright prism of a rainbow arching a mile across the sky behind them. One end of it came down in the spot in the field where they had taken refuge. Bobby wanted to go back to look for the pot of gold, but he knew better than to jump out of his mother's truck, so he and Renny planned it as a future adventure. Charlie remembers believing that the thunder had been God speaking, and she wonders what he must have wanted them to know.

The disembodied female drone's voice politely interrupts the reminiscing to announce that they will soon be making a brief stop at Nagoya station. Charlie and Brenda catch up quickly to the present day circumstances of everyone they know in common, and then the doors hiss open. Brenda makes a quick exit and the train likewise departs without lingering. Charlie notices a new face across the aisle as she returns to her original seat. A fully coifed, elaborately garbed, real-life-geisha has boarded her car. Charlie has never seen one before. *I'll bet she's actually a maiko, not a fully practicing geisha yet – she seems too young.* Charlie is fascinated.

The woman is wearing a grand, floral kimono of reds and yellows, belted with a heavily brocaded obi sash, so stiff at the waist that she sits ramrod straight and far enough away from the seat back to keep from crushing the huge knotted bow at her back. She is a rare site in modern Japan, exquisitely white-faced with a touch of cherry on her center lips, like a Chaplin moustache dropped an inch and dipped in strawberry jam. She sports a hard, puffy-curling hairdo criss-crossed with shiny and gently tinkling silver ornaments and what looks to be, but can't possibly be, chopsticks. She seems about twenty, though she might be even younger. She has a small silk bag in one hand. As she sits in the seat in front and across the aisle, Charlie can only see the back of her head, her neck and the side of her face when she turns. Charlie adjusts out of her slouch both in deference to and reverence for the elegance poised cross the aisle.

The train speeds out of Nagoya through a repeating series of rice fields, blue-roofed homes and factories. Charlie notices many contrasts here to the Tokyo "suburbs", but can't stop her eyes from wandering back to the maiko. The makeup is so perfectly applied, and the hair – *Is it a wig, so with no strand out of place?* The mystery of it, enhanced by the kimono, gives Charlie the feeling she is in a sort of dreamland – or on another planet.

Before long, however, the fantasy world fades to the mundane. The maiko's head bobs once, ever so lightly, to the left. *Ah*, Charlie thinks, *she still nods off on the train like a normal Japanese.* Charlie knows that the Japanese have a special talent for sleeping in any position, and are somehow especially unable to resist sleeping in any moving vehicle.

Then the maiko does something that surprises Charlie. In slow, choreographed movements, the painted lady lifts her head, opens her purse using both hands, takes out a small folded white handkerchief, and places it like a bib around her neck. *To protect her silk kimono from the white makeup*, Charlie guesses. And for the next fifteen minutes, the maiko's head bobs down and back up many times in tiny, rhythmic movements. Not once does her chin or cheek touch the handkerchief. The maiko, though not immune to the gentle, sleep-inducing rock of the train, does know her full range of sleeping motion and the proper etiquette to be observed with it.

Charlie takes a long look at herself in the reflection of the window-turned-mirror in the darkness of a tunnel. She wears khaki slacks, a denim shirt, and once-white socks with a small hole wearing through on the left heel. Her dark brown hair is now shoulder length and hangs in loose strands about her face. She's never liked tying it back even when it was long. She doesn't think of herself as pretty, though she has a decent figure, straight teeth, and eyes that seem large in her oval face. All that sounds good, but she considers herself middle-of-the-road, not a beauty but not a hag, and is glad she was spared the self-image doubt that plagues many of her girlfriends. Her smile is her strong point and she uses it often, mostly because she just likes to smile. The train emerges from the tunnel into late afternoon light and her image disappears into the countryside. *I wouldn't make a good geisha*, she thinks to herself. *Too clumsy.* She pictures herself in the black wig and traditional costume, spilling a drink on a client's lap or tripping over her own kimono. She has a good chuckle out loud, though nobody on the train seems to notice. *Hey, maybe I'm a geisha of sorts at Bar WhyNot? Hostesses do a lot of the same things, it's just the modernized version. It is curious how far I've come in the past four months.* At this moment she is miles away from Seattle, in place and in spirit.

Charlie purposefully follows the maiko out of the train at the Kyoto stop. She tries to imitate her short, tiny steps but stumbles when her tennis shoe sole catches on a bump in the tile floor. It lurches Charlie forward and she brushes the back of the maiko's sleeve with her hand.

"Sorry, sorry...gomenasai!" she says, glad she can apologize in Japanese. The maiko turns around and smiles at Charlie with her eyes, putting her hand over her mouth and bowing slightly. Charlie smiles back and returns the bow awkwardly, feeling foolish and laughing inside. She hasn't had much practice bowing in Tokyo. She walks more quickly out of the station and, after a couple of minutes of deciphering signs, marches in the direction of the guesthouse, which is less than a mile from the station. She is looking forward to meeting up with Marie. *At least I won't be so obviously out graced with her,* she thinks to herself, humorously. After asking only once for directions, she finds the guesthouse, checks in, and waits for Marie in the company of several maps and travel books.

Marie shows up that evening in good spirits. Her hair has grown out into an unruly tomboy mop over the last half-year and Charlie playfully tousles it when they greet. Until she sees her that night, Charlie hadn't realized how fond she had grown of the woman. Her defiant energy is infectious. They have a joyous reunion in their shared room over beer from a vending machine, reviewing and revising the information they had shared via e-mail during the past few months. Marie is glad to be back in Kyoto – she has been here once before. As a bonus, Marie knows a gaijin woman who works as a hostess downtown near Gion, the famous geisha area. They decide to try and find her tonight, venturing down Kiyamachi Street to taste the Kyoto nightlife.

Kiyamachi is a miniature version of Tokyo's Shinsaibashi. The main street, buzzing with neon and the crashing of pachinko balls, is always bustling with activity. The buildings are all three to six stories high and the clubs are crammed into tiny rooms on each floor of each building, stacked like poker chips all the way to the roof. Charlie thinks they will never be able to locate any particular club, but is really keen to see if the trade varies much between Tokyo and Kyoto. With Marie's strong sense of direction and the help of several slightly drunk salarymen, they do find Veronica at her club,.

The Mighty Beanpole is a salaryman's delight of stainless steel and silver and karaoke. The clientele is involved mostly in the green tea trade and tends to be older and more traditionally minded than your usual workaday stiffs. It is not a busy night, so Veronica is able to beg off early and join Marie and Charlie for a night on the town.

"I'm from South Africa," she states in response to Charlie's comment on her accent. Veronica is in her mid-twenties and has lived in Kyoto for three years already, all of them spent hostessing. She is as experienced in the trade as anyone else Charlie has met, and the two of them trade tidbits. Veronica is still wearing the blue silk blouse and a dark knee length skirt she put on for work. She looks more like a headmistress at a girl's school than a hostess on a work night. And she does know what is going on in her city. As it turns out, a stand-up comedy revue is slated for a bar nearby that night, and the performers are all foreigners. Veronica heard that one of the skits will be a spoof on the hostessing racket, so they dash towards the bar to watch the fun.

Not surprisingly, the place is filled to standing-room-only with gaijin, most of them still in their work clothes, coat and tie yet to be removed after the evening's work teaching English. The revue has started already, but they haven't missed much. Two overdone gay guys are in the middle of their stand-up routine on bathing at the sento – and getting some good laughs. Most of the crowd is raucous and rude, which suggests that the drinking started early and continues to be heavy.

The three women find a table in the back just vacated by three Japanese who must have finally admitted to themselves they were in the wrong bar. They order drinks. Marie recognizes someone a few tables over and goes over to say hello. Charlie watches her walk across the room and notices others, men and women, watching her too. During lulls in the act on stage, Charlie and Veronica chat about perverts at work, and Charlie's confidence evaporates in the face of the depth and breadth of experience Veronica has earned in the last few years. Not that Charlie congratulates or envies her, of course, but she is surprised because she assumed that the men would be better-behaved at the Beanpole than at Bar WhyNot? Veronica explains.

"The types of men who frequent The Pole – that's its nasty nickname – are indeed more traditionally minded than the modern businessmen in Tokyo. My customers therefore hold *more antiquated* expectations of women than your customers probably do. This is both an advantageous and a bore."

"How so?" Charlie is fascinated once again by the constant mix of old and new in Japan. Veronica continues.

"These green tea traders expect their hostesses to be entertaining, but not intelligent in the world of men. On the other hand, they also respect the hostesses more and are less likely to think of gaijin women as loose and easy. Kyoto has the reputation, in general, for maintaining the standards of old Japan."

"Charming," Charlie smiles.

Marie returns just as the comedy duo finishes their act and onto the small stage comes Veronica's friend, who introduces herself as "Kitty" with a deep, throaty voice. She is bursting out of her low cut, sequined, red dress with slits high up both thighs. The dress sparkles and flashes in the spotlight, sending mirror reflections off the walls and ceiling. Her make-up has been applied thickly and colorfully, painting a clear picture of her character for the skit. She oh-so-deliberately lights a cigarette and takes a deep drag. Her auburn hair is teased and piled high on her head, with a few strands left artfully and sensually hanging loose around her neck. The musical accompaniment suddenly comes on over the loudspeakers and Charlie recognizes the tune immediately. The three women turn to each other knowingly after the first few bars of music and smile in unison. Kitty slowly and meaningfully gyrates her hips to the hoots and hollers of the drunken crowd and belts out her whoreish tribute. Charlie knows it's a knock off of a real R and B tune, but doesn't know who sang it first, only that she first heard it in a TV commercial for perfume.. But Charlie has to admit that the new lyrics are hysterical.

> I can bring home the bacon-
> Fry it up in my pan….
> And make you just beg to be…
> A salary man….
> 'Cuz I'm a hostess baby…..H-O-S-T-E-S-S-
> Lemme say it again…
> 'Cuz I'm a hostess, lover….H-O-S-T-E-S-S

Kitty signals for silence by turning her back to the crowd, which silences them immediately. Then she slowly twists to face them as she launches into the last stanza with a diva's desire, and the once-howling crowd sits rapt in awed silence as she finishes with a sultry chorus that does Billie Holliday proud.

> ….
> Don't worry 'bout me baby
> I am not in a rut
> 'Cuz I ain't nuthin but a conversaaaaation sluuuuuuuuutttt

The curtain of applause falls long and loud. Kitty finishes to a well-deserved standing ovation. Charlie laughs to the point of tears. Kitty accepts the audience's adoration with grace, failing to flinch at the catcalls. She knows her talent well – she has a sexuality that cannot be denied and a voice that demands equal attention. A half hour later she joins the three women for a drink. They are effusive in their praise and she equally cool to it, like a star. Her name really is Kitty and she is French Canadian.

The show drones on late into the night, but much of the English-teacher and local gaijin-scene jokes are lost on Charlie and Marie. So they leave Veronica at the bar with Kitty and walk up the river back to the guesthouse. The night is mild and at 2am the streets mostly deserted. They are both mildly drunk and Charlie can't get the last line of the chorus out of her head, to the point of singing it every so often and gyrating her hips to boot.

"I ain't nothin' but a conversaaaation...sluuuutttt."

"Christ. Enough of that already." Charlie smiles in response.

"It's just too true. What do you think the men in conversation lounges really want?"

"That's obvious enough isn't it?"

"On the surface, maybe, but I don't really know."

"Come on. Men are the same everywhere." Marie then softens. "Though I suppose here they are a touch more off than the usual."

"Yeah. Look at us here. We're walking down a deserted street in the middle of the night in a big city and I don't feel any danger at all. What do you mean by 'off'?"

"I mean the Japanese are different. The women too. They say it themselves you know. That nobody not Japanese can understand what it means to be Japanese."

"But different in what way? We're here aren't we? That must mean that we are attracted to that difference..."

"No, I think we're attracted to Japan more because it's different than where we're from. We could be in China, or Mexico – because the grass is always greener. We're just glad not to be knee deep in the brown grass of home.

"So what's different here than back home?"

"Christ woman! Enough of the questioning!" Marie says it a bit too harshly and Charlie falls silent, stunned. They walk on silently. After a minute or so to collect her thoughts, Marie apologizes.

"Sorry for that. That's not directed at you personally." Marie keeps her head looking forward too intensely, so Charlie smiles and puts a hand on her shoulder, but doesn't say anything.

"I'm a little preoccupied, thinking about packing up and going back to New Zealand. I'm getting tired of it here. The problem is, I was tired of it there, too. So going back doesn't sound all that exciting, but at least it's something I know." They are silent again for a few moments.

"You can say something again now. I won't bite your head off."

"I ain't' nothin' but a..." Marie pushes her away in jest.

"Bitch!" she says with some mirth. Charlie acts offended and then takes a deep breath.

"What would you do if you went back home?"

"I don't know. What, who, even where? It's all a fuckin' mystery. I'm just getting' so tired of my life here. That routine back there just summed it all up."

"See, I told you it was all too true," Charlie says, trying to interject some levity, not wanting the frivolous evening to turn serious.

"Yeah, that's the problem you see. The whole fucking world wants you to whore yourself for a buck. That's how the Japanese are different, maybe. They're more innocent about it. They accept it more and it's lovable but it makes me sick. I'm tired of big tits and skinny legs and doing everything so it looks good on the surface but underneath is rotten and smelly. It's all bullshit."

"You mean just in Japan or everywhere?"

"I mean all of it. Do you know the Japanese term *tatemae*?"

"I've heard it, but I don't really understand it."

"It means the way you do things on the surface. It's bowing and smiling to someone when inside you hate their guts. They say that it's to maintain harmony, but I think they're just cowards, like the British. It's easier to push down all the noise and put on the face than it is to deal with it."

"So, what's that got to do with...." Charlie lets the sentence trail off, seeing the connection, but feeling confused. She continues, "I've had this odd feeling, since before leaving Seattle, that the way we're taught things are *supposed* to be isn't the way they *really* ought to be. Only I don't *know* how things ought to be, so I feel like I don't have the right to be too critical of what *is*. Does that make sense?"

Marie nods. "Well, a philosophical breakthrough. I might just make a real woman out of you yet." It becomes Charlie's turn to push Marie.

"You know the weirdest thing about Japan? Here is this culture with all this wisdom and culture and art. You'd think they would have an enlightened perspective on how the new world should be, how everyone could live in harmony? But they are just as fucked up as the rest of us. I mean, just look at this." They stop at a point where the view includes mainly concrete – the riverbed, riverbank walls, and the ten-story monolithic concrete structures that line the river with ugly and foreboding menace. Even in Kyoto, a city revered for maintaining the old ways and architecture, concrete is rapidly replacing the wooden past.

"But what's there to do about it? We have to go on. There's no sense in letting it all bring you down. You know, fight when you can, do the most damage, and move on. The Japanese *wa* has a lot going for it."

"But I don't believe in '*wa*'. Pursuing harmony is just a load of crap from the powers that be, intended to keep us in our place and things the way they are. I think the whole thing, the way we rape each other and the planet, needs to be shattered. And when enough of us get angry enough, it just might happen."

Charlie pauses to think about this. She knows Marie has had a few drinks, but this is sober commentary. In her own slightly tipsy analysis, it even makes some sense – the 'powers that be' part, not the 'lets start a revolution part'.

"The only problem with that is I don't want to live my life angry all the time. Yeah, there is a lot to be pissed off about, but it just seems a waste of time to dwell on it."

"So, what then? You just put on the tatemae and act like it's not there? I can't do that. It's all too much in my face and I can't pretend it's not."

They come to a row of cherry trees, the leaves gently rustling in the night breeze, unaware of the tribulations about them, or unperturbed. They stop to listen to the sound of river water flowing over the rocks, the wind whistling through the buildings, and the distant hum of the city they are a part of tonight. They walk on and Charlie picks up the thread.

"It's not all a waste. It's not all sad – I know a lot of it is, but not all of it. I know I'm naïve in so many ways, but I don't mind because I don't want to pay too much attention to the dark side. I'm afraid I'll get sucked in and I'll never come out." Charlie feels something welling up in her throat and draws a deep breath to calm the turbulence. Marie can sense the emotion of it and walks closer to give Charlie's shoulders a squeeze.

"Don't you pay too much attention to me now. We've all got our own little wars to wage and I don't need you waging mine for me. I need you to keep me looking towards the light every now and then – get me out of my funk. So I don't go off and strangle somebody."

They spend the next two days in Kyoto, visiting the famous temples of Kiyomizu-dera and the thousand Buddha statues at Sanjusangendo, among others. The stark contrast of Kyoto's old, wooden Japan and Tokyo's new, concrete Japan is powerful, lingering in the forefront of Charlie's mind during the train ride back north. The images of the past few days swirl in her mind's eye in a snapshot collage of sounds and colors. *It is odd*, she thinks, *that I would consider Kyoto as representative of the old when I kept hearing and seeing Marie's comment about the ugly concrete buildings surrounding the river the other evening. The theme reinforced itself as we meandered through the temple grounds.* Roaming through the thousand Buddhas, Charlie had been whisked from past to present by a hunched over, aging mama-san, dressed in blue and gray cotton kimono, dragging behind her a grandson toddler in a red wagon. The boy was intent on a hand held video game and was bursting from the wagon in his girth, his eyes hidden beneath a Chunichi Dragons baseball cap. Charlie's impulse had been to tip over the wagon, but of course she held back. The mama-san smiled cheerily as she passed and then continued her strange pilgrimage, straining at the wagon handle.

ଡ଼ଡ଼ଡ଼ଡ଼ଡ଼ ଡ଼ଡ଼ଡ଼ଡ଼ଡ଼ ଡ଼ଡ଼ଡ଼ଡ଼ଡ଼ ଡ଼ଡ଼ଡ଼ଡ଼ଡ଼ ଡ଼ଡ଼ଡ଼ଡ଼ଡ଼

Charlie lets the rocking of the train lull her into a reflective state. *Marie and I didn't talk much more in-depth after that first night, but I feel closer to her more than ever now. It was sad to hug good-bye among the pulsing crowd at Kyoto Station. I'm glad Marie got out of her funk, and that we'll get together again when she comes to Tokyo in about six months. It will be great to see her again. I miss her already.*

Continuing her journey home, Charlie is comforted with the nostalgia of returning to her station, her neighborhood, and her apartment building. In a country so foreign to her, she deeply values coming *home* to familiarity. Yet she is also dismayed at what is missing – things she hadn't noticed as lacking before her trip to Kyoto. There aren't any ancient structures in Tokyo. No green to the landscape. No evidence of the rich heritage she now realizes is the core of the Japanese culture. She knows this is true because the Kanto Plain, over which Tokyo stretches for ninety square miles, was virtually leveled by firebombs during World War II. The question that piques Charlie is: W*hy didn't they rebuild any of the city according to the old methods? No temples with huge, sloping tile roofs. No wooden houses with small gardens. It is as if there was a wholesale rejection of all that was traditional.*

There is more to it than a simple lack of materials or skilled workers in the traditional veins. Bury the past with the dead and look towards the future for those that survived? She recalls reading an article on Yukio Mishima and for the first time can really see what he was upset about now. He killed himself – committed *hara-kiri* with a knife to the belly on national TV in

1970 – to protest the national sellout of all that was uniquely Japanese. *Maybe he was a fanatic and maybe war did that to people, made them confused and unstable. But what if he was right? Why not rail against the forces of change and make your own change, put your own imprint on the new way?* She is beginning to understand this point of view.

Subconsciously, Charlie begins to compare her own self-view to how she thinks the Japanese view themselves. She replays the conversation she had with Marie in Kyoto and realizes she had been speaking with two voices –one speaks of the outside world she lives in, but the other, inner voice, reveals another truth. The Japanese penchant for *nihonjinron* – study of things Japanese, fascinates her. The Japanese say they can not be understood by the outside (non-Japanese) world, yet they themselves are ignoring, rejecting, and throwing away most of the cultural elements that have defined them for centuries. This dilemma mirrors her own internal conflict and is perhaps the same for those around her. *We idealize the past, but reject it to embrace the future. I desire stability, yet I know that change is the only constant.*

For Charlie, this is a clear parallel between the way the Japanese have dealt with change and her own life choices. She is tempted to dismiss and devalue the American, the feminine, and the Diaz experiences that formed today's "Charlie", and instead concentrate on newness, change, and survival in the modern world. She wants to view her past as just the past, and not as the basis for who she is now. But then, she realizes, she would be doing, in microcosm, to herself what Japan has done to itself.

As she makes herself comfortable in her own tatami mat room, nursing a glass of red wine, she realizes that what disturbs her about this new realization is the ugliness she sees in "modern" Japan: the concreted riverbanks, the litter, the noise and neon eye-pollution… The old Japanese ways were beautiful, but they are untenable in the current time, perhaps? The ways people now relate to one another has forced change. In the head down rush to catch up, aesthetic and spirituality have been sacrificed for brawn and money. *Do I have the same ugliness in the modern me,* she wonders, refilling her glass. *Am I a contradiction of myself and my words and thoughts?*

☯☯☯☯☯ ☯☯☯☯☯ ☯☯☯☯☯ ☯☯☯☯☯ ☯☯☯☯☯

Back at the University of Colorado, Charlie minored in Chinese Studies and her favorite class was a seminar called China Since the Revolution. Every class topic resulted in lively – sometimes-heated – discussions on the cultural purges and sacrifices that plagued the Chinese in the late sixties. Most members of the class were adamantly and vocally opposed to destroying cultural artifacts; these were the arts, crafts, teachings, and symbols that had brought China to the present. To deny their importance and influence had been foolish and criminal. A few of her classmates, however, argued that the purging had been necessary for the Maoists to take power because they had to create a blank slate. All preexisting institutions were a hindrance, a handicap, to Mao's Chinese, who had to be shown a new way. Charlie had been too timid to form, let alone give, an opinion, but in her silence she secretly sided with the minority argument. It seemed impossible to her for a people – or even a person – to create a truly new way of being unless the influence of the past were erased. *The problem is,* she surmised, *you can't erase the past – you can only destroy its features.*

There was the paradox of Mishima; by destroying himself, he furthered the cause of those he opposed because he wasn't around to oppose it anymore. The wisdom of the past was largely in those like him and not in the "things" about him. Charlie's past was physically 3000 miles away, but did she really want to destroy them – or her access to them – altogether? *Maybe I ought to just leave them for another time and place, for others to discover and value. Do I need my own cultural revolution? Or just to know that I have my own private Kyoto waiting for me back in America?*

She allows these questions to linger, unanswered, for weeks as she swoops back into her modern Tokyo life. She immerses herself in teaching and finally signs up for a Japanese calligraphy class in addition to her language classes. She decides that letter therapy is an appropriate way to help think through her life questions, and she seeks advice in several emails to Joan. She hints at her current dilemma (*is it smart to look forward and backwards at the same time?*) but stops short of asking for Joan's guru-wisdom. She still gets it.

Hi Charlie,

I've finally made the decision to pack up my bags and move to a place where old geezers like me are supposed to live – near San Diego! It's been a hard decision in the making. I've been in Seattle a long time and have a lot of ties here. I'd thought that I could keep the best of both worlds, but of course that isn't possible. You have to be where you are and not where you're not. When Alice and I first moved here over fifty years ago now, I never thought about what it would be like to stay in one place for so long. Well, Alice has been gone for some time now and I've continued on my way, but it's time for a change. Who'd have thought a woman closing in on ninety would say such a thing!? It just goes to show you, the only unchanging thing is change.

It sounds like you're enjoying yourself over there. I seriously gave some thought to a visit, but it just isn't in the cards. You know I studied calligraphy myself some years back. Maybe it was a lot of years back! I can't remember so well. I've kept a box of brushes and what-not from those years in the basement. I'm setting them aside for you. I'm not selling the apartment building, so I'll keep a storage unit in the basement for my things. Some of the other stuff you left with me can just stay there.

I haven't heard any mention about your love life. You know old women like me need those tidbits. Vicariously is the only way I've got left. I detect a little impatience in your letters. Remember, being antsy isn't a bad thing, just don't let it get in the way of seeing things for what they are. I'll sign off now. I'm keeping this e-mail address. Note the new real address at the bottom. I'll be there in a month or so.

Love, Joan

Charlie prints out a copy of the letter to keep in her day bag. She rereads it often and thinks of the words as wise and Joan as a sage.

Charlie's love life has been dead until just recently. Ever since Thierry she had no desire to be with anyone. She isn't pining for him – they were quite clear on "no expectations" – and never received a reply from the letter she wrote him months ago. She doesn't really expect one, but it would have been a nice surprise. She isn't ready to purge that part of her past quite yet. But she also doesn't want to be intimate with anyone physically right now. Pauline introduced her to a fellow Irishman, David, a few weeks ago, and they went out to dinner once. He is sweet and good looking, and he reminds her a bit of Renny. That is comforting but also a touch disturbing.

Renny has been on the road for a few months now. She is so pleased that he quit his dead-end San Francisco job to join the *real* world. But she is disappointed that he skipped over Japan on the first leg of his trip and headed straight to Indonesia. He is thinking about maybe working in Japan too, and that possibility brought joy to her heart when she first heard it. But now, she has a sneaking suspicion that she might be gone by the time he arrives! Anyway, she'll see him in just a month or so for the first time in almost a year!

☯☯☯☯☯ ☯☯☯☯☯ ☯☯☯☯☯ ☯☯☯☯☯ ☯☯☯☯☯

She and Pauline go out for coffee one afternoon after work. Pauline is going to Korea for a holiday and wants the scoop from

Charlie. Charlie did a quick trip to Seoul a few months earlier so she could reenter Japan with an official, school-sponsored visa in her passport. Charlie was in Seoul for only three days on her trip and it had been cold and rainy. The only real info she can relay is about the airport and a decent guesthouse.

Charlie and Pauline had chosen to meet in the same café where Charlie had sat with Marta, the apple thief. Charlie relays the story to Pauline, who reacts with interest.

"I've got a bit of that in my past you know."

"You're kidding. Come on, tell me about it." Charlie is all ears.

"It was in Dublin. I'd just graduated high school and it was the summer before I was scheduled to matriculate at Trinity. I was at a dress shop with some girlfriends and took a fancy to some black lace panties. I stuffed em' in my bag and wouldn't you know it, the clerk saw me and I was caught red handed." Pauline pauses there, sips her coffee and looks out the window.

"You can't just stop there! What happened?"

"Calm down dearie. The whole thing became a mess. Me Dad got involved and I thought he would beat the daylights out of me. If it got out I could've been expelled from university before I even started. Well, we paid the shop for the panties, I still have em' you know, and I had to write a letter of apology and that was that. Ma said a few novenas for my spiritual health and fretted over my damnation. I dyed my hair purple after that."

"What'd you do it for? The thrill?"

"I suppose. I don't know why really. Sometimes I want to do something that you aren't supposed to just because you're not supposed to do it. Do you ever get that feelin'?"

"Yeah, all the time. Only I've never really followed up on it. I'm too chickenshit."

"You are an innocent one at that, girl."

"I am not!" Charlie laughs as she said it, but truly feels indignant.

"C'mon. What's the worst thing you've ever done?"

Charlie has to think it over.

"See what I mean? Just that you have to think about it says that I'm right."

Charlie frowns. "I took some mushrooms in Thailand last year."

"Ooh. You're a naughty one ain't ya? Next thing you know we'll be seein' your picture on the most wanted list."

She has to laugh at that one. "You bitch," she whispers, then adds, "So what of it? Just because I haven't done anything too bad. What does that mean?"

"You tell me now. I'm not as worried about it as you seem to be."

Charlie nods. Pauline is way too quick to joust with. "Well it doesn't mean anything. It just means I've been a good girl," she says with a pout.

"My angel St. Charlie. No wonder I've left the faith."

"I want to see a picture of you with purple hair."

"Next time you're over, remind me. It wasn't so flattering after all that. That's the thing of it, you see. As much as I wanted to rebel, my vanity stayed with me. I wanted to look like the girls of Heart, you know, the band, but I ended up looking more like Alice Cooper." That gets another good laugh.

❧❧❧❧❧ ❧❧❧❧❧ ❧❧❧❧❧ ❧❧❧❧❧ ❧❧❧❧❧

Renny shows up two days later, excited and weary from six months on the road. *If he has been on the road for six,* Charlie muses, *then I've been gone from Seattle for almost a year – can you believe it? Time has flown, so I must be having fun.* Renny stays with Charlie for a week, sleeping the first couple of days away while she works. They compare travel stories of India, where it turns out that both of them have a "stalker" story to tell.

She feels some pride at being able to show him around Tokyo knowledgeably. She is still trying to adjust to his decision to find work and live in Kyoto. She just assumed that he would stay near her in Tokyo, but she should have known better. Kyoto seems more natural for the alternative-minded. And she only half-allows that Kyoto might have been a better choice of locale for her, too,

if she had done more prep before coming to Japan. Renny read up
on different cities, talked to travelers in Asia who knew Japan,
and made an informed decision that Kyoto would suit him better
than anywhere else in Japan. Charlie relishes her visit there, even
for all the feelings of self-doubt it brought up.

On his last afternoon in Tokyo, they have lunch at the
restaurant that Charlie has begun to call The Apple Theft, across
from her school. Renny knows it is a disappointment for Charlie
that he's leaving to explore life in Kyoto, but also knows she will
accept it without a fight. Still, he wants her to know that he
wishes they could live closer. "You're disappointed I'm not
staying in Tokyo?"

"Well, a little, of course. But now that I think about it, it'll be
nice to visit you down there."

"I know it was kind of a surprise decision – I just assumed I
would come to Tokyo, too, to mooch off you – but starting out in
Kyoto just feels right."

"When I was there last month, I could tell it would be a
different experience than being here. Tokyo's pretty cool, but it's
definitely got a Big City vibe."

"Yeah. I'm ready to settle down for a bit. Being on the road
was great, but I'm looking forward to an adventure that doesn't
involve finding a new hotel every week."

"So, you understand the visa thing well enough?" asks
Charlie, changing the subject and wanting to show her brother
she could still be of some use to him.

"Yeah. I think I'll look for work and if I don't find a school
that will sponsor me for a visa, I'll go the Seoul route and come
back in with a fresh tourist visa every three months."

"Well, you'll have to go even if you get on with a company
that will get you the visa, so here's the place I stayed at in Seoul."
They walk to the nearest subway station after she hands him the
address to the guesthouse and makes sure he has her email
address and phone numbers at school, home, and the club. It is
hard to let him go after all, even though he'll be living three
hours away by train – their closest proximity since college. She

finally waves good-bye to him as he bobbles his backpack through the turnstile at the station. He surprises her one more time by looking back and smiling, which softens the lump in her throat and allows her to flash her Charlie smile at him.

Afterwards she hops a train over to Harajuku to walk the Meiji Palace grounds, a favorite haunt because of the access to both a quieter Japan and the throbbing rock music one has to pass through to get there. Rows and rows of stylized and wannabe Japanese garage bands blare their music and cater to their groupies, playing everything from Elvis to the Sex Pistols to Run DMC. Charlie passes by the bands on her way into the palace grounds – into the past, where the serene garden underscores the contrast.

She noticed how Renny seems older to her this time. She hadn't noticed his aging before, any more than she keeps tabs on her own maturing. Now she wonders if time has taken its toll on her, too. It isn't so much a matter of looks – she isn't a vain person and knows that youth is a state of mind more than anything else. Will that attitude shift in the years to come, as she is fast approaching thirty? She thinks about Joan – approaching ninety and still embracing change! *"Everyone else always seems older than me,"* she has said several times, and that keeps her young at heart. But Charlie is beginning to see this for herself. *Everyone does seem older, and surer of themselves. I guess that is not a bad thing.*

As she walks out of the palace grounds into the mob of rockabilly cowboy bands and leather-coated punkers, she notices a Tokyo Billy Idol pointing at her and inviting her to join his groupies with a 'come hither' curl of his tongue. At least she thinks he is pointing to her. She walks over and stands in front him while he sings badly and gyrates wildly, rubbing his crotch and spraying the lyrics into the microphone. She grins up at him and smiles widely to herself and moves onwards. *Well, maybe not everyone.*

11

RENNY

SAN FRANCISCO	KYOTO	THAILAND	KATMANDU	LAKE TOBA	INDIA	IPOH

YEAR 1	YEAR 2	YEAR 3

THE NIHON WAY

Teaching conversational English in Japan was one of the best gigs I ever came across. While lucrative "privates" were hard to come by and were coveted by the free-lance English teacher, once you landed a few, it was Easy Street, Asian-style. The students were motivated, they had adequate disposable income, the hours were flexible, and it was all tax-free. But newly arrived job-seekers usually pursued mainstream teaching gigs in established schools. A BA, or at least a certificate that says you had one, was usually enough to get a job all by itself. That and cleaning up for the interview, though that wasn't always necessary. The Japanese place a certain intrinsic value on what we might call eccentricity, though we might elsewhere assign the same traits to being a slob.

Within four months in Kyoto, I was teaching twelve private lessons a week for a sum total of seventy thousand yen – about six hundred dollars – a week. Not too shabby for someone with no formal teacher training, working half time and enjoying the self-employed lifestyle. I had gotten lucky, it's true. It was all about being ready to open the door when opportunity knocked. In this case, the door to self-sufficiency hinged on being in the right place at the right time, and willingness to help a stranger.

I made my own initial attempts at finding legitimate ESL work in Kyoto, but was not very successful for several reasons. At the top of the list was the fact that I didn't really want a job. Next to that was the strange vibe I tuned into at a couple of interviews at small schools. I, reluctantly, assign the feeling to

226

bigotry, though, to this day I am not positive if that is the appropriate description. Japanese culture messes with definitions of social acceptability – creating ambiguity with issues that are more clearly understood elsewhere in the world. Roles of the sexes? Appropriate places for colored faces? Cultural perspectives are rarely predictable or transparent to the new arrival. Still, I know when I am being disrespected for something arbitrary and some interactions in Japan clearly tread that line. At two of the schools I applied to teach at, it was pretty clear I wasn't white or female enough to suit them, and those rejections fed my own apathy, fueling my desire to stay outside of the mainstream work channels.

The silver lining revealed itself about two weeks later. I was learning my way around Kyoto, enjoying the sights before taking another stab at the dreaded resume and interview grind. I was riding my bike back from a late morning at the rock garden at Tofukuji, a smaller temple complex tucked away in the southeastern foothills, all blissed out on Zen and peacefulness and goodwill. I happened upon a foreign woman at the side of a small alley struggling to get a very heavy Japanese chest through a doorway. I probably would have offered help even had she not been foreign, but I was already susceptible to that peculiar gaijin affliction of feeling akin to total strangers who are not Japanese. I think it had something to do with knowing we could never be "in", so we naturally bonded as outsiders. I pedaled down the alley and offered a hand.

Her need and my interest combined into a friendship over the next three hours as we hauled assorted vintage Japanese furnishings and accessories from her car into her new, modern apartment. She was, in her own words, "moving on up." She even sang it in the style of The Jefferson's TV show. I never asked her how she came to know the tune, since she was obviously British.

Martha was a university teacher in her mid-fifties. She had been in Japan for eight years, working several jobs and accumulating snippets of Japanese culture, in evidence among the furniture and knickknacks we hauled. But now she intended to spend more time with herself, less time teaching private lessons, and generously offered to gift some of them to me. Of course I said thank you and yes. These six private students led to referrals for three more, and I soon feared I would end up in Martha's world of coveting free time. I acquired three more through acquaintances at the guesthouse to bring me up to a full load.

There was, of course, the visa situation to deal with, but I wasn't worried about it. Official working visas required sponsorship and I wasn't in that loop. Furthermore, I didn't want to be. Taxes and mandatory health insurance were to be avoided, in my eyes, at all costs. It's hard to step off if you don't stay below the radar. I'd met some people who had survived for years without a working visa and that gave me confidence. Louise, for example, had spent the first 18 months in Japan by flying out to Korea and back every three months, returning with a fresh tourist visa each time. As it turned out, the immigration service started cracking down when I was there, thus my little caper with the washed out passport in Thailand when I returned for the third time.

Soon after acquiring work, I ventured out with Tony one evening, heading for one of our favorite spots – Yoshida Mountain – or hill rather, on the eastern side of Kyoto. There was a temple there, Shinyodo, where we hoped to absorb a calmer, Buddhist perspective, and the hill gave an expansive view of the city. It was a short ride to the base of the hill, and we rode it in silence. When we reached the bottom at the concrete steps that led to the top, we locked our bikes and began the long climb up through the woods.

There wasn't anyone else on the hill this evening, or so it seemed to us. A feral cat darted across the path up ahead and dried brown leaves rustled in the cool spring breeze. A clear quarter moon greeted us as we crested the hill and settled down on a concrete bench by a run-down playground. We listened a moment to the silence, to make sure that we had the place to ourselves. Tony took out his pipe, already filled for the occasion, and his trusty lighter. He allowed me the first drag, as was his custom, and we got slowly etherized. There were tantalizing glimpses of the city to the west, visible through gaps in the trees. We watched and listened, tuned to the night and the fading hum of the surrounding city. A gust roused us from our night meditation.

We arose without speaking and walked along the ridge path to the Zen sitting area of Shinyodo temple. The flat cushioned *zabuton* mats were strewn artistically about the polished wooden floor, awaiting dawn and the monks' behinds that would warm them. The place emanated a Zen serenity that may have been more in our minds than in the place itself. It doesn't matter, of course, since a place exists regardless of our feelings for it. A bustling city can be a sanctuary, or a forest glade an emotional firestorm depending on what you bring with you when you're there.

We continued walking downhill to our intended destination: a secluded cemetery adjacent to the temple grounds. We paused to listen and be sure the stone monuments were indeed deserted. The coast was clear, and we entered. We chose a large flat monument with a *torii* gate atop it and climbed up. The gate rose about four feet from the slab, which was itself at least four feet off the ground and about four by six feet square. We settled in under the gate and stared off across the grounds to the city beyond. The cemetery had newer monuments of clean gray granite scattered among the hundreds of older, weathered stones that had not seen care for some time. We loved this place. We discovered it three weeks earlier on a midnight jaunt, my first in Kyoto.

"What do you figure that fellow's story was?" Tony pointed two rows down at a moss-covered headstone about the size of a fire hydrant. The etched outline of a warrior holding a spear at his side was still faintly visible. The bright face of the moon lit the area well and added shadows to the mystery of the place. Silhouettes of temple roofs guarded the perimeter of the hill, opening up to naked tree branches with bulging buds scattered along its arms, embracing another rung of smaller house rooftops, beyond which shone the city lights.

"Died of TB just before the war started in '35. Never knew he'd be surrounded by concrete throughout eternity. Never knew of disco, cold wars, and karaoke. China was the foreign menace when he died, not the US. Worked in the rice paddies all his life, like his father before him. Had two boys killed in the war and a wife and daughter made poor by it. Though he never knew that, of course." I sighed at that last detail.

"Not bad," Tony mused. He liked this game even more than I did. "What would his life have been like?"

"Hmmm..." I paused for dramatic effect. "He patrolled the fields for loafers and thieves. Checked the roads for ronin trying to take advantage of the local women. He imagined himself a modern samurai, thus the symbol on the headstone. I don't suppose he was too different from you or me."

"I'm not so sure about that," Tony said. "He probably didn't travel much, never would have known what life was like outside of this little area. And he would have had a master, the rice plantation lord, who treated him like a slave, and could've killed him on a whim, if you believe what they say."

"Which I don't. History makes the samurai society sound like it was heartless. I don't figure it really was. You can't go around killing people for no good reason – especially when they work for you and you need the rice crop to be prosperous. There would be a revolt eventually. If you were this guy, you wouldn't put up with some local lord offing your father or brother because he looked sideways at him. You know, like in the movie <u>Shogun</u>, where the soldier cuts a guy's head off because he spills water, or something like that. So I guess the people of that time were more reasonable than they get credit for and the stories we hear are more for fright – to invoke some kind of reverence – than for real."

"Could be. This guy just wanted to have the same peace and prosperity that we do. Not have the boss breathing down your neck and all. I don't know about the revolt part though. People can be sheep. M'Dad worked thirty-five years at the same insurance firm. He said it was good and we benefited from it, but he pretty much just followed the herd."

"We can't all be lone wolves. There's got to be some who want to be in the herd. Most do, I think."

"Yeah, I guess that's true. We're all just animals in the end. That's a little frightening when you think about it. If it's true, then what's the point of it all? You eat, you reproduce, you get thinned when you're no good anymore."

We paused to consider the impact of those words. I picked up the thread.

"I think, sometimes, that everything humans have created, the rules and morality; it's all just a big load of crap. It's just because we can't accept that we're gonna die. The samurai saw that. They always tried to keep in their minds an image of their own death. That way they stayed pure, in the moment. They say you can't be frightened that way. I've tried it myself, to keep a picture myself at the moment of death in the back of my mind as I'm facing a new or fucked up situation.

"What's the point of that?!" Tony recoiled a bit, which made me laugh.

"Well, I can't decide if it helps or not, but I think it does. In the back of my head I see my own death, so the decision I have to make at any moment doesn't seem as important, or the risk seems less important, because I know that I'm going to die in the end, like everyone else. The question is, will I shit my pants the moment I see the truck bearing down on me or will I smile like the Buddha?"

"Well I can tell you that...." Tony's snide reply was cut short by my open hand, held out in warning. A soft rustling among the gravestones a few rows over startled us into silence. A momentary rush of horror ran through my veins accompanied by an image of an enraged samurai warrior getting ready to lop our heads off.

"Well, I don't know Tony, maybe it's the GHOST of a SAMURAI...." I nearly shouted, attempting to oust the invaders.

Quietly but swiftly, two crouched silhouettes rose from the ground maybe twenty yards away, picked up a blanket and hurried off towards the path down hill. It was obvious we had disturbed a pair of lovers who had sought privacy among the headstones. In Japan I hadn't noticed many options for lust-release for the young and still-living-at-home, other than checking into a hotel, which costs and in the end isn't so private to arrange. Privacy was a luxury. Tony and I sat in silence, soon realized that we were among other trysting couples in the cemetery. We resumed talking, this time whispering out of respect for these hearty souls making love among the dead.

"You just met Louise, right?" I nodded to Tony's query.

"Did you hear what happened to her the other day?" Tony asked. "It is a wild story. She was sitting on a bench over on the Philosopher's Path. Have you been there yet?"

"I've ridden past it, but I haven't spent any time there." The Philosopher's Path was a tree-lined walkway on the eastern edge of Kyoto that meandered along a creek, through old neighborhoods, temples, teahouses, and parks.

"Well, she was sitting on one of the raised benches, reading a magazine and having a coffee or something and she looks up. There's a guy sitting in a car parked across the road. He's looking right at her and he's jackin' off! No shit. Poor Louise, she doesn't know what to do at first, so she looks away. When she looks up again, the guy is still looking right at her, but he looks away when she sees him. She can see down into the car because the bench is set above the road. Now she's getting really pissed off, so she gets up and walks over to the car. The window is open so she dumps her coffee, not scalding she says, on the guy, calls him *skebbe*, the Japanese word for pervert, and goes back to her bench. The bloke is apparently some sod of a salaryman and he drives off in a hurry."

"This can be a strange country at times." I could only agree.

"So I ask Louise why she did it and she says she thought it was because she felt violated. There she was on the Philosopher's

Path no less, feeling all calm and full of bliss and here is this guy throwin' a kink in the works."

"The guy should've picked a more discreet spot." Was I trying to defend the guy? Louise would have socked me if she'd been listening.

"Yeah, that's what I thought, too." Tony agreed. "But, maybe that was the most discreet spot around! It's the same for these poor bloody buggers tryin' to make it in a cemetery for Chrissakes. They're just scratchin' an itch and there's no other way to reach it." Tony rubbed his back against one of the torii gate pillars in a mockingly sensual rhythm.

I laughed at the image, and his words made some sense to me, but I wasn't sure I had it all clear in my head.

"So, what are you sayin'? You don't think the guy was a perv or what?"

"Well, yes he was, but I feel badly for him too. I mean, here's this bloke who probably works all day and maybe has a time of it at home and all he wants is to get his rocks off."

"What about the shower, or the toilet stall?"

"I haven't got all the bloody details worked out! Maybe he has to shower at the frickin' public *sento*. Maybe the toilets at work don't offer enough privacy. I'm just sayin' that maybe he's like these poor horny folks here, doing it in a cemetery. Maybe he's just acting on his animal instincts is all?"

"Yeah, I guess I feel sorry for him, too. But I like Louise's reaction also. It's like the ultimate rejection. Her response was as primal as his whacking off."

Tony paused before agreeing. "I hadn't thought about it that way, but maybe you're right."

I leapt through the philosophical window Tony had opened for me. "The problem is, in our society we can't act on our primal instincts when it hurts others. That's why we have culture. Otherwise we'd be killing each other."

"News for you, chum – we're already killing each other. Culture can't keep your primal instincts from taking over sometimes. You can't help feeling some things."

"But look at the Zen masters. It's Buddhism in your face again with some answers. They say that you can wade through it all – fear, hate, lust, and all that – and overcome it by just observing it there and not acting on it."

"That's maybe true for the monks, just like some people can run a hundred meters in under ten seconds, but most of us can't do that." I knew Tony admired and respected Buddhist teachings, but he was skeptical of how they could work wholesale, in the real world.

"Ah, the limits of the body and potential of the mind are two different things, Grasshopper." I gave him my softest kung-fu master whisper.

That stopped us both cold and started us laughing.

"It's all just pissin' in the wind. I guess we all just have to find our own way through this surreal world." Tony stood up and stretched his arms over his head. I did the same before we both hopped down and strolled back towards the bikes. We stopped again at the meditation room, looking about with new perspective.

"You know what the wise old monk said about meeting the Buddha on the road," I commented off-handedly, knowing Tony would take the bait.

"What nonsense are you going off about?"

"Kill him," I said. Tony gave me a 'fuck-off' sort of look and started to say it when I interrupted. "Meaning, there is no way to enlightenment outside of your own self, your own hard work and persistence. Following the Buddha as your savior will gain you nothing. So we should eliminate that distraction – the temptation to see the answers from outside of ourselves – and kill the Buddha if we ever see him taking up space on our superhighway." I'd taken to this saying the last week as a way of reminding me to do my own thing and not follow somebody else.

"You better lighten up on the Zen shit before you end up in the loony bin."

"Could be worse places."

Our whispers returned to normal voices as we headed back to the bikes. Taking a detour through a second, smaller cemetery, we unintentionally spooked another couple out of the shadows and sent them scurrying off. I don't know why they just didn't let us pass and then go on with their business. You'd think a couple of gaijin passing through wouldn't alter hormonal urges that much. We could only see their dark outlines and hushed voices against the wall three rows over from the path. If they had stayed quiet, we wouldn't have known they were there. Instead, they hurried off, bent over, arms full of blankets and whatnot, in the direction from where we'd come. Maybe they figured they would have more luck at the larger cemetery we'd just vacated.

Tony laughed. "*They're* the ones thinking this was a surreal night. Tomorrow they're going to say to their friends, "We just wanted to make out, but there were these crazy gaijin yelling in the cemetery."

"Serves 'em right. They should just park their cars by the Philosopher's Path next time."

❀❀❀❀❀ ❀❀❀❀❀ ❀❀❀❀❀ ❀❀❀❀❀ ❀❀❀❀❀

One of the luxuries I afforded myself in Japan was an every-other-day trip to the neighborhood *sento*. These public, segregated baths are common in Kyoto, since many of the older houses weren't built with bathing areas. Even the newer apartments might only have showers and this denies one the pleasure of the hot soak. The Japanese have made bathing an art form. An evening soak, I soon discovered, is one of the purist forms of pleasure available to an unaccompanied individual. To the Japanese, bathing is as much for spiritual and inner cleansing as for removing physical dirt and grime. As a matter of fact, one never enters a hot bath without first thoroughly cleaning the body outside the tub. This often confused and embarrassed the newly arrived gaijin, who view the bathtub as the place for soaping up. The poor fool who enters the common tub with soap and dirty feet might get away with a stern scolding in rapid Japanese. Or he might experience the ultimate humiliation when he realizes why other bathers had left the tub as soon as he entered, and waited for the staff to drain, clean, and refill it before they returned.

My guesthouse had adequate, shared shower facilities, but for less than three dollars I afforded myself a little slice of heaven three times a week. To me, the sento was a sensual paradise. I enjoyed walking down the street in the late evening with my small shower bucket filled with shampoo and soap and a tiny cotton towel. Obviously headed for a bath, I was a gaijin neighbor wanting to fit in, often treated to warm smiles, nods and grunts, or short greetings from the folks tinkering with their flowerpots or bicycles. "You are going to bathe? Ahhh, very good. Enjoy yourself. Thank you. Wonderful evening, isn't it?"

I learned the ritual from observing other bathers. Sit on the small plastic stools or on the floor in front of one of the dozen shower nozzles mounted three feet up the wall. Douse yourself with water from a bucket or from the showerhead. Soap up, rinse well. Once clean, choose one of the three main tubs, with water temperatures ranging from nice and warm to scalding. Slip in, place your tiny towel on your head, and enjoy.

Occasionally, when I felt adventuresome, I would try one of the smaller, less popular tubs – one had an herbal scent and color, "Good for healthy" I was told once by another bather. I've been told the greenish hues that show up every so often are radon baths. Why? I can't be sure, but why not? The Japanese are way ahead of the curve in the ablution arts, so I didn't question it too deeply. The other alternative therapy offered was the electric tub – full of low voltage juice – but I was way too smart to get into that one! My routine developed quickly: soak, cold plunge, sauna and repeat. By the end of three months, I could just manage five minutes in the scalding tub at the end of the circuit. All this for less than the price of a cup of coffee – the best deal in the country.

One evening, after I had been in the country almost a year, I was soaking in one of the small tubs, sento towel folded and perched atop my head, minding my own business. About a half dozen other guys were there, in different stages of cleaning and relaxing. In came a very old fellow, hunched over and weathered. I recognized from other visits. I had watched him with interest for weeks, wanting to know his story, trying to make eye contact. He had, on several previous occasions, answered my smiles and hellos with awkward grunts, the same way he interacted with just about everyone, so I didn't take it personally. He just performed his ritual, and after washing headed straight for the hottest tub, located in the middle of the room.

This particular evening I was in a tub next to the wall and as the old man circled the central tub he surprised me by stopping right in front of me and looking directly into my eyes. It was a piercing, intense stare, and I had no idea what he meant by it. Before I could even acknowledge the gesture, he stood straight upright, rigid, and tipped over backwards onto the tile floor. His head hit the tiles with a distinct thud and he was out cold, motionless and stiff like the dead. His bright red blood started to pool on the tiles underneath his head. Every head in the room turned towards the sound, but the rest of their bodies were frozen solid. The two guys washing up at the showers stopped mid-scrub. The two others soaking in tubs looked but their faces did not register any emotion whatsoever. I tried to make eye contact with one of my fellow bathers, thinking, *OK, I am the only gaijin in here and I don't know shit about how to handle this. Stay cool.* But their eyes were glued to the prostrate man's body, like they were seeing their own demise and were mesmerized by it.

After seconds that seemed like an eternity, I got up out of my tub and approached the splayed body. I wadded up my little towel and placed it under the man's head. Still, no one else moved. I motioned to a man near the door to go to the reception area to call an ambulance. I must have spoken in English, and I don't know if the man understood the words, but of course the meaning was clear. The only sound in the room was that of the showers streaming water onto the floor.

There I was, squatting, naked, next to a dying old Japanese man, in a room of other naked Japanese men who were all just staring at the two of us. It was utterly surreal, and time passed slowly. The man I'd sent out returned and joined me next to the old man. Just then the old man came to and tried to get up. He seemed confused and started to mumble and shiver a little bit. We tried to comfort him, holding his shoulders down and telling him to stay calm. The blood was thick on his head, shoulders, and the tiles.

Before long, we heard the ambulance siren outside. The paramedics came and took over, quickly getting the old man wrapped in blankets, onto a gurney and out the door. Then an old woman came in and silently cleaned up the blood. I returned to the tub and tried to soak out the accumulated tension. Just before I turned completely prunish and was ready to get out, I realized that the paramedics had taken my towel along with the old man. *Just as well*, I thought, *since it was covered with blood. But now I have nothing to cover up with as I walk to the dressing area. And I'll have to buy a new one.* I looked around for something to wrap around me and caught the eye of the man who had called for help. I patted my towel-less head and shrugged, intending to share the joke. He seemed to understand, went out to the front desk and returned with a brand new towel. He brought it to me, stammering,

"You are…. very…kind!"

"Arigato. You too." I smiled as appreciatively as I felt.

He was pleased with this exchange and so was I.

I walked, genitalia modestly covered, from the bath area to the dressing room and noticed the stares I was getting. *Only in Japan*, I thought. I wish I had a picture of that room full of naked Japanese men and one gaijin, frozen in place. I wondered about the old man, whether he'd hurt himself from the fall or maybe had a stroke or maybe was just dizzy. The look he gave me just before he fell led me to believe he knew something bad was happening or about to happen. I later asked the sento staff about it, but was unable to get any clear answers. I never saw him there again. The next week I was back, this time in the afternoon, and met a different clientele.

Occupying the bathing area were only three other fellows. Two of them were seated on the little stools in front of the showerheads on the left wall. I could just make out the wild tattoos around their torso area of colorful green and red images, but I couldn't see the detail. The third wore a pink ribbon around his head with an elaborate bow to the front. He was washing the backs of the other two with a loofa sponge and his body had a cherub softness to it, in stark contrast to the hardened muscles of the others. *Yakuza with a femio*, I recognized. The punch-permed hair, unusual in a land where almost all have it straight black, was the deciding clue, though the tattoos were a dead give-away, too.

I'd never encountered the yakuza before so close. Literature and folklore refer to them as a sort of mafia and that may be true, but I associated them as more akin to a Rotary Club with an attitude. They stepped in and got things done where the local bureaucracy couldn't. Many of the Japanese seem to accept and even appreciate their presence. The yakuza apparently controlled neighborhood discipline, such as which street vendor got to set up where, disposal of eyesores, and supposedly prostitution and the distribution of drugs. The femio was a man-girl, accepted by the toughs for the contrast and service, I suppose. Not all femios are Yakuza, mind you. Tony had pointed out the phenomenon to me my first week in the country, when I was fascinated by a waiter wearing heavy makeup, earrings and a tight skirt.

The three noted my entry without apparent interest and I sat along the wall on the opposite side. After cleaning up, I settled into the medium-heat tub. The femio was cleaning himself at the shower since he had just finished washing his "friends". The smaller of the two tattooed blokes came over and dipped into the tub across from me. He had noticed my glances at his tattoos and stood up in the tub. A short tile wall separated the two tubs and I leaned onto it in interest.

"You like eh?" He smiled and stood up fully, opening his arms and turning like a runway model. A red and blue dragon wound around the man's abdomen, the head breathing orange fire over his chest and the tail wrapping around his back and ending

239

in a dagger of a point near his navel. It was spectacular. The rest of his torso canvas was crowded with other designs – trees, bamboo, a sword, and other symbols I didn't recognize or understand. I wanted to look more closely, but didn't want to be rude. "It's beautiful."

"You are the gaijin who save the grandpa here last week."

"Well, I didn't *save* him, but I was here." I shouldn't have been surprised that he spoke English, given my newly chosen profession, but the words did startle me.

He looked at me seriously. "Good thing. Brave man." I didn't know if he meant the old man or me. Was this man really the old man's grandson? He reached over and shook my hand heartily. Then he burst out laughing before settling back into his bath.

"Do you know what happened to the old man?" I ventured.

"Oh. He is OK. Almost dead before fall." He laughed again. Normally this would have unnerved me, but after a few months in Japan, I had learned to accept the incongruous.

"You speak English very well." I wanted to hear more from this guy.

"I live in San Francisco three years." He held up three fingers. I was expecting to see a truncated pinky, the sign of a harsh yakuza disciplining, but was disappointed. "I was chef at a Japanese restaurant. I was no good. Bad chef. They send me back." His laugh really roared this time, attracting a glance from the other tattooed man, who said something to him that I couldn't understand. My new friend replied in equally unintelligible tones – it sounded to me like the deep, gravelly samurai dialect you hear in an old black and white Kurosawa movie.

"I lived in San Francisco for a few years before coming to Japan." I said once he turned back to face me.

He liked this immensely. He reached over to shake my hand again. "Nishimura desu."

"Nishimura-san, *hajimemashite*. Renny Diaz desu." This generated another hearty laugh, but I knew he was not laughing at me – he liked my Japanese greeting, unfazed by my poor pronunciation.

He pointed to my eyes. "You are some Japanese maybe?"

"A little Chinese maybe, and Mexican."

"American! Ah, yes. So mix up. Many people, all mix up. Good good. Japan people same, all same." He was pleased with himself for knowing this and settled deeper into the water with a long sigh.

With that, the dragon-covered Nishimura-san tuned me out, so I focused my attention across the room, where an equally bizarre scene was taking place. The femio had donned a shear pink robe with a white feather collar. He was also wearing clear pink plastic slippers that were way too small for his feet. He trotted over in a pigeon-toed gait to the second tattooed man, who had just exited the bath and was standing near the entrance to the locker room. The femio proceeded to dry the man with a small sento towel and then brush his hair. It was a comically sweet sight, with the pink robe fluttering about and the boa feathered femio first reaching up to comb the stoic head of his master, then sitting him down on a stool to complete the job. The yakuza now and then grunted instructions to the femio, who answered in a demure cooing tone, fretting like a mother before sending her son off to school.

Nishimura had been listening, perhaps observing with his eyes closed, and abruptly arose. He strode over to the electric tub in the corner and looked over at me. "You like *denki?*" I recognized the word for electricity and I shook my head in an emphatic "no." He wasn't going to get me zapped in the electric tub!

"Come come. You try. Good for muscle."

Reluctantly, I got out of my tub and padded over. He had already stepped in and beckoned me to join him. I looked down into the tub, expecting to see the water vibrating. Tony had explained that small electrodes send a current through the water and it felt like a thousand tiny creatures stinging you. The tub was only two feet deep, but the yellow and red lightening bolt warning sign above the water had always scared me off. I knew I would end up hopping a lively polka as soon as my foot touched bottom and I was torn between the fun of bucking conventional wisdom and the potential stupidity of taking a toaster into the bath with me.

I hesitated, and he grunted *"Gambate"* by which he could have meant "congratulations", "good luck", or literally, "do your best". Not to be embarrassed as a sissy in front of this Mafioso, I stepped in. The first sensation, a soda pop tingling, was not altogether unpleasant. I went to sit on the edge of the tub and noticed that the closer I moved towards one side, the stronger the sensation got. I was careful to keep the family jewels out of the tonic water, and experimented with dipping my hand in first. To my surprise it spasmed with the electric current. Once I got over the initial shock (pardon the pun), it did feel oddly relaxing. I dipped my whole arm in but was only able to keep it under a few seconds. Nishimura showed his pleasure at my persistence with a toothy smile.

"You show good spirit. You make good warrior!" He nodded and then grunted, like a soldier. His friend echoed the grunt from his perch near the door. The femio said nothing, fully occupied in powdering the man's back. Nishimura submerged his body to the neck. We stayed in the tub for only a few minutes before I knew that I'd heated up enough for the day and had to go. Nishimura got out with me.

In the dressing room, he bought a large bottle of beer from the vending machine and took two glasses from the water cooler. He poured a glass for each of us. We toasted with a whispered *kampai* and drank in silence. I wasn't sure how smart it was to drink beer after an hour in a hot tub, but I couldn't turn it down. Nishimura traded jokes with the old lady at the reception counter. She was there about half the time I came through, so I figured she knew my face, if not the rest of me. Now she pointed at me and broke into modest chuckling. Nishimura translated.

"She say you always welcome. She say you have good body for gaijin." He slapped me on the back and we both laughed at that one.

"You can do better maybe, eh?!" Nishimura nodded towards the old woman. "Want young Japanese girl? I set you up with real nice!" He held his forearm out in front of his groin, imitating a hard on. "Strong!" What could I do but smile?

"I have a girlfriend already" I lied., "but thank you - arigato."

He grunted and nodded his head.

I never saw them at the sento on my subsequent visits. I considered that afternoon to be one of the highlights of my time in the country. Whenever the stress of the unexpected starts to fry my nerves, I still think of the tattooed Nishimura and the femio with his robe and slippers and the gravity of the moment fades to pink.

12

CHARLIE

SEATTLE	TOKYO	THAILAND	LONDON	THE PHILIPPINES	INDIA
YEAR 1		YEAR 2			YEAR 3

INSIDE OUTSIDE

She can't make out the entire letter, but knows from what little kanji she can read that it has something to do with healthcare and that it is official. Charlie shows the letter to Shoko, whose English nickname is Sandy in deference to that Japanese penchant to acquire a new name for new endeavors. Sandy is the office manager and the one who does everything, as far as any of the teachers can tell. She is happy to help with translations, but takes on a serious look as she reads Charlie's letter.

"It is from the tax department. They need to have a copy of your health insurance policy."

Charlie opted out of "mandatory" Japanese premiums for the national health insurance, knowing it was very expensive and that she was not likely to ever need it. Foreigners are allowed to do this (but Japanese nationals are not) as long as they have health insurance coverage from elsewhere. Charlie, like many foreign workers, said she did, which was the truth at the time. When she left Seattle, she declined the option to extend the health plan from her former employer. It would have cost about three hundred and fifty a month and, given her travel budget, had been out of the question. Three hundred dollars could be a month on the beach in Thailand!

Besides, not having insurance gives Charlie an odd thrill – both fear and excitement. Sure, she had been scared of disaster striking – a broken arm in England, dysentery in India, malaria in Thailand... but the excitement of being a sort of rebel against convention is a stronger emotion. That, and the fact that the cost of healthcare in the developing world is reasonable, though in Japan it is not. Her parents were outspokenly critical of her decision, a rare thing for them, but she had been firm.

Her rationalization: *Everyone assumes that health insurance is a necessity, but it's really a form of modern slavery. People will stay at a job they hate just because "the benefits" – primarily health insurance – are good. Never mind that most people never use the insurance to the degree they pay for. That doesn't seem to matter – it is the security of having insurance that is important. And what the hell, I'm young!*

Eric Diaz had been very concerned about this. He and Helena had lived their entire lives as upright and responsible adults. They bought Charlie a six-month travel insurance plan as a gift. This ran out about six months ago and since it wasn't renewable for someone "living overseas" she had been without insurance ever since.

"I thought they just took your word on that?" Charlie tries to negotiate with Sandy, misguided and fruitless though it may be. Sandy has nothing to do with it. She shrugs her shoulders in reply.

Charlie thanks Sandy for the info and takes the letter back. She needs to give the situation some thought.

What are they going to do, deport me? Sandy would never do that, but the school director, Okuda-sensei – I wouldn't put it past him. "Officials" in Japan are such sticklers for rules. But, I do have my visa and it's good for another three months. It might become a problem when I have to renew it, but I'll deal with that when the time comes. She files the letter away and forgets about it for the time being.

Charlie prepares to receive her first group of visitors next week. Marie is flying up from Miyazaki for a conference and Renny is coming by Shinkansen from Kyoto with a friend to see the sights in Tokyo. Their visits will overlap for two days and Charlie is looking forward to introducing Marie to her brother. Renny and his friend Tony will crash at her place, but Marie will stay at a hotel near the Imperial Palace, compliments of her company. Still, there should be plenty of time to get everyone together, and she enjoys having a distraction from work. Renny did come through in a flash on his entry into the country five months ago and now wanted to take some time and "get the feel" of Tokyo. Charlie is hard pressed to decide what will best give the "feel" of the city and settles upon planning to just walk around the markets and through the main neighborhoods.

She takes the subway to Ueno station to meet the two coming up from Kyoto, buying a platform ticket so she can go in to meet the train. Almost half a year has passed since she's seen Renny and, though they had spoken and written during the interim, she is excited and even relieved to see him again. She misses being in the presence of someone to whom you need to give no explanations and from whom there is no hiding.

Tony stands back while the pair reunite, then gives her a warm handshake and smile. Charlie feels immediately at ease with him, feeling like she knows him already through Renny. She grasps his outstretched hand with both of hers and he blushes just slightly and she also looks away and smiles in her own wave of confused, pleasant feelings. They head to a café to chat because none of them want to settle in just yet. It had only been a mere three-hour train ride, after all. Tony banters with the twins for fifteen minutes and then asks for train directions and a phone number so he can run some errand and find his way back to Charlie's later.

"You two have a lot of catching up to do." Tony winks as he generously leaves the siblings alone to talk.

Charlie and Renny decide to walk most of the way back to her apartment, catching the subway for a short distance and getting off two stops earlier than normal to stroll the rest. On the way, Renny relays his sento story of the old man teetering over and whacking his head, to Charlie's fascination and horror. While marveling at the strangeness of it, another part of her inner self is wondering, *what would I have done? Here Renny doesn't want to get involved in these things and ends up having to and here I am*

246

inclined to insert myself into any cultural situation, like with the crying woman in the park, but I can't seem to be able to do it right. What does that mean? It jars her momentarily and she sluices it away by telling Renny about the insurance letter.

"So how come Mom and Dad bought you travel insurance and not me?"

"I don't know. Maybe they thought you were the more responsible of us and so of course you would buy it yourself."

"Or maybe they just love you best." He is kidding, but his words have a sarcastic bite.

She takes it more seriously.

"C'mon, you know that's not true." She knows there is some kernel of truth to it, though. She was always the "good girl" and Renny her foil. In comparison, her grades, friends, and choices always seemed, in the eyes of their parents, more responsible and upstanding. That she was treated preferentially looked obvious, now. She hasn't thought much about this as a possibility, and doesn't want to cater to it. But Renny doesn't let go of it easily.

"Well, it sort of *is* true, but it's not a big deal. Because you got better grades, you got the Jeep and I got the beat up old VW Thing."

"Which you loved. About the insurance, I..." Charlie interjects.

Renny smiles and interrupts. "I never brought it up with them, so they probably didn't think about it either." Renny has the gift of being able to move on from discussing a heavy topic and wait for a better time. He leaves his ego at the end of a long leash, and she loves him for it. She doesn't dare bring up the five hundred bucks Dad had slipped her at the airport.

"Part of that is bullshit, really. Dad thinks of you as a strong, capable man and me as a vulnerable little girl out in the wild world. He sees that you're independent, but still wants to take care of me."

"Naw, he doesn't really trust me and the decisions I make. He always wanted me to be more focused, more stable, like you.

Maybe that's why I wasn't. One reason for it, anyway. I don't think I could handle doing things the way Dad did."

"I was just a goody two shoes, obedient daughter. And give me a break – you focused well enough."

Now he means to drop the subject for sure. Shrugging, Renny says, "I've got an angle on how to fix up the healthcare thing with the tax people. Show me the letter for the travel insurance."

She retrieves the paper from her day bag and they look it over.

"See, all we have to do is change the dates on this thing and you can provide them a copy. They don't need to see the original." He smiles his sly smile.

"I don't know, Ren." Charlie isn't so readily able to delve into the underworld of forgery, as evidenced by her deeply furrowed brow and jaw clenched in contemplation. "What if I get caught?"

"C'mon Miss Goody Two Shoes, they won't even question it. You're just getting audited, like by the IRS, and they just need a piece of paper. They don't really care if you have the insurance or not. You're just some lowly gaijin after all."

"How would we change it?" Charlie reluctantly ventures forward.

"White out and a typewriter."

"Are you sure this will work?"

"Of course, I've done this kind of thing before." A conspiratorial look comes into his eyes and he emits a low "heh heh heh." She looks at him dubiously, asking "Like what?" with her eyes.

"I forged the AAA stamp on my international driver's license with a bar of soap, so I could drive a motorcycle. Nobody has asked to see it, but check for yourself." He pulls the small booklet from his pack and shows her. She can't discern the difference from the other stamps. He is pleased.

"I have many hidden talents, fraulein," he winks in his best Colonel Klink imitation.

Tony arrives at the apartment to find Renny and Charlie sitting on the front hunched over the letter.

"A couple of tittering little field mice we have here."

"Okay. I think there's an old manual at work. I'll see if I can borrow it." She ignores Tony's comment and looks squarely at Renny. "I guess you want to take care of me too, huh?" He smiles.

"It goes both ways, sis. I guess I still owe you for covering for Greg and I in the garage that day."

"Naw, I think you've paid that balance off over time." She starts to smile at the memory, and he can't resist retelling the tale, part for Tony's sake and mostly for his own satisfaction in verbalizing a fond memory.

"God that was funny. Greg and I were hanging out in the back shed this one afternoon, practicing our toking techniques, as always. Then all of a sudden I hear you yelling at Dad to help you fix the car door or something stupid. Then I hear Dad answering from just outside the door! Man, we almost shit out pants. You got him to turn back to the house but we had to think fast because we knew we couldn't just walk out of the shed. So we grabbed rakes and strode out like we knew what we were doing."

"Yeah, and you should have seen the smoke billowing out behind you. You're SO lucky that Dad didn't notice, or at least he didn't let on." Charlie relaxes back against the wall, as if they had just gotten away with it again.

"He asked us what we were doing with the rakes and we had to say that Mom wanted us to clean up the vegetable garden." Renny nods his head at their successful deceit.

"It's a dangerous game to play one parent off the other. It seemed to work that time, though. Mom never said anything about it. Neither did Dad. But *you* held it over my head for years!"

"Yep, I got a lot of good paybacks for that afternoon. I guess Miss Goody Two Shoes was on vacation that day." Charlie smirks with self-satisfaction.

Tony sits quietly among them, listening with interest through the freely associated recall of the two. He sips on a beer he brought with him, drinking straight from the one liter bottle. "What's the worst thing you ever did in high school?" Renny asks him.

"We're good boys in Britain," Tony counters, "Never do anything untoward or mischievous. I was a good lad." He passes the bottle to Renny.

"C'mon, you're disappointing me." Charlie baits him, smiling as she takes the bottle from Renny and knocks back a deep draw.

"Well, we snuck into Stonehenge one night. My family was living not too far off and a few mates and I drove over and snuck into the grounds after they closed. I was fourteen then. We hopped a fence and crouched through the fields trying to play Mission Impossible, but we didn't do anything much once we got there. Played like Druids making a sacrifice of a pint or two, but that was it."

"Did the Druids actually do sacrifices?" Charlie has always wondered about that.

"Fuck if I know. Didn't see any evidence of that on this particular night."

"Fair enough. What else? You must have done *some* naughty stuff." Renny seems reluctant to believe Tony is so squeaky clean. "If you're not as experienced with criminal activity as we are, the least you can do is make up something good."

"I don't think I was as delinquent as the two of you appear to have been." Tony takes on an admonishing tone to match the frown on his face.

"Well, Renny broke some rules, maybe. But I was basically a good and proper girl." Charlie flutters her lashes and purses her lips.

"Pleased to hear it madam." He bows his head low and takes her hand to give it a shake. *He is quite a charmer*, she muses.

"Mademoiselle, if you please."

"Please forgive me." He bows again.

"Jesus Christ!" Renny breaks up the moment. "And I'll have you know I was not a juvenile delinquent. I just experimented with what was there. Blame it on the whims of adolescence," the last bit accented a la Terry Gilliam.

That gets a good round of harrumphs from the other two.

"So you haven't yet evolved into maturity then?" Tony mocks.

"That's why he needs to see me more often. A prim and proper sister's advice can keep him on the right path."

"And just where would that path lead if I did follow your lead?"

"Obviously, you will never know." Charlie feigns disappointment in the voice of Maggie Smith and Tony shakes his head in mock disgust.

"Can I puke now? Or should I wait for y'all to kiss first?"

❧❧❧❧❧   ❧❧❧❧❧   ❧❧❧❧❧   ❧❧❧❧❧   ❧❧❧❧❧

The next day while Charlie works, Renny and Tony explore Harajuku, hoping to see the line-up of rockers, but it being a weekday, there is only a tenth of the weekend throng. It is still fascinating but they soon move along to the nearby temple grounds. Charlie meets them in the late afternoon near the Imperial Palace and together they rendezvous with Marie at her hotel. She was to have arrived around noon and by now would be eager to get out on the town. Charlie expertly guides the men through back alleys and down side streets to the New Hachiyama Hotel, a drab ten-story businessman's accommodation of concrete and mirrored glass.

Charlie phones from the lobby and Marie comes scurrying down in a minute, indeed itching to wander out in the big city.

"If you guys don't get me outta here quick, I'll get sucked back into going out with 'the colleagues'." This is the introduction. She looks around in a comically criminal fashion and then practically pulls Charlie outside in a getaway with the others hastily following. As they walk down the block, Marie gives Charlie a joyous hug and lets out a whoop. "You must be

Renny," she says, offering a hand. He takes it and Tony follows, introducing himself.

"Glad we could abet the escape," he says.

Marie smiles appreciatively and explains to the other two, "I really don't mind the people I work with, but Christ, I have to spend all of the next two days with them." She blows out a long, forced sigh and squeezes Charlie with an arm around her shoulders.

"Tokyo seems like a breath of fresh air, culturally, compared to Miyazaki," Marie continues, in rare form.

"Funny how that goes. I'd bet many people living here would love to escape it for the less bustling pace on Kyushu," Tony comments.

"That's probably true. The grass IS always greener. I hate to hear myself say this, but it's awful nice to see new gaijin faces about. Miyazaki can get lonely that way. I must know every gaijin in town by now. Not that I mind the small town vibe, since that's why I left here in the first place. But I do like coming back to the energy here." She skips out ahead of the group and does a slow pirouette, looking up at the surrounding city with fresh wonder and infecting her companions with her enthusiasm.

They choose an Indian restaurant Charlie had read about in a monthly gaijin magazine. Nobody is offended that they don't go for Japanese food – and afterwards, they wander off to a cozy little bar in Shibuya for a nightcap. The place is decorated in rustic log cabin style on the inside, with huge split horizontal timbers lining the walls. There are several long, low tables shared by several groups at once – family-style drinking. They remove their shoes and step down into the cut-out flooring beneath the tables to sit at knee-level benches. The walls and ceiling are completely covered with photos, postcards, posters, poetry and various other scribblings donated by its patrons over the years. This is Bar U, a favorite haunt of the local expats.

They share the end of a long table with a group of Japanese college students, nodding hellos and ignoring their giggles. Charlie orders four large Sapporos and some mushroom snacks and edamame, and they make themselves comfortable. Tony soon becomes absorbed with the various writings and drawings on the walls.

"Here's one I like; 'Ignorance is knowledge. Peace is hate. Love is death.' Sounds right up your line, Diaz. The wayward one, that is," he says, pointing at Renny but smiling at Charlie.

"Sounds like the author had a bad evening to me," Charlie replies.

"I don't know about that," Renny pipes up. "He sounds pretty bright to me. The opposite of a thing often defines the thing itself. Take the ignorance part there. You don't really know anything until you know what it is you don't know."

"Hmm...that's a lack of awareness maybe, but not ignorance," Charlie rebuts.

"You're being too literal about it," he retorts.

Marie jumps in. "What they needed to add to the end of that set of lines there is that it's all bullshit. Ignorance, knowledge, peace, hate and love and death. Got a pen?"

Charlie fishes one out and Marie proceeds to write her amendment underneath the lines.

"Such a cynic we have here," comments Tony. "I'll go along with it, on one level, but you can't live that way all the time."

"What way, exactly?" Marie inquires.

"Thinking everything is bullshit."

"What makes you think not?" Marie challenges him with a squinty look. Tony flinches slightly and then smiles.

"Then you might as well kill yourself. Give up. What's the point if everything is just bullshit?"

"The point is only to see it for what it is, and live without the delusion that it's something more than what it is."

"That sounds like Renny's Zen bullshit." Tony baits Renny now.

"As long as you're calling it what it is." Marie raises her glass and smiles triumphantly.

"I think some things are bullshit, but not everything," offers Charlie. Marie puts her arm around Charlie's shoulder and frowns and nods.

"Case in point – here's my idealist, middle-of-the-road, girlfriend. She lives life like Mary Tyler Moore. Everything has gotta be okay in the end." She is merciless in her sisterly chiding. Charlie gives her a feeble punch in the arm and blushes at the truth in Marie's assessment.

"She's always been like this you know," Renny adds, as if speaking of a naughty child. "It's a good thing you had me around to balance you out." He gives her a patronizing look.

"And what did she balance out in you? Your stupidity?" Tony comes to her rescue.

"Don't change the subject now!? It's just getting interesting. C'mon Charlene, what really sticks in your craw?" Marie challenges.

"Nobody calls me Charlene except my late Grandma Maxi. But in the interest of keeping the evening entertaining, I'll overlook your little indiscretion. Besides, nothing really sticks in my craw. What's a craw anyway?"

"Not a clue," says Tony.

"Tell us something you think is bullshit," prods Marie.

"How come you get to ask all the questions now?"

"It's good to put the shoe on the other foot now and then." Renny, her twin brother of 28 years, looks at Charlie with sincere curiosity.

"Bullshit is having to put up with the Japanese government wanting to see my health insurance verification. What a pain in the ass." She pauses to sip her beer then turns to Renny. "We can use the typewriter at work, by the way." He nods and Charlie briefs the others on their scheme.

"You know what else is bullshit?" Charlie is now wanting to vent. "All this brave-new-world crap of passwords and email names and credit cards and insurance. Who the hell cares about any of that? I don't want any of it, but I have to deal with it because if I don't then I can't be here. So there, is that what you wanted?"

Everyone is silent, lightly stunned and amused by the passion of her words. Then Charlie breaks out in a smile and the others join in. "So, like I said, some things are bullshit and others aren't."

"I think we could use another round here," Tony says as he waves to the bartender across the room, holding up his bottle and four fingers.

"But you want to be here, so you're willing to put up with the B.S. – play the game – in order to get what you want," Renny prompts her..

"Maybe. I don't really know what I want."

"You want to minimize the bullshit," says Marie, authoritatively.

"But you just said that everything is bullshit, so how can you minimize that?" Tony pretends to be confused.

"Just because of that. If you see everything that way, as meaningless, as bullshit, as a game, then that's half the battle. You don't make it bigger or more important than it really is."

"Kill the Buddha," Renny says.

"Christ, not that bullshit again." Tony rolls his eyes.

"Exactly." Marie raises her glass to Renny and they toast the point.

"So what's *not* B.S. then?" Tony asks, glancing pointedly at Charlie.

"Being here with you guys. Listening to a nice piece of music. Walking in the park. You know, stuff like that." Charlie's voice softens a bit.

"Now I know we are *all* full of it – me included – so I'm proven right yet again." Marie blows on her fingertips and polishes them on her shirtsleeve.

They drink until late in the evening. When the alcohol and the cigarette smoke become too much, they walk Marie back to her hotel and arrange to hook up again the following evening. Back at her apartment, Charlie sets Renny and Tony up with futons, pillows and blankets. She puts their futons near the kitchenette, leaving her sleeping space intact across the room.

"I picked these up on one of the big garbage nights. Don't worry, they've been cleaned and you'll be quite comfy on them. Just keep the snoring and farting to a minimum." Charlie gives an admonishing look towards Renny and tries to carry it over to Tony, but finds herself embarrassed to hold his glance. "Okay then," she continues, "See you in the morning." She kisses Renny on the cheek and Tony leans over for one as well and she, only in fake reluctance, obliges.

She lays awake for some time, listening to the rhythmic breathing of the two men just across the room. As she finally lapses into sleep, the bullshit conversation seed sprouts into her dreams.

I am walking around some big, ancient city. I don't know what city this is and it doesn't matter. I'm running some errands, going to the bank, buying groceries. As I am doing these things, I begin to notice that it's my body doing the transactions, but it's not really me. It's like I'm watching a television screen through my eyes – those are my hands, my arms, and my legs performing the actions, but my mind, my self is disconnected from my body. Then my arms and legs start to stretch far away in front of me, getting smaller and smaller. But I can't be sure if they're stretching out or if I'm receding into some far away place?

Now I'm in a room, sitting in a comfortable recliner. My limbs are grossly swollen – arms puffy and pink, legs bulging and the skin tight around my thighs. But I am still inside my head, watching as if it's a video in a letterbox format. I try to feel sensations through my fingers, but it's all distorted and all I can feel is a numbing buzz. But this doesn't alarm me at all. I begin to focus on the buzzing sensation and soon I can feel it all throughout my body. I feel giddy and punch-drunk.

I start to focus in on my foot, which is the size of a watermelon and throbbing like a vibrator. I play with it in my mind, trying to make it bigger, then smaller. I can't tell if it is working. I look up to see myself transported, in the comfy chair, deformed with swollen limbs, onto the canvas of an oil painting. My body is in the painting itself, but I can see it like it's hanging in a museum. There are other figures around me – people I don't know – with the same deformed and disproportioned features. But they are not grotesque. There's a cow in a field, and its four legs are all pointed upwards. It's next to a flowering tree with white blossoms the size of basketballs. I stare at myself in the painting for some time, observing the images and feeling the sensations in my body. For a moment I believe I am fully awake, or just on the edge of it, but then I realize that only in this dream place can I see things like this. I begin to back up, watching my image fade. Black space fills my eye's frame until the images shrink to a pinpoint and then vanish.

She awakes with a gasp, curiously wide-awake. The dream images are still vivid, but the queer feeling is gone, except for the clear memory of it. It is still dark outside the window, and as she looks around the room she sees the silhouette of Tony sitting up. He gets up and goes to the kitchen, returning with a glass of water. He sits beside Charlie.

"I heard you gasp in your sleep, and…"

"Sorry about that. I must've been having a bad dream." She reaches over for his glass and sips, slightly embarrassed.

"No. I was awake. It's always hard for me to sleep in a new place."

He reaches over and brushes a stray hair from her cheek.

"I'm feeling a little restless," he says. "Would you like to go for a walk?"

She looks over at Renny, observing his chest rising and falling in deep sleep. The clock reads three fifteen. Charlie nods and slips back the covers. She throws a sweater over her pajamas, and Tony pulls his jacket on over his sweats. They step quietly into their sandals and out into the spring night.

They walk in silence along the deserted street, their footfalls echoing off the concrete facades. Charlie steers him towards the small neighborhood park. Once there, they skirt around a couple of sleeping figures lying near the path and sit on a pair of swings. The sky is partly clear, with dull twinkles peeping through the city haze. The air feels clean and comfortably cool.

"What goes through your mind when you can't sleep?" she asks him.

He shrugs. "I don't know. This and that, the usual nonsense." He smiles when she chuckles and goes on. "Tonight I was thinking about how I'd been such a good boy, growing up. Like you." He gives her a gentle glance. "I wish I'd been more naughty. Like your brother."

"Doing what, for instance?"

"Like playing more pranks or being more..." He stops.

"More what?" She is curious and tries to coax him out.

"I was going to say 'more aggressive with the girls', but...aw, I don't know." He laughs. "What about you, what were you dreaming about that you woke up with a gasp?"

She looks away, not sure how much she can remember and how much she is willing to share with this attractive friend of Renny's. The creaks of the swing chains make a strange, sad music in the still night air.

"I was dreaming about..." she finds it hard to describe in words, "It was like I was falling, only *up*, in the opposite direction, and then suddenly I noticed something that scared me. It was....." Her voice trails off as she knits her brow, trying to remember. Tony waits, saying nothing. One of the sleeping figures on the ground on the other side of the park turns over noisily, grunts, and then settles back down. Charlie continues.

"I was dreaming that I was looking at myself through a kind of window. You see, I've seen this window before in my dreams, but I've never wanted to look through it because....because I thought it …. frightening." She fumbles for the words. She has never revealed her dreams before, let alone to a perfect stranger. She has only known this guy for a day.

"What did you see? If you don't mind my asking." He is genuinely curious.

"I'm not really sure. I was looking at myself from a different point of view, but I don't know what it means. I can't remember much more. Let's get back to your insomnia. What do you mean – you should have gotten into more trouble as a kid?"

He pauses a moment, collecting his thoughts, then says, "I was so proper growing up. My parents were good, upstanding royal subjects and I was taught to follow along, you know. Be a good lad, eat your peas, do your homework, play football, ...soccer. But I think a lot of that was,…well….bullshit. Not to beat the dead horse. I don't mean I should have been a rebel against the establishment, like the Sid Vicious or something. I'm talking about more subtle rebellion, like bad manners when called for or not going straight to college. Don't get me wrong, I'm glad I went to university and all, but…Christ, I sound like an idiot! Sorry." He looks away, embarrassed and amused at his honesty with this new friend.

Charlie laughs in sympathy. "No. Don't stop." She reaches over and squeezes his hand where it gripped the swing chain. His fingers tighten up and then relax, but Charlie doesn't let go. "C'mon, keep going."

He exhales deeply. "I'm just trying to figure it all out, really. Some of the things that I always accepted as the way life's supposed to be don't seem that way anymore. That's good I think. It's good to see things for how they are, whether or not you think it's all bullshit, like Marie does. I know we were kidding around a bit tonight, but there was some real wisdom there. Somewhere." She lets her hand slide from his and starts to swing back and forth.

"I think all that partly triggered my dream, too. In the dream, I saw that what I *think* I am is not necessarily how others see me. I don't know why that matters either, but it does." She starts swinging harder, pumping her legs underneath her, and Tony joins in. They are too big for the swingset but it holds as they swung hard and fast for a good ten minutes. At one point, the sleeping figures both sit up and yell something at them, the signal to stop swinging and pipe down. They let the swings slow of their own accord, feeling like two kids who've being scolded to act their age. They walk back to the flat in silence as the city begins to wake up around them. Renny is still fast asleep when they come in, but they are too wired to sleep anymore. Charlie quietly makes a pot of tea and they go back outside to sit on the front step and silently watch the day break.

Renny wakes up around six, unusually early for him, and can immediately see in the small room that his sister and his friend are gone. It takes him a full minute to open the front door and see them there. He blows out a long sigh, half to clear the cobwebs and the other in admonition. "Turning into old folks," he mutters, sitting beside them.

They head out for an early morning breakfast at a little greasy spoon a short walk from Charlie's apartment. One of Tokyo's great features is the magical presence of just about every kind of restaurant imaginable – often in the most surprising places. This little restaurant, The Little Easy, actually serves an American breakfast – eggs, bacon and hash brown potatoes, on formica countertops and in tiny padded diner booths. It is located in the basement of an older brick building, below an ink-stamp maker, in a little alley that never sees the light of day, let alone the traffic of tourists.

"You guys need to work on the no sleep thing. It's not good for you." Renny warns them, even though he has more of a bleary eyed look than they do. "It's not good for me either."

"You were up yourself at six, my boy," notes Tony.

"Yeah, but I wouldn't have *stayed* up."

"Grumble, grumble, grumble. You're as bad as the guys sleeping in the park." Tony turns and gives Charlie a wink.

That day the three of them tour the Imperial Palace – not just the park grounds, which they had seen yesterday. And then they walk the streets of the city for hours. Afterwards, the boys return to Charlie's to take a nap while she goes off to work. She meets up with Marie at her hotel after that.

Marie is still in good spirits. Her conference is one where she can go on autopilot and she, in spite of herself, enjoys chitchatting with co-workers. Charlie is wired from too little sleep and too much on her mind. The presence of family and friends keeps her revved up and she just goes with it. They decide to walk and chat.

"Whatever happened with the idea of heading back to New Zealand?"

"Oh it's still the plan. I just haven't pinned it down yet."

"Are you becoming one of 'the jaded'?" Charlie chides.

"Jesus, I hope not. I told myself I'd never stay so long that I became...blasé, but then most of the jaded say that, don't they?"

"I suppose that's a way to look at it." Charlie purses her lips in thought and then adds, "We all swear to never go there, but..."

"I saw myself in a different mirror this morning that only brings it all too close to home." Marie slows her walk and looks over at Charlie with raised eyebrow. "You sure you want to hear this now?" Charlie nods enthusiastically, tuning out the signs of spring and becoming all ears and eyes tuned to Marie.

"Okay. There is this guy I worked with here in Tokyo a couple of years ago, lets call him Bob. I see him now only at these sorts of get-togethers and, well, this year I noticed the metamorphosis. I mean, okay, the money is easy and we're free, sort of, but why drop into this hate mode? Christ it scares me because I know I've got much more steam to blow off than Bob and he's been here only a year longer than me and he wasn't half bad to have a drink with way back when!" Marie blows out a "whoosh" and then smiles to the sky and jostles Charlie with her shoulder. "I swear right now that I want you to shoot me down, you American with a gun, if I ever become one of the living dead."

"Not much chance of that," Charlie says.

"I wish that were true. Fuck me. At least I haven't jumped into bed with every little Japanese boy that came my way. Though, that's not a bad idea when I think about it. When I see Bob and his whiny tone I think, there's no way I'm that far gone. But I do find myself ranting about stupid little things like how can the trains be so damn punctual? And what is it with the cutesy and high pitched giggle that makes me want to strangle the next office lady I see? Do you see it now? I am becoming one of them." Marie stops in her tracks, clutching her head in thespian despair. Charlie halts alongside and laughs, copying her gesture.

"Ohhhh noooo, it's true. I've lost you to the dark side," she says theatrically.

They continue to walk. "I shouldn't be joking about this, really," Marie continues. "I noticed the other day that I am starting to sound Japanese. Another telltale sign. I've caught myself saying things like, Japanese hate war, or, it's very violent in America. Christ! How long have I been using such generalized tripe? Do I want to belong here that badly? Hell no! So tell me now, have I gone over the edge yet? Is it so obvious to everyone else and I just can't see it?"

"No, you're not one of the jaded – *yet*. You've been a bitch since the first day we met, so we can't say that Japan has changed you into a cynic."

"Not bad Charlene." She nods approvingly at Charlie's barb. "So, I can't figure your brother out. Is he more or less like you?"

"Yes, he's more or less like me." Charlie smiles. "He's a good guy. He's a little freer than I am, but also more insecure."

"How can he be both?"

"I don't know, but he is. He's flippant to an extreme sometimes, but underneath that brash exterior, he's aware and watching and he cares what people think and say. I can read him because I'm the same, only in the opposite."

"Well that's easy to understand!" She laughs as Charlie shrugs and continues.

"When you're a twin, people always ask you what it's like. It's strange really, because how would I know what it's like *not* to be a twin? What have I got to compare it with? It's like asking, 'What's it like to be you?' Granted, there is something about sharing the same birth-space that creates a unique bond. We are connected, that's for sure. Maybe not as much as identical twins are, but again, how can I say? I only know what I am. What we are."

"I'll bet it's cool not to have been born alone. You've already kicked part of the 'born alone, live alone, die alone' mentality the rest of us have going."

"I don't know about that. I can sure still feel lonely. Back to the *point*, what's keeping you from pinning down New Zealand?"

Marie doesn't answer right away, instead pursed her lips in thought. "It's whether or not going to New Zealand is what I *should* do. I'm thinking about going to London also. There are good opportunities there and my mother would be close by."

"Sounds like you're just in the same place as the rest of us, out here floating in the current, tacking across it and trying not to swim against it directly." Charlie animates her advice, her arm movements attracting some attention from passers-by. Marie tries to ignore them, which only encourages Charlie to be more expressive. "...trying to choose which shore we wash up on. Do we set the most direct course, doggie paddle our way along, with or against the current, the tide, the shipping lanes? Maybe you need to drift a while longer and save up some more energy." Marie nods and rather than provide a pithy retort, remains silent. Charlie sees she might have exposed a nerve, and leaves it alone.

They decide to go roust the boys from their naps. Rush hour is still a half an hour away, so they catch the next train and are at Charlie's flat in no time. The nappers are still down as the women enter, but they awaken at the slamming of the door. Renny sits up and stretches, letting out a loud groan. Tony copies him.

"That was civilized, truly," Charlie jabs. Tony lay back down to stretch his long limbs.

"Fuck civilized, it was necessary," responds Renny.

"Let's head over to my school. We can grab a bite to eat nearby and you can fix up my health insurance paper."

They are ready and out the door in less than ten minutes.

The forgery effort works beautifully. Charlie leaves a copy with a note on Sandy's desk, feeling the sin more venial than mortal, and ascribing that to the abetting presence of her brother and cohorts. The four then proceed to spend the evening walking through Akihabara, the vast electronics retail neighborhood, both marveling at and bemoaning the latest gadgetry.

"Here's the paradox," states Renny, "embrace it and become enmeshed in acquisition and obsolescence. Shun it and get left out of the loop." He sweeps his hand across rows upon rows of cellular and recording devices.

"There's never any middle ground for you, is there?" Tony jests.

"Once you're in it, you're in all the way, baby, whether you admit it or not."

"You are so full of it, Ren," says Charlie. "Why can't I have just a little and enjoy it? We can stop short of becoming co-opted."

"Just one little bite of the apple, eh dear sister? I don't think it works that way."

Marie laughs, observing them both closely, then says, "You two are too cute. I can't tell if you're opposites or the same."

"I am not the same as my poor, misguided brother," Charlie protests.

Renny puts his arm around her and becomes the world's worst used car salesman.

"Hey Little Missy, could I interest you in one of these new-fangled, state of the art, gotta get em' while they're hot MDs? Maybe a cell phone with web access at a gajillion bytes per second response time, all in a fashionable red alligator skin case?"

"I already have a cell phone, which *you* borrowed yesterday, by the way." Charlie nods to the others in triumph.

"Yes, and have you checked your e-mail account today? Wouldn't want to miss anything would you?" Tony jabs.

"I am a flawed human being," Renny says, oh-so-humbly. "I can see the way, but it doesn't necessarily mean I can live it."

"*Do what I say and not what I do*?! Oh pul-eeze." Charlie rolls her whole head.

"So are you enmeshed in the system or out of the loop then?" asks Tony to Charlie.

"I'm stuck on the fringe of the loop. I can't get out, because I can't let go." Charlie grins at her self-assessment.

Marie snorts in approval. "Very poetically put. I like it. I think I'm right there beside you."

13

RENNY

TEXAS	KYOTO	THAILAND	KATMANDU	LAKE TOBA	INDIA	IPOH

EARLY YEARS	YEAR 1	YEAR 2

THE WAYS OF THE EAST

The squeak of the porch swing is the only sound that breaks the intermittent drone of the dry wind through the sagebrush. Renny looks over from his perch on the corner of the porch railing to see Charlie and Grandma Maxi flipping through a worn photo album. He is sixteen and bored stiff after five days in the desert wasteland of southern Texas. He is more than ready for his parents to return from their 'second honeymoon' on South Padre Island. He stands up and looks over at the neighbor's house, about a hundred yards away. No movement. Nothing moves out here, he thinks, except the dirt and the sagebrush in the wind.

"René dear, come over and join your Grandma."

Renny shuffles over, swishing over the deck planking with his basketball shoes, and sits next to Grandma. It's a tight squeeze for the three of them on the old wooden swinging pew and he looks up cautiously as he lowers himself, wondering if the chains can take it. Grandma is holding a different album now. The cover on this one is faded and cracking cowhide leather and across the front, at the bottom in barely legible golden letters, it reads 'Maximilliana Diaz'. Grandma squints at the cover and chuckles a Diaz chuckle. She carefully wipes away some non-existent dust from the cover and sighs. Charlie has wrapped herself around Grandma's right arm.

266

"You turn the pages Charlene," Grandma says to her. Charlie reaches across her lap and carefully lifts the cover to reveal a page of badly yellowed black and white photographs. Renny leans on Grandma's shoulder with interest now, his curiosity getting the better of him.

"This would be your Great Grandpa, my father, Maximillian Alvarez." The picture shows an average looking young Mexican man dressed in a black suit and a white button-down shirt. He stands stiffly in front of a general store, as if he's still waiting for the photo to be taken. "He died before you two were born. He's about twenty-five years old in this photo. Behind him is the family store. They closed it around 1935. I was about sixteen then, your ages." Grandma Maxi chuckles again, the mirth beaming from her eyes as she leans over and kisses Renny on the forehead. "And there's your Great Grandma Alvarez in front of our house." They pause for a respectful moment –less interested in Grandma's mother, and then Charlie turns the page.

They flip through the first few pages of the album, Grandma narrating each picture with the names and places and stories of times past. Charlie sees a face she doesn't know.

"Who's this Grandma?"

Grandma Maxi lets out a high-pitched "whooo" and smiles a broad grin. She looks conspiratorially at her grandchildren and says, "Well...I guess you're old enough to hear about it now." This, of course, has the twins on edge and even Renny perks up at the hint of intrigue.

"That there is Mister Charlie Chou." Charlie's head jerks up in surprise, she's heard this name mentioned before, though she can't remember where. Grandma folds her hands over the photo and looks off into the desert as she speaks.

"He was one of the main hands at our family's small ranch. Before my father moved up to El Paso to open up that store. We lived out here, not too far from this very spot, but over closer to Harlingen. We lived on a small spread and raised a few cows." Grandma became lost in thought for a few moments. Renny looked over at Charlie and could read in her eyes that there was a good story coming.

"There's a story that Mister Chou is your real Great Grandfather. My real father" Both children jerk upright, startled expressions and questioning eyes, but Grandma Maxi just breaks out giggling until she has to wipe the tears from the corners of her eyes. "Oh dear. I've done it now," she says to no one in particular.

"You see, my father – your Great Grandpa – wanted a big family, but for some reason, they just weren't coming along. Nowadays, you could go to the doctor and get everything checked, but this was the old days and you just didn't talk about things like that." Grandma takes a deep breath again, saying "Aye yi yi, Dios mio" as she exhales with a smile. "I think my mother finally gave up waiting and decided to have a child any way she could. I think she had a little fling with Mister Chou. She never told me that herself of course, but rumors went around, especially when I was in school, since I always did have that look to my eyes. You both have it too. I think the rumors got so bad that your Great Grandpa had to up and leave town. He took me and your Great Grandma away and opened up that store. The funny part is, his plumbing started working after that. It must have got jarred loose because your Great Uncle Javier came along within a year. He'd already saddled me with his name by then.

"Whatever happened to Charlie Chou?" Charlie leans on Grandma eagerly.

"I never knew. He left the ranch before I was born. He went back to China to be with his family, or so the

story goes. I never could talk with either of my parents about it, of course, but that's what your Great Aunt Veronica told me. Your father knows the story, but I don't think he puts much faith in it. I don't know where he thinks he got the slanty eyes then."

❂❂❂❂❂ ❂❂❂❂❂ ❂❂❂❂❂ ❂❂❂❂❂ ❂❂❂❂❂

Dear Charlie,

I was just thinking about the time we spent that summer with Grandma Maxi in southern Texas. I'm in southern Thailand now, in the village of Songkhla, and everywhere I look I see Charlie Chou! I never planned to come to this place, but you know how it goes. I was on Koh Samui for a couple of weeks and ran into this American guy, Richard. He works for the Peace Corps and is based in a little village just outside of Songkhla. He's helping set up a bakery operation there so the locals can make some bread, and he invited me to visit. Since I'm planning on going down to northern Malaysia anyway, it was on the way. I like being on the road. What's it been now? Almost two months since I left San Francisco. Feels like longer. I went up to northern Thailand like you suggested and had a great time. I did a trek out of Mae Hong Song for four days and then hung out in Chang Mai.

I met up with Richard on my way south and ended up here after I had my fill of the beach life. As it turned out, there was a festival happening in Songkhla on the second evening I was here. What a trip! I'm still not sure what the festival was about – some Buddhist holiday. It was mostly an opportunity for people to party.

Let me give you a little taste of this festival. Early in the evening, a bunch of kids got up on a dinky little stage in the middle of the village and started singing some traditional folk songs. It was a nice, slow, moon-gazing sort of thing. Next thing you know, a guy comes in and sets up an amplifier next to them and starts banging out some accompaniment on an electric guitar! It was like having Jimi Hendrix playing the national anthem next to a barbershop quartet. Then they brought out two other amps and all you could hear was this cacophony! The kids were still mouthing away at whatever tune they were singing and nobody seemed to care that they were completely drowned out by the guitars. Amazing. Is this progress?

Then I got to meet the mayor. Richard notices him sitting down front and he drags me over to introduce me. We go over to the fellow – he was right in front of the speakers and I'm thinking Richard is going to move the conversation to where we could talk. But no! Right there, Richard yells something in the mayor's ear, he nods, we shake hands, he says something to me, then I nod, but I couldn't hear a word he said! I swear I wasn't tripping either. The music is coming out at a hundred decibels plus, and there we are chatting with the mayor, but we're all acting as if it's all perfectly normal. The funnier part is that the mayor somehow then gets a call on his cell phone and proceeds to have a phone conversation right there. There's no way he could hear anything on that phone. It was all so surreal.

Then there was this one cool Buddhist game that I had to try. Get this: a Monk Money Toss. There's about a dozen of these kinda scarecrow-looking figures dressed in orange monk robes – on a merry-go-round! Each monk figure is standing around the perimeter of the circle holding a brass begging bowl. A live monk keeps the contraption spinning slowly while people throw coins into the bowls as they go around. Of course I couldn't pass up a chance to improve my karma, so I took a handful of one baht coins and proceeded to toss. I was hot! I got something like ten out of fifteen shots, and guess what I won?! No, not a giant stuffed Buddha (though that would have been NICE!). I won a blessing from the monk. There was an older woman watching the whole thing and she told Richard that I had some major good karma coming my way.

Okay, so back to the Charlie Chou story. Richard took me on a walk around the town and I noticed a Chou Dry Cleaning shop. Of course I had to check it out. Inside was an elderly couple that didn't speak English and they must have thought I was whacked when I proceeded to ask them, via Richard's excellent Thai, if they knew anything about a Charlie Chou who lived in Texas. Richard told me that "Chou" is about as common as the name of Johnson, so I shouldn't have been surprised by their head shaking and blank stares. We left the shop and went back to the party.

I'll be coming into Tokyo in another month and a half. I think I'm going to go with the Kyoto option for work. I know it would be great if we were working in the same city, but Kyoto just sounds more like my pace. But I'm flying into Tokyo so I can see you first – can I crash with you for a week or so? I'm getting ready to head into northern Malaysia. I don't really want to spend much time in Malaysia now – too expensive, so I'll catch a ferry from Penang down into Sumatra and stay there for a month. Then I'll return the same route and head your way from Bangkok. You've got my flight info, right? Hope you're doing well, Sis. Tell Mom and Dad I'm OK when you talk to them.

Love, Renny

I caught the train into Malaysia and made my way to the island of Penang, just across the bridge off the mainland border between Malaysia and Thailand. On Penang, in the city of Georgetown, I immediately caught the overnight ferry to Medan, the biggest city on the northern part of Sumatra. I had heard about Sumatra from Richard, my Peace Corp friend, and was anxious to hit Lake Toba and the orangutan reserve at Bukit Lawan. Both areas are in the northern half of the island, so I didn't plan on too much moving around. I sat by myself on the top deck of the ferry radio tower platform all night, surrounded by ocean.

Sitting there, above it all, I thought about my decision to leave my job, San Francisco, my country. It had been so much easier than I thought it would be. Yes, the money had been good and the work in the accounting offices engaging and the thrill of tracking the market almost addictive, but I knew it wasn't for me in the end. How could you get so excited about a few percentage points going up and down? That thrill was bound to have worn off soon. It was all just a legitimized and semi-respected form of gambling – ultimately boring. We partied when it went up and drank when it went down. The same story either way. It was good to be away from it – smart, even – and it was good to be having an adventure and seeing life from a different perspective.

Since the ferry was an overnighter, it arrived in Medan in the morning. Not having any desire to stay in the city, I made my way from the port to the bus terminal and caught the next bus towards the orangutan reserve. Bukit Lawan was going to be a bitch to get to, with countless hours of crowded local buses and potholed roads, but it was worth the trip – like everyone says. I jostled for a seat with the horde of locals going the same direction.

A striking German couple squeezed onto the crowded bus just outside of Medan. There were no pairs of seats open, so she sat next to me, the seat vacated just then, and he sat several rows in front. I offered to trade seats with the guy, but she shook her head and settled in. We nodded a greeting but she seemed disinterested in making conversation, so I pulled out my book and started to read. My seatmate perked up when she recognized the title – Beneath the Wheel, by Herman Hesse. I had found the book at a restaurant in Penang while waiting for the ferry, trading for it with Edward Abbey's "Monkey Wrench Gang." It was hard to concentrate as the bus bounced the words all over the page, so I soon closed the book and rubbed my eyes.

"Hesse is too much for you now?" I looked over to see her smiling. She had long brown hair tied back in a ponytail and gray eyes.

"Any reading is too much now." I introduced myself and we got to know each other over the next few hours becoming, as travelers so often do, almost intimate friends by the end of the ride. Her name was Sophia and her traveling companion was Franz, though she said they weren't a couple. They were classmates studying anthropology at a university in Munich. Sophia in particular was keen on primates and full of information on these orangutans.

Franz joined our conversation, sitting on the armrest of Sophia's seat – whether to assess my intent or exert his status, I couldn't be sure. When the bus arrived in Bukit Lawan, I had no idea where to go and was happy when Sophia asked me to come along with them to a guesthouse she knew of. I was more surprised, however, when she and Franz invited me to share a room. There was one available with three single beds and since we were all adults and on a budget, I said yes.

We were all tired-but-wired from the trip and as the evening came on Franz pulled out a joint and the three of us enhanced our already-altered state on the porch just outside our room. I toted my book along, more as a prop than with the intention of reading it, since Sophia seemed to know Hesse.

"You are going to try again?" Sophia had brought some loose-leaf notes about orangs with her and was feigning to read also.

I looked off into the dense thicket of jungle just a few yards away. "Not really. I just like carrying it around." Franz passed the joint. I didn't like the tobacco mixed in with the hash, but pulled a few drags just the same. I remembered to hold onto the joint for a few drags rather than pass it right along. It is a European custom not to pass too quickly – you might only get one turn in a crowd. I remember accusing a Frenchman of "bogarting" the smoke in Chang Mai – all in fun, of course, but that sparked a thirty-minute diatribe of how crude and impatient Americans are. I took the blows in stride but didn't want to recreate that scene here. Still, I smiled as the memory came to me, and Franz saw it.

"So just carrying Hesse makes you smile?"

"Oh, I was just thinking about how Americans and Europeans are different."

"Oh? How so Mr. American?" Sophia looked ready for a debate, smiling and eager.

"Well Mr. And Mrs. Deutschlanders…"

"That's Ms., if you please."

"Okay. Miss. And Mister. I don't know exactly how we're different. I was just thinking about it is all. Take this joint, for example." I passed it to Sophia and she passed it to Franz without partaking. I explained about bogarting; that it had something to do with Humphrey Bogart and how he used to hold onto his cigarette butt long after it had burned down to nothing. I don't know if this is the true origin of the phrase, but I'd heard it before and it made for a good story. They had seen Casablanca, and liked the imagery. But Franz pointed out the irony of Bogart being an American who held onto the smoke like a European.

"So what does that say about how Europeans and Americans are different?" Franz asked.

"I'm open to suggestions. You've read Hesse right?" They nodded. "What would he say about it you think?" I was pleased with myself for passing it back.

Sophia and Franz looked at each other and exchanged something in German.

Sophia spoke. "We are more uptight about things than you are." This sent her giggling and Franz frowning.

"Maybe," I replied, "but we are more stupid." This yielded a protest expression from Sophia and a nodding grin from Franz.

"See, Franz agrees."

"Yes, with both of you." Franz entered the fray. "For Germans, smart and uptight can be a bad combination."

"I haven't read much of this book yet, but I've read some other Hesse and I think he speaks for everyone. For Americans, stupid and carefree can be a bad combination also."

"But you are all not stupid." Sophia came to our defense.

"I don't mean literally. But Americans are naïve, I think. It's hard to talk about hundreds of millions of people generally, but, what the hell."

"Hesse saw the problem, I think." Franz had stretched out in his chair, the smoke wafting about him. "We can't go with the old ways. It has to be new."

"Yah, but the old ways aren't all bad. Some things, we need to go back to them. But factories and everything with pollution. This is a bad thing." Sophia added thoughtfully.

"So Sophia, you'll take a boat back to München rather than fly?" Franz said with a wink.

"If I don't have to listen to you, maybe." Sophia laughed again, merrily. I liked bantering with her, but noticed that Franz kept a serious look – yin to Sophia's yang.

"So the question then," I said, "is how to find a new way?"

"There is no map for this thing. You just have to do it," Franz said.

"So we just need to step off the wheel before it spins too fast?" Sophia asked.

"But what does that mean?" I was hooked in now. "We're all on the wheel, one way or another. We all live on Planet Earth and it's going wherever it's going. Some would say "down the tubes" and others say we're spinning out into the stars. Whichever is right, we can't really get off." I reached over for the joint.

"Yes, yes, the bogarting. Here." Franz smiled.

"There are wheels within wheels I think." Sophia's eyebrows were knit. "True, we can't step off the big one, but we can step off the little ones. I don't have to live like my parents."

"We are all fucked anyway, so why worry about it," said Franz. "We know that we *do* have to do some things differently, the question is *what*? Since the sixties, maybe, you know, with rock and roll and all that, everyone knows the old order is kaput.

But nobody has come up with a new order. It's still money, money, money."

"Europe and America are the same. We act like we're different, but we are all ruled by money and power. This is no different than it has ever been. Anywhere, anytime," I replied.

"This is what happens to you when you study anthropologia," Sophia said, jerking her thumb at Franz and rolling her eyes, smiling. "I think the primates, like the orangs, are a higher order than we are. They don't need technology like we do."

Franz had the last word. "Yah, they just need to worry about being crushed by ours."

ᖇᖇᖇᖇᖇ   ᖇᖇᖇᖇᖇ   ᖇᖇᖇᖇᖇ   ᖇᖇᖇᖇᖇ   ᖇᖇᖇᖇᖇ

I spent two weeks in Bukit Lawan, most of the time I walked the trails of the sanctuary and visited the tourist center. I wasn't so much interested in the primates as the jungle. I felt a curious sort of sadness whenever I saw the orangs, which was rarely. The purpose of the center, after all, is to ensure and rehabilitate their innate wildness. I couldn't help but feel they are doomed, limited to this little corner of the world in a kind of zoo while people like me visit and intrude. I didn't want to be a downer about the experience though, so I "forced" myself to enjoy the exotic jungle environment, losing myself in the massive foliage among the odd, tiny creatures of the undergrowth: the voracious leaf-cutter ants, the colorful geckoes with their throaty refrain.

Sophia and Franz often walked along with me, or I with them. After a week, Franz left for the northwestern coast to surf. Sophia and I continued sharing the same room. . She slept in the nude and made no attempt to hide this as I stole glances at her, surreptitiously, during the first week. But I was convinced that she and Franz had something going on, so the thought of getting physical with her had stayed in the fantasy realm. She surprised me one evening by slipping into my bed. She did this with a light heart and a curious spirit.

"Have you discovered a map yet to get off of your wheel?"

"I've already stepped off without one," I answered, "and I don't see a reason to go searching for a map now."

"You don't need a map for tonight." We kissed and grinded the wheel of passion instead.

❦❦❦❦❦ ❦❦❦❦❦ ❦❦❦❦❦ ❦❦❦❦❦ ❦❦❦❦❦

I left Sophia and Bukit Lawan, with some regret but knowing I needed to keep moving. The road drew me forth and I couldn't resist the lure. I was also ready to venture onto Lake Toba and then curl back northward to the mainland. Movement seemed key at this point. All of my experiences in between these encounters blended into the wake, dragging behind me as flotsam and memories.

Back in Medan, I stayed the night in a seedy little motel near the bus station and then caught a mini-bus to Lake Toba the next morning, about a five hour ride southward. In the middle of the lake is Samosir Island, a lush donut hole in a jungle mountain lake surrounded by steep, verdant cliffs and open sky. I caught the first ferry over to the island and got off on the first pier we came to. Just up the road I found a small bungalow complex right on the water's edge. I took the first cottage I was offered and collapsed on the porch hammock.

I was still in 'the travel zone' – that zombie-like state arrived at from inhaling diesel exhaust, hearing the constant hum of engines and feeling the rhythmic drone of tires on pavement and gravel. My senses were alert in one way, to direction and stoppages, but dulled in another from sensory overload, the humidity, unvarying lush jungle vegetation and the smells of fellow travelers. I was ready to breathe deep of the quiet and the still new (to me) Indonesian aroma in the air.

The next day, I planned a walk around the island, or at least ten or so miles of it, but cut it short after two hours when my energy level ebbed to nothing from the heat, humidity and just plain tiredness. I cut across the island, bushwhacking a beeline back to the bungalow, and wasn't too surprised or concerned when I realized I was lost. One can't really get lost on an island, but the pathways that meandered around the hills that crown Samosir Island are a tangled maze indeed. After a half hour of wandering around in an attempt to get reoriented, I decided to sit down and rest a minute. But where to do that? I spied a hill about a half-mile away and made for it with gusto, striding confidently across an empty field so the owners wouldn't mistake me for someone who might be lost.

As I crested the hill, I stopped to admire its dimple of a crater and the small wooden hut it cradled at the bottom. It looked like the hermit's residence I had imagined in my daydream on the bus from Nepal – the place I went to after leaving my beautiful sixteen-year-old Indian wife for more peaceful environs. I couldn't tell if anyone was home or not, so I approached cautiously and, not seeing anyone, sat on one of two logs placed deliberately in front of the hut in a "V" shape – to welcome guests, I hoped. The view from the bottom of this bowl wasn't so great, but the place itself was serene and very calming. Before long, I was down on the log and fast asleep.

I awoke to the sound of footsteps walking very near. I shot straight up, trying to startle the newcomer more than he had startled me. I checked quickly to see that my bag was where I had left it. Just as that thought slipped by, I heard a lighthearted chuckle. I looked towards it. About five yards away from me, perched on the end of the other log, was a weathered old man with a long wispy white beard and a balding head. The few loose white strands that still grew there were anchored to his skull at random. He wore clothes that looked like they were made of burlap and no shoes. He held a long vine switch and was doodling with it on the ground in front of him. He didn't seem angry to find an uninvited guest awaiting him upon his return home. He didn't seem disturbed at all.

"I'm sorry to have intruded," I said. "I was lost and I just needed to rest and..." I cut the apology short when he started chuckling again, this time louder and more like a full-on laugh. Then he grinned a happy grin, revealing two rows of shiny white teeth. They looked out of place against his ragged clothes and filthy feet, and at first it unnerved me a bit.

"You sure have white teeth for such a ...a.... poor looking guy," I thought out loud, thinking my English wouldn't be understood.

The smile vanished immediately and I wondered if I'd screwed up.

"I didn't mean to offend you, I'm..." The smile returned. But he didn't speak or signal anything to me, so what could I do but keep babbling?

"My name is Renny." The man's face softened and took on a faraway look. Then he looked at me again. About half a minute passed as he sized me up.

"Tomonori-des." He stared at me some more.

"Tomonori. That sounds Japanese." The man grunted in assent, but said nothing more. He was still moving the switch across the dirt. *Hmmm, this is getting more interesting by the minute.* I looked down at the doodling and was surprised to see the ground wiped clean, like a sheet of new rice paper, and on the sheet of dust Tomonori had drawn out what I thought were Japanese characters. Boy, what I would have given to be able to read them. "That's Japanese?"

The man looked up. "Chinese and Japanese," he said. His English pronunciation was flawless. I should have known.

"What does it say?"

Tomonori shook his head. "It say nothing. Is just practice. Mmmm. English not so good now. Need practice also." He scratched his head and stood up.

"I'm sorry, I should go." I said that but I really didn't want to leave. I felt drawn into this isolated vignette and wanted to see where it would go. The man didn't acknowledge my apology and offer to leave, instead he walked over to the hut and went inside. I waited a minute, confused but still too curious to give up so quickly. After several minutes I figured he meant for me to leave, but as I started to get up he came back out with a bowl. He walked over and offered me one of the three rice balls that were nestled at the bottom of the bowl. I took one, gratefully, and he nodded. We sat back down in the same places.

"Your name, Lenny," the man said, nodding.

"Renny, that's correct. I'm from America. Most recently from San Francisco. In California."

The man's eyebrows rose at this and he nodded, knowingly.

"This is very good. Thank you." The rice ball had a piece of pickled cucumber, or something like it, inside.

"Sumatra *onigiri*," he said, pointing to the rice ball. The man laughed heartily at this, amused at something that was wasted on me. Not until a few months later would I learn that onigiri is a popular Japanese rice snack, usually white rice with a dab of fish or meat or vegetable, wrapped in dried seaweed.

"San Francisco nice place," Tomonori said, looking thoughtfully at the sky.

"You've been there?"

He nodded but said nothing more.

My sense of adventure overcame my otherwise cautious inclination to be polite and not pry. "I don't mean to be nosy, but how did you get here?" He looked at me with a puzzled expression. "You're Japanese right? But you live here, it looks like." I felt foolish and let the words die, thinking it was hopeless and half-sorry that I'd been so rude.

"Nosy." The man pointed to his nose but said it to the ground. "What is nosy?"

I laughed without thinking and the man smiled. "It...it...means that it is none of my business, but.... I want to know." Tomonori looked at me, cogitating, then broke out in a wide grin. "Nosy." He nodded his head in understanding and repeated the word. "Nosy. Nosy. Yes. I understand." He chuckled again and then became quiet. I sat in silence with him for what seemed like a full ten minutes. Just as I was giving up any hope of communicating further Tomonori said, "North Beach. I like this place. You go to North Beach?"

"Yeah. I like it too. I worked downtown. When were you there?"

Tomonori exhaled deeply and looked to the sky. It was like the question had metaphysical ramifications and required deep thought.

"About twenty years before. I have been since many times, but for a few days only." His English was improving with each utterance. Tomonori fell silent again, seemingly in contemplation. I squelched the urge to say something else – to ask another question – some inner instinct told me to sit in silence. It was uncomfortable at first, but it was obvious that Tomonori liked silence and was not one to be pushed into talking. Besides, the quiet of the countryside was a welcomed sound.

"I work for a bank for many, many years. San Francisco, my first job out of Japan. I was young then, your age maybe. Good times." He laughed. "You. What you do there?"

"I worked for an accounting office." Tomonori pursed his lips at this. Silence again.

"You quit your job?"

"Yes." More silence. "Did you quit your job too, Mr. Tomonori?"

"Tomo. Call me Tomo." He nodded. "Yes. After long time."

"How long have you been here? On Samosir Island?" More deep contemplation.

"Where you stay at?" He didn't seem to want to answer any questions about time.

"At Misty Bungalow. Over that way, I think." I pointed behind me, uncertain.

"I think maybe this way." Tomo jerked his left thumb to the right.

"The truth is, I got lost and was trying to see where to go, so I came up here."

"Get lost is not bad thing."

I stood up, taking the hint. "Do you want that...I should go?" Tomo looked straight at me again, scratched his beard and grunted. I felt like I was in a Kurosawa movie.

"Sit. Sit." I sat. Tomo started doodling again. "You know kanji?" I shook my head. Tomo drew two characters in the dust.

"This mean *'jiyu'*. Freedom. I come to Sumatra for *jiyu*." Tomo mumbled something in Japanese. "Some years ago, my bank send me here to look at finance for logging. I come to Tobako, Lake Toba, and like it very much. I finish finance project, come back here. Stay forever."

"You quit your job?" I asked a bit too emphatically.

Tomo looked up sharply, then smiled.

"Job no good. Job very sad. Very bad. I..." Tomo took an imaginary blade in both hands and thrust it into his belly, turning it to slice a *hara kiri* incision across his abdomen. He slumped forward slightly to put a fine point on his demise, and then let out a hearty laugh, pleased with his acting.

"How long did you work there?" I wondered if he'd answer this one.

"Mmmm. Twenty seven years."

"And you've been here how long?" Tomo looked at me, mumbling something in Japanese and pointing to his nose. "Nosy." He laughed.

"I'm sorry. I'm just curious."

Tomo erased the kanji characters and redrew them, clearly more satisfied with this second rendering.

"More than three years now. My family still in Tokyo. They never come here." Tomo broke out in a roaring laugh, as if that fact in itself was hilarious. I couldn't help but join him.

"You have children?"

"One boy. One girl. Both now grow up." Tomo was softening up now, becoming more animated and at ease. I began to wonder if the surly hermit routine was an act.

"Why don't they visit?" Tomo looked at me with surprise. He stood up and waved a hand at his hut, speaking something in Japanese that I guessed meant, "It's obvious, isn't it?

"They think I'm crazy old man. Ha! Maybe they right!" Tomo proceeded to dance an improvised jig around the log.

"Why was your job no good?"

"Mmmm." Tomo continued dancing, but at a slower pace. "Job was like...*shabu shabu*." He shook his head violently and made a swishing sound. "Work work work. No play. Money ichiban!" He pointed his forefinger upward, but his face mocked the meaning: number one. "Rush rush. No time for spirit." His words and gestures were dramatic and overstated – I could feel the raw emotion that fueled them. "And you! You young man. Why you quit your job? Ha!" I stood up and did a few stretches over the log. The morning had become afternoon, and I wanted to match Tomo's animation. And I was happy to talk about leaving the working world behind.

"I quit because I wasn't having fun."

"Fun?! What has this to do with work? Ha!"

"I needed to know there was something more out there in the world. I wanted to explore and just do something else."

Tomo looked at me seriously. "What about family? You have wife or girlfriend?"

'No no no no no. No wife. Too much responsibility just yet. And my family was cool with it." I couldn't tell if Tomo really understood me, but decided not to worry about it. "What about your wife?"

"My wife!? All she like is Gucci Gucci Gucci!" He spoke the name in a little girl's voice. "Ha! I say no! Cotton cotton! Ha!" The jig started up again. Between bounces he said, "She stay in Tokyo. Keep all my money, except for just little bit. What I need it for?" He gestured around, looking at the hills and the sky. "A little for rice. That is all."

"What about your colleagues?" I asked. Tomo surprised me by stopping in his tracks and peering at me over his shoulder. He put a foot on the log and scratched his beard.

"Colleagues. Mmmmm."

"You know, your co-workers."

"Shhh! I understand, foolish young man. Shhh!" I zipped my mouth and waited. "I was Vice President, overseas loans. I had power!" He thumped his chest, with apparent pride, and then laughed. "Power over fools! Ha! Good money, good position. Wife very very happy. Children at Todai – big university. But it was no good!" He shouted the last sentence. "My spirit was in a bottle. I need to open the bottle. To break the bottle." He mimed the smashing of a glass, flinging it from his hands to the ground. "My bank very unhappy. Ha! They think I need to see psych...psycho..." He spoke the word in Japanese.

"Psychiatrist?"

"Shhh!" He looked menacing. "Yes. Maybe. I say no! I need jiyu, free. I see men work to death and never have jiyu! Tsk tsk tsk." He wagged his finger at me as if I had been naughty. "So now I am ronin. No master! Haha!" He skipped off to the crest of the hill. Once there, he threw his hands up in the air, yelled something in Japanese, and then shrieked with ferocious joy. Before the sound dissipated he was running along the perimeter of the dimple, stopping at each of the four cardinal points, I guessed, to repeat the gestures and yells. I watched with amazement, sharing the elation.

Tomo returned to the hut, huffing and exhilarated, and ran inside. He came back out with a bottle of clear liquid and two plastic cups. He poured a drink into each and shoved one of the cups into my hand.

"Sake. I make myself," he said proudly. We drank and he refilled and we drank again, and again. After an hour, we still had not moved. We sat on the same logs, becoming sleepy in the afternoon heat. Tomo lay on the ground next to his log and I stretched out on mine. We both dozed off within minutes.

Again, I awoke with a start. The sun was just kissing the horizon and the air was thick with the fragrance of orange. I looked around, but the hilltop was quiet and Tomo was nowhere to be seen. The sake bottle and cups were gone. The switch was gone. Separating disappointment from concern, I pulled myself slowly upright. I called out Tomo's name. No answer. My head was pounding and my mouth felt raw. *Sake – homemade – I should have known better.* I walked over to the hut, looked around the hillside, and then pushed the door guiltily open. The room was sparse. A crude mat lay on a platform in one corner and a small wooden table and chair in another. The cabinet next to the table was leaning precariously to one side, and a few cooking utensils were hanging from the walls. I felt like an intruder, so I backed out and closed the door.

I walked the perimeter of the hill, looking for signs of Tomo or anything that would let me know he had been there. Nothing. No sign, no clue. *It wasn't a dream was it? It couldn't have been! My aching head proves that!* I looked around the ground nearby. The only footprints I could make out were my own. Then I saw the spot where Tomo had been doodling in the dirt. *Thank god – I'm not crazy.* The two kanji characters were still imprinted in the dust. I took a notebook out of my daypack and copied the characters as best I could. Then I knew it was time to get moving. Tomo had pointed the direction back to my bungalows so I headed that way. As I reached the crest of the hill, I turned to look back. The hut and log area were quiet, like I'd never even been there. I turned again to look down the hill and could see the lake in the distance.

Before I could leave this place I knew what I had to do. I raised my hands over my head and screamed at the top of my lungs – not imitating Tomo but sending up my own prayer to echo his. I screamed a high-pitched whine and then a low moan and then I stopped fashioning my plea and just screamed for the joy of it.

I returned to the hilltop two days later, but there was again no sign of Tomo. I waited an hour, but felt no presence or invitation to wait, so I went back down to the lake. I repeated this again two days later, and again two days after that, but not a glimpse of Tomo or a wisp of the daily life he must lead up in the hills. On my last visit before I left, I left a note on the table in the hut:

"Tomo –
Jiyu be with you.
– Renny"

14

CHARLIE

THE LITTLE THINGS

Charlie keeps her gig at Bar WhyNot the whole time she is in Japan, which is well over a year and a half by now. Her shift was whittled down to one night a week since the teaching work expanded, but that makes her time there all the more enjoyable. It is still lucrative and she welcomes a regular clientele each week that she enjoys talking with. They tip well and still behave themselves.

Today is Charlie's last official day at the bar. She has been greeting and parting from many of the regulars all evening. Mr. Shinmura, her very first client, just gave her a farewell gift of five hundred dollars. Charlie feels warm, loved, and already nostalgic about the good times. But she also feels a tremendous sense of relief. *I won't miss the uneasiness of being a hostess. That little voice inside my head keeps reminding me I am a sort of prostitute. I will miss the easy talk, the façade of happiness. It's so easy to fall into fooling yourself – and my clients – that life is carefree and happy. Sometimes just acting like it's true makes it true. That's my big take-away from this job. Maybe from Japan as a whole.*

The night comes to a close and the bar crowd dwindles. Mr. Soto is unusually ebullient and she is happy to finish her last shift with him so engaged.

"Remember my first day?" Charlie dares to bait him. "You weren't so sure that I would be a good hostess, were you?" Soto ignores the comment, lighting a cigarette and looking out into the lounge.

She's tempted to try again – to see if the boss will admit that the job is all form over substance, but decides not to be so cynical on her last night.

A small crowd is still left at closing time. There isn't an official closing time, really. If a customer is spending big money, the bar stays open. Around a table by the window sit Mr. Ando and Mr. Tanaka, both regular customers of Charlie and Andrea. Tanaka-san has adopted a European air of late, taken to wearing berets, silk cravats and double-breasted suits. Tonight he sports new, round, wire-framed glasses in addition to the maroon beret which has become his favorite. Flanking the two men are Tanya and Julie, with Andrea nestled in between. Charlie watches them from the bar. *They are good*, she notes to herself, *...acting like the conversation is the most interesting they've heard in a long time. Beautiful smiles and clothes and I sure am happy to be done with it.*

Andrea sees Charlie watching them from the bar and waves her over. She waves back but signals she is having a conversation with Tonto, their nickname for Tano the bartender. He has been a reassuring constant for Charlie over the last year. Shy and professional, he has always been there when she needed him, ready and willing to help. He is probably in his mid-fifties – some Japanese faces were amazingly age-defying – and he smiles only in private.

"I'm going to miss you most of all, scarecrow," she teases him. He nods almost imperceptibly, and lays a card on the bar in front of her. The surprise lasts only seconds before she takes it up with both hands and opens it. A pressed white flower covers the front, and inside he has written, "I will miss you. Tonto."

He probably spent an hour thinking what to write, she thinks, choking a bit on the lump in her throat. *Better not cry, though. That would embarrass both of us.* She walks around the bar and stands on her toes to kiss him lightly on the cheek. He just keeps on wiping the spotless counters, but she catches the shy smile and returns it.

She goes over to join the group at the table by the window and easily slides into the conversation and the cliché. But it is getting late, and within minutes the party breaks up and Andrea and Charlie walk Mr. Tanaka downstairs. Out on the sidewalk, Mr. Tanaka stops and turns to Charlie. He takes an exquisitely wrapped gift out of the shopping bag he'd been carrying and offers it to her. She feigns surprise and glee as she opens the silver and white paper to find a leather handbag, a Coach.

"I bought it in Paris and I hope you like it. Remember me." He says.

Charlie whistles in appreciation and guesses it cost him five hundred dollars or more. She accepts it graciously, though she has come to secretly loathe such ostentation. *He should have given me the money*, she thinks, but is happy all the same and thanks him.

Then an odd thing happens to color the evening. The three of them are standing on the sidewalk, still streaming with pedestrian traffic despite the late hour. Walking past just as they look up is a friend of Andrea's, another hostess and fellow Aussie who Charlie doesn't know.

"Hi Michele!" Andrea says. "I'm almost done for the night – wait a sec and I'll go up to get my things."

The woman nods and stands aside to have a cigarette as Charlie and Andrea say goodbye to Mr. Tanaka. Charlie gives him a warm hug and he kisses her on both cheeks. He repeats the gesture with Andrea. He then reaches over to Michele to kiss her on the cheek and she reacts with alarm. She doesn't know this man from Adam and isn't looking at him as he nears her. When he tries to kiss her cheek, she immediately slaps him hard on the face. He freezes in shock, glasses askew on his face full of incomprehension. He is instantly brought out of his reverie and Charlie feels for him as his shoulders slump. A tear swells in his right eye. Charlie isn't sure if it is from the slap or from shame.

"I.....I....just....wanted..." He turns, bows, and flees down the sidewalk. The three women stand there for a few moments in silence. Mr. Tanaka's figure recedes in the distance, bent over and almost running. Michele is breathing hard.

"Christ! What happened just now? I thought he was *skebbe.* I'm sorry," she says to Andrea.

"Don't worry about it love, he has to learn. He's not a pervert, that I know of." Andrea has the resigned air of a longtimer who's seen it all. She speaks of Mr. Tanaka like he is a child and in a way he is. He had been innocent and unaware.

Charlie thinks: *It's a horror to be brought out of blissful ignorance, but when reality beckons, what can you do? Most western women in Japan, and especially those in the hostessing trade, end up dealing with perverts, or skebbe men, as we call them, at one time or another. In that regard, the reaction Mr. Tanaka received wasn't out of the blue. This situation is so uncomfortable I don't know what to make of it!*

The three walk upstairs, Charlie with the uneasy feeling in her gut that the world around her has gone haywire. She decides right then that she is ready to leave Japan and do some traveling again. She knew the decision wasn't far off. By quitting at the bar, she is hoping to give herself some free time to enjoy the country more before she leaves for the next adventure. She hadn't decided the *when* part of the scenario yet, till now. *It's going to be soon.*

❧❧❧❧❧ ❧❧❧❧❧ ❧❧❧❧❧ ❧❧❧❧❧ ❧❧❧❧❧

Two weeks later Charlie is on a train going north of Tokyo with Pauline and Andrea. They are headed for the little town of Ashio to spend some time in the forest and visit Nikko National Park. Pauline had arranged a house swap with Mark, a teacher from Ashio who was itching for some time in the city. The suburbs of Tokyo extend far to the north, but after two hours the concrete gives way to rural landscape and then thick forest and mountains. An unusual characteristic about Japan is that, despite the huge population confined to such a limited land area, open space is plentiful in the rural areas of the country. Most of the people reside in the urban centers and these are enormously crowded, but the countryside is open in an unexpected way. The contrast takes hold of all three of the city girls and they fall silent, watching the train wind its way through the trees. They put down their magazines and books and sit staring out the window. After a long stretch of this, Pauline interrupts the reverie.

"So there's this train and on it are an Irishwoman, an American woman and an Australian woman." She stops, the others awaiting the punchline.

"Yes.....?" Charlie prompts.

"That's it. I thought it might go somewhere, but no." She picks up her book and pretends to read.

"Well, the Aussie and the Yank are wondering what the hell they've gotten themselves into by traveling with the Irish one." Andrea smiles and Pauline sighs deeply and puts down her book with equal exaggeration.

"They're finally going to see how to do things right is what I reckon." Pauline looks out the window and purses her lips.

"Is that so?" Andrea retorts. "I didn't think the Irish knew much about doing anything at all, let alone doing things right."

"That coming from an Aussie?! Maybe I'll just follow you, but do the opposite."

"So long as you follow me, I don't care."

"I'm just along for the ride," Charlie says. "If you two want to do all the things that need doing, I'm just happy to tag along."

"Ain't that just like a Yank?" Andrea says to Pauline, who takes up the cue and turns her remarks to Charlie.

"Just mooching off the hard work of others and acting innocent."

"If the two of you are hard workers then I really want to see what easy street is like."

"And she's cheeky to boot!"

"So the Irishwoman and the Aussie throw the American off the train and...."

"And end up falling off with her because they are so naturally uncoordinated."

"I've taught this one well," Pauline says to Andrea.

"Don't swell her head any more than it is already, naturally, being an American and all that." She looks at Charlie with mock condescension.

"I think you both are just needing a beer."

"It just so happens….." Pauline reaches down into her daypack and pulls out a bottle of Sapporo. Andrea does the same and reveals a bottle of tequila. They look at Charlie expectantly, but she just shrugs.

"Didn't I tell you about the mooching bit?" Pauline says, looking disgusted.

"I'll see if I can get some cups and ice," Charlie volunteers.

"That's the least you could do. I think we better save this one for later." Andrea tucks her bottle away as Charlie heads for the dining car. She returns with the goods, including an additional bottle of amber. They chatter and banter and try to keep the volume down until the beer is gone and the train eventually pulls into Nikko. From there they hop the next bus and ride forty-five minutes into Ashio.

Once there they find the apartment with ease using Mark's crude map, for it really is just a small and charming village. The few locals out on the streets gift a few long stares to the trio as they walk along, but this is not unexpected or misinterpreted. They find the key under the mat and make themselves at home.

They are in the apartment less than an hour when there is a knock on the door. A colleague of Mark's, Hasegawa-san and his wife Yumi, are just checking in to make sure they are OK. He insists on taking the girls on a tour the following morning and they happily consent. Instead of shooting tequila that night they opt for a sound and early sleep in the eerie silence of the Japanese countryside.

Sega and Yumi show up promptly at nine the following morning and treat Charlie, Andrea and Pauline to a day unlike any they could have predicted – uniquely Japanese in its effusive hospitality. The couple is in their mid-thirties and adopts the girls like they are long lost siblings. After a sumptuous brunch of fish, omelets, and salad, they tour the now-defunct local copper mine, which had been the mainstay of the local economy for decades, up until the early 1980's. After riding the little train car through the hillside tunnels, it's a walk in the forest to tea and scones at a mountainside resort, then nine-hole three-par golf, and finally a dinner party complete with karaoke. Sega and Yumi refuse to let the girls pay for any of this, insist though they do at every opportunity.

"This is getting ridiculous," Pauline whispers, after being scolded for trying to pay for the golf. "This day must be costing them a couple hundred bucks. All that for friends of a friend!"

"Truly amazing, isn't it?" Charlie marvels.

The most that Sega and Yumi will accept from the girls is an excruciating karaoke rendition of 'I Will Always Love You', sung Whitney Houston style, sort of. The three of them sing it together, without harmony and after two bottles of sake between them, to the rousing applause of everyone present. The three get dropped off after dark with sincere "thank you's" and *arigatos* from all sides. As they climb the stairs to the apartment, Charlie comments, "I wish I had a recording of that, if only for how bad it was."

Pauline replies, "I'll bet they do also, so they can have something to look back on and cringe at how they wasted a load of money on gaijin who couldn't sing."

The following day, Mark's dilapidated 1972 red Toyota compact is suitable enough to take the girls on a full day of touring around the Tokugawa mountain retreat and burial ground.

"These are the folks who founded and ran Japan's last great, pre-western contact dynasty." Pauline is up on the history and speaks authoritatively. She proves to be an adequate guide. The setting is gorgeous and the structures powerful yet simple. Of particular interest to all of the tourists at the memorial for the first of the family's shoguns, Tokugawa Ieyasu, is a carving over a gateway that features three monkeys. One has his hands over his eyes, one is shielding his ears and the last is covering his mouth.

Visitors stop and gawk and take pictures of the monkeys as if it is the prime reason for coming. Charlie is not impressed.

"I think it's sort of anticlimactic," she whispers to Pauline and Andrea as they pass underneath the doorway, hardly pausing. "The monkey figures are small and pretty uninspiring. But I guess they're famous – and I didn't know they were originally Japanese! I saw another rendition of these monkeys on a t-shirt once. But there was a fourth monkey added, holding his hands up in the air. It said, 'See no evil, hear no evil, speak no evil, have no fun!'"

"No shit," Andrea agrees.

They return to Mark's place after dinner at a ramen shop near the apartment and pop the bottle of tequila. It is a beautiful evening and they sit on the floor in front of the main and only window of the apartment looking up and out at the stars. Andrea finds Mark's stash of small sake cups and they drink shots from them.

"Do you suppose those monkey carvings are the original?" Andrea asks.

"I think the idea has been around longer than the couple of hundred years those monkeys have been sitting up there," replies Pauline, "but I'd guess those are certainly the most famous."

"So, just what idea is that, Herr Professora?" Charlie slurs the last word on purpose.

"I think whoever added the 'have no fun!' part hit the nail on the head," says Andrea before Pauline can reply. Pauline gives her a pained look.

"I'm surrounded by small minds!" she sighs.

"How did I get thrown in?" Charlie protests.

"By association!"

"Sorry girl. Luck of the draw," Andrea says to Charlie with a shrug and a smile.

"The idea," Pauline continues pointedly, "is that *evil* is a creation from the self, and if we choose not to see or hear or speak it, then it doesn't exist for us and we don't give in to it." She punctuates the point by slamming back another shot.

"But what is evil?" Charlie replies, ready to delve deeper. "Does this qualify?" She points to the half-empty bottle.

"I haven't gotten that far yet in my analysis." Pauline furrows her brow in thought and refills her cup.

"I don't think anyone can say a particular thing is evil or not. Outside of the obvious, that is, like murder or rape and stuff like that." Andrea says this dispassionately while looking up through the window, and it takes the other two a moment to take in the tone. She continues, "My Dad used to be into reading religious philosophy. Still is, I suppose. He used to tell us, growing up, to always have a 'pure heart'. I asked him what this meant and he said he couldn't explain it but that we would know someday. So, I think that evil is the opposite of having a pure heart, whatever that means." She smiles sweetly and pours another round.

"I like that," Charlie says. "Pure heart. So you're saying that there is no standard by which to judge if something or someone is evil. Hmmm."

"I don't know," interjects Pauline. "There are standards out there, but I guess how they get applied is anybody's interpretation. The poor guy who steals food to feed his family breaks the rules, but is that an evil?"

"But how, then, can you know what is good or not? Everything, every action could be viewed as acceptable, given the right circumstances." This debate becomes an itch that Charlie needs to scratch.

"You can't know for sure," says Andrea. "You only can know in your own heart what is good."

"I'm more curious about the see and hear no evil part of it," says Pauline. "I can figure out how you should *speak* no evil, or *think* no evil, but how can you not see or hear it? Does that mean I am supposed to ignore an atrocity because I don't want to be infected by the evil of it? That doesn't make any sense to me."

"Ah, but it's not taking it *inside* of you that you can control. I'm not saying there is no objective for goodness out there – though fuck if I know what it is – I'm just saying that you can control how it affects you." Andrea keeps on surprising Charlie.

"So then, you admit that it exists. That evil is out there, that circumstances can't in some way legitimize every heinous act?" asks Pauline.

"I don't..." Andrea begins a reply but Charlie interrupts.

"How, then, are we supposed to know how to act? There has to be some way to know if a thing is true or not, or good or bad."

"I think you act, hopefully, in a way that you know is right. Like the bloke who steals the food, there is no objective way to look at it," replies Andrea, again the sage.

"Now I don't want this to go to your head or anything," says Pauline, looking at Andrea, "but you're right, I think. Or I'm right and you're right in agreeing with me." She smiles. "You can't let evil come in or out of you. The monkeys are right on it. No matter what's out there in the world – and it covers the gamut – the pure heart idea, I think, is to protect your innocence, by not internalizing the evil."

"It's like confession then," Charlie offers. "You're saying that we can be innocent, or made clean, even if we've transgressed."

"That's a very slippery slope, St. Charles," retorts Andrea, "But I don't have the Catholic thing going for me like the two of you have. Lets just agree that, as long as we can have our fun, not hurt anyone, and not become maddened by the nastiness of the world, life is good. Here's to a pure heart."

☯☯☯☯☯ ☯☯☯☯☯ ☯☯☯☯☯ ☯☯☯☯☯ ☯☯☯☯☯

On the train ride back into Tokyo, Charlie decides to give two months' notice at the school and to leave Japan soon after. Pauline isn't surprised to hear it. She says she's been thinking about it also, but will probably wait it out another year. Andrea doesn't comment.

The next day, Charlie begins to put things in order, preparing to go. She decides to travel around Asia for a couple of months before returning to The States. Charlie phones Renny in Kyoto. He is surprised and pleased to hear she is ready to move on.

"Hey bro, it looks like it's me following your lead this time," Charlie says, referring to Renny's impending departure from the country in a week.

Renny chuckles, "About time I got on the other end. "So what's the plan?"

"There is no plan, yet, just an itch."

"Well don't start winging it too much, I wouldn't want you to get too close to my operating style."

"What? You don't think I could handle it?" she teases.

"It's not so much handling it as putting up with it. And be careful what you wish for, sister of mine."

They work out a plan to just meet somewhere on a beach in Thailand in three months – details to be worked out later.

As it turns out, Charlie's two months carry over into almost three. Part of her reluctance to stick to the schedule is a feeling of obligation to minimize the disharmony her leaving will cause at the school, for the students and for the staff. In her almost two years in Japan, she had gradually and subconsciously become tangled in a web of *giri*. The dictionary defines it as "obligation", but to some it is a Japanese version of duty gift wrapped with a smile that says *sucker,* and subtly pressed into an unwilling palm. Giri is a basis for relationships, stressed in every corner of the country and every aspect of the culture. Combining giri with her dormant Catholic guilt, it's a wonder Charlie does not stay in Japan for another year.

But she also wants to match schedules with Marie's exit and to meet up with Renny. When Charlie breaks the news to Marie, a lightning bolt of energy sparks through the phone.

"You have got to be kidding me," Marie shouts! "I'm coming with you! I can't call myself a Kiwi and let my girl here, a Yank at that, show me how it's done."

"You just can't keep up, old lady," Charlie replies.

"We'll see who can't keep up."

Marie calls back the next day to confirm the dates and her commitment to the adventure, which makes Charlie ecstatic. Marie had been a great traveling companion through India and, while Charlie liked the challenge of a solo jaunt, Marie's company is always full of surprises. In truth, Charlie wonders to herself if she can keep up with Marie. During the next couple of weeks the two women talk regularly to compare travel books, highlight maps, and work out a plan to meet up with Renny in Thailand. After that, they will go south together into Malaysia and maybe The Philippines. Just as the plans are finalized in their minds, Charlie gets a call from Cheryl in Seattle. She has a couple weeks' vacation coming to her and wonders what Charlie might be up for.

In the end, they arrange to meet up in Bangkok. Charlie wonders what Joan or her Grandma Maxi would say about coincidences like this one. Funny how these things have a way of working out.

Closing up shop in Japan and bidding a fond *sayonara* to her friends, co-workers, students, and clients leaves Charlie feeling a little blue and more than a bit nostalgic. She writes to her parents:

Dear Mom and Dad,

...I've made some good friends here during the past twenty months. It feels sort of like graduating from high school or leaving the dorms at college. I know I haven't made many – any – close Japanese friends. I think it takes longer than a couple of years to do that. Maybe the Japanese don't readily befriend foreigners because they know that sooner or later we leave. This bothers me a little, but I chalk it up to my inability to speak the language well, my busy work life, and, yes, I always knew this was a short stop for me on life's highway. I hope that it wasn't because I am too closed-minded or unaware.

Did I ever tell you about the Japanese concept of tatemae? It's about the "face" that you show to the world around you being different from the real "you". When they talk about "saving face" they mean keeping relationships honorable and respectful to maintain the harmony. It's not OK here to show your real face, your real feelings, if they will upset the balance of this finely integrated society. Tatemae, both theirs and mine, is definitely part of all of the relationships I made with Japanese people,. I suppose the concept applies to a lesser degree with everyone in any culture. I wonder how much anyone can really connect with another person? Maybe finding a best friend – a soulmate – is a rare occurrence in this world. But I see that you two managed to find each other. And I feel lucky because I was born with one, in a way. It's a rare and lucky thing for me to have Renny...

Love, Charlie

She hopes the letter give them some comfort, in case they think their little girl is miserably lonely and losing it. Or in case they start to worry again when she gets back on the road.

Charlie begins to see Japan differently during her last weeks there. The little things jump out at her – like the pungent smell of ramen noodles from the neighborhood shop, or the cooing of the pigeons under the eaves next door. She stops to fully smell and hear these things, as if for the first time, and knows she will miss them. She also witnesses more incidents like the one that shocked and confused her on her first day in Tokyo. By now, Charlie wonders if she has mastered the art of nonjudgmental patience that would have helped her understand the incident when the old woman was hit by the car at that intersection. Her test comes one morning at the subway station as she waits in line to buy her ticket from the machine.

As she starts to put her coins in the slot, she drops one and bends to pick it up. But when she stands up to try again, an impatient hand knocks hers aside and slips his coins into the slot as her coin and purse full of coins go flying. He doesn't acknowledge Charlie or her coins, as she stands there, dumbfounded, between tears and anger. He grabs his ticket and runs off. Another man in a suit is standing behind her and sees the whole thing. As Charlie bends once more to retrieve her scattered coins, she lets the emotion drain away. The man behind her waits patiently by the machine until she stands up. He asks where she is going in simple Japanese, and she answers politely. He buys her ticket, bows his head curtly and hurries off. She accepts it all. She is grateful, and not confused.

Another test comes on a late night train home just two weeks before Charlie is to leave Japan. She is standing in the middle of the car, in "the train zone" – a state of semi-consciousness that most commuters adopt, lulled into it by the soothing rocking of the car, the drone of the rails, and the mindless jumble of images speeding by the windows. In the train zone, you don't notice who sits next to you or where the train is until it arrives at your stop and some sixth sense shakes you back into the world.

On this occasion, a young couple boards and stands against the sliding entryway doors. As the train starts to move, the young woman, maybe twenty years old, unbuttons her blouse and the man begins to rub his hands and face over her breasts, moving with the gentle sway of the train. He kisses her nipples and licks wildly. She looks like she is enjoying it immensely. Charlie snaps out of semi-consciousness at the incongruity of what she sees, and looks around the car to see that a few other passengers are also watching, but without any emotional or judgmental response, like it is an everyday occurrence. The rest of the passengers don't appear to even notice. The show goes on for several minutes and Charlie watches openly, a little embarrassed but mostly amazed. As the train pulls into the next station, the young woman buttons her blouse and the couple dash out of the train as soon as the doors open up. Of the passengers who remain on board, Charlie notices no shared glances, no change of facial expressions. It is like the incident never happened, and no one but Charlie will remember or ever talk about it.

She meanders throughout the city more frequently now, both as a meditative exercise and as a tourist seeking to burn onto the retina one last memory of a special place. Charlie's inner self begins to overlay memories onto fresh observations, and an internal dialogue develops between the past and the present Charlie. As she passes images of herself in shop windows, she stops seeing the outward, obvious way she "looks" and instead peers inside of her reflection to see if she can observe anything else. She twice catches herself staring blankly into a window for minutes, at essentially nothing, and wonders if she is becoming kooky. Her internal dialog is confusing and soothing at the same time.

The Query: *What's up with this country? Who are these people and why do they act the way they do? There's the elderly woman at the coffee shop who spits in her coffee cup before drinking it. Or the elevator girl in white gloves and pink fedora who chatters away in high-pitched, department store girlspeak, even when nobody is around to care what floor ladies' lingerie is on – except for me who's spying on her from behind a clothes rack. I don't mean to imply that everyone in the country is off their rocker. In Japan, this is most likely less the case than in the States. It's just that I can't find the norm. Is there one?*

The Reply: *I'm afraid the Japanese social fabric is not a continuous, flawless weave of smooth silk. I'm afraid it's quite ripped up – tattered in places. There is form, but to what end and over what substance?*

Confusion: *So why do I care about that? Why do I give two hoots about here?*

Reason: *Because you're attached to it, that's why, girl. Because you've lived here and grown to like it, and know it a little. And maybe you're a little bewildered because if Japan isn't what it seems, then what is? Maybe nothing?! Would that be so bad?*

Understanding: *Yikes! That is both heartening and disturbing. Maybe it says more about me than anything about them. Why do I take notice of these things, and also notice that almost everyone else doesn't seem to notice? Maybe this sort of thing has been going on forever, and I am only now coming into the loop. Did living in Japan bring me into the loop? Would I have made the same discoveries if I had chosen Australia? India? Madagascar? I am less surprised now by the unusual and even eerie vignettes that play out around me. I guess that's why I left the mainstream in the first place.*

Reassurance: *I know, I know. Some – like Renny – might say that I never left the mainstream. That following the lead of thousands of other English teachers and gaijin hostesses is not exactly blazing my own trail, but hey, give yourself a break. There may be a whole network of secondary paths to take – all offering a better way than the main route. I may have left the big river and maybe I spent the last couple of years on a rather large tributary, but I at least did paddle out of the crowded current. And it's an added bonus that, out here in the world, there's a whole regatta of people who are paddling for another flow. The mainstream has become too polluted to sustain the spirit; to maintain a pure heart.*

Hope*: I am ready to seek out new adventures. Time to get myself out of this newly acquired security trap I created for myself. It was a good thing – a kind of stepping stone – and I ought not put myself down about it. I've done pretty well for myself in Japan. In twenty months of working, I managed to save eighteen thousand dollars, more money than I have ever had in my entire life! I will spend a bit on seeing some more of the world, but I'll* *save some to start up something new back Stateside. Or wherever I end up.*

During her last week in Tokyo, Charlie gets an unexpected visit from Tony. They had kept in touch through letters and the occasional phone call since his visit with Renny five months ago and the two have come to know each other little by little. Their relationship has begun to develop into something.

He is in Tokyo for just one evening on business for his school and they hook up for dinner. Over the entrée, Tony hesitates before talking about the future.

"So, you're going to meet up with Renny in a couple of weeks?"

"Yes. In Bangkok. And then down to some island. Why do you have that mischievous look in your eye?" She smiles.

"Well..." he stops to sip some wine, prolonging the drama. "Renny mentioned this to me before he left and I've thought about trying to meet up with him for a couple of weeks and, as it turns out, next week I am at the start of a holiday, so...." He looks away and then back at her, matching her smile.

"I wonder if you could still get a ticket?" Charlie says with animation, which pleases him.

He purses his lips as if pondering, then says, "It just so happens that....I've already booked one. I haven't paid for it yet though." He looks at her squarely, asking the question with his face, but doesn't add any more.

Charlie laughs and lightly kicks him under the table. "Well, you better get on the phone then before it's too late."

"Alright then," he replies, acting casual and getting up to go to the loo.

Charlie thinks, *I do like his company and I'm attracted to him, but I've got to take it slow! Intense and sexual and then over is OK, but does everything need to be that way? I think he's a little uneasy because he's close with Renny. He sure is cute, though.*

They figure out his flight is the day after hers and Marie's and she agrees to wait for him in Bangkok. After that, they walk to the station holding hands. Outside of the train station, as they prepare to go in different directions to catch different trains, he leaves her with a long, soft, lingering kind of kiss. Just a light brushing of tongues – enough to hint at more, and enough to allow Charlie to feel his lips for many hours to come.

Marie shows up in Tokyo three days before they are scheduled to leave and helps Charlie haul boxes off to the post office. Neither of them knows where they will end up next, so they spread their belongings among family and several friends, hoping not to overburden any single one. Charlie mails half of her boxes to her parents and the other half to Cheryl in Seattle, just as Marie sent half of hers to New Zealand and the other half to England. Charlie feels less apprehension about traveling than she did when they first met, two years ago in Heathrow Airport. She feels like she and Marie are on more of an equal footing, though Marie still often acts like an older sister.

On her last night in Tokyo, Charlie goes out on the town with Marie, Andrea and Pauline. Their mood is subdued rather than celebratory, underlying the interrupted friendship that they knew was inevitable.

"Do I detect an undertone of travel envy?" Charlie fishes for some support or passion.

"Maybe a tad," Pauline says, acting jealous.

"It's good to come and it's good to go," Andrea comments with nonchalance.

"Aw, I think you're both bordering on being a lifers," chides Charlie.

"So, you've bought a one-way ticket then?" asks Pauline.

"Tokyo to Bangkok direct. From there it's anybody's guess."

"Same with you?" She nods with her chin to Marie.

"That's right. Though it's not so open that we can't guess where the possibilities might lead."

"Not me. I am an open book of blank pages and I don't want to know," Charlie says.

"When will you be back through Tokyo?' Andrea asks.

"In a few months. I'll need to clean out my bank account and tie up loose ends. But I think this is it for Marie."

"Amen to that," Marie answers. "Who knows when I'll be back here."

"And you're leaving us here to rot and mildew," says Pauline.

"Speak for yourself," replies Andrea. "We'll be relaxing in the first world while these two are getting flea bitten, dysentery, and vaginal warts."

"And sunburned on the beach, drinking martinis," Charlie counters.

"I always considered that "first world-third world" designation to be strange," says Marie. "And just where is the second world? How come you never hear about that?"

"Strange maybe, but true," says Andrea. "Technology, democracy, institutions, you know, the little things that keep us out of the gutter."

"Not necessarily quality though," says Pauline. "Quantity maybe, but not quality."

"I see lots of quality here, I just can't get you poor fools to see it," replies Andrea.

"It feels good to be free with just my backpack. I could forget about all the rest of it. It's all just bullshit," says Marie.

"Nice to know you haven't changed too much," says Charlie, challenging the old theme.

"I calls it like I sees it."

"Well, I see work in the morning, and you two are off early, eh?" Pauline, ever the realist. They nod. Charlie and Marie are crashing on Pauline's floor this last night, having already given up the apartment earlier today. As they exit the restaurant, Charlie and Andrea say their goodbyes. Andrea taps Charlie lightly on her chest as they break their hug. "Stay pure inside there."

"I'll follow your lead in that," says Charlie. Andrea rolls her eyes and grins, turning to stroll away.

The three catch a train to Pauline's neighborhood. Walking from the station, Pauline asks Charlie a question out of the blue.

"Do you remember when we went gomi-hunting for furniture and we saw that couple fighting in the park?" Pauline muses.

"Yes," Charlie replies, and explains it to Marie. "I think about it every so often."

"I'd have kicked his ass," Marie replies and gets a laugh from the others.

"I'm sure you would have. Why do you ask, Pauls?"

"We just passed a similar couple back there a ways, up one of the alleys." Marie and Charlie turn, but only see people walking down the street.

"They weren't quite in the same mess the other couple appear to have been in, but this woman didn't look too happy either. Do you want to go back?"

Charlie just looks at her – it feels like a test. "So, what are you saying? That I'm one of the jaded now?" Charlie says this a bit too loud, with a slightly defensive edge to her voice.

"No, no. It's just that you act a bit more Japanese about the world now," says Pauline, hugging Charlie's elbow.

Marie laughs.

"Is that a good or a bad thing?" Charlie ponders, out loud.

15

RENNY

SAN FRANCISCO	KYOTO	THAILAND	KATMANDU	LAKE TOBA	INDIA	IPOH

EARLY YEARS	YEAR 1	YEAR 2

FISHES IN THE STREAM

It was March 15th. The sky was clear and pale blue that morning, unusual both for the time of year and the place. I was standing on a corner in western San Francisco, at the edge of the Inner Sunset district, waiting for a bus to take me to the N Judah line and into the city center. The pavement was damp from the night's rain and the gleam of the rising sun was all that much brighter as it reflected off of the still-wet surfaces all around. Pockets of steam wafted up here and there as they caught the first rays of the day.

There was a new face at the bus stop this morning. A young woman standing two yards away, dressed all in black: shoes, stockings, mini skirt, leather jacket, wrap-around sunglasses and shoulder length, jet-black dyed hair. There was no other color on her except her white skin and silver earrings. She smoked ferociously, forcibly and loudly exhaling the smoke upwards and wasting no time before inhaling another drag. I shook off my staring and came back to life as soon as I heard the gaggle approaching. They departed their bus a block away and headed for this corner with determination. As it did every morning, the sight gave me a warm feeling.

Five days a week for the last two years. I still didn't know where they came from, where they were headed, or for what. To church, maybe. During my first week at the stop, I had patiently waited, gentlemanly, as the dozen (it seemed like more) short and aged Chinese women boarded my bus in a rush. The first few times I let them all in ahead of me, and there was room to

306

squeeze in behind them. I only half-expected a nod or two of appreciation and was only half-disappointed when they didn't even acknowledge my gesture. But then one day there wasn't enough room, and I missed the bus for lack of space. The next morning, politeness be damned, I went straight for the door when the bus pulled up, instead of allowing the group in ahead of me. Then I got some recognition, alright. The lead matron gave me such a harsh look that I blanched with guilt. I thought for a moment that I might be assaulted by swinging handbags, but of course I wasn't. But I had learned my lesson, and held my ground every morning after that, often boxing out the little biddies with my butt and elbows while trying to guess the exact point where the bus would stop. It became a game for us, but I'm not sure any of them really enjoyed it.

This particular splendidly sunny spring morning, the group was more audible than usual, speaking in rapid and clipped Chinese. Nothing like the sun to bring out the chirping, I mused to myself. The bus came and I let them board ahead of me. After all, this was the last day of the game. It felt only right to finish it this way. And it didn't matter that none of the beneficiaries of my kindness even glanced up in my direction. The woman in black was visibly flustered at the aggressive gaggle as she ground out her cigarette on the sidewalk. She inserted herself into the middle of it with audible frustration. I sent her a smile of camaraderie, which she ignored, and then I squeezed in behind the group, just able to fit inside the door as it closed behind me.

I was really loving the morning commute today, savoring the lingering aftertaste of dread that had accompanied me for most of the last year. It had almost completely faded, replaced by a sort of premature nostalgia. I changed from the bus to the street car ten blocks later. I scanned the passing cityscape through the window. The rows of Victorian fronts were glistening pink and yellow – magnificent! – and the downtown skyline, varied and jagged, was a human-made arête of concrete and glass. The streetcar plunged underground and the view was lost in darkness, punctuated by flashes of light from passing stations and streetcars heading back out. By routine, I exited the streetcar and the downtown station, joining the throngs of work-a-day Joes and Janes as we all aimed for the office.

This day I strolled a little more lightly than the rest of the suits on the sidewalk. Why be in a rush today? I sat on a park bench just outside my office building, a block off of Market Street, and watched the figures scurry around me. It was amusing, for the first time in two years, and I was glad for that little comfort.

When I stepped off the elevator, the office was already abuzz with activity. Half of the staff had been in since four a.m., when the office opened to be ready for the New York opening. I was glad I graduated from that shift after my first year. Today I didn't really have much to do aside from cleaning out my desk and saying goodbye to co-workers. I headed to my cubicle, the contents of which had already been crammed into boxes or given away to the office vultures. I was lucky to still have an office chair. I decided to just sit down and look around. What *was* all this stuff? Did any of it matter at all? Then I saw them staring down at me, smiling, one of the last signs of my personal life left up on the cubicle bulletin board. Mom and Dad and Charlie, in a photo taken during our last year of college during Christmas vacation. We were all in Miami for a Diaz reunion....

Uncle Jorge's house is a sprawling six bedroom suburban stucco affair with huge, blossoming gardens. Almost all of the clan is gathered: Grandma Maxi and her four children and their kids as well. There are twenty in all, just one cousin missing because she is taking her sophomore year abroad in Madrid. In fact. cousin Carla's travels in Spain are the current topic of discussion. Her father, Uncle Marty, is waxing on to Charlie and me about sowing our wild oats. Anton, Uncle Marty's eldest, joins us. He's now a lawyer with a big firm in Chicago, and indulges his father's jolly mood – enhanced from four hours of vodka tonics.

"You gotta get those adventures in while you're young. Lemme tell ya, 'cause boy, when yer older, the bills and the responsibilities take hold and the chances just ain't there anymore. Ain't that right my boy," he says to Anton. Anton nods thoughtfully and Uncle Marty asks Charlie to make him another drink. She happily obliges. We've just had our 21st birthday and joining the relatives in a cocktail is new and exciting.

Anton looks serious and proper, dressed in a button down light blue oxford shirt, khakis and penny loafers. I've never really enjoyed his company, though we have always been pleasant to each other. His extra five years have been too much for us to bridge in order to become close. And his frat boy style makes me want to spill a drink on his perfect look, but of course I don't.

"I think that's right, sir" Anton says. "I like having the money from work, but extra time is non-existent." Charlie returns with a set of glasses and gives one to Uncle Marty, keeping the other.

"Thanks darlin'," he says in his best good ole' boy accent. I laugh, inside, because I have always been amused by Uncle Marty's contrast to the rest of the family. He is married to Dad's younger sister, the proper and society-conscious Aunt Elena, and he owns and manages his own auto parts store. He always seems more interested in having a good time than in being serious, so we kids naturally gravitate towards him. "So, what are you two gonna do now?" he continues. "Yer finishin' up school by summer, ain't that right?"

"Keep your fingers crossed," Charlie replies, raising her eyebrows.

"I really don't have a clue what I'm going to do," I tell him. "I'd travel if I had the money, but I'll probably have to find some work first."

"You're majoring in economics right?" Anton says this with a frown, so I nod more enthusiastically than I feel.

"Have you thought about graduate school? Or law school maybe?"

"I want to be done with school. I'm tired of it."

"Well, it's the best avenue to getting a better paying job. It's well worth the investment of time and money. I'm proof of that."

"Yeah," says Charlie, *"But do you really like it? I mean, doing the eight to five routine just seems so...so...boring."*

Uncle Marty lets out a *"whooowhee"* and then adds, *"Ain't that the truth, child. You keep that thought and remember what I said about gettin' yer adventures in."* I turn to observe Anton squirm at his father's advice.

"But you're a business owner, father," he says. *"You know it takes hard work to get where you want and there's no substituting for it."* Anton unconsciously fingers the buttons on his shirt front and then runs his fingers through his hair and looks over at his mother across the room. Following his glance, I notice he is his mother's son, perfectly coiffed and proper. I wonder, momentarily, how Aunt Elena and Uncle Marty ever hooked up?

"That's mighty true, but all good things in due time. It's good to know first what you really want though, 'cause yer likely to get it." Uncle Marty drains his drink in one gulp and smacks his lips in satisfaction.

"What do you want, Anton?" asks Charlie.

"What do you mean?" he replies, turning towards her with a frown. *"The same thing everyone else does. Nice things, like a car and clothes and a house or apartment, you know. It's more than that too. I also want to be recognized for my work, to feel satisfied knowing that I can do something well."*

"And what's it you're working on now?"

"I'm lawyering, you know, writing contracts and negotiating."

"For...?"

"Most of my clients are businesses, like in banking or finance." He appeared satisfied with his answer, himself and the importance of his work.

"And overall, your happiness quotient is...?" I waited, but he didn't bite, so I let it go. I didn't want to push Anton to make a point that I wasn't quite sure about myself.

My nostalgia was interrupted by a throat being cleared outside my cubicle.

"Hey, Earth-to-Renny." It was Lena from Marketing, a buddy from the early shift of a year ago. We had since become less close, more from lack of proximity than anything else.

"Oh, hey. Hi Lena. I was just reliving my recent past." I showed her the photo. "That was taken five years ago, in Florida. And now I'm off for who knows how long? And who knows where?"

"So, now what, are you having second thoughts?"

"Naw, I'm just not sure what I'm looking for. What I want. To wander. To be free. That's about it."

"Well, don't be a stranger." She gave me a wink and wandered off, leaving me with a vague feeling of inadequacy. Why? I haven't figured that out yet.

I spent the rest of the morning cleaning up my files. By lunchtime I was ready to leave for the day and be finished, but hey, I needed the money so I decided to gut it out until the end of the day. I was up to the 6th level in Galactic Battle Cruiser when Patrick and Shari showed up to take me out to lunch.

Patrick worked in Lena's department and Shari was done for the day, being one of the lowlifes from the early shift. We had been comrades in arms, railing together against The Man, while still accepting our paychecks, of course.

"Lets get dogs at the stand, walk down to the Embarcadero and sit by the fountain." I suggested this, since it was my favorite way to spend the noon hour in San Francisco when the sun was out. The bright day had clouded over, though, in typical San Francisco fashion; tantalizing you with beauty one minute and hiding it the next. Not that it was truly hidden, mind you.

Shari had a new design shaved into the crew cut around the perimeter of her head. It was a series of fish swimming clockwise with a few strands of seaweed in between. The hair on top was longer and dyed green. Her head looked like a tropical island. This was the fourth design she had had in the past two months, and I had to say something about it to her.

"Nice reef. Good to be able to change the scenery at your whim."

"I'd change it every week if I could," she replied, "if it didn't run fifty bucks a shot."

"I like this one better than the triangles and squares," said Patrick.

"Oh really? I'd have thought that one would have suited you better," she replied. Patrick frowned and I smiled at the joust. She never let up on his mostly mainstream tendencies. While the three of us considered ourselves on the fringe, each perceived it in a different way. For Shari it was raging against the socialized image and limitations for women; for Patrick, it was whining against having to work at all when baseball and other pursuits were clearly more desirable. For me, well, I was against it all.

Shari and I had enjoyed a brief fling a few months back. I was taken with her brashness and beauty, enhanced in a mildly vulgar way by her wild adornment of it. The affair lasted only two nights but the sex was as raw as I had hoped. On the third evening, I went to see her recite one of her own pieces at a poetry reading in the Castro District. She exhorted passionately about Nicaragua, the pain of the people there, the oppression of the heat, the poverty and the government.... and it wasn't half bad. But the only call to action it incited in me was between the sheets, and when she sensed my ambivalence, that was all she wrote. We traded notes through Patrick, just like in high school, and remained friends. She was a good egg, really. Not the maniac in black that some folks at the office thought her to be. A little bit of rebellion is healthy for everyone. Looking over at her that last afternoon at work, I wondered if I could have mustered more enthusiasm for her cause. *That was truly moving...and the meter was right in sync...* But who was I kidding?

"I think this one's one of your best. Right up there beside the chessboard," I said, meaning it as a sincere compliment.

"That one ran me eighty bucks," she said, "and the pieces grew back in within a week. The price we pay for our art." She said this last part with exaggerated pain and it got chuckles from me and Patrick. "I see you've cleaned up your act now that you're quitting and going out into the unknown universe." She nodded towards my new 'do' – short on the sides and top, and clean-shaven cheeks. I shrugged.

"Couldn't have done this while working now, could I?"

"You're still a bum. Nice hair can't hide that," said Patrick. We reached the Embarcadero fountain and, after purchasing our wieners, found a place to sit near the water and away from the suits. We were within shot of the occasional misty spray and we didn't mind.

"Aren't you going to miss this wonderful place?" Patrick swept his arm about.

"It really is wonderful," I had to agree, "and yes, I'll miss it, a little. I'll miss the homeless guy over on the wall feeding the pigeons and guarding his cart. And of course, the prime viewing of the latest designs." I reached over to give Shari's head a gentle caress. She stiffened a bit at first and then, uncharacteristically, leaned over and nuzzled my shoulder so I got a face full of green bangs..

"We'll keep you informed of any major changes," Patrick promised. I only barely heard him through the mental haze brought on by Shari's closeness.

"Ground control to Major Diaz! Hellloooo?" Patrick waved a hand in front of my face. Shari sat up and smiled up at me. It was a special gift to see her smile.

"Is it all just too much for you? Maybe you should just stay put?" she jested.

"He's been doing this more often lately, you know," Patrick confided. "Higgs caught him day dreaming during a staff meeting two weeks ago, and what did our good man say when his reverie was interrupted? He laughed – a predictable 'HA!'." Patrick spit out the mime.

"Mr. Higgs didn't laugh with me, as I recall," I reminded him. "But fuck him. I had just given him my notice the day before. *'Don't think you can skate through the end of your stay with us, Mister Diaz.'* What an asshole." My impression of the stick-up-his-butt Mr. Higgs got a smile from my friends.

We sat for a few minutes longer and then started walking back to work. As we reached the building, I hesitated and tugged on Shari's arm to slow down. Patrick got the signal and went in, leaving us alone outside. After an awkward moment, I gave her a hug. When we separated, she looked up and smiled again.

"I don't know why I'm telling you this," she said, uncertainly, "but you're probably the last man I'll ever sleep with." It wasn't funny, but I smiled.

"Giving up the bi route and focusing solely on your own gender, eh?"

"Something like that."

I nodded. I hadn't known about her open-gender policy until after our first night together. Upon hearing her new direction, part of me – the manly ego part – was pleased, but the other part was curious. "I hope I haven't put you off of men altogether?"

She laughed. "Don't give yourself too much credit. Or blame." She tiptoed up and kissed me on the lips, hard, but without passion, more as a statement of her power than in affection. She walked me to the elevator and we stood silently waiting for it. She turned away as I entered and I winked goodbye as she looked back before the doors shut.

Back upstairs, I wasted another two hours playing computer games and stealing a few office supplies. By three o'clock, I couldn't stand it anymore and started to make my exit. In the accounting department, I made the rounds, saying goodbye to those with whom I had worked, but knew very little about. It felt anticlimactic and yet satisfying, perfunctory but sincere. Saving the best for last, I rounded the corner to Mr. Higgs' office. He spotted me and, to my surprise, smiled and beckoned me to enter.

"Glad to see you stuck it out, Renny." He rose and shook my hand.

"What else could I do?" was my pithy reply. Then he reached into a desk drawer and handed me what I assumed was my final paycheck.

"You don't need to stay the rest of the day if you don't want to. Best of luck to you." I shook his outstretched hand once again and considered a parting shot, but then thought better of it. I choked out a "Thank you, Mr. Higgs" before he dismissed me with his broad back as he turned to work on something that caught his attention. I wandered away, a free man.

I returned to my cubicle, picking up a little spring in my step with every stride. I retrieved my little box of mementos from this phase of my life and headed towards the elevator, passing Patrick's cubicle on the way out.

"They let you out early?"

I nodded and smiled a big one.

"See you back home then?"

"Yeah, let's hit The Haight tonight."

I reversed the morning ride on public transportation, back to Patrick's apartment, which was just two blocks away from my old flat. He had been generous to let me doss here for ten days so far. Two more until my flight. But I was too antsy to wait here until he got home. I dropped the box off on the kitchen table and caught a bus to Ocean Beach. I wanted to walk along the surf for a couple of miles one last time. Or at least for an hour.

It was still sunny out on the beach, in contrast to the usual misty fog. I would have taken that as a good omen, if I believed in such things. The beach was relatively quiet, but probably typical for a weekday. There were a few pairs of people starting to walk the sand, taking advantage of the rarely-seen sun. I started walking.

Down the dune a stretch I saw an old man sweeping the sand with a metal detector. He was wearing earphones over a faded plaid golf cap and he was whistling.

A sharp beeping coming from his wand caught my attention as I approached him, and the man dropped suddenly to his knees and started to dig with his hands. He seemed to have found something, but was struggling to uncover it, stopping after a minute and exhaling a long breath. I went over to help him and dropped to one knee next to him. He looked up, at first with alarm, and his arm came up to fend me off.

"Need any help, mister?" I offered with a smile. When he saw I just wanted to be friendly, he relaxed and pulled off the earphones and cap, revealing a shiny pate. He was already sweating and unzipped his khaki jacket. The breeze felt unusually warm.

"Sure thing, son," he replied. "Much obliged. This old body don't work like it used to." I dug down into the sand a good six inches and found a rounded edge. I tapped on it with my fingers – it appeared to be a hubcap. We both stopped for a moment, peering down like archaeologists at a newly uncovered treasure. We dug it out finally and brushed it off. It wasn't a hubcap at all. It was some sort of shield made of metal, with a well-worn image of a yin-yang symbol surrounded by a dragon. It seemed to be etched in silver on a round metal disk. I turned it over and discovered a picture hook.

"It must be a wall hanging of some sort." I offered.

"Heh heh," the old man chuckled. "Would you look at that? You never know what you'll find." He was clearly pleased with the treasure..

"How do you think it got here?" I wondered out loud. "It doesn't look rusted enough to have spent any time in the water."

"Somebody probably tossed it from their car window, like a Frisbee." The man turned it over in his hands and then made a motion to toss it away himself, but didn't. Instead, he laughed again. "I used to have me a pendant with this symbol on it when I was in the Navy back in 1949. I got it in Manila. I gave it to my grandson a few years ago and now look, I've got me one again."

"Do you know what it means?" I did, and I thought he did, too.

"Oh, it has something to do with male and female. Can't have one without the other you know." He looked over at me with a devious grin and then back at the disc, flipping it over as if studying it. "They say it's all about balance in the end," he said, still contemplating the object.

"Well, have you lived a balanced life?" I asked, half-jokingly.

He looked up at me, but had a faraway look in his eyes. "Oh, I suppose so. I never did go in much for eastern ways of thinking. I only wore that pendant because it was given to me by the sweetest looking girl I'd ever seen. A little Filipino gal named Rita. I met her at a USO club. Our boat had been put in the yard near Manila for minor repairs and we sailors pretty much had a month of liberty."

"So you fell in love and brought her home with you?" I guessed this wasn't the case, but the thought just came out of my mouth.

He shook his head and looked down. "I always meant to go back for her. I told her I would, but I never saw her again. We left Manila and I left the navy when we got back to Alameda and then…" His voice trailed off into a distant memory. "My wife died about three years ago."

"I'm sorry to hear that. Maybe you should go find that Rita."

The old man looked perplexed for a moment, then broke out in a cackle that tied him up for half a minute.

"Wouldn't that be something? I sure hope time has been kinder to her than it has to me." He became silent for a moment, then continued, "I'm ashamed to say it, but I've been thinking more about Rita than I have about my wife since she passed on. Forty two years we were married, and now that she's gone I spend more time thinking about a woman I spent only three weeks with, forty somethin' years ago. Go figure. Naw, I think that the time for me and Rita is half a century too late, but it's a fun thought. Just remember, you never know what's going to happen out there in the world, young fella. Just keep your eyes open is all I can say. Take a risk once in a while, but don't be stupid."

"I'll keep that in mind, sir." I got up and brushed the sand off my pants. "Be careful with your back now."

In my mind's eye, the old man became my high school physics teacher, who said to me, *"Inertia is one of the most powerful forces in the universe. The energy that pushes us in one direction requires a concentrated, opposing energy to slow down, stop or redirect us...and a huge force of energy to reverse it completely."* That young sailor in Manila had all kinds of energy propelling him towards the American dream of a wife, kids, and a home in the suburbs. Would his life have been better – or worse? – if Rita had been a more powerful force? Or if inertia had been less powerful? Time can't be reversed, of course, and regret is a wasted emotion. I knew then and there that I would face the next year or two with no regrets, to see where I ended up. I wished for balance and adventure, but knew that chance was the big unknown, as it should be.

☙☙☙☙☙ ☙☙☙☙☙ ☙☙☙☙☙ ☙☙☙☙☙ ☙☙☙☙☙

It was the night before I left the city – the country, for that matter – and Patrick and I were out on the town in the North Beach neighborhood. We met up right after Patrick finished work and hit all of my favorite haunts: North Beach Pizza and the Savoy Tivoli. Now we were winding down the evening at Mr. Bing's, a tiny, smoky, dimly-lit hole in the wall in the red light district. We discovered this bar a year earlier and liked it for the seedy feel and the fact that it had beatnik ties. The patrons these days were mostly in their 50's and 60's and had quieted down from the ranting pranksters depicted in the posters and poems at the bookstore just up the street.

The bartender at Mr. Bing's knew us and let us run a tab. "The usual," I said to the barman with a wink. He just looked at me like I was stupid. We hadn't been in here *that* often, I guess.

"Two shots of your best tequila with beer chasers," said Patrick, bailing me out.

"Hey, I don't want to overdo it." I faked some concern. My flight left in the early afternoon. Patrick rolled his eyes at me as we took two stools at the bar.

"You're gonna have to keep me apprised of how Japanese baseball compares to ours," said Patrick.

"My guess is they're better than the Cubbies at any rate," I said. Patrick snorted at the comment, but didn't reply. We met during my first week at work and became fast friends. Patrick was a sports fanatic and seemed to think of all aspects of life in that frame of reference. It made for good conversation and banter around the office, though I was looking forward to escaping the daily routine of checking scores.

"They have a few pitchers over here now, but I haven't yet heard of any hitters or fielders to come this way yet. Though there is some talk of some guy coming on with Seattle soon. Ichi-something? That makes sense in the evolution of the game, I think. The pitching comes along before the hitting does." I adopted Patrick's authoritative air.

"What the hell do you know about it?" he took the bait. "I don't see the same thing happening to the Central American players." I loved it when he challenged my knowledge of the game.

"That's true, but look at a regular season," I replied. "The pitchers always have it better at the beginning than at the end. That's because it takes time for the hitters to figure them out."

"So how does that explain Japan's baseball evolution?" I couldn't tell if he was feeding me these lines as a last-night tribute or if he really didn't know.

"Very simple, Watson. Japan plays in a more conservative style, if what I'm reading is correct, and I assume it is. We know they have major league grade pitchers, so the hitters face real heat. My guess is that, because hitting takes a certain amount of aggression, it's taken them longer to develop kick-ass hitting. I'm sure it will come, though."

319

"My friend, the baseball philosopher." Patrick raised his glass in a toast.

"A noble undertaking, often misunderstood, but clearly a way to truth and beauty," I countered as we clinked our glasses and downed our shots.

"Maybe the skills of the Asian players are more suited to pitching and it's just a matter of simple genetics, you know, like the Kenyans in the marathon or the Brazilians at soccer," I added cautiously, not wanting to get into a deep discussion about race and sports.

"There may be something to that," Patrick said, seriously. "Though I think it's more a case of it being up here." He tapped the side of his head.

"Everything is up there in the end."

"Not everything. Sometimes it's here too." He tapped his chest. "Without the will, all the ability in the world is nothing."

"But there's more to it than just heart. I know emotion plays a big part, but without the talent, heart is courageous, but not enough. Think about it. We've both known guys who had all the drive in the world, but lacked the talent to make the big leagues."

Patrick nodded, looking contemplative. He signaled the barman for two more shots. "You need to be able to recognize where to put your energies, that's true. I wanted to play shortstop as bad as anything I've ever wanted, but I'm just not quick enough. I'm glad I recognized it early. But you have to be able to dream don't you!? If you don't dream, then what is there?" He said this without any emotion. The shots arrived and he tipped his back immediately, following it with a healthy slug of beer.

"Yeah, you have to dream, but recognize where dream and reality diverge. That or be strong enough to make them converge." I didn't know where that sentiment came from, but I knew it was true as soon as it came out of my mouth.

"If half the people out there who made it had listened to the odds makers, they'd be sitting here like us, talking about it instead of doing it. Not everyone is an all-star. That's the beauty of it. And some who have the talent don't make it because they don't have the heart or the discipline to develop their talent. Or sometimes there are too many nay-sayers." Now he was getting into the fray.

"That's true of everything. The thing that gets me is, why do some people that don't deserve it still get there? I think luck plays a big factor."

"No doubt. Luck and balls. If you ain't got the *cojones* to try a thing, then you don't deserve to have it. And if you do go for it and don't get there, then hey, at least you can say you tried. There's got to be some satisfaction in that." We toasted the point.

"So what about the other half?" I could see that Patrick's light was burning bright now and I didn't want to turn it down just yet. Sometimes I tired early of his sports enthusiasm because he tended to go off, way out into the stratosphere, but tonight I wanted to go along with him.

"The other half. The other half. You mean the people who just don't have the sense to know not to try a thing? Well, they're saps, I guess, but still, you gotta like that they give it a try. It's like the guy in Kesey's book who tries to lift the refrigerator, or whatever it was. He knows deep down he can't lift that thing, but there is just this *inkling* of hope and he latches onto it and tries anyway. That's admirable, man. You can't fault somebody for trying. And for those who made it without really having to try, well, shit, we all wish we were like that. Everybody wants to win the lottery, but you can't bank on that." He was rambling now.

"You can't really bank on anything when it comes right down to it." I supplied the obvious closing comment.

"We can bank on your leaving tomorrow." Patrick was back on the ground now.

"I suppose that is something. What about you now? You'll stay with the market game? What about that sports bar you keep talking about?"

"Someday. When I can pull together the cash and get my shit together. For now, I'll stay where I am, though this move of yours has me thinking." He finished off his beer.

I knew that Patrick would continue to immerse himself in the Giants and the 49ers and the Warriors and the rest, leaving him with little free time to truly explore his own path. It was both a beauty and a bane of sports and entertainment addiction. Of any addiction. You spend the better part of a day under its influence and that keeps the dread at bay. Not a bad way to go about life, all said and done. We anesthetize ourselves in one way or another to avoid having to engage in our own lives. Self-medication is the modern way, part of American culture. Whether it be booze or Ritalin or Prozac or the TV. Patrick wholeheartedly and sincerely dove into the information flow every day, in the hope that it would sweep him away completely, to the point where his decisions were all made for him. I thought of it as a sad comfort – easier for pain relief in the short term, but hell to look back on from your 60th birthday, unless you never look back. Or up, or down, or anywhere beyond your tiny place in the world. I sometimes wished I had that talent. Maybe Patrick got it right. Maybe there was nothing else except the passion of the trivial pursuit, so why get all bound up in trying to find something else? Good question. All I knew was, I had to go.

The next morning, I woke early and made Patrick a nice omelet to go with the two ibuprofen and coffee we both needed. We kept the conversation light, knowing it would be the last for a long time. A handshake, a back pat, and a smile at the door, and Patrick was off to the grindstone, leaving me to create a path leading away from that wheel.

Me, my bags were already packed and I had no last minute errands to run, so I left early for the airport. I took the same route as I would have taken into work, only extending it a leg further. It was different riding in the mid-morning on a weekday. I couldn't tell if it was me or the crowd. I was relaxed and excited in the throes of seeing the city in farewell mode. The ride seemed to go both slower and faster at the same time and I pondered my exit from this city, my home for two years.

I read somewhere that the relativity of time is dependent on perspective, so that five seconds touching a hot stove could feel like an eternity, and likewise an hour with a pretty girl could flash by in an instant. I wondered what Einstein would have said about both perspectives existing simultaneously from the same point?

Maybe all points of view exist at the same moment and what you see laid out before you depends solely on what you focus your attention. The wheel we are on rolls along at its own pace. If you peek around the edge, you see it moving quickly, but if you're standing at the hub, it seems to be rotating slowly. So, what does that mean? I can't say really, only that, as I watched San Francisco recede into the horizon, I could also see the wheel's hub and its edge at the same time. That was a new perspective for me, and I was pleased to be able to realize it.

I sat in the gate lounge watching the parade of people pass. I read newspapers, finding the sports sections of four different ones, and downed enough coffee to keep me wired for hours. When they finally called my flight for boarding, I was jittery and excited – from the coffee or the anticipation, I wasn't sure. But I was elated and scared and oh-so-ready. I almost bounced down the gangway, ducking my head through the plane doorway and entering the cocoon of the 747. I would spend the next 12 or so hours in a suspended state – traveling from one world, one way of being, to a whole new one I knew almost nothing about. As excited as I was, after a few hours, I found myself nodding off into a deep sleep. I missed two bad meals and three even worse movies, awakening just an hour before landing. Not a bad way to start it off.

16

CHARLIE

SEATTLE	TOKYO	THAILAND	LONDON	THE PHILIPPINES	INDIA

YEAR 1	YEAR 2	YEAR 3

WHAT TO DO

"C'mon – you've been getting ready for this ever since Nikko. The only thing you've forgotten is to buy *my* ticket!" Pauline feigns disgust.

It's the morning of Charlie's departure, just before they all head out the door – Pauline to work and Charlie and Marie to the train station. She's really happy for Charlie, and only a little jealous. Charlie offers her a cocked-head smile and Pauline softens.

"Don't worry, darlin'. If there's anything you've missed, just let me know and I'll take care of it if I can."

"Thanks, Pauls. What am I going to do without you?" Charlie gives her a quick hug.

"Lord knows how the world manages without me backin' 'em up, but they do." They all walk out together that morning, Pauline with her small and light daypack of ESL books, Marie and Charlie with their big, heavy backpacks. At the train station, they hug again and this time Charlie doesn't let go so quickly and Pauline squeezes back. They part and Pauline winks and darts off into the crowd. No words are passed.

On the way to Narita, they let the excitement of the adventure emerge and take hold. The bustle of Tokyo station has Marie snarling and Charlie smiling – at the crowded energy and at Marie. Marie catches on and reacts.

"Christ! Don't tell me you're enjoying this?"

Charlie smiles and shrugs her shoulders, then puts her hand on Marie's shoulder. She lets it rest there as they weave their way through the morning rush hour throngs to the airport express. As they board the train, even Marie begins to lighten up.

"Fucking Japan!" she says out loud to the platform, and then more quietly to Charlie as they sit, "It is an oddly beautiful place, in spite of itself. In spite of me." Charlie leans over and kisses Marie's cheek. They speed onto Narita airport in silence, each soaking up views of the city and lost in thought. There is no apprehension as they shuffle through lines and board the plane. Before they know it, they are descending over the Gulf of Thailand.

It's great flying into Bangkok a second time. I feel like an old hand at this Southeast Asia route! Charlie muses as they arrive. As they disembark, she lets Marie take the lead in customary fashion, but with amusement this time rather than relief. Charlie knows Marie has to deal with the world in her own way and it's okay. The new country jitters are almost absent as they sail through immigration and customs, exchange money and hail a taxi. The entry is almost automatic, as their hotel is predetermined and Cheryl is already there, having arrived that morning.

She and Charlie haven't seen each other in two years and the reunion in the lobby is loud and physical.

By mid-evening, Charlie leaves Marie in their room to sleep and goes to Cheryl's room to chatter away. After only three less-than-neighborly fist-taps on the thin walls, they decide to take the conversation outside. They roam around the Banglamphu district.

"Man, Bangkok is a zoo!" Cheryl exclaims. "But look at all the foreigners around!"

"Khao-San Road is just that way," says Charlie. "I don't really like it, but it's easy." They meander through alleyways and down to the river. The streets and the shops are familiar to Charlie from her first visit here.

"Easier than I thought it would be. The taxi driver from the airport just assumed I was coming here! So, look at you – more than two years since you were here and you seem to have slipped right back into it."

Charlie laughs. "If you only knew the truth. Though I guess I am not as green as I was when I first started out."

ⒶⒶ Ⓐ Ⓐ Ⓐ   Ⓐ Ⓐ Ⓐ Ⓐ Ⓐ   Ⓐ Ⓐ Ⓐ Ⓐ Ⓐ   Ⓐ Ⓐ Ⓐ Ⓐ Ⓐ   Ⓐ Ⓐ Ⓐ Ⓐ Ⓐ

Tony shows up late the next evening, as planned.

Tani, the owner of the guesthouse, is quite apologetic when he tells them that the place is full – an unusual situation for Bangkok in March. He's sorry, though glad for the business, and suggests that they work out a sharing arrangement. It's just for one night, after all. Tony doesn't react visibly, despite Charlie's questioning glance.

"Just a sec," she says, taking a step back and approaching the other two women, who are reading at one of the lobby tables.

"You'll never guess....." Charlie opens as she sits down. Marie is ready to do battle with Tani, but Charlie asks her not to, making light of the situation.

"It's no big deal. We'll be off tomorrow morning and it'll be done with."

They decide to switch – Cheryl and Marie agree to tolerate each other for one night so Charlie can share with Tony.

"I feel a little awkward about this, but hey, we're friends, eh? *Gambarimashō*," Charlie says with a promising smile and a bow.

"Yes, let's 'do our best'." Tony picks up on her Japanese. "Or should I say, *mai pen rai* – as Renny taught me. It means "it can't be helped, so live with it" in Thai. A very helpful little phrase, isn't it? We'll just have to make do." Tony blows out a long sigh and acts the stoic one, though Charlie can detect his amusement.

"Don't get any ideas now," she teases, to which he puts his arms up in feeble defense. Its late evening already and the group trundles off to bed, anticipating the next morning's journey to the island. Charlie catches Tony peeking at her as she dresses for bed, and he blushes as he turns away.

"Er...sorry. Well...no...I'm not....but I'll blame the jet lag if that's alright?"

Charlie smiles sweetly in reply, saying, "Forgiven." She steals glances of her own, though more discretely. Their flirtation has a seriousness and intrigue that promises a passionate culmination some day. By some electric but shared instinct, they make a tacit agreement to engage in days, rather than minutes, of foreplay. Instead of rushing into an affair, they both are happy to play the game as the stakes get higher.

The next morning at breakfast, Tony casually touches Charlie's back as they climb the steps to the café. During the meal, Charlie lets her knees bump up against his under the table. He pretends he doesn't notice but she is sure he's well aware of her body.

At ten a.m. the group leaves for the beaches of Koh Chang to meet up with Renny. They share a minibus with half a dozen others for the five hour ride.

They catch an easy connection to the ferry from Laem Ngop. But upon arrival at the island pier, their camaraderie morphs into chaos as the group tries to figure out how to get to the beach where Renny awaits them.

"Lets walk out to the main road and get away from these guys," says Marie, referring to the jitney drivers plying the ferry pier.

"But why not just go with one of them," says Cheryl.

"Maybe we should go the other direction, to the village first," adds Charlie.

"Trying to get four westerners to make a decision is an exercise in anti-Zen," Tony mutters to a passing backpacker, but lets the women squabble, standing a couple of paces off, silent and smiling. Charlie takes charge by flagging down the next available taxi and negotiating the fare. The others follow. Marie seems at a loss for words, but smiles her surrender as Charlie winks at her.

Renny seems happy to see everyone then puts on a pout about their being a day late, but everyone knows it's just for show. The others are good about leaving Charlie and Renny be for the rest of the day to re-bond. Charlie is keen on getting his story about Malaysia and he's excited to tell it.

"My plan is to go to Malaysia with Marie after this. We'll split up for a few weeks after we get to Penang, and then she'll go on to Java. I'll stay in Malaysia and hit the Cameron Highlands, and I don't know where else, before heading for Singapore. Then we'll meet up in Manila and travel together again there for another month." Charlie relays her itinerary as if it is a flight plan. Renny just laughs.

"Sounds good. Unless you two have a blow out fight, or you meet another sexy scuba instructor or...." She punches him in the arm to interrupt him but he continues, retelling stories from the road that she has already heard or read. But now she's paying attention to the details.

The group quickly settles into a beach routine. Everyone is ready for it, each needing some time to unwind from the Japan pace – or the Seattle pace, for Cheryl. The second morning at breakfast, there is a flap over rooming, with a German fellow claiming Marie's single bungalow as due him. Marie, having been primed already by the situation at Tani's Guesthouse in Bangkok, is not about to let it go and holds her ground, even winning over the German, Kris, and inviting him for a drink. Tony and Renny half-heartedly invite the girls to go for a hike up the mountain behind the bungalows, but they decline in unison. Marie has noticed some of Charlie's interest in Tony and they discuss it as the boys head off.

"Not a bad catch of the day, as far as men go," Marie says as they watch the two men start up the beach.

"What are you inferring..."?

"Hey, you can't fool me, girl, so don't even try it."

Charlie blushes slightly and looks down. "Alright. What of it? I'm allowed."

"No doubt. I even encourage it. I think."

"How's it going with your young German over there?" Charlie juts her jaw towards Kris and his comrades over in the lounge. Marie looks over and sees them taking bong hits and laughs, shaking her head.

"You'd think I'm a cradle robber. Christ! Nice hard little body though. So long as I'm toking with them, I don't notice his age, or lack thereof."

"What do you make of Tony?" Charlie surprises herself by asking. She had not been one to share details about relationships with anyone, but with Marie it is different.

"Like I said. Not bad. Your brother seems to like him. That's a good sign. Just remember, it's all fishing."

"I've heard that metaphor before," says Charlie, recalling Joan's words from long ago Seattle. "But it sounds so...crass." She laughs again at herself and the world.

"See, so long as you're laughing, it stays in perspective."

"Yeah, yeah," Charlie replies. "I do like the game."

"You don't even know all the game yet, sister, but you're getting close."

"Fuck you," Charlie kids.

Marie nods her head lightly and smirks, looking first at Charlie and then off into the horizon.

Charlie looks up later that afternoon from the dining area to see Tony and Renny sauntering back from their hike. The boys are jovial, though looking pretty worn out.

Marie looks up from the next table over and smirks, noticing their shirtlessness but not the scratches. Walt, a new acquaintance and his beau Spencer snicker and whistle in agreement. Charlie launches herself up and out of her chair as they get close.

"Oh my god, what happened to you two?!" she cries.

"Tony sprained his wrist doing some Tarzan stunt. I told him not to try it, but hell, he's a pig-headed Brit." Renny kids him.

"It's swelled up like an apple!' Cheryl says as she gets up to review Renny's damage, looking over at Tony. Charlie is surprised that Renny lets Cheryl baby him, even accompanying him to the shower. Charlie is obviously concerned about Tony's injuries and takes both pain and pleasure in examining his body for scratches.

"C'mon – lets go wash out some of those wounds." She tells him as she leads him towards the waterfall shower. Marie rolls her eyes and makes another comment to Walt and Spencer, but Charlie doesn't hear it. Charlie realizes that she not only cares for Tony, she's quite aroused by his form and vulnerability just now. Her face, calm and purposeful at first, does not betray her building excitement.

She leads Tony by the arm towards the back of the bungalows. The bathing area is a cascading waterfall behind the bungalows that is open to public view by passers-by strolling the beach. It bothers Charlie a bit at first, but she sucks in her modesty and decides to just enjoy it. They arrive at the shower area as Renny and Cheryl are leaving and the four exchange glances, but no words.

Tony is a wet and grubby mess and she gently helps him out of his shirt. Tony dips his head, then his shoulders and back, under the flow as she reaches for the bar of soap among the rocks. Charlie steps under the flow with him and begins to soap up his torso with a circular, sensual motion. They are both getting soaked but neither seems to notice. Or perhaps it is *all* they are aware of. Her initial concern about his injuries soon dissipate, and her thoughts turn to more pleasuring circumstances.

Charlie is wearing a bikini bottom and sleeveless t-shirt with nothing underneath – which becomes more evident with each drop of cascading water. *God, this is right out of a Playboy video*, she thinks, glancing around to see if there's an audience. *I feel a little self conscious. I hope nobody is watching. It's not like we would really do anything in public, it's just so intimate, and I feel so exposed. Isn't it funny how some of the most intimate moments don't involve sex at all?*

She shudders – from the cold water or from the building sexual tension, she isn't sure. She washes Tony's back, rubbing up and down with his now-clean bandana. First he's kneeling in front of her, his head nuzzling her breasts, as she washes his hair and scalp. Then he stands to rinse and she stands back to watch his physique emerge from the soapsuds. She turns him around and presses her body against his backside, bringing her arms around him to gently soap his chest from behind.

Tony keeps on his trunks, but she can tell he is excited. His hands folded in front half-cover the bulge, as he makes his own attempt at modesty. Passion soon gets the best of him too, and he turns to watch her, smiles at her erect nipples poking through the wet t-shirt, and puts his hands on her hips to draw her closer.

I'm glad there is water pouring over us because I am dripping down my thighs, Charlie thinks. But rather than explode into a sexual frenzy, the shower remains almost innocent. They both rinse the soap off and, after finishing cleaning, just sit and let the water run over them, Charlie curled up in his arms, careful not to bump his wrist but otherwise without a care in the world.

When Charlie finally shivers with the cooling breeze, they get up from the rocks and kiss tenderly and yet deeply – a light touching of tongues that leaves both of them hungry. The fiery passion has simmered to smoldering embers, but is far from extinguished. Charlie feels it in every cell of her body, every pore is open to it, and she grips his arms and digs her face into his chest to hide it. He responds with a possessive hug and gentle stroking of her wet hair.

Charlie grabs a drying towel from a nearby clothesline and they pat each other dry, Tony carefully dabbing around Charlie's breasts and not looking her in the eye when he does so. She is equally cautious around his trunks as the bulge starts to rise again. She squeezes him on the arm and lets him go.

"You should rest up now," she manages to say, and he nods with a grin. He kisses her cheek before heading back to the restaurant to get some more ice and take a nap. She watches him go.

Charlie is still too aroused to return to the café and chat with her friends, so she takes a walk down the beach instead. The waves lap her feet. She doesn't notice the music blaring from the bar at the other end of the beach. Her inner voice assesses her feelings.

The last time I was on a beach with a man, it was Koh Tao and Thierry – god, how long ago was THAT? Hmmm…didn't we have great shower sex that one time? That was raw passion. I had never done anything like that before. It was scary and exciting and wonderful. I miss the excitement of new love, but I don't miss Thierry, exactly. I would love to see his smile again, and the way he touched me – wow! With Tony, I feel, I don't know, like I'm in uncharted territory and I need to go slowly so as not to stumble or get lost. I'm not scared of falling into the black hole anymore though. Tony touches me in a way I don't understand and it makes me feel silly and confused, but delighted! But jumping right into bed...I'm not sure that's a good idea. I don't want to be a tease, but the seduction and the foreplay is such a big part of the thrill. The journey IS often more exciting than the destination – that's true in more contexts than I had previously imagined.

I want to understand the unknown, but it has to be at a pace I can comprehend. This is all so weird! Maybe I need to toke a little with the gang, get some different perspective. Now I understand why Renny and his buddies smoke ganja – having a little help to buffet the crosswinds before they toss you too badly about isn't a bad thing. I think I'm still going to get blown across the map, but it'd be nice if I found a way to cushion the blows. Maybe I need to just bob with all the waves until they stop being unusual?

That evening the group gets into a heavy conversation about the meaning of it all and Charlie gets drawn in against her will, finding herself revealing ideas she didn't know she felt so passionately about. *Do I really feel so strongly about not wanting predictability in my life? Why am I so indifferent, even adamantly against wanting to project a shape to the future?*

Charlie and Tony swap glances and inadvertent touching all evening. The sexual tension between them is almost visible, but no one does anything to facilitate action. Charlie leaves the group on the beach, giving Tony a light kiss on her way out, and goes back to her bungalow to ponder the evening

Renny can get so wound up about things! How did I let him draw me into all that psuedo-philosophy bullshit? I suppose he has a point, though. Why am I trying to escape? Or better yet, what? It's not like I have a plan or anything. Though I wish I did.

What would that plan be? Win the lottery and travel forever. Right! Might as well try to fly to the moon! But why not travel forever? I mean, at least in my mind. Why can't it all be an adventure? I really don't want anything other than that! So, how do I keep that perspective? I can't evade responsibility my whole life, can I? I just don't want to be bored! Well, it's not boring now, that's for sure. This thing with Tony, damn! Why am I being so cautious? Am I just a game player? No...maybe...who cares. Just go with your feelings, Diaz. Stop being such an analyzer, like you accuse Renny of all the time. At least he's honest about it.

After dinner the following evening, Charlie and Tony take a late night walk down the beach. At the far end, the bars and cafés peter out and there's a stretch of white, moonlit sand stretching for a final quarter mile. They're holding hands, splashing in the gentle surf, and falling in love. At the end of the beach, they turn to walk back, but Tony pulls Charlie gently back towards the row of sentinel coconut palms, and they sit on the sand.

"If I touch your knee, you're not going to haul off and whack me like Marie did to that fellow last night, are you?"

Charlie smiles. "I am so sorry I missed that, and half glad too. I've seen Marie in action and, no, I won't take you out. Down, maybe, but not out." She blushes at herself and he reaches over and kisses her, gently at first and then they are both overtaken by passion built up from days, months even, of foreplay. As the heat intensifies, Tony interrupts.

"I...um...don't know if this is appropriate for me to say or not, but...um...I don't have a condom with me and..."

Charlie giggles. "You are sooo British." She playfully slaps him on the cheek.

Tony sighs deeply. "I suppose I should take that as a compliment. I think," he adds, uncertainly.

Charlie pushes him down and straddles him playfully. "That's right."

Those are the last words they speak for the next fifteen minutes.

The following morning at breakfast, Charlie, Cheryl and Marie are sitting together while the boys remain slumbering away.

"We missed you last night playing cards," Cheryl says, casually, while buttering some toast.

"I figured you were all so stoned, nobody would notice," Charlie replies.

"Oh yes yes yes my good friend. Come on, out with it." Cheryl stops eating and folds her hands in front of her, like a Mother Superior wanting a confession. Marie smiles nonchalantly from across the table, but she is clearly interested.

"Well, since you asked....Last night we went in for the full dry humping routine. That sounds so vulgar! There must be a better word for it." Charlie is all of a sudden shy and tries to distract herself by eating.

"No, go on, I know what you mean, I think, but details would help," Cheryl eggs her on. Marie is nodding in agreement.

Charlie pauses, then leans forward and the other two lean forward with her for comical effect. She whispers. "We made love without taking our clothes off. Well, we left our undies on. Our hands and tongues were all over each other, though it was all above the waist and my god, his tongue! I'd never cum like that before. It was a...a...revelation. He just exploded into his trunks and I could feel his pulsing and it was incredible. I felt like I'd gone somewhere new." Charlie's voice is low and racing as fast as her heart.

"Calm down, girl, I don't want you to have to run off to the bathroom or anything. Shit, I might have to run off to the bathroom myself with this level of detail!" Cheryl invites Charlie to pause, then continue.

"I don't think we were planning it. Consciously, that is. We just sat down on the sand and..." she shrugs.

"And...?" Marie makes a circular motion with her index finger, telling Charlie to continue.

Then all of a sudden we're...you know." She stops and snorts.

"No...." says Cheryl.

"Then I'm rubbing up and down on top of him and – just as it happened! His orgasm was so powerful it led me to go off at the same time." Charlie pauses again to catch her breath.

"Why didn't you just strip off and do it normally, naked?" Cheryl asks.

"Oh, I don't know," she lies. "Heat of the moment, I guess. But does it really matter? And what is normal, anyway? We both got some pleasure out of it and it leaves something left to play the game for. Oh, not that I consider this a game. I think?" She looks up to see Marie arch her eyebrows and smile.

"This guy is different. Special." Charlie's voice trails off, along with her gaze.

"Yeah, sure honey. They're all special." Cheryl is not convinced. "How did you clean up? That couldn't have been very romantic."

"We took a swim. There was a lot of phosphorous algae glowing in the water, and that reminded me of a night in Koh Phangan with Thierry. I told you about him, right?"

"Oh yeah, the scuba instructor. He sounded pretty special, too." Cheryl winks to Marie, who nods.

"Well, I felt a twinge of guilt about that, but mostly I noticed how last night felt different. This time had more to it. Or maybe less to it, as a matter of fact. I don't know how to describe it."

"Love's a beach." Cheryl says, signaling for another coffee.

"Everything's a beach," says Marie, her first words of the conversation.

Charlie acts offended and gives them both the finger, then breaks out in a titter.

"Oh my God. I can't believe I'm talking about it like this? What are we, in high school still?"

"Never left it I think," adds Marie.

☯☯☯☯☯ ☯☯☯☯☯ ☯☯☯☯☯ ☯☯☯☯☯ ☯☯☯☯☯

The other events happening around Charlie seem like sideshows for the rest of the time on the island. Cheryl and Renny have their own mating dance going, but Charlie is wrapped up with Tony and with trying to put her last two years in Japan into some perspective. She unwittingly starts that process by mostly escaping into books and naps and beach walks. She isn't reading anything with any heft to it, some science fiction and a crime novel. She tries latching onto some more serious reading in an attempt to challenge herself more, but after a few pages, can't get behind it.

She has this idea to get through <u>Ulysses</u>, but finds her mind wandering every time she picks it up. She gives up after a few tries, but still totes it around. It is part of her illusion of looking impressive to whoever needs to know such a thing, including herself. And she realizes this deep down, but still carries the tome out of some misplaced respect for what has been proclaimed real and unique. She ends up toting the damn book all over Asia!

Renny is running the beach the next morning and Charlie and Marie lay into him.

"So, this is the answer to masturbation?" Charlie kids.

"It's either that or rope swinging. And we know where that leads," adds Marie.

Renny answers them with his middle finger. "It's better than paying homage to the great Joyce by toting a five pound hunk of paper around as exercise."

"Hey," Charlie shouts defensively. "Don't dis the master."

"Master of what?" he replies.

"Master of something different than your nights." Renny continues running and Charlie turns to see Cheryl approaching. As she sits on her towel, Charlie asks, "So, what's the deal with you two?"

"None of your beeswax, sister."

"Oh no. Not after my little confession. Out with it. Now!"

"I'm with her," Marie adds in support.

"You're with whoever leads to sex," says Cheryl. Marie nods. Charlie gives Cheryl a 'come-on' wave with her hand.

"Well, I like your brother. That's all there is to it."

"So, you're not sleeping with him because you like him?"

"It's not like we have the best situation now," Cheryl says, looking around. "And not all of us are outdoor exhibitionists." She gives Charlie a disapproving look.

"No excuse. Though, I know what you mean. About the situation, that is," Charlie replies.

"I'm taking his sister's lead here. Why rush things?"

"Because all we have is now!" Marie exclaims. "Why rush things? Sheesh! Between the two of you, you'd think this was a fifties beach movie."

Charlie ignores the comment. "I'm not trying to get my brother laid now, I'm just trying to figure this all out."

Cheryl offers, "It's like you said the other night, Charlie – I don't know what I want. And I don't think Renny does either. That doesn't mean I should get my rocks off just because I can."

"And you don't think he wants to?" asks Marie with disbelief.

"I think all men want to. All the time. Hey – we're having fun. It's not like there's nothing happening. Isn't it you who's always talking about the game?"

Marie nods in thought. "Okay. You've got me there. I just don't see the big deal."

☯☯☯☯☯   ☯☯☯☯☯   ☯☯☯☯☯   ☯☯☯☯☯   ☯☯☯☯☯

Cheryl leaves for home two days earlier than the rest of group and Charlie isn't sure whether she and Renny ever do get it on. Charlie finally does get a bungalow to herself and she and Tony use it fully, shedding all of their clothes in privacy and not feeling self-conscious. There is something urgent about their lovemaking that excites and disturbs her. It is intense beyond her experience. The relaxed and playful feeling she'd had with Thierry isn't here, with Tony, though in being honest with herself, the timing and circumstances aren't here either. There are too many distractions around, both physically and emotionally, for her to be free enough to know what she is feeling. Before she knows it, Tony has to get back to Bangkok for his flight back to Japan and Renny has to go off to meet a professor in the northeast somewhere. The four of them pack up and depart

337

together, shedding Renny at Laem Ngop to go north, with the rest of them heading west. Tony's schedule is tight and he needs to leave for the airport soon after they arrive in Bangkok. The minibus drops them all off near their hotel. Marie and Charlie check into a room and Charlie walks Tony out to the street to flag a taxi to the airport. They don't say much and it is probably better that way.

"I'll write you from down south somewhere."

He nods, squeezing her hand. "I'd like to pick this back up again."

She doesn't reply, only squeezing his hand in return. They hug long and hard and he leaves her with a last kiss and a clearing of his throat. She watches the taxi drive off and wonders what the hell she is doing and whether she needs to get a new grip. She asks Marie about it that evening and Marie is her usual non-committal self. "Just go with what feels right."

Great, Charlie thinks. *Nothing feels right. What is right?*

Marie and Charlie hang out in Bangkok for almost a week, visiting temples and arranging visas for Malaysia, Indonesia and The Philippines before Renny shows up again. He has hatched some cockamamie scheme about smuggling hash back to Japan and The States and Charlie doesn't know what to make of it. To Charlie, his behaviors have always bordered on the outlandish and she loves and accepts this about him, but the potential consequences with this scheme are terrible and she doesn't know what to do.

She knows she can't talk him out of it and he can see her dismay. She decides not to let it drag her down and puts it back into a little mental box, hopefully never to be retrieved except for a nostalgic chuckle. Renny accompanies Marie and her to the train station a couple of days later as they're ready to depart southward and the box opens up a little. She sits, holding hands with him on the platform, fearing that she might have to do it next through prison glass. She shuts the box again, hugs him tightly, and says goodbye.

Charlie and Marie take the local trains down to southern Thailand, which takes them a couple of days. They stop for a visit to a temple in Songkhla and then head over the border into Malaysia. Charlie is preoccupied with Renny and Tony and doesn't really pay much attention to Marie, but Marie is okay with that. Both women are preoccupied with just having left Japan and contemplating the future, but trying to stay in the present.

At Butterworth, just inside the Malaysian border, Marie continues south towards Indonesia and Charlie slows her pace even more, deciding to see some of the spots Renny raved about in Malaysia. The women reconfirm plans to meet up again in Manila in a month, arbitrarily choosing a guesthouse from the guidebook. They part with kisses to cheeks, both in their own world of thought.

The next month is a blur of memory. Charlie traipses all over the peninsula, keeping to herself, chatting up neither tourist nor local, but reading escape novels like they are going out of style. Even now she doesn't attempt to delve into her thick Joyce novel, but nevertheless refuses to leave it behind. She challenges herself to have physical days, walking for hours in the quiet jungle paths of the Cameron Highlands and through the jumbled concrete streets of Kuala Lumpur. She doesn't worry about being a single woman walking by herself, and the vibe she puts out says as much, because she is never bothered. *This is one advantage of traveling in a Muslim country: the respect is there, even if the rights for the native women are lacking.*

She spends a week on a beach on the east coast, looking for the famed and elusive sea turtles, and is disappointed to see so few. She finally departs in a fury after seeing a guide and his assistant push a tired turtle back up the sand so his next group of tourists will have something to gawk at. The turtle had just finished laying her eggs in the foredune and was making her exhausting return to the sea. Charlie tries stopping the guide, but he waves her off like it is a common thing to do. She heads inland.

Renny had intrigued her with wild stories about piercing rituals in Ipoh, but she doesn't see any when she wanders that city for a few days. And still, as her month alone on the road nears the end, Charlie keeps herself distant from potential new acquaintances, not making eye contact and keeping information exchanges to a minimum. In fact, she has so much on her mind that she rarely notices opportunities to interact. *I must seem like a cold fish to my fellow travelers. But so what? I just don't have room in my skull for any more complications!*

Soon enough she is on a plane out of Kuala Lumpur to Manila. She finds the guesthouse, with Marie patiently awaiting her in the lobby, as if the many miles and days since Thailand passed in an instant. Seeing her after being alone for so long is wonderful.

"What a sight for sore eyes," Marie says as she hops up to greet Charlie.

"Likewise Kiwi-girl," Charlie answers as they hug. They pull back and then lean forward and kiss on the lips, lingering for just an instant before pulling back, both chuckling and smiling.

"Bali was great," Marie continues. "Especially after getting out of the hellhole of Jakarta. But that was then and now is good, good, good." She tousles Charlie's hair and takes her bag, leading her to their room.

"My God, the last month is a blur," says Charlie. "I don't know why, but I feel like I can slow down now. So tell me about Bali!"

Marie tells her tales like they were no big deal, though to Charlie they are seeds to be sprouted on some future trip. Likewise, Charlie recounts her journey with nonchalance, as both are engrossed in the physical presence of the other and their talk is just filler.

They decide to spend their time in The Philippines away from Manila. Northern Luzon seems like the ideal destination, with it's many out of the way villages nestled in the jungle.

"Lets find a spot to spend the whole three weeks – or at least most of it. I don't want to hop all over the place," Charlie pleads, unnecessarily.

"I'm all for that. The last month has been great, but it has worn me out!" Marie agrees. "Lets just find a little place we can sink our teeth into and just enjoy each other's company."

"Deal," concludes Charlie.

That place turns out to be a village named Batad. It is remote and takes some effort – two trains, a ferry and a bumpy converted pick up taxi – to get to, but the setting is Shangri-La and the people friendly. Batad is a mountainous village with rice terraces and wild bamboo hillsides. The two women feel as safe as cuddled babies, and go walking through the village at least twice a day. They visit secluded waterfalls and chat with the people they meet along the way, getting to know the locals a little. One of the locals that befriends them immediately is a black mongrel. He follows them around the village, or wherever they go on a walk. At first Charlie is annoyed with him, but soon starts to expect and enjoy his company. He is rather thin, but clean and peppy. As a matter of fact, that's what Charlie and Marie decide to nickname him – Señor Peppy.

There are a few other foreigners staying in the village, but Marie and Charlie discretely avoid them. Charlie begins to realize how traveling, especially this second time around, can lead to introspection despite the obvious pushes and pulls to go outside of yourself. An alien environment forces you to be sure of your own footing. *You can only distract yourself to a limited degree with foreign sights and sounds,* she thinks, *"though God knows if you keep moving fast enough, the distraction can become the focus. I guess that is what I learned the last month, traveling by myself in Malaysia. I made the world my TV, but I have not much to show for it.*

Charlie gets to know the outlying hillsides pretty well and is comfortable walking there by herself when Marie doesn't want to come along. She can count on Señor Peppy to accompany her. They don't know where Peppy lives at night or who, if anyone, feeds him. Charlie and Marie give him the small food scraps they sometimes have at the bungalow. The girls feel a little sorry for the numerous dogs they see everywhere which are, naturally, none too welcome in the public eating areas. The dogs survive mostly, Charlie guesses, on tossed out food. Señor Juan, who runs the bungalows and restaurant where they are staying, can often be seen shooing away strays from around the kitchen back door. He is an elderly man who wears just a white wraparound tunic and slippers. His thick hair is peppery black and his skin a leathery brown, and his smile reveals badly crooked and yellow teeth. Whenever he takes out the trash to the burn pit, the dogs seem to know and follow closely on his heels. Outside of one or two special dogs that are clearly privileged to be owned specifically by neighborhood families, most of the dogs appear to be wild, and always hungry.

The women eat mostly at Señor Juan's, occasionally venturing off to try out other places, but no place they find is as friendly or offers food as good. Señora Colavera, Juan's wife, is a happy, rotund woman, always in a flowery dress and apron. She is an excellent cook and takes great delight in Charlie and Marie's appetite and extended stay.

Marie's goal for their time in Batad matches Charlie's. She had been in and out of Japan for the better part of six years and this transition to the next adventure looms large for her. They both have no idea of what lies ahead, beyond a visit with their parents.

"Are you still toying with the idea of moving to London?" Charlie inquires over dinner one night.

"Yeah, I guess. But I don't know about jumping into another hectic scene. London can be a bloody mess ya know." Marie's voice trails off.

They avoid talking about the future too much. The now is fine and neither of them want to look too far ahead to something that is going to happen whether they dwell upon it or not. However, as the final days of their stay in Batad approaches, talk of "what's next?" is inevitable. They choose one of their last walks together to talk openly about the coming weeks and what awaits them after that.

"So, Seattle and the Midwest for a month. Then what?" Marie begins by giving Charlie the first turn.

"I don't know. I certainly won't hang out too long with my folks. I'm thinking Seattle again for a bit, though this traveling routine suits me well."

"What about your brother? He's back with your folks now isn't he?"

"I think so. My guess is that he'll be back on the west coast too. He talks about grad school, but who knows? What will you do if you stay in New Zealand?"

"That's just it. I don't know either. I've thought about starting up my own business. Maybe a travel agency or something like it, but I don't know if I have the discipline to be self-employed."

"And if you go to London?"

"The same, I don't know." Marie laughs melodically. "We sound like broken records. I'm wondering if this feeling ever changes? Maybe we all just go to the grave wondering what's next?"

"I can't quite imagine knowing what a long term plan is, let alone *making* one. I don't really want to know. Sure, the uncertainty can be a little unnerving, but any illusion of certainty is even worse. Let's just let ourselves sound like a broken record."

"What, and live like Señor Peppy here?" The mutt wags his tail and entangles himself in their legs. Marie reaches down to pat him on the head. They don't pet him too often out of fear for fleas and bugs.

"Yeah, that's right." Charlie answers. "He doesn't even have a concept of the future and it doesn't matter."

"But it does matter to us, don't you think?"

"Yes. And no. Ashes to ashes. We'll earn the same outcome as our little friend here in the end."

"But what do I want? That's what gets me. You'd think I'd know what I want after all this time of specifically trying to figure that out, but I don't. I might as well have never left New Zealand at this rate." Marie is upset, and Charlie tries to comfort her, putting an arm around her shoulder.

"You don't really believe that."

"Of course not, but I still wish I had more of it figured out."

"Maybe it's like you said, we never figure anything out. I'm beginning to think that's the case. I'm coming to the conclusion that I don't know a fucking thing." Charlie purses her lips and looks at the sky with knitted eyebrows, dropping her arm.

Marie laughs at this and says, "Remember when we first met in the airport at Heathrow?"

"I thought you were the wizened travel guru. Look where it got me." Marie reaches over and puts her arm around Charlie's waist. Charlie does the same, and they walk the path together that way. *It feels good to be close to Marie – physically and emotionally,* Charlie thinks. *I get the impression that Marie doesn't open up with too many people. I'm honored. I wonder if sisterhood feels like this?*

They continue walking, arm in arm, with Señor Peppy circling their feet in oblivion.

"If I didn't think it would mess things up, I'd kiss you now. I mean, really kiss you." Marie looks over with sly eyes and Charlie smiles back. Charlie reaches over with her free hand and strokes Marie's cheek with the back of her fingertips. They stop then, in the middle of a forest path on the edge of a rice terrace. They both lean towards the other, bending formally at the waist and kiss lightly, and then passionately, letting their bodies get close and their arms intertwine around heads and shoulders. Charlie is thinking all the while, *I don't know about this...Wow!...This isn't half bad...who am I kidding?...It feels fantastic...*Marie abruptly pulls back. They both chuckle nervously and Marie strokes Charlie's face.

"I don't think we should go there," Marie says. "Not that I don't want to, but..." Her words trail off as she looks away. Charlie picks up Marie's hand and swings it gently as they continue walking and thinks, *"I guess she's right in terms of it complicating things, but it can't get anymore complicated, can it?"* This time Charlie stops and leans over to kiss her again, hard, and then pulls back. Marie is surprised by her aggressive move, but likes it, and Charlie can tell. They continue walking, hand in hand, Señor Peppy circling their feet in oblivion.

Back at the bungalows, Señor Juan informs them he would like to have a feast the following evening, their last night in town. The women happily accept his offer and begin to anticipate one of Señora Colavera's unique dishes. The following morning, they begin to pack up their belongings, write their final postcards, and of course, take one last walk through the hillsides with Señor Peppy. Upon returning, they meet Señor Juan on the path near the bungalows.

"You are ready for feast tonight?" He is full of mirth and carrying a machete and a sack. "We have a very special dish tonight."

"We're ready and game for anything," replies Marie. Señor Juan nods, smiling. He then walks over to Señor Peppy and in a single fluid motion, brings the full force of the machete, blunt side down, on Peppy's neck. There is a loud pop and Peppy crumbles to the ground, instantly dead. Señor Juan looks up, teeth flashing yellow, in a gleeful smile. "This very very good."

He gathers the dead animal into his sack and walks back down the path to the restaurant. Marie and Charlie haven't said a word. They are both shocked beyond speech. They stand in the path for a few minutes, numb and paralyzed. Slowly, then profoundly, Marie begins to chuckle, then snicker and then break into a bellyful of laughter that has her doubled over in hysterics. At first, Charlie can't comprehend the reaction.

"This is not funny!" Charlie protests. "Well...uh...but he....um..." She fumbles for words but can only latch onto Marie's laughter. In seconds, she is not able to prevent a little smile from forming on her lips. This just makes Marie laugh harder.

"It isn't funny!" Charlie rasps through her tensed throat. There are tears in her eyes from the shock and the sadness and the laughter. She can only join Marie in a belly-aching shout at a world gone mad. When the moment passes, they sit on the ground in the middle of the path, breathing heavily and wiping their eyes.

"There is no way I'm going to be able to eat tonight." Marie declares, exhaling deeply.

"Come on, even in honor of Señor Peppy?" Charlie can't tell if Marie is joking or not.

"You're serious?" Marie is startled a bit.

"Well, sort of." Charlie considers backtracking.

Marie laughs again, involuntarily. "Just what else are we supposed to do? Protest like good PETA supporters?"

"But…. Señor Peppy! Oh my God! What…..?" Charlie is again at a loss for words.

"Didn't I hear you say yesterday that you didn't want to know what was around the corner? Well, this is it girl."

"So this is my comeuppance for wanting spontaneity in my life?"

Marie doesn't answer and Charlie doesn't expect one. They sit in silence for a few moments.

"I'm glad he didn't tell us beforehand," Marie finally says. "I'm not sure what I would've done. I mean, it's not like we were going to take Peppy with us tomorrow. Maybe some of the meat we've been having all along…."

"I don't want to know," Charlie interrupts.

"Fair enough."

"I need a drink."

They go back to the bungalow and sip some cheap whisky. They fall asleep quickly and are unawakened by each other's snoring.. A knock on the door from Señor Juan does the job, signaling that dinner is ready.

The feast is a beauty. Señor Peppy has been incorporated into a stew, with some slices on the side that look like dark turkey meat, along with a large drumstick. There are bowls of stewed carrots and other vegetables strewn about in bowls on the table. With some hesitation, both Charlie and Marie gratefully accept the bowls of stew offered by Señora Colavera.. They peek over at each other, seeing who will sip first, and end up synchronizing their spoonfuls. It is really quite good.

Charlie can't bring herself to eat the meat slices directly, though she does ask for seconds of the stew. Marie is digging in with gusto. Señora Colavera tries to push the drumstick off on Charlie a few times, but she is staunch in her refusal. She keeps thinking of Señor Peppy as she eats him and it leads to a feeling of giddiness that stays all evening. Señor Juan is pleased and satisfied with the feast, and the four of them end the evening stuffed and punch drunk. The women head back to the bungalow in high spirits.

Marie lets out a sonorous belch and then says, "Señor Peppy speaks."

Charlie follows with a dainty burp of her own and in her best Darth Vader voice, says, "I am with you always my children, feed me well." She pretends to wag an imaginary tail and pants in short, quick breaths, like Señor Peppy did just this morning. Exhaustion sends them both into a deep, dreamless sleep.

They take the following two days to make their way back to Manila for a final night there before departing. Charlie is heading for Tokyo and Marie for Auckland. On their final night, they dine out at an upscale restaurant. Marie orders a steak and Charlie a vegetable curry, wondering if she will forever swear off meat.

"You've been vegetarian since three days ago," Marie says.

"You've noticed. I haven't decided whether to make it permanent."

"A one dog woman is it?"

"There's only been one Mister Peppy. I'll never have another like him." She exaggerates a sigh of nostalgia and sadness, tinged with happy memory.

"This steak is oddly reminiscent. I wonder where it came from?"

"Don't even go there."

"Where to then?"

"How about Kiwiland. Is your Dad going to pick you up?"

"God no. He wouldn't come into the city to save his life. I'll stay with some friends for a couple of days before heading out to see him. After that..." Marie shrugs her shoulders and looks down.

"London still on your mind?"

"More and more. I could do something professional there more easily, though I'm not crazy about that option, professional work that is."

"I think I could live in London for a bit."

"Are you serious?"

"Sort of. I don't know. Getting work there would be a problem, as an American that is, but I'll bet there's a way around that."

"There's ways around everything. So, what are you saying, that you'd like to go to London and get a flat together?"

"Ever to the point I see," Charlie smiles.

"You wouldn't want me any other way."

"True enough."

"I'd be lying if I said I hadn't thought about asking you to come with me. I'm not exactly sure what we have here just now, but you're not half bad to hang around with." Marie gives her a sincere smile.

Charlie takes that for the compliment it is. "Same here. I think we've established that I don't want to know what's around the corner. I can't decide if I'm crazy to be thinking about living in London or just crazy to be thinking about doing it with you."

"I really don't know what I want either, you know." Marie looks serious and sets down her fork and knife and takes a deep breath. "I can't promise you all good times, but I'm sure you'll have your moments as well. And you would be in England, surprise-surprise, if and when Tony comes home."

"I've thought about that. But that wouldn't be the only reason. Not even near the top of the list." Charlie is convincing, even to herself. "And what are the alternatives? Marie's Travel Barn in downtown Christchurch? And me, Assistant Marketing

Analyst with title-itis to boot? I just don't see it. Makes me want to become an alcoholic."

Marie says nothing.

"Do we really need to reintegrate? The thought scares the hell out of me. There's got to be some other way." Charlie almost sounds desperate.

"Create our own, that's about all we can do," is Marie's simple answer.

"I wish I could say I had your confidence in the matter. I think I need to let the Señor Peppy philosophy take hold." Charlie finishes off her wine.

"And that is…?" Marie cues the line.

"Live for the moment." Charlie smiles.

"Ah, I have taught you well. Just don't let the "beaten and boiled for dinner" part come into it. Then you become like all the rest."

"The rest of whom?"

"Of the followers. Of those out there you're scared of becoming like. The lemmings that jump off the cliff." Marie reaches over and lightly pats the back of Charlie's hand.

Charlie covers Marie's hand with her own and holds tight "I'm also scared of becoming like you," she says, smiling. "I don't want to know as much as you do."

"That's wise. I don't want that either," Marie says wistfully. "You don't want to know what goes on behind these calculating eyes."

"Same ole' same ole'," Charlie responds. "If you had any idea of what goes on in my corrupt little mind, you'd just wither up right there in your little ole' seat."

"Do you really think so?" Marie is incredulous.

Charlie knows it's an exaggeration, but she wants to sound tough. Underneath though, she knows she is still a sophomore.

"London's expensive, you know," continues Marie.

"So," Charlie replies. "You're rich aren't you? You can be my Sugar Momma."

Marie spits out a 'HA' and sips her beer. "And I'm not so poor myself in the end," Charlie adds.

"We're all poor in the end, honey."

"I can see we might have to discuss terms of endearment at some point."

"So, where does this leave us now?" Marie sounds hopeful.

"Thinking."

That night they sleep, innocently, like children who have never known of sex and all that goes with it. Charlie isn't sure if she is a wannabee or really bi. In the morning, she awakens to Marie's caress on her shoulder. She pretends half sleep as they slowly explore each other with their hands, kissing and rubbing faces. Marie knows her business, which half surprises and half terrifies Charlie. Marie pops a breathmint in Charlie's mouth and then her own and then they trade them in a kiss. Charlie is a little nervous, but it works its way out amidst the caressing and stroking. It isn't an earth rocking experience, but it is gratifying and new and she likes it. More than that, she likes being with Marie. She trusts her, which says a lot and means more. Attraction is an odd thing just in itself. You can ride it for quite a ways, but it changes and morphs over time and space. The physical allure is present, but there is more to it than that, only she can't put a finger on it and doesn't want to try too hard. Emotions and thoughts are swirling around that morning. Both Charlie and Marie shunt them aside as best they can.

By late morning they are packed up and heading to the airport together. Their flights are three hours apart, Charlie's leaving later, and the airport seems the best place to hang out in the meanwhile. They arrive later than they expected, leaving Marie with having to rush, which is just as well. They run to her check-in line, wait together until she has her boarding pass, and then run to her gate. A quick hug and a promise to call each other in two weeks is all the goodbye that fate allows them.

Charlie is happy for the quick goodbye, but as soon as Marie disappears onto the gangway, Charlie feels a deep emptiness too.

Meandering around the airport she wonders; *Just what is happening to me? My confusion over where I want to be, when, and with whom seems to have sprouted new tentacles.* She boards her flight in this state and it nags at her all the way to Tokyo.

17

RENNY

SAN FRANCISCO	KYOTO	THAILAND	LAKE TOBA	INDIA	MIDWEST USA
EARLY YEARS			YEAR 1		YEAR 2

IN THE BEGINNING

The underbelly of the VW Bug looked to be intact, though we had no flashlight to inspect it more closely. The front bumper rested firmly on one side of the ditch and the back bumper and one rear wheel on the other side. The space underneath was about four feet of vacant air. Greg and I squatted below the passenger door, our necks twisted at a funny angle to look up at the undercarriage.

The ditch was bone dry, thank God. This was late winter and the grass around us was a withered brown and tan. A slight breeze made swishing sounds in the grass and caused a ripple effect that made waves in the night light. We tried rocking the car to get if off its perch, and even got some motion side to side.

After a minute of this, we stopped. It wasn't getting us anywhere and could lead to a worse predicament. I circled the blue vehicle a couple of times, inspecting the scene. Greg spun the free wheels playfully, making 'whoo' sounds as he did so.

Then I crawled underneath the vehicle to look up at the undercarriage again, this time more closely.

"No apparent damage," I ventured. Greg made no reply, instead crawling under to join me reclining on the ground. We just lied there for a few moments, feeling this was a unique situation and one we ought to savor.

"We're totally fucked," said Greg, calmly.

"It would seem that way," I added.

Realizing we were out of options, we locked up the bug and walked briskly back along the road, which was actually a pair of dusty parallel dirt ruts in the earth.

"Lets get to the main ditch – there should be some people there." I said more confidently than I felt. "We can get somebody to help us lift the bug out and back on its wheels."

"Yeah, I guess it's about two miles to the county road, and it's a nice night for a stroll." Greg added, in the moment as always. After a few minutes, his focus drifted back to the "incident".

"I just didn't see it coming and when I did, it was too late. So I gunned it thinking we'd jump over it and...." Greg's voice trailed off. He was wound up and worried and a little drunk. I walked beside him, saying nothing. It was cold out, but thankfully dry. We both brought our light denim jackets and had our hands dug down deep into the pockets of our jeans. Standard posture and uniform, no matter what the occasion or weather.

Greg pulled out a fifth of cheap tequila, now half empty, from an inside pocket and gulped a slug. He handed it to me and I did the same. The liquid affected a sharp burn down my gullet and into my belly.

"Aahhh..." I smacked my lips and exhaled heartily. The internal heat felt good in the cold night air. And I felt manly, in retrospect, to be downing hard liquor as I also silently savored the faux rituals of my continuing initiation into adulthood. We followed the winding tire tracks back through the grass and brush and sage of the plains. The crescent moon lit our way and produced long shadows from off to the right.

"My Dad's gonna fuckin' kill me if he finds out," Greg began to let the fire of the tequila heat up his words. "We gotta get that moved, man! Fuck Me!" He screamed to the sky, flailing his arms at an unseen enemy, and I chuckled.

"Stop your worryin'. We'll get it out of there. It may take all night, but we will." I started thinking of excuses to explain why I would be out so late, even though my curfew was one a.m. and it was only eleven now. Three weeks until graduation and the school year had progressed to a close with little fanfare due to my decent grades, so I wasn't too worried about this minor setback having long-term repercussions at the Diaz house.

"Oh shit!" Greg frantically patted down his pockets. "I left the weed in the bug."

"You dickhead! Goddammit!" I was only feigning the disgust. "Let's go." We turned and headed back to the car. Once there, we both climbed into the bug, which rocked back and forth as we hopped up. We left the doors open and this gave both of us an odd view over the ditch, being a yard or more above it.

We smoked there, quickly passing the joint back and forth and inhaling as deeply as we were able. Greg overdid inhaling on one toke and subsequently sputtered and coughed and cursed.

"Fucking amateur," I responded, taking the joint from him. I slouched back in the passenger seat and exhaled a long slow breath.

"Don't bagart man," said Greg reaching over.

"It's bogart you idiot." I held the joint out of reach and then took another toke before handing it over with disdain. Greg took it with equal contempt.

We sat in silence, looking out at the distant lights of a farmhouse on the horizon and the headlights of a car moving towards it.

"So the Diaz twins are off to Colorado. Man. Who'd have figured? I can see your sister, but what do they see in you? They should've asked me." He shook his head with a sneer on his face. I laughed contemptuously and sneered back.

"You gonna stop by on your way thru to California?"

"If I feel like it. We'll have to see what's going down at the time."

"It's that or you'll be sleeping in this rattrap in a rest stop in Nevada."

"Whatever it takes, bro. So long as I'm on the road, baby." Greg whooped out a war cry to the night sky and I joined him with my own version of a wolf howl.

"You've gotta stop to drop off some of that hydroponic on the way."

"Yeah. But that's all for cash only man."

"You don't think a bunch of college types are going to want to pay? That's one of the best markets there is."

"As long as it's cash down and no hassles."

I paused to add unnecessary emphasis on my next question.

"You gonna stay with it?" I ventured cautiously.

"Why not? It's good money and so long as I can stay away from The Man."

"That's just the problem. At some point it's gonna catch up with you."

"But you're talkin' about more than just The Man now, dude."

"No I'm not. That's your main danger as I see it."

"It's definitely there, but it's not the A1."

"What is then, Mr. Know-It-All?" I snorted, dragging out the last word with a rap emphasis.

"It's getting sucked into the machine, dude! Once the hooks get into you, there's no getting out. It's like being caught in a giant fishing net, no matter where you turn, the net is there and you just get tangled up more and more until you can't move. You can't swim, you die. So watch out!"

"That ain't all you're saying, man. The trap is there, I agree, but you can stay out of the net if you keep a look out for it."

"Famous last words, bro."

"Let's walk." We started back again towards the road, this time at a less frantic pace.

"So you're going to California to sell weed and get rich. You gotta be looking further down the line than that, man."

"To what? You're missing the point, jerkoff!"

"Which is?"

"To stay out of the grips of The Man, the machine, the life sucking dickhead motherfucking plight of the masses. I don't want no part of that. No part. Whatever it takes to avoid it, I'm there."

"But why can't you avoid it without putting yourself at such risk?"

"Man Diaz, you are a geek at heart, dude. I'll come visit you someday in the burbs – you with your two point two kids and soccer mom for a wife. You'll be seeing it my way by then, but by then it will be too late. Taking a risk to avoid that life sentence is part and parcel of the whole thing. If there wasn't any risk, then everyone would be doing it." He paused to take a thoughtful breath. "And then it would be co-opted by the machine and no good anymore."

"And maybe I'll come visit you in the pen, and then you'll be seeing things *my* way. But it will be too late for you then, too."

"Prison one way or the other, bro."

"Yeah, but mine at least has the illusion of freedom. Given a choice, I'll go with that one."

"Given a choice. Ha! You really think you have a choice in this world? The choices are limited to the number of cogs in the machine. You mold yourself like one or the other and fit in and do your duty. I say fuck the machine, man! Throw a wrench into the works and let it choke itself to death. It's happening already. Look at global warming and population explosion. It's just a matter of time."

"But it's not all darkness, man! There must be some righteous beauty out there for us to latch onto without us having to go to the dark side."

"Yeah, but what's the dark side man? Is it really the evil bogie-man or is it what's passed off as "The Force"? That's where you have to be careful about how much crap you swallow just because it's spoon-fed to you. Even the most vigilant can get overtaken. Look at Darth Vader, just a dude out there getting what he could until it overtook him and he began serving it."

"That's a fucking movie dude, I'm talking reality here." At least I thought I was.

"There ain't no reality anymore. It's all mixed up into one so we can't tell what's real and what's not. The beauty you're talking about is out there, but I don't believe you'll find it by following the well-trampled routes. You gotta break out on your own trail is all there is to it."

"Yeah, but it's easier to get stuck in a ditch that way."

We came to the main drainage – a one-lane ditch that connected to the main county road another mile to the east. Our tire-track path met the ditch about two hundred yards from Moose Loop, an area that was hidden from sight of the road and well known to local partiers who wanted some privacy. I didn't know how it got its name; it was just a spot in the bottom of a ditch that got washed out every time there was a thunderstorm. For a Friday night, there weren't that many – about ten – people gathered about. A bonfire blazed from a fire pit about a hundred yards away, and we jogged to it and warmed ourselves. One of the faces looked up as we arrived.

"What happened to you losers?"

"Stuck tight. We could use some help. I got a nice fat doobie to pass around for any volunteers," said Greg.

One of the fireside crowd had an old Chevy pick up, so three of his buddies and the two of us hopped in the back as he drove us back down the ruts to the waiting bug. The six of us were able to lift the bug out with appreciable effort, sliding it back the direction it came and onto the dirt tracks. Greg paid them off and we could see their lighter flash as they drove back to their fire.

Once again, we were left sitting in an old beat up VW out in the middle of a deserted field to ponder our futures. We waited for a few moments, listening to the Chevy recede until the swishing breeze was all the sound that was left. Without a word, Greg started the engine and drove us along the track again, slowly this time, following the direction of the truck.

"I see you're heading for the established road because it's the easiest way out." I couldn't resist commenting on the irony.

"Use what's there, but don't think it's all that's there."

"What, do you have an answer for everything?"

"Follow me, Diaz. You might actually get somewhere."

"That's what I'm afraid of."

"That's your problem, dude. You are a chickenshit deep down. Until you get past that, I can't help you."

"That's good 'cause I'm not asking for your help."

"Just as well."

Greg did stop in Boulder that fall and made a killing on weed sales in the dormitory. He headed out to California after that and I got a postcard a year later. He was living the high life, just as he had predicted, and he invited me for a visit. I took him up on the offer during Spring Break of my third year. He was living in a split-level house near Laguna Beach with three roommates. He had adopted a "surfer dude" mentality and look, not surprisingly, sporting long, sun bleached hair, baggy shorts and flip-flops. He'd traded the jean-look for one of a slacker.

We hung out in a stoned stupor for a week, leering at girls on the beach, eating falafels and occasionally venturing into the water. I sensed an increasing cynicism coloring Greg's rants. Growing up, I'd always seen him as an idealist wrapped in a cynic's shroud, screaming at the world more out of passion than disgust. But in LA, the bitterness was more evident and his rants more bile than rebellion, and one night I called him on it.

We were sitting out on the beach and it was early evening. There was a commotion in the parking lot behind us and we turned to see two patrol cars cornering a small red pickup. The cops were cuffing the two guys from the pickup – two black men in white sleeveless t-shirts and black bandanas worn low on their foreheads.

"Fucking fuzz!" Greg spat out. "Just pounding on the brothers 'cause they can. Ain't no justice in this world, man."

"You're so full of shit dude," I countered. "Who knows what the fuck was going down over there. Maybe it's bullshit, but maybe it's not. We don't know." Greg gave me a withering look and shook his head in disgust.

"Don't tell me you're taking the side of The Man, man! They don't need any more help!"

"So what are you saying?" I jousted. "We don't need cops around? Of course we do! I'm not saying I like them, but, shit, there's got to be some order."

"College has fucked you up, dude. It's just like I predicted. You get to where you can't see the forest for the trees. The cops is just a tool of the powers that be! Plain and simple. Their idea of order is oppression."

"So, what, you're going political on me now? I thought it was about finding your own way, not joining in some fake revolutionary fist-waving, feel-good spew."

Greg looked over at me with a piercing gaze. Then he looked over at the police cars, and then out to the water, letting out a heavy sigh.

"Fuckin'- A Diaz." He nodded and dragged on his cigarette. "Fuckin'- A."

"At a loss for words? Shit. That's a first."

We were silent for a few moments, and then he said, "I don't want you to get to thinking you know anything or anything, but maybe you're onto something there. I've been thinking something like that for a while now. I mean, I hate the fuckin' cops. And they *are* a tool of The Man. But... shit! I don't know, dude?! I find myself spewing about shit I don't really believe, or only half believe, because it's the thing to do, only it ain't on the mark because...because of what you said."

I chuckled in partial victory, partial confusion, and nodded.

"Don't be smug. You're still a wuss, Diaz. I can see that hasn't changed."

"So, what of these thoughts you've been having," I said, keeping the conversation on track. "And by the way, screw you."

He sneered. "You know, it's like all these dudes I've been hanging with out here. They like to spew on how radical they are, but we don't really do shit except smoke weed and watch the boob tube! It ain't a bad existence, but it's not... I don't know, satisfying."

"What would you rather be doing?"
"That's just it."

❧❧❧❧❧ ❧❧❧❧❧ ❧❧❧❧❧ ❧❧❧❧❧ ❧❧❧❧❧

By the end of my five years in Boulder, I had almost become a respectable human being. It took me a year longer than Charlie to get the degree, but I got it all the same. Looking back now, I wish I'd have taken even longer and not 'buckled down' at the insistence of Mom and Dad. After graduation I spent six months on hiatus, doing absolutely nothing, and then did a year in Indianapolis, clerking in an accounting office and wondering just what the hell I was doing. I didn't feel "on my way" towards anything. I didn't really do anything in those years except watch football and give the straight and narrow life a try. I was good at it, I guess, but bored to death. I quit clerking after the second year, floated around between the folks and friends' houses for a few months. Then I went to LA to look up Greg.

It had been four years since I'd seen him in Laguna Beach. I learned from his parents that he was now living out in a remote area of the desert near Joshua Tree. I decided to drop in unannounced and found his little trailer in the shade of a big cottonwood tree. A small, well-tended garden bordered the trailer and I wondered if I had the right place. A young woman was out front, suckling her baby.

I introduced myself to Candy, who was pleasant, but reticent, clearly engrossed in her new infant. She wore a blue sackcloth dress and had long black hair. She continued to nurse the baby as she showed me around the area. Greg was out at the store and expected to return within half an hour.

As Candy didn't invite me in, I walked around the neighborhood for a bit until Greg showed up in a beat-up blue Toyota pick-up. He had grown his hair longer and now had it tied back in a pony tail. He looked both more radical and more responsible at the same time.

"Renny Diaz. It's been a few years dude." He gave me a bear hug, which was a first for all of our time together, but was a nice twist. "You've met Candy and Summer, I see. And you've gotten a tour of the McGann luxury estate." He swept his arm across the desert horizon, a wide smile on his face. We walked into the trailer and I was pleased to see a warm and cozy home inside and not the bachelor pad of my prior visit. We grabbed two beers and went back outside to the picnic table that was next to the vegetable patch.

"This is...different," I commented. "I like it."

Greg chuckled. "Yeah. Been out here for over a year now. The LA scene was getting too hectic. I still go in a couple of times a month, but I get out as fast as I can now."

"Still in the biz?"

He looked up and stroked his beard, smiling and nodding. "I'm not doing direct sales now, though. Wholesale is better. Less risky, sort of."

"Less risky! Coming from you? Glad to hear it, I think."

He looked over at the trailer. "I've got more to think about these days. I even got a regular job over at the video store three nights a week. She don't like the other thing, but it's good dough and, hey, I know the business well enough."

I nodded in appreciation for the situation.

"But don't think my outlook on life has changed too much, now, if that's what you're implying." His voice rose a notch, approaching the pitch I was so used to.

"I can see that," I smiled.

He continued. "I've just figured...am figuring out a better way to get free of it."

"What's "it"?"

"You know dude! The wheel. I'm just tryin' to get off. Stay off. That's all. And look at you now. What was it you were doing in Indy?"

"Accounting. It sucked, big time. I guess I agree with you after all."

He laughed. "Yeah. So it goes."

I hung out there for a week and we went hiking in Joshua Tree Park and had all of our meals at home. Candy warmed up to me – once she figured out I wasn't a dealer, maybe. It was like old times for Greg and I, but even better. I left with a promise to keep in touch and feeling like the world was a new place.

From LA I headed north to San Francisco. It was just for a visit, but I ended up getting a job there and that was that. I wasn't looking for one, but that's how it goes sometimes. *When you want something it isn't there and when you don't, it falls in your lap.*

I crashed on the floor with Jeff, a buddy from the dorms in Boulder. He was working for a company in the stock market, and knew my background and wanted to help me out and one thing led to another. This type of job was relatively new to me – Associate Clerk, tracking trades and charting which categories and trends were most active. It seemed exciting, sort of, and the money wasn't half bad, so I took it without considering many other options. Jeff got promoted and transferred to Dallas after I'd been there just three months, but it didn't matter too much by then. I'd settled in and gotten to be buddies with Patrick, so I continued on with my almost-professional life, albeit in my own way. I lasted that way for two years.

Just after Charlie ventured away from her professional gig in Seattle, I got a call from Candy. Greg had been killed in a car accident out near Bakersfield three days earlier. They were having the memorial service the coming weekend. It was Tuesday when she called and that Friday I drove south. The ceremony was in Inglewood, near Candy's folks. She was moving in with them, giving up the desert life for the time being. Summer was toddling around and oblivious to what had happened. The service was decidedly mainstream, much to my surprise. Candy's parents had made the arrangements and, being solid Presbyterians, followed that vein. I figured Greg would be churning with his ashy remains stored in the ceramic urn with a cross on it. Greg's parents were gracious, but utterly bereaved and I kept my distance. He had no brothers or sisters. After a forgettable hour of strange words describing little of the Greg I knew, we went to a reception at Candy's parent's house. I only knew one other person there, a roommate from Greg's LA house, but we had nothing else in common, so the conversation didn't last long. I wandered around the crowd of mourners and drank to numb my brain. As I was getting ready to leave, Candy came up to me and asked me to follow her upstairs. Sitting on the edge of her bed, she pulled a small envelope out of the nightstand drawer and handed it to me. I opened it and found the pendant Greg had always hung from his rearview mirror. Candy tearfully got up and walked away, squeezing my shoulder and leaving me to be with the gift. I delayed only a few minutes, then left the house without saying goodbye to anyone.

In my hotel room that evening, I twirled the half dollar sized piece of metal in my fingers and mused about past and present. On one side of the pendant was an engraved angular peace symbol, superimposed on a barely legible marijuana leaf. On the other side, pasted over the smooth back, was a faded sticker of a fist with the middle finger sticking up.

"Classic Greg," I whispered. I remembered the pendant from our days in the VW bug, but the sticker on the back was different then. He replaced it every so often with a new image. The first one I remember was of a motorbike with the outline of a busty babe on the seat. He had scraped that one off to put on a VW logo with the word "Dude" underneath by the time he came through Boulder. I remember telling him that the marijuana leaf was a stupid thing to advertise where a cop could see it. He shook his head at me in disgust and gave me his typical "You're an idiot" response. I couldn't agree more now.

Back in San Francisco, I went on autopilot for a month before deciding to pack up my bags and head for Asia. I decided to follow Charlie's lead and go out and see the wide world. *It was an escape*, so I told myself at the time, *or maybe a quest. Maybe both. Quest for what, I still can't say*. I do know that it all started way back on that night with Greg in the stranded bug, and the quest (or escape) is ongoing. So, just what is it I am running from? Or to? Still can't say for sure.

❀❀❀❀❀ ❀❀❀❀❀ ❀❀❀❀❀ ❀❀❀❀❀ ❀❀❀❀❀

So, there you have it, the brief history of Renny Diaz, or at least the parts that bear upon my frame of mind as I sit here on this plane about to land in San Francisco. I hope some sewage vacuuming dude checks her haul tomorrow and finds a nice surprise for herself. I suppose all of these reminiscences still beg the question: Why? Why attempt a new career as a smuggler? I'm not sure I can answer that easily, if at all.

Why is it we do anything that's out of our ordinary routine? I believe that most of our actions are automatic. It's not that we don't have choices, though Greg might disagree, but our inability to fathom the range of choices open to us limits what we can be.

Think of it another way. If I had the ability to understand all of the variables that go into the equation that makes up my life, would I be any better off for that knowledge? I think not. We might think we want to be God – being all-knowing of all things – but I don't believe that's really what we want. We can't possibly see all of the choices available to us out there because there are essentially an infinite number. But even if we could know them, it wouldn't help us out because we would become paralyzed with the bewildering array. I'm obviously not a believer in pre-ordination, nor in fitting your shape into the slot just because it does fit. I used to think that everyone needs to find a slot to fit in, but I'm beginning to question that. No reason why you can't create your own slot if you can't – or don't want to – find one ready-made for you.

Is mine a new lost generation? No, not lost – like the children of the 60's or the Beat Generation of the 1950's or of the 20s. What might be missing is that we have no shared identity gained through a war to end all wars, or a depression, or a Vietnam. I can't say, 'Hey, I marched through the streets in protest, drank whiskey with Faulkner, and rode the rails with the migrant movement.' I am left wandering because I haven't paid my dues or shed my blood and tears for the cause. I lack that license to do whatever the hell I want because I've walked the line and gotten to the other side. That is the character of my times. Our times. Our fame is having no fame, our standard no standard.

It's all been said before. "Go your own way." Chanted musings from the young and jaded, the middle-aged and cynical. And it's difficult to argue with. *So what?* I say. It needs to be said and done again and again and again. Our collective memories are short beyond comprehension. We need to have it emblazoned on our foreheads and into the back of our eyeballs. Our collective automatonic responses are so ingrained now that even the rebellious reaction is well scripted and predictable. The rebel has become the icon – the co-opted symbol of the machine surging forward into new territory. Not that I'm a rebel, mind you.

So what am I saying, that I am some new explorer in uncharted territory? Well, to myself only, yes. But I'm still searching for that new standard against which I can measure myself and say, yes, I hold up and the trip has been worth it. This is not a measurement in scientific terms, or course, another symptom of our delusion that assumes everything can be measured and judged based on an objective ruler. The standard I seek is unique to me. I can't be compared to another person in the same way that the taste of an apple can't be judged to be better than that of an orange. And so I flirt with the fringe of acceptability in the hope that I'll bump up against my own standard, even if by accident, and know it for what it is.

In the hindsight perspective of this backwards glance, my epiphany is normalcy: I have done what has come naturally at the time. I suspect that I will keep reminding myself of this over and over again, and I'll rage against the dulling conformity around me, knowing all the while that it is only what it must be. And it's all the same. The absurdity of our times is its only truly redeeming quality.

18

CHARLIE SPEAKS

SEATTLE TOKYO THAILAND LONDON THE PHILIPPINES INDIA

YEAR 1 YEAR 2 YEAR 3

REVELATION

The polite Japanese voice over the loudspeaker switches over to English with a British accent, calling for Mr. and Mrs. So-and-So. The rest of the words are a garbled drone as I bend over the sink and soothe my face with cold water. I look up in the mirror, swabbing off excess water with my hands and run my fingers through my hair. *I've got another hour before my flight to Seattle. What's another hour after the last three days in Japan? The last three months all over Asia, for that matter? It is time for me to meditate over it all. Take your time.*

I notice the voice again, just for an instant before I hit the steel button of the air dryer. My immediate world is overtaken with a swoosh of hot air and noise rumbling off the tile walls. I like the escape and the sensation and hit the button twice more, redirecting it on the third time towards my damp hair and face. Anything to get away from this jumbled up mind.

I arrived back in Tokyo three days ago from Manila. Unsettled as I was departing Manila, I was able to put it aside for the practical part of traveling back into Tokyo. I called Pauline but was only able to leave a message. I thought about calling Tony in Kyoto, but wasn't sure what I wanted to say. As soon as I got through customs I took the express train out of Narita. I had forgotten nothing about navigating the Tokyo subway system in my three months away. Taking the Yamanote Line towards

Pauline's flat, these thoughts and images keep clouding my awareness.

Shit, are you toeing that fine line between 'relaxed' and 'neurotic?' You can't go around obsessing on mini-dramas all the time, can you?

There is a place for them of course, but to keep them in the forefront of my thoughts all the time is too destructive. All things happen on their own good time and that's about all you can say about it. My drama with Marie – and with Tony – is certainly on my mind, but don't let it overtake every waking minute!

But Charlie dear, isn't that what you're doing now?

I stow those thoughts back in their box in my little mental attic and, for the moment reflect on my short transit time in Japan. What hit me the hardest upon coming back into Tokyo were the contrasts – in wealth, the environment and the symbols. I remember earlier discussions about first world/third world differences, and how those definitions seemed so straightforward then. Now they appear more obtuse.

What is the significance between having a material thing available or not?

By chance, someone is born with access to a greater level of material wealth than someone else. The question is why do we consider the *having* so much greater than not having? I'm not talking about having clean water, food and shelter, but about having *wants*.

Charlie, you like the good life as much as the next.

That's true, but now I'm wondering if the good life is all that much better than a simpler one? Having money and clothes and entertainment all around, plus toys and gadgets to keep you distracted – this is all well and good and even fun and challenging, to a point. I question people who say that they could lose it all in a moment and not care; that it's all just "accessorizing" in the end, and unimportant.

In the 'first world', the accessories are becoming the end, the goal itself.

And that is causing so much confusion, so much senseless wandering. We're up in a balloon with no tether. It's exhilarating at first, but once you realize you're at the mercy of the crosswinds, you want to land but can't. Or you try to enjoy the ride. Maybe that's not the most accurate metaphor, because we're all at the mercy of the winds of chance. The point is the danger when we believe the accessory is the necessity. When that happens, we've lost sight of what is truly necessary.

The anchoring points have all been washed away. The navigation maps have faded beyond recognition. And we're all – well, Charlie Diaz is – searching for new ones.

God, I'm beginning to sound like Renny. He always harassed me for being a material girl, and now I know he was right about it. I'd like to think I've evolved a little, at least. I've always followed the path well-traveled by, towards what I believed to be good and solid. And now I see more clearly how valueless much of that was.

So how come I still want to buy that two hundred dollar pair of shoes?

I know that they are just symbols of quality? I can argue ten different ways about why those shoes are worth it for the fine craftwork and treated leather and design, but deep down I know that going barefoot is superior.

And just why is it that we are all so gullible? Accepting the images that are force-fed to us, believing what someone else tells us about what is right or chic or important?

The whole world has this disease and I recognize the symptoms in myself, but I'm not sure what to do about it. My ego won't allow me to disregard the opinion of others as unimportant or misinformed. But why *do* I care what somebody else thinks? So what if someone sees me walking around in ten dollar shoes?

That would almost be preferable. If someone judges your character based on such a thing, then you don't really want to get to know them anyway.

I snap out of the "train zone" and begin to notice around me all of the attention paid to form and the unimportance of any substance behind it. Above my seat is an ad with a man standing out on a deserted beach. His pant cuffs are rolled up and he looks dapper and contemplative. A cigarette dangles from his fingers. Underneath the photo, in big white letters: Smoking Clean.

Across the aisle, a young girl in a schoolgirl sailor uniform dress deliberately applies glue stick gunk all around her calves. She pulls up her white tube socks and carefully matches the rim with the gunk line, pressing firmly to keep the socks from sliding down. Inside, I roll my eyes and snicker.

How can this country still seem so foreign even after I've lived here for a couple of years?

☯☯☯☯☯   ☯☯☯☯☯   ☯☯☯☯☯   ☯☯☯☯☯   ☯☯☯☯☯

When I got to Pauline's, I found a note on the door that said the key was in one of the flower pots and to come on in and wait. I let myself in and slept for an hour. When I awoke, it was six-thirty in the evening. I called Tony, knowing he'd still be at work, and left him a message to call me back. I knew Andrea was visiting in Australia, but I called her also and left a message on her machine, just saying hello. Pauline showed up an hour later.

"Hey, stranger!" she surprised me by returning a hearty hug.

"Hey yourself! It's great to see you"

"I can only stay for about twenty minutes, then I have to scoot out to an appointment," Pauline apologized.

I gave her the whirlwind account of three months in twenty minutes. She did indeed hurry out the door within a half hour of breezing in, and I was surprised to be glad for more time to myself. Tony called back just then.

"Hi, Stranger," he said instead of hello.

"Hello there my English gent."

"Your English gent? I like the sound of that. At your service." I could feel his little bow through the phone and my heart skipped a beat.

We caught up on the particulars and then peeked into the black hole.

"I'd like to see you before you leave Japan." His voice was tentative, but warm and assuring and I knew I wanted to see him just by hearing it.

"I only have three days before my flight out, but maybe we could..." My voice trailed off.

"I'll do a round trip from Kyoto in one day, no worries." He suggested more cheerfully than he could have felt.

"Are you sure?" I offered him an out. "It's three or four hours each way on the bullet train and a couple of hundred bucks! It would make for a long and expensive day..."

"I'll be there late morning the day after tomorrow."

The following morning I took care of some final banking chores and other errands. I was pleased with the results, finding I had spent only twenty five hundred dollars during the past few months. I had sent home six thousand before the trip and still had ten in the bank here. I pulled it all out, mostly in traveler's checks and a couple thousand in US dollars. I still felt nervous carrying around so much cash, but that's the way it's done in Japan and I knew it was safe. Still, old habits die hard, and all morning I tried to keep aware of my surroundings and vulnerability, and was relieved to finally get back to Pauline's to stash my cash and wait for her to come home from her morning shift.

"You seem very distracted for someone just having come back from a long holiday." Pauline and I were walking in the Imperial Park and aiming for a particular restaurant that served great *okonomiyaki*, or Japanese 'pizza'.

"I'm sorry, I was just spacing out on this being one of my last days in Japan." I had actually been thinking about Mr. Peppy and how absurd that incident had been.

"Lucky you. Though I can see how you would miss some of this." I looked up at the budding trees and smiling faces drenched in sun.

"Well, at least it will soon be summer stateside also. Not a bad time to be going back."

"What is that amused smile all about?" I told Pauline the story of Señor Peppy.

"Can't say I've ever had dog before. How was it?"

"Not so bad taste-wise. It makes for a good story."

"So long as you can say that about most things, then I suppose you're doing alright." Pauline was philosophical.

"You really think so?" I wasn't so sure.

"Yes I do. Life is really just a series of amusements. At least that's one way to look at it. You could look at most of the same events as tragic also, but what's the point of that?"

"But there are other sentiments in the mix, don't you think?" Pauline didn't catch how I was trying to adhere to my love life lessons of the last few months.

"I suppose, but I can't be bothered with them too much. Why get all twisted up with them? Stay light is what I say."

"I'm trying."

We reached the restaurant and placed our order at the little counter. We grabbed a booth near the grill and watched the chef silently. Soon our lunch arrived and we were both mesmerized by the tiny, wispy fluttering fish flakes dancing on the surface. Shaved, dried bonito is a taste we had both acquired over time.

"Remember how grossed out you were when you first saw this?" Pauline said with a twinkle.

I nodded. "And now here I am seeking it out as a lasting memory. I suppose I am flexible after all." Pauline smiled and we dug in with gusto.

We spent that afternoon and evening together, amusing ourselves with bits and pieces of Japan I'd been curious about but had never delved into. We played pachinko for half an hour and I won a thousand yen, though I'm not sure if the incredible sensory overload was worth it. Squinting from the neon and with our ears still ringing and clothes smelling of cigarette smoke, we moved on to the electronics district. I bought a portable CD player just for the hell of it. Per Pauline's directions, the evening remained light and I slept that night dreamless and easy.

The next morning, Tony called and relayed his arrival time. I went to meet him at the station. It felt good to put my arms around him and feel his around me. I fought the melting feeling briefly, thinking I needed to keep my shield up, but soon I forgot about it and let the emotions flood in. I thought about Pauline's approach to life – keep it light – and decided I needed to work out how to be light without suppressing emotions.

He was upbeat and happy to see me and it was infectious. We walked over to a café just two blocks from the station.

"A bit different than a walk down the beach, though equally as nice with the company." He slipped his hand into mine and playfully swung it back and forth, not letting go when it stopped.

"Well," I mused, "I don't think concrete beats sand or skyscrapers blue sky, but I agree on the other bit." We reached the café and found a small table. After some more banter, the subject of Renny came up.

"My brother got off OK last month?"

"Yes." Tony smiled and started to say something, but stopped short and looked confused for a moment. "Did you...oh...never mind." His words trailed off.

"I know about his little escapade," I said. "At least he made it through Japanese customs without getting caught."

Tony laughed and breathed a sigh of relief. "A ballsy brother you've got there. I wasn't sure whether to hug him or punch him when I found out."

"I'm not sure ballsy is the best word to describe it." I was smiling, but also shaking my head, still a little worried. I was sure I would have heard from the folks by now if Renny was in jail. It was just too much to contemplate or worry about.

"What about you, did you do anything illicit after we left Thailand that I should know about?"

I shook my head no, but blushed slightly. I think he noticed, but didn't say anything.

"I'm thinking about moving to London for a spell. I thought I'd room with Marie and see if I could find work there."

"Really?" He was obviously intrigued with this idea.

"Are you going to stay in Kyoto forever?" I was kidding, but he got the point. He shuffled his feet under the table, resting his calf against mine. "I haven't thought about it too much," he lied believably. "London would be a logical next stop, if and when it happens. I could end up in Kyoto for the duration. It's not so bad when I think of it." He looked me in the eyes and raised one eyebrow.

"C'mon. Be serious with me." I wanted some truth.

"Well…..what….I don't really know….I am being serious." He was faltering badly, so I interrupted him with laughter and a playful kick on the leg. At first he was nonplussed, but then smiled shyly.

"Nice to know there can be a hiccup to the suave Englishman routine."

"I am not suave," he said with a strongly-offended tone.

"No offense intended, sir."

"What would happen with….What about seeing….you know…. Do you *want* me to come to London?" I hadn't been sure until that moment. I hated being weak and needy, but that was the way of it. I stroked his hand on the table and smiled. "Yes I do." Then the full tsunami of emotions burst through surface. *What had I said*?! What did I mean?! I felt confused and deceitful all at once, yet at the same time, open to whatever might come out of it.

"But …what?" He sensed my state and was clearly concerned.

"But…I don't want to make any promises. I…I don't know just what I'm doing now and I don't want to cause things to go bad. I don't want anyone to get hurt, me or you or anyone else."

He was silent for a few moments. He looked at me with confusion on his brow and I could see he was experiencing his own tsunami.

"But, you do want me to come to London?"

"Yes. Yes absolutely I want that! But you have to come because it's right for you and not just because of me. I want to see where this goes with us and ….and….Oh I don't know? Why is this so hard? I just want you to come. That's all."

He smiled then, gently and beautifully.

"And stop looking at me like I'm a mad woman. I mean, maybe I am, but don't rub it in." He looked down, but kept the smile.

"Alright then, I'll come."

"Just like that?"

"Is that a problem?" he jested.

"As long as it's not just for me, right?"

"Okay then, however it needs to be said."

"But that's…." He put his finger to my lips to stop me and took a deep and deliberate breath.

Still smiling, he said, "Stop worrying about that. I'm a big boy. I've lived in London before and I've expected my path to circle back there. This is just a catalyst. I want to see where this – you and me – leads also. I'm not going to tell you I haven't thought about this already. Let's just see what happens. As it is now, we've never even lived in the same city. I'd like to see how that would work."

Damn. I couldn't have written that better, so why did I feel so bewildered by it?

We spent the rest of the day walking about the city hand-in-hand, stopping for a meal or a drink when we were tired. I was glad we got "the talk" done early in the day so we could enjoy the rest of our short time together without that hanging over us. He told me about his family and growing up and we compared the similarities and differences. Renny was a common thread through the conversation, as we both knew him so well. It was like Renny was the medium through which Tony and I began to understand each other better. By mid-evening, we were back at the train station and hugging on the platform.

"A little different from Bangkok," I said, looking around at the disapproving Japanese faces.

"Not so much. I don't really notice much else when you're around."

"Very smooth, sir. I'm on my guard for that. You better get on your train." We kissed, briefly, but passionately. This is Japan after all, home of the sublime.

The overhead buzzer screeched it's warning of the doors closing. He jumped aboard and just as the hiss of the sliding doors threatened to decapitate him, he said, "Hey.....I love you." The doors closed on him and we locked eyes as the train pulled off.

He probably sensed my stunned reaction and confused smile. Talk about a tidal wave! But I liked that he said it. It made me feel tingly and pleasantly odd.

What is it about those three words that can jumble up your head even more than it already might be?

I was tempted to be angry with him for laying it on me like that, but that temptation dissolved. How can you be mad at someone for saying such a thing?

I made my way back to the flat in a daze and started repacking for my flight the next morning. Pauline was working late and came in around ten. I was exhausted and so was she, so we both allowed the evening to fade quietly. Anticlimactic to my day, let alone my three-year adventure in Asia, but appropriate.

That night I tossed and turned and harbored a general state of agitation. I wasn't well rested in the morning. Images of racing trains and smiling faces and dogs wagging their tails were all I remembered of the night.

At seven o'clock, I gathered my bags and headed for the train station. Pauline walked me out to the street in her pajamas and hugged me goodbye before I turned to hail a taxi. It left a sweet and savored image of her in my mind: hair all mussed up, arms crossed, and launching a cavernous yawn in her checkered red and white flannel nightshirt, which hung down to her ankles and failed to cover the little white bunny slippers on her feet. When I think of Pauline, no wonder I always smile.

I arrived at the airport a couple of hours early and breezed through check-in and immigration. I still had my gaijin card and thought about turning it in, like you're supposed to. *But why? Who would know?* I liked the "bad girl" side of this decision. And what if I changed my mind and wanted to come back to Japan next year? Having that card would ensure an easy return. I guess I also still liked having insurance.

I settled into the lounge near my gate, turned off my radar on the environment and I went back into my own little world: the land of Charlie's heavy baggage. Images started to fly past and I can't hold on to them, or don't want to. There goes the hat in the river and then my Grandma's rocking chair superimposes itself upon that, again to be replaced by three monkeys, hands down and staring at me, and so on. I find my shoulders getting tight and a headache coming, so I just start to walk.

☺☺☺☺☺ ☺☺☺☺☺ ☺☺☺☺☺ ☺☺☺☺☺ ☺☺☺☺☺

So, I end up here, in this airport potty, trying to dab away the film that seems to be covering my brain and the rest of my insides, making everything blurry. The cold water makes me feel better on the outside, at least. It's forty-five minutes before my flight and I let the film re-coat my senses. Auto-pilot clicks on and gets me on the plane and in my seat, strapped in for the duration.

Whether it's the culmination of being on the road, leaving an adopted home, or facing a new landscape, my consciousness escapes into a dream state. There are a number of Japanese on the plane, naturally, and these innocent folks become cameo actors in my waking dream. Mr. Tanaka's pained face of rejection from an attempted hug races by. I can feel his pain squeezing my chest. Peppy is chasing after him, in a pet carrier being pulled along by an old woman. She runs into a young man in the aisle. She's the Mama-san who pulled the wagon and the man has the face of the boy. My mind's eye witnesses these events with amused and horrified fascination.

I look at my reflection in the window and see myself sitting silently in my car in front of my old office building in Seattle, staring with mouth agape at the smooth glass windows. A few rows up are the ugly tourists from the London coffee shop. A woman passes me in the aisle in a long coat and I think for a moment it is Marta, but the woman just keeps walking and I never see her face. When I look down the aisle, I see a Japanese woman look up and I swear it is the woman from the park. The woman makes eye contact with me and then looks down, but I feel a burning inside. I see a man get up from across the plane and he looks like the Indian man I pushed in the puddle.

Get a grip Charlie! Snap out of it!

The plane is quiet, with most of the passengers engaged in the movie or napping. I rise from my aisle seat slowly, feeling woozy and uncertain. I stumble to the bathroom and latch the door with finality. Maybe I can shut out these images with physical action.

I splash water on my face and try some calisthenics in the limited space, but it doesn't work. Sobs start welling up from my chest and I can't stop them. I don't understand what is happening. I kneel by the bowl and vomit up some soda. This makes me feel better for a moment, but the purging brings some mental clarity. I stare at my reflecting in the mirror.

What were you thinking? Inviting Tony to London. When you'll be living with Marie!? What are you, nuts?!

The whole premise of my adventure now seems to be a joke. I am a hypocrite, plain and simple. I said I wanted to understand myself and the world about me on this journey, but truly I seem to want only the security of control and the image of quality. I *am* the ugly tourist. I am the man in the puddle, only I hide it behind a pretty smile and pleasure seeking. *Disgusting!*

I claw at my belt and pull out the hidden wallet strapped beneath it. Unzipping it, I grab the traveler's checks and scrunch them up into a ball in my fist. I knead the ball ferociously. *This is the absurdity of it all. Money isn't the answer and I need to get free from it. This fucking paper is the evil and I've allowed it into my life and become infected.* I flush the commode and watch the blue swirl circle the steel bowl, washing over my opaque reflection. I rip off a chunk of the wadded checks and drop it into the spiraling liquid, feeling cathartic and vengeful. Then the inner voice screams.

Stop, you idiot! You don't need to go there! Nothing is final. Sit back for a moment.

Tears are streaming down my face and I am trembling. I am sitting, slumped in front of the bowl and shaking with sobs.

"What am I going to do now? There is no answer to that, I know. There is no answer to any of it.

You just go on. You can know you've been sincere and continue to be more so. The inner voice finally becomes a comfort.

"But what about my hypocrisy? Dumping this wad of cash – the goal I did pursue instead of the one I should have gone after – of finding what's authentic in the world and in myself – I need to atone for that. I need to make it right."

That's being a good catholic girl. But why don't you make your penance a sincere life and a pure heart?

The simplicity of this realization strikes me dead center. I take a few deep breaths and wipe the residual tears away. I hear a chuckle escape my lips. I push my way up from the commode and look in the mirror. I am a sad sight.

I'm going to be all right, I inform my reflection. I set down the wad and vigorously wash my face and comb my hair with my fingers. I then unwad the checks. Parts of four checks are missing, gone to blue heaven in the bowels of the beast. It all seems so comical. It will make a good story for the teller at the bank when I go to cash them in.

You see, I was in the bathroom and my waist pouch fell in and I... With a last audible, deep sigh, I unlatch the door and go back to my seat.

The plane interior seems brighter now. I hear a child laugh and it causes me to smile. People's eyes are glued to screens, but I can't be bothered to look at what they are watching. I have my own melodrama to follow and that is more than enough for the moment. I am exhausted, but clear-headed and even giddy. I start giggling and attract the attention of my seat mate before I get control of it. I try to put some perspective on it all.

Live a sincere life. Keep a pure heart. So this is my great revelation? You might as well say, 'be happy and good'. Just how do I go about such a thing? So here I sit, hurtling through the sky in a tin box and wondering still what it's all about. Does the sum of my experiences make up who I am? Does it really matter? I feel washed over in a way, like I've been baptized anew. I chuckle again. The world appears more absurd and unstable than it ever has, but somehow it doesn't bother me anymore, or at least just not right now. I can accept it.

The stewardess comes by and takes orders for dinner. I order the meat. Be light with me Señor Peppy!

THE END

☯☯☯☯☯   ☯☯☯☯☯   ☯☯☯☯☯   ☯☯☯☯☯   ☯☯☯☯☯

John Arbogast

Acknowledgements

First and foremost, for my wife Nancy, without whom
this book would still be sitting as a bundle of loose-leaf paper and
I would still be mumbling about it. This book's existence is as
much due to her support and persistence as anything. Her
editorial advice has been invaluable.

Secondly, to all those who contributed comments and
editorial advice, encouragement and feedback, including; Annie
Dochnal, Tom Bickle, Richard Wilen, Koa Roberts, Eben Fodor,
Jean Hahn, Nicole Westrich, Dennis Ramsey, Dawn-Lee Ricard,
Barbara Shaw, Tom LoCascio, Trina Duhaime, Randy
Harrington, Justin Fernandez, and my father, Bill Arbogast and
twin brother, Tom Arbogast. Thanks also to Sandra at Paintworks
for help with the cover. If I have omitted anyone from this list,
my apologies and thanks.

For all those with whom I've shared experiences on the
road during these past few years. My imagination has prospered
from our time together.

About the Author

John Arbogast lives in Eugene, Oregon with his wife Nancy and two cats. He started his education in Kingston, Jamaica, continued it through to a BA from Boulder, Colorado and an MS from Eugene, Oregon. He has worked a slew of different jobs, including as an English teacher in Kyoto, Japan, Archaeologist, Nursing Home Administrator and Assistant Caretaker at an Arboretum. He has spent a good many years living and traveling outside of the U.S., including in Thailand and Germany. This is his first novel.

About the Cover Photographer

Photographer William Bloomhuff travels documenting the world's traditional people and their cultures. He resides in San Diego CA. www.bloomhuff.com

John Arbogast